I0675152

Maven's Crown

Trevor Parker was born and raised in London
where he lives with his family.

Trevor Parker

Maven's Crown

Published in 2009 by New Generation

Copyright © Trevor Parker

First Edition

The author asserts the moral right under the Copyright, Designs
and Patents Act 1988 to be identified as the author of this work.

All Rights reserved. No part of this publication may be reproduced,
stored in a retrieval system or transmitted, in any form or by any
means without the prior consent of the author, nor be otherwise
circulated in any form of binding or cover other than that which it is
published and without a similar condition being imposed on the
subsequent purchaser.

For Janet

Characters

Some of the leading personalities of the time find their way into the story. I have taken some liberties with their motives to fit the plot.

George I, the Elector of Hanover

Succeeded to the throne ahead of more than fifty others with a stronger claim after his mother, Empress Sophia, died. There was some doubt whether Queen Anne was as happy with the son as she was with the mother. The Elector spoke no English and was reputed to have little regard for the nation. Marlborough, though, had courted him earlier in the century while visiting the continent.

Bolingbroke

A leading Tory and possible Jacobite sympathiser, he had much to lose from the arrival of the Georgians. He had made himself an enemy of Marlborough by signing the Treaty of Utrecht in 1711, effectively bringing an end to Britain's involvement in the war.

Bothmer

An aide to the Elector.

Duke of Marlborough

The Duke of Marlborough (then John Churchill) triumphed at Blenheim in 1704 and endeared himself to the nation. By 1714 he had amassed great wealth but had fallen out with the political leadership. His wife, Lady Sarah, had been a lady in waiting to the late Queen.

Duke of Shrewsbury

Appointed as the Queen's first minister (there was no "Prime Minister" at this time), Charles Talbot was the ideal choice to keep the schemer Bolingbroke out of office. By 1714 he was quite ill but retained his mental agility. A successful and peaceful coronation would mark the peak of his administrative achievements.

Blenheim, 1704

John Churchill sat astride his stallion and surveyed the scene before him. From this vantage point the whole theatre of battle was laid out before him and he was pleased to confirm with his own eyes what his scouts had already told him. Progress had been exceptional. The future Duke of Marlborough grunted his approval and prepared to dismount.

In the undergrowth not thirty yards away a dark haired rifleman dragged himself up the slope, his stomach flat to the uneven ground. Luke Maven's eyes focused on his quarry, a lone sniper, but also swept left and right in case the Frenchman was accompanied. Maven sat up and leaned against a tree. He raised his weapon and began the laborious loading process, tipping powder into the pan then priming the mechanism. The sniper found a patch of ground and settled in for the kill, resting the weight of his weapon on his elbows, his back arched to form a cushioned frame. Maven knew that his chances of taking out the attacker were less than even. The flintlock musket was an unruly beast and accuracy was never her strong point. He watched the sniper settle and steady his breathing, watching and waiting. The sniper was too far away to be rushed. There was movement in the middle distance and it became clear to Maven who the Frenchman sought. He followed the sniper's line of sight and muttered an expletive. The General.

The big man got down from his horse and handed the reins to an equerry, stomping his boots on the ground to get some life back into his feet.

Maven reviewed his options. The chances of the enemy hitting his target were good but not guaranteed. If he fired at the Frenchman and missed then he would create a diversion that would enable the sniper to move closer and perhaps get a better shot. Maven placed his rifle on the ground, gathered himself and sprang towards the nearer of his two objectives. At full speed and ten yards from the General he shouted. The big man turned to face him so that he was side on to the sniper. Maven flung himself at Churchill's waist, clasping him around his ample midriff and knocking the breath from his body. As they fell to the ground the sniper pulled his trigger and the crack echoed through the trees. They felt the ball rush inches over them and the General's white stallion screamed in pain as the ball hit him in the flank. The animal reared up and wheeled around, its forelegs scrambling for thin air, its eyes wide with terror. The horse tumbled backwards and writhed in agony in the dirt and then was stilled.

The commotion drew members of Churchill's office and three of them ran towards the sniper, knowing they had half a minute before the assailant could reload. The Frenchman knew he had used his one opportunity and elected to run from the fray, downhill, rifle in hand. Maven allowed himself a rueful smile.

There was a sharp report from an English rifle and then a scream. The escaping sniper was hit in the stomach from a distance of no more than twenty feet. The ball passed out of him next to his spine, sending a shower of blood over the feet of the chasing pack.

At the top of the hill, the General sat upright and did his best to regain some dignity, brushing away the attentions of his officers. He fixed his gaze on the man who had so roughly hurled him to the ground. "Who the devil might you be, sir?"

"Maven, sir, of General Cooper's Foot."

"Close call."

Maven looked at the horse, lifeless on the ground behind them. "I am sorry, sir. Had I been closer I would have shot him but I could not guarantee ..."

"Nonsense, man. It was excellent work. The blighter had no business getting so ruddy close." This last comment was directed at the red-coated officers flapping around their commanding officer.

Maven continued, "We tracked him from the river. He was alone but too quick for us to stop him."

"So you are not alone. Who administered the coup de grace?"

Before Maven could answer a short, rotund Cornishman presented himself, looked down at the seated pair and saluted loosely, adding, "Bleddy 'ell, tis Mr Marlborough 'imself," and then to Maven, "You done good there, boy."

London, 1714

1

In the streets around Covent Garden the October day yielded to a chilly autumn night. The stiff breeze had cleared the area of its more peaceful denizens, hurrying them off to their cold damp rooms in the alleys and passages that soaked up the population like a sponge. An elderly watchman sat alone on a rough wooden bench, his torch in his hand. He stared ahead into the middle distance of Drury Lane as if troubled by something and his face glowed red and orange and yellow as the flames flickered. He coughed as the air about him dried and irritated his weak lungs. His eyes followed the tall, broad stranger as he made his way out of the gloom. The new arrival wore no periwig and he was dressed shabbily in a brown leather sleeveless tunic. What most intrigued the old man was that the visitor carried himself like an officer, upright and purposeful rather than one who was tired by the day's labours. The sleeves of the white blouse were too clean, he decided, not those of a working man at all. The watchman hawked and spat on the ground. The stranger's presence would only lead to trouble, he decided.

Luke Maven felt the watchman's rheumy eyes on his back as he entered The Bull Tavern armed only with a name and a vague description. Maven chose a table near the door and ordered beer from an attractive maid as she passed. The tavern was crowded and noisy and there were groups of men engaged in loud and humorous exchanges. Prostitutes weaved in and out of the conversations touting for business, mostly without success. A fug of tobacco smoke hung in the air, trapped by the low ceiling, and caused the laughter and the cursing to be punctuated by bouts of coughing.

Maven leaned his elbows on the table. The maid smiled each time she passed. Maven nursed his tankard of ale and watched her breasts heave as she walked. He smiled back and allowed his mind to wander. Then he was shoved to one side by the sharp elbows of a woman trying to create enough room in the crowded to get herself a drink. Her name was Jenny Salmon, brought to the capital by her husband, a Worcester tradesman, and then abandoned when the rogue had discovered the other delights that were available in the big city. Maven ignored her. He was busy looking at the small, rat-like man in a scruffy wine-coloured coat who had risen from a distant table and was making his way to the door. The wretched Ged Marrow looked much like a thousand other men in this abysmal city, trying and struggling to make a living. The thieftaker was hated equally by both the law abiding and the thievery and his appearance suggested he was close to giving up his contest with life. He looked at Maven and their eyes locked for less than a second but it was enough to tell each of them that his rendezvous with the stranger was on. Maven watched the little man make his way to the door, dodging between the various groups. Jenny Salmon took Maven by surprise.

"Not seen you about before, love."

She had made up her pock-marked face earlier in the day with a foundation comprised mostly of brick dust, a good portion of which had now come off, lending her a comical look. Maven ignored her and tracked Marrow, who by now was just a few feet behind them. The maid returned with the woman's jug of ale and paused for payment but Jenny Salmon was preparing her second assault. The maid had seen this exchange more times than she cared to remember and, whilst the cast changed, she knew what the outcome was likely to be. She raised her eyes and smiled at Maven and withdrew to serve another customer, chalking up the penny to the whore's slate on the way. Jenny Salmon took a long pull on the beer and wiped the overspill from her chin with her sleeve.

"Look at me, love, you might like what you see."

Ged Marrow opened the door and was about to slither out when he paused to allow a new customer to enter. Maven decided that his reason for being here was now ended and any hope he had of following the small man outside discreetly could be destroyed by his new acquaintance, who was becoming friendlier by the second. The woman poked him in the arm, leaving a black mark on the sleeve of his white shirt. Maven turned towards her and rose from his stool, pushing her aside with more force than he had intended. Jenny Salmon smiled and revealed a chaotic collection of rotting teeth.

"Like it a bit of rough, do ya?"

12

The waft of strong drink on her breath and the sudden change of temper caused Maven to reel back.

"I'm up for it if you are love. You scared? A bit of a coward are, ya? Don't worry, I won't tell no one. It'll just be our little secret."

Maven turned away. Her expression changed and her smile became a sneer.

"What're ya doing here anyway, stranger? Up to no good?"

She grabbed him by the arm and held on. Maven could go nowhere without pulling Jenny Salmon off her stool.

"Let go, madam. "

She leaned into him and sighed.

"Make me."

She released her grip and poked Maven's sleeve again, leaving another mark.

"Oh dear," she slurred," I've marked your pretty French shirt."

Maven wondered how far Marrow could have travelled in the few seconds since he had left the pub. He shrugged the woman off and, as he stepped toward the door, she slid to the floor, her arm outstretched like a lover begging her man not to leave. Nobody chose to notice Jenny Salmon's fall. Maven moved swiftly to the door and left the tavern. At his back he heard the whore's plaintiff cry, "Bleedin' Jacobite."

The watchman sitting outside held out his palm and offered to light the way. Maven declined.

"The small man who just left here. Which way did he go?"

The watchman considered the question then pointed his bony hand in the direction of St Giles. Maven sighed,, cursing his luck. Only a fool would go into that dangerous, overcrowded rookery after dark. He hoped he could head him off before he got there. Maven set off quickly and, his eyes not yet accustomed to the darkness of the street, walked straight into a man, an inch or two shorter than him but of considerably larger girth. Neither yielded and they stood face to face. Maven was the first to speak.

"My apologies sir, I didn't see you." Then, expecting no further discourse, he moved to one side and made room for the large man to walk past. A waft of malodorous, alcoholic breath hit Maven's face.

"You wanna be a bit more careful, son."

The man's left hand made an unsuccessful search for the billy club that protruded from a pouch on his belt. Maven sensed the danger and darted out into the narrow street, covering twenty feet before the larger man had turned. He swayed a little and steadied himself. The watchman's torch silhouetted his obese outline.

"Come back 'ere and identify yourself!"

Maven ignored him and disappeared into the quiet darkness, hoping the man would find the Bull Tavern a more enticing prospect than a run down the street. Unfortunately, Jenny Salmon now blocked the doorway and she treated the man, with whom she was evidently on first name terms, to a tale of how a French stranger had engaged her services then run off without paying. The constable turned and gave chase. Maven eased himself into a narrow alley and cursed as he stood in a puddle and his boot leaked what he hoped was rainwater. His pursuer lolloped along with his left hand pulling the billy club into action and the right hitching up his breeches, which were slipping down as he ran. He was followed by the limping watchman who waved his torch about, risking the safety of the timber buildings on either side of the lane. By the scant moonlight Maven could see Ged Marrow not far ahead, walking down the centre of the road. Then Marrow stopped and turned and looked back. Then the little man was disturbed by the fat man's calling and continued on his way.

Maven stepped out of his hiding place and caught the constable full in the face with an open palm, the shock sufficient to knock him to the ground but not enough to cause any lasting damage. The agility of the man took Maven by surprise and he rolled and made a grab for Maven's boot, then sunk his teeth in just below the knee. Maven stamped on the man's hand and he rolled away, brought himself upright and came straight at Maven with the club swinging. Big mistake, thought Maven, I can see exactly where it is going. As the club swung towards his face, Maven caught the weapon and held it firmly in his hand, then brought his left fist across and connected with his opponent's ribs. The constable's grip on the wooden implement relaxed and Maven relieved him of the club. But rather than accepting defeat, his attacker came towards him again, this time with both fists clenched. Maven speared him in

14

the chest with the blunt end of the club then followed up with a punch to the face. The constable wavered then fell backwards, just as the wheezing watchman staggered up, illuminating the scene with his torch.

The altercation had alerted Mr Marrow that something serious was afoot behind him and, as was the way of any sensible citizen these days, he removed himself from the vicinity as quickly as possible, melting into the shadows and the den of vice that was St Giles. After a brief search around the dark by-ways off Drury Lane Maven cursed and gave up and went back to his room at The Star, taking a longer route so as to avoid his new foe. He knew the ways of the thieftaker and would wait for the next offer. It would not be slow in coming. Marrow had the items and they were worthless to him but he knew their owner valued them considerably. He would find Maven soon enough.

In the morning, lying fully clothed under his blanket, Maven was woken by the sound of Trescothick, clomping up the stairs in his heavy boots, cursing in a Cornish accent that had never succumbed to the London melting pot. Trescothick banged on the door of the room opposite. He hollered just a little too clearly, something about the constable about to come in on a search. In the few seconds of shouted instructions and muffled responses, Maven ascertained that the male guest of the room had apparently paid his female companion to stay the night, a common enough occurrence but sufficient to give a certain kind of constable adequate grounds to arrest the landlord for keeping a bawdy house or, more likely, to shake him down for a few shillings.

The thought dawned on Maven that the spectacle was being staged for his benefit. He twisted his upper body round so that he could peer through the crack in the door where the rusty hinge had worked away the frame. If the episode was for show then the landlord took no chances for he put on a good demonstration. Trescothick shooed the alarmed and half dressed guest into a cupboard at the end of the narrow corridor and slammed the flimsy door shut after him, ignoring the plaintiff cries. Maven watched, vigilant but unconcerned, and reached out a long arm to gather his only meaningful possession, a small pewter trinket box and stuffed it deep into the pocket of his tunic. He recognised a voice that filtered up from the saloon. The voice fitted the man perfectly: big, ugly and drunk. The constable clattered up the stairs and made heavy weather of it.

Maven peered through the gap. The constable wore the same heavy clothes he had had on last night: brown boots and a leather tunic, soiled over many months from the mud and dung that spattered up from the London streets. The landlord blocked his way and made a fuss about opening up the room opposite, fretting over a large bunch of keys and muttering incoherently. The law officer filled the corridor. His eye was blackened and he had a dirty bandage wrapped round his right hand. There was a trace of dried blood between his nose and top lip. Last night, recalled Maven, he had looked like any other London tradesman on his way to the pub. He cursed under his breath.

Maven pulled his boots on and gathered his heavy jacket about him. He eased open the window and looked left and right into the yard below to see whether the constable might have brought some assistance. Apart from a pair of thin brown chickens that dug among the thin earth there was nothing down there. He clambered out of the window and hung by his fingertips then dropped, rolling onto his side as he landed, scattering the chickens to the edge of the yard. The ground was cold and damp and hard. He picked himself up, rubbed the grit from the palms of his hands and swept back his long dark hair. Assured that no one had seen his escape, he strode down the side of the building to the wide gate, which was being opened by a drayman, who had just arrived with his beer delivery. The drayman recognised Maven and raised his hand in salutation then swallowed the hullo when he sensed that his friend had other matters to attend to. Maven hesitated and thought about Westminster. Then he changed his mind and turned left towards the City.

The first light of the October morning was breaking through, edging aside the London night, bringing with it grey clouds and the threat of yet more rain. Later on in the day, Long Acre, though narrow, would be a busy thoroughfare carrying traffic from St Martin's Lane to Drury Lane. At this early hour, though, the street was quiet and only the delivery men disturbed the peace. The sounds of hooves and wheels on the hard surface of the road competed with the cries of shopkeepers berating the boys who brought the fresh goods in from the wagons. A skinny black mongrel weaved in and out of human feet, barking when he judged that a boot had got too close.

Maven spied a fine black coach on the opposite side of the street, drawn by two smart, aloof black horses oblivious to the action around them. The drayman's heavy horses stood just a few yards away from them and the two pairs faced each other in a companionable silence, though the animals were as far apart in class as their owners. Assuming the coach was the transport of a gentleman come early to a Covent Garden shop, Maven processed the information and decided the carriage posed no threat. He walked up Long Acre towards Lincolns Inn, still annoyed with himself for not avoiding last night's altercation. Regardless of a personality flaw and fondness for ale, his new enemy was a parish employee and enjoyed an invulnerable status. The constables got to say who plied their trade locally and who didn't. It was Maven's bad luck that he had stumbled upon one who seemed like he derived maximum enjoyment from his freedom. He needed to get over the boundary into the next parish as soon as he could. With luck, the constable there might fit the more traditional picture of a retired tradesman who sought only a quiet life whilst leaving the street to get on with managing itself. Maven would get a note to Trescothick later to thank him and apologise for bringing the law onto the premises again. As he walked, Maven reflected on the threat he faced. The constable could have him charged with any number of unsolved crimes and, for good measure, invent a few new ones. There was no justice to be had unless you were a gentleman and could pay your way out of trouble. But then, gentlemen did not move around the unsavoury parts of London after dark dressed like dockside porters. Nor would a gentleman ever give his address as The Star Tavern, Covent Garden. Arrest was an option to be avoided at all costs.

Maven strode toward the junction with Drury Lane, calculating how soon he could reach Lincoln's Inn. He heard horses behind him and turned. The coach that had been parked opposite The Star drew alongside and he tensed, wondering who might be lurking behind its leather curtains. He stopped walking and braced himself for one or two men to jump out or, perhaps, a pistol to appear through the window. He faced the door of the coach and waited, his senses alert and he was ready to roll under the vehicle and out the other side at the slightest sign of trouble. He flicked a glance back towards the tavern to see whether the constable had completed his search of the premises. The curtain at the carriage window twitched and a woman leaned forward, her pretty face filling the frame. "Luke Maven?" said the woman, just loudly enough for him but no one else to hear. Then, taking no response as an affirmative answer she added, "Get in, Captain."

The team of three arrived for its prearranged rendezvous at the Royal Naval Dockyard in Deptford. One of them, William Taylor, was a former soldier who had seen active service on the same battlefields as Luke Maven, though they had never met. A short, stocky individual, he had been stood down following the signing of the Treaty. Like many others, Taylor had been aggrieved that the country had been taken out of the war when, in his humble and ignorant opinion, there was plenty of payage still to be liberated from the French nation. He had been dismissed from his regiment with most of the pay he was owed and the battered uniform he stood in.

He now ran a timber yard in Lambeth for a tradesman who had been successful enough to adopt the manners and behaviour of a gentleman. William Taylor was left alone to look after the business. As a result, he had not only honed his skills in false accounting but also gained enough spare time to augment his income with occasional work helping gentlemen of a certain kind deal with projects that required the sort of ability that could only have been acquired on a battlefield. Business disputes were becoming increasingly bitter and the law was a long and arduous process that could be circumvented if one of the parties were to meet with an unfortunate accident. Taylor had warmed to his new career. He was handsomely paid and he would never again find himself half starved to death in some freezing corner of Europe waiting for a French dragoon to cut him down.

Yesterday, Taylor had taken a half-full wagon from his yard and hitched two spare horses to the back, as if he were taking them to market. He had driven out to Camberwell, where he rested the horses then turned north-east to Deptford. The roads were poor and the ruts were wet and deep so that progress was slow. He carried with him paperwork confirming that his load of timber came from Kent and was destined for a customer in Lambeth. He also carried spare cash since it was not unknown for local constables to introduce their own turnpike charges as the mood took them. On board were several weapons, among them a cudgel, a pistol and his prized possession, a Spanish blunderbuss that had come home from Flanders with him.

This pair of gentlemen met his limited requirements: they were discreet and they paid well. They needed both qualities, for the work they were doing would see them all hung, drawn and quartered at Tyburn if they were caught. The first, Mr Webb, had set out last night at sunset and drifted down with the tide in the failing light. As a boy, he had acquired the skill of piloting river craft in and out of the larger trade vessels that clogged the Pool of London. Unable to pass upriver beyond the Bridge, ships queued, sometimes for days, for the right to unload their cargoes, causing congestion as far back as Blackwall and the expertise needed to move in and out of the vessels without collision was considerable.

The final member of the trio was the Colonel. He was angular, ugly and kept his short fair hair under a powdered periwig. At a little under six feet, he was the tallest of the three. Very much the dandy gentleman, he had hired a boat yesterday to take him down as far as Greenwich. He succeeded in restraining his flamboyant urges and passed unnoticed to his destination where he paid the wherry man generously and went to find his lodging in the town and to check on the shipping movements. This morning the Colonel had taken a shallop back up to Deptford. He had arrived on time, paid the driver and taken refuge in a coffee house near the dockside to wait where he knew that a gentleman drinking coffee and perusing the newspapers would attract no attention.

Mr Webb had woken early, roused himself from under the canvas and washed off the grime of the night with river water. He cursed under his breath for having to spend the night in a dusty hole, since the boat had been used sometime recently to ferry coal ashore, probably from one of the Newcastle craft that plied the east coast route. He breathed deeply and reassured himself that this was to be his last outing. In less than a week he would be rid of the tiresome Colonel and free of the erratic and dangerous William Taylor. He untied the boat and slipped away from the shore, rowing into Deptford, where he tied up at the edge of the dock and went in search of Taylor, checking all the while in case he had been followed. On this occasion, more so than any of the previous meetings, he wanted to abort the mission if they were in danger of being apprehended. The instructions had changed at the last minute, which meant that someone higher up the command had decided it was time. But change brought added risk.

Mr Webb bought a piece of greasy pork from a street seller and a tankard of ale to wash it down then leaned against a wall to observe the comings and goings of the dockyard. Within half an hour, the timber wagon hove into view. Webb threw the remains of breakfast into the gutter and returned the empty tankard to its owner. Taylor drove the wagon past the quay and onto the quiet road that led south. Webb followed then strolled passed the wagon and stood by the horses at the rear. The driver jumped down and walked round to the back where he met his colleague. Webb removed his heavy black coat and threw it to Taylor, who stowed it under the canvas. In return, the driver pulled out a sack of replacement clothes and the boatman changed from river worker to gentleman in the space of a minute. Now sporting a maroon overcoat, a cravat, a sword and a clean peruke, he slipped Taylor's cudgel into an inside pocket and strolled away.

2

Had it been a man, Maven would have suggested that he step down and have the conversation by the roadside, but he was not used to being invited into ladies' carriages: even the harlots who plied their trade around Covent Garden were rarely this brazen. It was an unthinkable breach of etiquette that he should receive this request. However, in a fraction of a second the niceties of London society were expelled from his thoughts by the appearance on the street of the constable, spilling out of The Star and stumbling towards the next tavern in search of his man. The constable looked up and saw him. He was fifty yards away. The officer gambolled along in his peculiar lop-sided fashion once again, one hand supporting his breeches to prevent them from slipping to his knees and the other waving at Maven. His strangled shouts suggested to all onlookers he wanted Maven to wait. The woman threw open the door.

"Get in, we can talk on the way."

Maven bundled himself into the carriage, his broad shoulders almost too wide for the narrow aperture. She reached out and slammed the door closed before he settled onto the bench seat. Without waiting for instructions, the driver pulled away towards the safety of Lincolns Inn, sending an elderly pedestrian scurrying for cover amid a welter of shouted abuse. Maven's hostess turned in her seat and peered around the curtain that draped the rear window. She turned back and smiled.

"You must have upset him terribly."

"I don't like the company he keeps."

Maven's fear of an accomplice proved unfounded, not to say impossible in the confined space, where his bulk took up the entire bench that backed onto the driver. Whoever this woman was, she had sufficient confidence in herself and enough faith in the honesty of her passenger to retain only her driver as protection. After the initial burst of speed they travelled slowly in the traffic, not much faster than the constable could run, in fact, but their steady pace and his lack of stamina forced him to give up the chase by the time they reached Drury Lane. The carriage rocked from side to side. There was, apparently, a way of riding comfortably in a London carriage but Maven had not mastered it. The trick was to pick up the rhythm and move in much the same way as if you were riding the horse rather than riding as a passenger in the carriage. He tried to find the pattern now but only succeeded in knocking his broad shoulders against the wooden panelling.

Anxious to prolong the silence for as long as possible so that his hostess might take the initiative, Maven examined the inside of the vehicle and tried to avoid meeting her gaze. Having exhausted the drab wooden interior, he paused at her feet, where delicate black leather shoes were partly obscured by the blue silk of her dress. Since the ending of the war the previously contraband French silks had become easily available and fashionable ladies could make more overt use of the skills of the Huguenot weavers in Spitalfields without fear of retribution or scandal. Those who wished to cut a particular dash would send out to Paris and have the cloth imported directly. Wherever she had got it, the dress would have cost her handsomely, thought Maven. It was a fine cloth and was finished with Flanders lace. It was cut low at the bodice but not so much as to suggest impropriety. It suited her, he thought. She was slim and pretty and her dark hair tumbled to her shoulders in curls. She had hazel eyes, which shone, even in the subdued light of her carriage. Maven guessed her to be less than thirty, purely from her clear, healthy skin. She was, he decided, a truly beautiful woman.

Her black leather perfumed gloves were a discreet sign of respect for the Queen and a downgrade from the full mourning dress that many ladies wore after the monarch's death. One hand rested in her lap while the other dabbed a perfumed handkerchief to her nose in an attempt to protect herself from the noxious odours of the city. Maven moved his attention to her hat, also of blue silk to match the dress. Her ears were adorned with what appeared to his untutored eye to be genuine pearls and there was a matching necklace about her throat, where he settled for a moment. By now they had reached Lincolns Inn and Maven knew he could jump out and be safe enough from the constable's revenge. But he was intrigued. Why would a woman he had never met before come looking for him in Covent Garden and then call him by name in the street? Had he met her before? He searched his memory for clues and came back empty handed. She would have stayed in his memory, of that he was sure. In the end, her reticence proved too much and he admitted defeat.

"I'm sorry, ma'am" he said, "but I don't know your name."

"Kathrine," she replied, holding out her right hand, which he took gently and nodded, any kind of bow being out of the question. She was not forthcoming with a surname. He looked again at her slender neck.

"Are you admiring the jewellery?" she asked.

"No. I'm afraid I have no understanding of such shiny trinkets, ma'am. I was more interested in the scars about your skin there."

She was offended but recovered quickly.

"That is not something we need to discuss and I shall thank you, sir, to avert your eyes."

"Ma'am," he assented with a nod and noted how her skin coloured. She raised her hand to her chin and contrived to find something of interest in the street. Her delicate pale skin made him aware of the dark stubble on his unshaven face. He swept his hand across the rough beard and he felt like a lumpen oaf. He busied himself with another survey of the vehicle. The coach was newly built and the leather bench seats showed no wear at all. The wood veneers bore no scratches, something that was inevitable once the carriage had been in use for a while, especially around the doors. They put Lincolns Inn Fields behind them and turned right onto Holborn. Maven eased back the curtain. The traffic here was even heavier, comprised of pedestrians, commercial wagons and hackney cabs. London was awake now and it would be quicker to walk. Everyone, it seemed, had a trade and insisted on performing it in the street: every few yards, hawkers and sellers tempted passers-by with all manner of goods from fruit and vegetables to second hand clothes. The hum of human interaction and the clatter of wheels and hooves set up a great noise.

"Could you tell me your surname, madam? You seem to know well enough who I am."

She allowed the leather curtain to drop back into place. She paused and then replied, "First, I should like you tell me what you are doing in London, Captain."

He could see the outline of a wedding band on her finger beneath the glove. A widow then, he decided. He was sure she already knew the answer to her question.

"I'm visiting."

"A tourist? Surely not. Only foreign dignitaries come to London for the sights."

"I came to pay my respects to the Queen and stayed for a while. It's been some time since I was here. I thought I might take in the coronation. "

He cursed himself for the amateurish lie.

"Covent Garden is an odd place to choose for a holiday."

"It represents good value."

The carriage turned a sharp left. The sudden movement surprised him and threw his weight against the side of the carriage. His head followed half a second later, knocking painfully on the wood.

"The horses know when they are nearly home," she said, smiling at his discomfort. "You shall be released from this cell very soon. You know, I hadn't realised how small this carriage was until now. But then I suppose it wasn't designed for someone like you."

They were in Hatton Garden, just outside the city wall and far enough from the Fleet Ditch and most of the populace to be a pleasant place to live. To his left the fine houses were arranged in the terraced style. The front doors gave onto a pavement of flagstones, a novelty reserved for the better districts but a luxury that made the road narrow. Opposite, there were open fields, although it would be only a matter of time before an enterprising builder persuaded the parish to allow him to begin yet another development.

The carriage stopped so that the mistress could step down in front of the house. The front door was blue, a shade not unlike her dress. A short, stern woman dressed in a white and grey outfit stood on the doorstep, waiting for her mistress. The footman jumped down and opened the carriage door. Kathrine allowed the man to take her hand as she stepped out then turned to face Maven.

"Thank you Hammond. Will you come in, Captain?"

Maven eyed the property with suspicion.

"You are quite safe, Captain," she smiled.

He stepped down from the carriage and followed his hostess. Her footman stood guard, occupying the ground between Maven and the lady with a spiteful and insolent look in his eye. He was a middle-aged misery of a man who looked from the small scars about his face and the powder burns on his hand like he may have once seen action. Infantry, thought Maven as he took in Hammond's scowl. The servant held open the door and stared at the officer malevolently, starting at the dirty boots and moving upwards with contempt to take in Maven's full height of six feet two, overly tall but not enough, clearly, to deter the surly inspection. Maven returned the stare until his accuser relented. Maven stepped into the house and the carriage door slammed shut behind him with more force than was necessary.

Maven looked at his smart surroundings. The ceiling was high and there was a delicate paper on the wall, a light cream with a maroon pattern repeated at regular intervals. An occasional table bore a china vase of bright red flowers he had never come across before. There was a wide staircase and its balustrade was painted white with the handrail stained to match the shade of the table. Everything gleamed. Yes, he thought, this was a fine house.

"Do come through. Sarah will bring us some tea."

Maven followed her into the drawing room looking all around in case there should be some surprise waiting for him. This room was also tastefully furnished and, once again, there was a delicate paper on the wall. A feminine choice, he thought. The room smelled of paint and warm comfort. There was a large white fire surround in the French style above a marble hearth and polished brassware. The room faced west and the fire burned just enough to take the morning chill off the room. Above the fireplace was a portrait. Its male, uniformed subject stared down hard and rendered Maven speechless.

"You recognise my husband?"

Maven brought himself to attention before stopping at the last second.

"Lady Cooper. I beg your pardon ma'am. I didn't realise ..." and suddenly his thoughts were accelerating in directions that had not occurred to him until that second.

In Whitehall, Charles Talbot, the 1st Duke and 12th Earl of Shrewsbury sat upright behind an immense desk staring at what he considered a damnable, never-ending pile of state papers. The poor light was causing his good eye to hurt and he knew he must soon stop and rest. Aside from the ticking of a large gilded clock on the mantelpiece all was silent until he leaned forward and coughed, rasping for several seconds until, at last, he regained his upright position red in the face and breathless. He wiped his mouth with a handkerchief and surreptitiously checked the contents for traces of blood.

"Crouch, are those blasted foreigners here yet?"

Outside, sitting at a desk in the anteroom among a library of leather bound books, Gideon Crouch sensed the Duke was troubled, and he had good reason to be. The clerk had been around the great man for long enough to recognise all his moods. That Shrewsbury had been reluctant to take on the role of Lord Treasurer was discernible only to those close to him even before that warm summer afternoon when the Duke had returned from the Palace and marched directly to his private office, slamming the door behind him and demanding to be left alone for the rest of the day.

Two months had passed since the appointment and the subsequent death of the monarch and the Duke had mellowed little. He was sustained in his work by the thought that he had kept the schemer Bolingbroke out of the office most had assumed would become his on the termination of Harley's appointment.   The Queen, however, had had other ideas, and Bolingbroke had once again underestimated her majesty's political skills. Bolingbroke had scuttled off to his father in Battersea and was hardly ever seen in town. It was just as well, thought Crouch, for Bolingbroke's stock had plunged with alarming speed. Rumours abounded that he was to be found skulking in the company of Jacobite noblemen whilst another that suggested he was planning to abscond to France. Even in his absence, Bolingbroke was never far from the centre of political intrigue.

Crouch smiled at the thought then stood and walked to the window, searching for the guests. The clerk was a not a short man but a childhood illness had left his frame twisted so that when he stood he appeared to be forever searching on the ground for some lost item. He looked from the street like an evil butler peering through the window, an image made more accurate by his beaky nose and pale complexion. Ten o'clock, Bothmer had said, so ten o'clock it would be. The Hanoverian was the most punctual man in the country, it seemed. Impatient, the clerk returned to his chair and sipped on a dish of coffee, a decadent indulgence encouraged by his master who believed the new drink to be more appropriate than ale and too useful to be left to the ever increasing numbers of coffee houses.

"Crouch!"

The clerk sprang out of his chair and made for the main office, dropping the china dish into its saucer as he passed. He flung open the doors and executed a deft about turn to close them again. In his urgency to serve, Crouch skipped across the room and bowed then stood as upright as he could and waited for his instructions, his shoulders hunched and his neck twisted. Shrewsbury continued to scan the paper in front of him for another minute then, his task complete, looked up at his clerk as if confused about why he was there. The recall of the instruction was delayed by another coughing fit and then, once the handkerchief was stowed, the Duke recalled why it was he had summoned Mr Crouch. The flaw in his left eye lent malevolence to the great man's stare so that he always appeared to be looking beyond the object of his attention. Crouch had become so used to it that the odd look no longer registered but it remained disconcerting for those who were meeting the Duke for the first time.

"Do you have news from the city?"

"I do indeed, sir."

"Then you had better share it, man. I should like to know before Bothmer gets here."

"I believe we have the complete picture."

"Confound it all! How is it that the Semite merchants get to hear such important news before Whitehall?"

He waved his hand at Crouch to indicate that the question was rhetorical.

"But of course we already know, don't we? Money speaks louder than politics; at least it does these days, eh?"

"Indeed sir, I fear you may be right."

"I am right, Crouch, I am very right, and it will be the undoing of us, mark my words. Before we know where we are it will be the merchants sitting here running the country and they shall be running it for their own ends, damn them."

Crouch spoke in little more than a whisper.

"I have taken the liberty, sir, of making enquiries and was able to ascertain the appropriate information. Lord Audley's movements seem to be quite well known and he makes no secret of his associations."

"Has he no shame?" shouted the Duke, rising from the chair, "and what, may I ask, is the point of paying our own informants if they deliver their news after it has already become common currency in Exchange Alley?

Crouch pressed on.

"There is a good deal of suspicion circulating, sir, and I regret that it all concurs with what you believed to be true. With regard to Lord Audley's, erm, associate, Mr Matthew Webb, there is much to tell. He consorts with the lower orders on Audley's behalf, he frequents taverns where a gentleman would not be welcomed and he meets with half-pay officers and vagabonds of the worst kind. The rumours suggest he arranges safe passage for funds that are intended for the Jacobite cause. They say that Webb ensures the gold makes its way safely to the north of the country."

Crouch paused while the information sank in.

"Rumours also imply, sir, that the gang has begun to bring in men from the continent. Professional soldiers."

Crouch knew this was the development that the Duke had been dreading. Shrewsbury turned toward him.

"If that is true then we have begun the Pretender's endgame. If that news reaches the Palace my life shall be made intolerable. It may already have reached the ears of Herr Bothmer. A little bit of warning would have helped us to plan, eh, Crouch? Am I right? But what of Audley? Which gentlemen does he meet?"

Crouch knew the Duke was fishing for a link with Bolingbroke.

"Discreet sources suggest that he is making arrangements to flee."

"Flee? Flee where?"

"To Scotland."

"And these discreet sources are not in our employ, I suppose?"

"They are not, sir. Our own people have been less than helpful."

"You know, Crouch, I think we should sack the lot of them and install someone to drink coffee and chocolate with the Semites and send us a note at the end of every day. We'd have a sight better idea of what was going on then, eh?"

Crouch elected not to tell the Duke that this was precisely how his intelligence was sourced. Instead, he replied, "Very good, sir. I shall have someone attend to it immediately."

The Duke sat down again and regained his composure. The timepiece chimed the hour and a liveried servant knocked lightly and entered the room.

"Herr Bothmer, is here to see you, sir."

Johann Caspar Graf von Bothmer stood in the reception area downstairs and looked around, taking in the fresco on the high ceiling and the delicate blue walls. He especially liked the brightly decorated bow fronted cabinet that the duchess Adelhilda had brought from Italy and he allowed himself the guilty pleasure of resting his hand on its marbled surface. He wondered idly whether the Duke understood how lucky he was to be married to such an attractive woman. One day, thought the German, he should like such a trophy himself. He caught sight of his reflection in the glass and decided he was a handsome sight in his black garb. He overlooked the way his portly frame stretched the material.

It was Gideon Crouch's usual practice to keep visitors waiting for at least ten minutes and the less favourable the visitor the longer was the hiatus before they were permitted to enter. On his first visit to the Duke, Bothmer was kept waiting for half an hour. As a result, protocol had been discussed in tones of forced politeness and now the Hanoverian contingent could expect to be ushered through without delay. In response to that minor diplomatic episode, Crouch had had the chairs removed from the reception room just to be sure that their most frequent visitors were not made to feel too comfortable.

"Good morning, sir," said Crouch, entering swiftly from the anteroom. He bowed and the visitor returned the gesture, "Will you come this way?"

Crouch deposited the guest in the presence of the Duke. There was no exchange of formalities. "Will you be requiring coffee, sir?"

The Duke nodded his assent and Crouch paused for the next instruction.

"My clerk has news for us, mynheer. Do you wish to hear it?"

Bothmer shook his head and waved his hand imperiously and Crouch withdrew to make the arrangements for coffee. Bothmer smiled. His English, though learned only recently, was impeccable and he spoke in clipped, formal tones.

"Our friend Mr Audley has been busy, yes?"

Shrewsbury had long ceased to be annoyed at the Hanoverian's supposed ignorance of British titles.

"The news has reached you quickly, sir."

"Audley is indiscreet. His Highness is concerned. His advisers are concerned also."

Shrewsbury knew that the King was kept in a state of blissful ignorance by his advisers.

"Quite, I am sure you are."

"And you are not concerned?"

"Of course I am concerned for his majesty's safety, Herr Bothmer. However, we have matters under control and the King is quite safe. We understand that Audley plans to leave London very shortly for Scotland. We shall have him followed and his movements will be monitored. I am sure he realises the futility of any action against the throne. He will pose no threat."

"On that note, at least, you are quite right."

The Duke looked up, puzzled by the response and Bothmer continued.

"My colleagues and I have put in place a plan of our own. Just to be sure."

The Duke sighed. The colleagues to whom Bothmer referred were the Counts Bernstorff and de Robethon and the three of them made a formidable triumvirate. It was rumoured that the King made no decision of any consequence without referring to them. Moreover, it seemed that most of the monarch's decisions originated from his advisers.

"Would you be in a position to share this plan with me?"

"In time. For now, I should like you to carry on. You and your people," he sneered, "may continue with your intrigues with your self-important noblemen."

Maven walked to the fireplace and looked at the portrait. Kathrine had taken the seat on the far side of a polished table and looked out of the window while they awaited the arrival of tea. As was the fashion with pictures of this kind, it was full-length, the General standing in full uniform, sword in hand. At his feet sat two spaniels, alert and ready to do their master's bidding. The background was common to many pictures that Maven had seen, a gentle green landscape unblemished by buildings of any kind, representing the England whose interests the subject had fought so hard and so successfully to advance. Sarah, the same servant who had received her mistress at the door, delivered the tray of tea things with much ceremony, removing the china cups and teapot as if they were the implements of a delicate surgical procedure. He waited for the servant to withdraw and unwittingly rested his gaze on Kathrine for a second longer than was acceptable, making her uncomfortable.

"I had heard that General Cooper had passed on. I'm very sorry," said Maven, trying to recover. He sat opposite her without waiting to be invited.

"Thank you. It was, in the end, a blessing. He suffered a stroke after his retirement and then a second finished him about six months ago."

General Sir George Cooper had enjoyed a formidable reputation. He was honest in his dealings with his men, paid them on time and often shared plunder with them. Most of the others, recalled Maven with disdain, used the commission they had purchased to inflate their incomes while leaving the men starving, not to mention short of key supplies like warm clothing and ammunition. General Cooper was a fine soldier and an honest man, fiercely loyal to Marlborough, but he demanded the same honesty and commitment from his men. Many lost their lives serving him.

Lady Kathrine served the tea herself and, once again, he was grateful for the interlude to collect his thoughts. She poured the golden, greenish liquid like it was a precious and fragile commodity. It would no doubt be the best quality, he thought. There had been gossip in the mess about the young bride Cooper had taken when he returned to England after Malplaquet and most of it had been of the unsavoury kind. At the time the General would have been a few years shy of fifty years old which meant his wife was barely half that age. Cooper had sold his commission then and there had been no opportunity to bring the lady to any functions. As a result, the rumours about her background had persisted in the General's absence. The woman before him did not seem to be capable of the crimes that had been suggested in the mess. Suddenly, she was speaking to him.

"So, Captain, I discover you climbing out of a tavern window dressed as a stevedore and chased by the constable. Do you still expect me to believe that Captain Luke Maven of Marlborough's Office is a tourist?"

"No, ma'am," replied Maven who could then think of nothing else to say.

"The General spoke fondly of you," she said, filling the pause. Maven wondered whether the lady addressed her husband by his rank when he was alive. He imagined the old man barking orders and running his household in much the same way as he had run the regiment.

"Why did you leave the army?"

"I had had enough," he said, "the Captain-General was in Marlborough House by then and I didn't want to push pieces of paper around. There was no fighting to be done and I could conceive of no role I would want in politics."

"You could have remained on the continent with Prince Eugene, could you not?"

"It had been a long time since I had seen my home."

"So you became a tourist?"

She smiled at him and he knew he was being mocked. Maven smiled back and sipped his tea, being sure not to spill any in the saucer or to make any slurping noises. He burned his top lip and felt like an oaf, out of place in these fine surroundings.

"Hugh gave me a letter, just before he died. It mentioned your name."

Maven's stomach tightened as he narrowed down the options for what the note might contain.

She stood and walked toward the fireplace, looking all the while at the portrait. "I miss him, you know," she said, gazing up at her late husband's likeness, "more than I would ever have expected. It was not as though becoming a widow was ever a surprise, after all he was considerably older. I just didn't expect to be alone so soon."

She continued to gaze at the portrait, addressing her comments as much to her late husband as to Maven, "Some said it was an arrangement rather than a marriage and, at first, I believe it was. My father was especially pleased, as you can imagine."

She was contradicting the mess story that she had been a harlot on the make but if what she now said were true Maven could imagine very well. It was clear from her accent that she was no aristocrat and it was a treacherous business being the father of daughters in the middle classes. Aspiring parents, seeking to ape the ways of their betters, made it their business to seek out desirable young men for marriage. Unfortunately, desirable young men were in short supply, the army and the navy taking the fittest and strongest away to fight, often never to return. So the balance of supply and demand tilted in favour of the young men left behind, many of whom were far from suitable matches for well-bred gentlewomen. A bidding war of sorts was often entered into if a father was to be successful in getting his daughter away. It could be an expensive business and Maven was certain that the General's interest would have been welcomed with a huge sigh of relief by this lady's parents.

"He told me about the battles. It was simply unspeakable. Did Marlborough really have to be so brutal? I'd rather Hugh hadn't told me ..." she tailed off and raised a hand to her mouth. "Was it as bad as he described?"

Maven was unsure how to answer. He never reminisced, preferring to put the memories away in a place where they were unlikely ever to be found. Mess room conversations were always about the pranks and absurdities. Never would they reflect on the horror of it all.

"We had a job to do. We did it and then we came home." He was uncomfortable now. "I'm sorry you didn't get to spend more time with him. He was a good man."

"I learned a great deal from him, you know. Most soldiers don't tell their wives anything. Hugh shared everything. It was his way of getting the war out of his mind, I think. He told me the story of how you came to be promoted Lieutenant. You were very brave. Saving the life of the country's leading General. I suppose if you cannot be promoted for that then ..."

She was waiting for him to say something and, when he remained silent, she sensed his unease.

"Have you ever killed anyone?" she asked suddenly, and then went on, "obviously, I know you have. What I meant was, have you ever been face to face with your enemy, seen him as a man and then had to, well, choose?"

"Sometimes."

"That's what battle is all about, though, isn't it? Being brave enough to look the enemy in the eye and then kill him."

"It isn't something I ever dwelt on. If I had then I wouldn't be here to have this conversation. I expect your husband would have said the same thing."

She returned to her seat, adjusted her dress and turned slightly to face him, her hands in her lap.

"The note that Hugh gave me. It confirmed something he had said to me before, when he was first ill. It said that if I ever needed assistance I was to seek you out."

It made sense, thought Maven. Cooper would have been more concerned about his young wife's safety than his own impending death.

"And you need my assistance?"

"Yes, I believe I do."

"Why didn't you send me a note? Was there really a need to collect me from the street?"

Maven guessed that, like Cooper, she was not the sort to sit at home and wait for things to happen.

"A note would have been a warning rather than an invitation, would it not? And if I had asked Hammond to collect you then I suspect you would have offered some resistance."

"Fair enough."

"Hugh said you owed him the repayment of a debt. A debt of honour."

Here it comes, thought Maven.

"Do you recall?"

"I believe I do," he said.

"Good. The assistance I require is a little ... delicate."

34

"Go on."

"I would like you to find a gentleman."

"Fine, that is what I do. But there are no guarantees. People sometimes don't want to be found."

She fixed him with her gaze.

"When you have found him I want you to kill him."

3

In the Deptford coffee house the Colonel sat with his back to the far wall, and he could see everyone who came in and out through the front door. There were no windows apart from a single dirty pane next to the open door and the clientele had to make do with candlelight by which to read their newspapers. There were three long wooden tables running across the room with bench seats either side. There were shelves running down each side of the room. The Colonel spied a bayonet and a musket, neither of which had seen recent use. On the wall behind him was a framed abstract of the Act of Parliament against drinking, swearing and profanity, which had been damaged, perhaps as the result of being thrown, and then returned to its rightful place on the wall. He had finished his first dish of coffee and had called for a second. His earlier research had indicated that the owner was quite relaxed about his coffee house being used as a place of business provided regular orders for coffee and food were placed. As the second dish of coffee arrived Mr Webb presented himself. Younger than the Colonel by around ten years and of a darker complexion, his black hair was now hidden under a grey wig. He took a seat at the Colonel's table facing the door and left his coat on despite the warmth. The weather-beaten owner saw him and swept by to take his order.

Over the next half hour the coffee house filled up to the extent that there were only two or three spare places. The owner, assisted by a young serving boy was kept busy delivering lunch to the customs men, traders and naval officers. There was a steady hum of conversation, much of it earnest and discreet but punctuated with occasional laughter.

The guest, due some two hours earlier, seemed not be coming after all. It happened in their line of work and it would not be the first time. The boy brought a platter of bread and meat on a wooden platter with two knives. The pair set about their luncheon.

Presently, one of the customs men stood to return to his office. As he did so a slim, fair-haired man slipped into the empty seat and heaved a canvas kitbag over the bench and let it rest between his knees. The new arrival took a clay pipe from an inside pocket of his plum coloured coat, emptied the contents onto the floor, refilled it and tamped down the new tobacco. He laid the pipe in front of him and scanned the room.

The Colonel spoke briefly to Mr Webb, who took a final hunk of bread and pushed it into his mouth. Still chewing, Webb walked towards the door. As he passed the new arrival, he withdrew from his pocket a slip of paper and dropped it into the courier's lap. By the time the recipient had registered the delivery Webb was in the busy street. The Colonel watched the target open the paper and read the single word. Had they chosen incorrectly the response would have been for the new man to twist in his seat to search for an explanation. This man needed no clarification. Instead, he looked forwards into the crowd of customers in search of his contact. The Colonel was the only singleton. He met the arrival's look and nodded, using the smallest movement but it was enough to convey the message. The courier fingered the paper and passed it from hand to hand. Then the boy arrived with meat and bread, which he proceeded to eat. The Colonel and the courier completed their luncheon in silence. Then the Colonel removed some coins from his pocket and laid them on the table, being sure to leave more than was required but not so much as to draw unnecessary attention.

The Colonel edged his way to the door and looked up and down the street. He saw Webb to the right, about fifty yards away loitering among some packing cases. The Colonel walked toward his colleague but did not cross the road, remaining instead in the shelter of the buildings. He walked slowly and when he was level with the wooden cases he turned and looked back toward the coffee house.

The courier stood in the doorway looking for him, taking the care that had kept him alive for so long. As his head turned to the right he located the Colonel and walked towards him, his kitbag slung over his left shoulder the heavy weight causing him to stoop. The Colonel gauged the speed and ambled along the busy dockside road, dodging porters and barrows. Webb followed about twenty yards behind.

William Taylor sat on the wagon and dozed. He had fed the horses, checked the fastenings on the cart and brushed the mud from the wheels. He had ordered, eaten and paid for his luncheon from the dingy sailors' tavern fifty yards back up the lane and the serving girl had come out and collected his plate and tankard. Then, as planned, he had saddled the spare horses. In the absence of anything better to do he had climbed back up on to the driver's bench. A sixth sense woke him, just as the Colonel turned the corner. Taylor jumped down and went to the rear of the wagon, where he untied the canvas cover and waited. The Colonel slowed and allowed the target to catch him while Matthew Webb waited at the corner. The courier spoke for the first time, the voice of an educated gentleman with the trace of a Scottish accent.

"You want me to travel in there? They usually send a coach."

"Our job is to deliver you safely," replied the Colonel. "A coach would no longer be safe. Times have changed." He nodded to the back of the wagon. "There's a change of clothes in there for you."

The driver edged closer to his disappointed passenger and breathed into his face.

"'Tis clean sir. I washed it down myself, sir."

He reached into the wagon and brought down a grubby upholstered footstool and placed it between the courier and the vehicle. The gentleman hesitated then heaved his bag aboard. He stepped onto the footstool and clambered into the wagon, making hard work of it then rolled away from the flap that Taylor slammed into place.

"I needs to tie this cover down, sir. We can't be too careful 'ereabouts. You never know who might be lookin'."

Taylor rolled the canvas and tied it off at each corner. The Colonel gestured to Webb and beckoned him to come down.

Taylor climbed up and grabbed the reins while the other two untied their horses and mounted. The horses were pleased to be moving and showed their displeasure at being tethered for so long before their riders settled them down into a slow trot past the wagon, leading the cortege from Deptford town towards the City.

"You cannot be serious."

"Oh, but I am, Maven."

"Lady Kathrine, this is London not the colonies. There are laws. You simply cannot take offence at someone and have them killed."

She sat back in her chair and sighed. He had thought she might be acting but then decided that her hurt was genuine. Had she believed he would accept her order and then swagger off into the city to carry it out? Apparently she did.

"Perhaps there is another way. What you proposed was a solution. Tell me the problem then I may be able to assist. Who is it you seek?"

Her features hardened. "May be able to assist? Aren't you forgetting something? My husband died believing you would protect his widow. He believed you were obligated to him, sir, even after his death."

"Look, I will help you find whoever it is you are looking for but I cannot carry out a cold blooded murder. A debt of honour is one thing but I'm damned if I will swing for it. "

She looked at him and waited for the apology that would surely follow his profanity but it did not come. They sat in silence for a while, each of them unsure how to resolve their respective dilemmas. Maven searched for polite excuses to leave and came up empty handed. There was no doubt that he was honour-bound to help her out of the tight spot in which she found herself. On the other hand, murder was murder, even in a society that seemed to have lost all sense of order.

"Tell me who it is you need to find," said Maven.

"You will help?"

"If by help you mean kill someone, then no, I will not. But if the person you seek threatens you then I will honour the General by providing you with protection."

She stood and moved to the fireplace, the better to be nearer to her late husband, perhaps, and looked up at his likeness. She stood there for a full minute, each second of which made Maven more uncomfortable as the wait threatened to become interminable. Then she turned and her expression had changed from confident gentlewoman to that of a frightened child. He wanted to reach out and hold her.

"Won't you please sit down and tell me the whole story," he said.

Her expression changed and she looked as if she would throw him out into the street. He could see childish petulance in her eyes, something of the fiery young woman Cooper had married. Then her mood passed and she returned to her chair, sat back and took a deep breath.

"His name is Edward Audley."

"Lord Edward Audley?"

"There is only the one, thank heavens."

Even Maven had heard of Audley.

"Madam, merely wishing him dead would be proof enough of your insanity. If you were to succeed in ridding the world of his presence then Parliament would turn every stone to find who was responsible. You would surely be found and hanged, along with anyone who provided assistance."

She turned so that the left side of her face was revealed.

"You asked me of this earlier. Do you recall?"

She twisted her head to the right and looked up to the ceiling. She was showing him the bruises about her neck. He leaned forward in the chair to get a better look and she reeled away from him.

"I wasn't going to touch you," he said, "I just wanted to see what sort of wound you had there."

"The marks are from a sword, Maven. The brute believes he owns me. He wants me for his wife."

"You are searching for a husband?"

She turned to face him.

"Good God, no. Sorry, I didn't mean... well, I am sure you weren't offended."

"But he has the pick of the whole country. I can think of no reason why he should have to force you into a contract against your wishes."

"A fact I have suggested to him. He has decided that a rich widow suits him rather better than a virtuous young thing. It is likely also that his pride is damaged by my rejection."

"Most women would be flattered by his attentions."

She admonished him with a silent stare and then continued.

"Have you met him? No, you haven't or you would not say such a thing."

"And the wound? Can I take it that he did not take kindly to being rebuffed? Perhaps you were not as polite in your conversation as you might have been."

"Do you read, Captain?"

Maven read newspapers in coffee houses but suspected that was not what she had in mind.

"I read something by Mr Swift a few years ago, but…"

"Swift is enough to put one off reading for life. You would not, I suspect, have discovered the work of Mary Astell."

Maven had not heard of the author. She stood and walked to the low bookcase under the window. The books were the type that people bought to read, unlike the tomes he saw in the army, which were shipped out by weight and selected for an officer's shelf on the basis of the uniformity of the binding. There were two long rows of books and he was not surprised to see her reach for a volume at the far left of the top shelf. She flicked through and found the mark she was looking for.

"If all men are born free then how is it that all women are born slaves?"

"You said that? I am surprised you are still alive, madam."

"Don't mock me Maven, it does not become you. It happens to be my opinion. I shall never marry him. Or any other man for that matter."

"And he assaulted you because you quoted some text at him? That hardly seems the act of a gentleman."

"He could hardly challenge me to a duel, could he?"

She swallowed hard and stroked her neck.

"He was remarkably calm. That's what was so frightening. He grabbed me by the throat and held me there. I thought he was going to strangle me. Then he took his sword from its …"

"Scabbard."

"Scabbard, yes, and rested the edge against my throat. He said, more or less as you did, that there are hundreds of women who would be happy to take my place and I should be grateful for his attentions. Then he said …"

"Go on."

"Oh God," she said and lifted her hand to her mouth as she began to cry, "he said if I wasn't married to him by the end of the year he would kill me."

"Did anyone else witness this, one of the servants, perhaps?"

"They certainly heard him shouting. Sarah came in to see what it was that disturbed me but by then they were gone."

"They?"

"Audley and his companion, Matthew Webb, my brother-in-law."

"This other man stood there and let this happen to you?"
"I am glad he did. If Matthew had stepped in I am sure Audley would have run him through. I shall never forget the look in his eyes."

"Was that the last time you saw him?"
"Yes."

"Is there someone you can stay with? A relative, perhaps?"

"I have only one living relative, my sister, Matthew's wife. They live in the country not far from my parents, but Audley knows the house. He will surely find me there."

From the window of the large Battersea manor house, Henry St John, the Viscount Bolingbroke stood and looked north across the Thames towards Westminster. He was tall and handsome for his thirty-six years despite having inherited his father's taste for pleasurable, almost rakish living. The pair of them had long since agreed that active and vigorous socialising was the secret to a long life. His father, sitting behind him on the large settee in the rudest of good health was proof of the philosophy. Both of them gripped large glasses of red Burgundy wine and the decanter that sat on its silver tray next to Henry St John Senior was almost empty. It was the older man who broke the silence.

"You must stop your fretting, boy. Even you cannot argue about this outcome. As soon as the lady upped and died events were taken from your hands. If you want my advice I'd suggest you lie low for a few years. The buggers will demand your return soon enough."

"There is no need to be so casual about it, father."

"I am not being casual. I am merely reminding you that the position is one you cannot now control. You play a dangerous game. The Whigs see you as a died in the wool Jacobite. And need I remind you that Marlborough has returned to London? He of all people would dearly love to see you perish in the Tower."

"We were just days away, father, just days."

"It is a shame that the dear Queen did not hold on for just a while longer but she did not and there we are."

"And we know why she did not hold on, don't we? Can it be an accident that the warmonger Marlborough returned to these shores the very day after her majesty passed away?"

"Now, do stop this Harry. There is absolutely no evidence and the price you will pay for starting rumours of conspiracy will be death. Worse, they will brand you an outlaw and your family will be punished as well. I have always said I would live to see you hanged, but I fear that I shall see you beheaded."

Bolingbroke turned to face his father.

"Events have a way of working themselves out. We simply need to apply reason and the word of God."

His father slurped his wine.

"Hah, it is the word of God that has brought you to this point, Harry. Let it be, will you. You want for nothing, after all. Leave the country to the Whigs and their tradesmen for a few years. They shall be so busy with their noses in the financial trough that they will forget all about you soon enough. You may return when they have made a thorough mess of things, as they inevitably shall. I don't suppose Walpole and his cronies possess the grace to ever forgive you but that does not preclude him needing someone of your intellect at some point."

"What I desire, father, is not land and money, but the right future for this country and I sometimes wonder if I am the only one who does."

"And that future is a Jacobite future? Harry, if you persist in this charade then you shall only lead us back into civil war. Without a party behind you it will be a short and bloody one at that."

"The Hanover Tories are small in number. The rest will support me once a Tory lead has been shown."

"I should have that confirmed in writing if I were you."

Bolingbroke smiled for the first time that morning then rang for the decanter to be replenished.

Two hours later Taylor had steered the wagon to the outskirts of Camberwell. He had driven slowly to ensure they were not followed and to allow his colleagues to ride ahead. He turned the wagon into a narrow lane, barely wide enough for the vehicle. The thornbushes scraped on the panels of the wagon. The lane continued for about a hundred yards and took him out of sight of the main road then reached a clearing. His two colleagues had earlier dismounted and tethered their horses. A third man, a thin and pallid individual, was with them, still on his horse. As the wagon pulled into the clearing the stranger urged his mount back into the shadows.

Webb and the Colonel walked to the back of the wagon and untied the ropes. The courier rolled to the edge and dropped to the floor, landing unsteadily on his feet. As he brought himself upright the Colonel caught him squarely in the midriff with a punch and followed up with a second to the jaw. He silenced the groaning with a kick to the back of the head. Webb reached into the wagon and dragged the heavy canvas bag toward him. He untied the cord and forced his hand inside. The chink of metal could be heard by all of them. The pair smiled at each other.

Taylor joined them and brought a knife from the recesses of his coat, a vicious, serrated thing that had a blade longer than a man's hand. He rolled the victim onto his back and unbuttoned the coat. Starting at the hem, he began ripping the lining with the knife. After six inches of cutting he paused and laid down the knife, felt inside the coat with his right hand and smiled. He withdrew his hand and held up a gold coin.

Taylor tore into the coat then. His enthusiasm for the task did not wane and it took him less than five minutes to empty the coat of its contents and place them into the sack. He checked the man's outer pockets and found a small leather purse containing more gold and a selection of foreign coins. Taylor crouched down by the man's head and rested a finger against his throat, as if testing for a pulse. Finding no sign of life he looked up at his colleagues for guidance. The Colonel nodded to the thicker forest. Taylor searched the pockets for anything that might identify the corpse then dragged the victim into the trees at the rear of the clearing and kicked a pile of leaves over the body. Webb tied the sack securely and threw it into the wagon, tying the ropes down again. The trio looked toward the stranger who remained imperious on his mount. He nodded his approval then kicked his mount into life and galloped past them through the clearing towards the main road.

When the servant had left the room with the empty decanter and his father had replenished their glasses, Bolingbroke withdrew a note from his waistcoat pocket and passed it to his father. The paper was heavy and bore a red seal that had been broken.

"What is this you show me Harry? If it is a matter of state secrecy then I fear I should avert my eyes for my own safety."

"I should like to conclude our business before the drink takes you father. Read it, please."

The older man took it and looked first at the seal.

"Atterbury? My goodness you do mix with some dubious company."

The older man read the letter. His face reddened with anger.

"The man is a damnable fool. Aside from committing such seditious thoughts to paper he has named his colleagues. Moreover, he has sent the damn thing to you. What will you do about it?"

Bolingbroke took the letter from his father.

"I think it unlikely that Bishop Atterbury, Ormonde and the Earl Marischal will find the courage to stand at Charing Cross and proclaim James the true King but I think I should like to be there to witness the event if they did. The looks upon their faces when they are apprehended would be something to cherish."

"I fear you treat the whole thing with too much levity, Harry. Surely you can see that even these friends of the Pretender recognise that theirs is a lost cause. The time is not right for an uprising and they have said so."

"Actually, the text of the letter says the time might not be right."

"It is one and the same thought. If there is doubt among men of their rank then any plot is doomed. You shall be isolated."

"Father, you are correct and your counsel is as wise as ever."

His father took a long draw on his glass. He puffed out his ruddy cheeks.

"And Audley, what of him?"

"He seems to have his hands full with that ungracious harlot."

The father stared at the son but his thought remained unspoken. Instead, he said, "You know, I believe Atterbury and his fellows would spend a good deal longer dithering about which of them would make the announcement than on the proclamation itself. The populace would doubtless walk away bored and our three wise men would have to chase the crowd up The Strand to get their message across!"

He laughed at his observation.

"I have something else. Something rather more important than the scribblings of a timewaster like Atterbury."

Bolingbroke removed another folded piece of paper from his pocket. This one also bore a red seal but it was wider and thicker.

"More intrigue, Harry? What is this?"

"It is my policy of insurance."

"Like they sell at Lloyds Coffee House?"

"This one is a little more reliable."

Bolingbroke handed his father the letter and the older man unfolded the paper and read its contents. He stared at his son but said nothing.

"You see, she had changed her mind. Had the poor lady lived for just a few more days the arrangements would have been made."

"Does anyone else know of this?"

"I was with her when she wrote it. We were alone."

"Then it will be denounced as a fraud, as will you."

"I fear you may be right. But the Hanoverians are searching for it nonetheless. Which means the lady discussed it with Shrewsbury."

"They will kill you for it."

"They may kill me when they find it. Until then they dare not harm me."

"What are you going to do with these papers?" asked his father indicating the first letter.

Bolingbroke looked at Atterbury's note then removed the pages that bore any reference to his name. He strode to the fireplace and dropped the offending items into the flames. They watched as the paper dried and curled and the seal melted. The treacherous thoughts of the three Jacobites turned to smoke and disappeared up the chimney.

"These," he said, brandishing the Queen's letter and the remainder of Atterbury's note, "I shall keep."

4

Three evenings later Maven and Lady Kathrine Cooper rode in her coach to Chelsea to attend a drawing at the home of Lady Mazarine. It was a society event and she was worried that Audley might attend. Apart from a discreet return to The Star to see Trescothick and gather his kitbag, Maven had spent all of the time with his new employer. It had not taken him long to conclude that she found the engagement more to her liking than he did to his. Several times, he had been shown off to her friends as if he were a talented musician or a Moorish slave and he feared this evening's outing would be much the same. There had, throughout his assignment, been no sign of Audley.

He had recovered his old uniform from Trescothick's store room and was pleased to find that, despite having lain there unused, it bore no damage, although the epaulettes could have been cleaner. Maven found the whole business of dressing up tiresome. Nonetheless, it was with some pride that he had examined himself in the looking glass earlier, taking in the polished square toed black boots, the grey breeches and the white shirt that Sarah had insisted on washing and then drying over the fire. Sarah had tried to convince him to shave his head and adopt one of the General's perukes but he had decided that he would not break his habit of wearing his dark hair long. Kathrine wore a dress similar, he thought, to the outfit he had seen her in a few days earlier, only this one was in a dark brown shade. The weight of the material and its cut suggested it was an expensive luxury, one of many he had observed about her. Maven wore a sword, ceremonial, he hoped, since he had never been much of a duellist, preferring a brawl to the finesse that swordplay required. In the event of trouble he had more suitable weapons to hand. In his right boot, he had stowed his short handled knife and he took care to walk in front of the looking glass to check that he did not draw attention to the weapon. For good measure, he had come down earlier from his attic retreat and hidden a pair of pistols in the coach.

The journey to Chelsea was uneventful, if longer than he had expected, through the ever-growing village of Kensington and the fields that he was sure would soon be home to the expanding swarm of London. Hammond drew the coach to a halt in front of the double doors, which were held open by a pair of liveried servants, resplendent in dark green with gold trimmings. Just inside the door was a woman in an ivory gown who Maven took to be the hostess. With her was a short, plump man, Lord Mazarine perhaps, looking like he would rather be anywhere else in the world right now. Maven helped Kathrine down from the coach and watched the servants consider what circumstances would have led a mere Captain to be invited.

Kathrine took his arm and they went through the formal pleasantries. The chubby bored gentleman was, indeed, Lord Mazarine, and his ribald remarks about Prince Eugene and the army prompted a silent rebuke and a thunderous look from his wife but a wry smile from Maven. Maybe it would not be so bad here after all, he thought, and was pleased when Mazarine said he would seek him out later so they could talk about the war.

Kathrine had assured him that there would be only a small gathering but she must have been misled for the main drawing room was home to at least a hundred people, about two thirds of them women. Of the men, barely a handful wore uniform and the few scarlet tunics drew the eye like red roses in a summer garden. Pleasant chamber music from a quintet in the corner filled the room and competed with the murmur of conversation.

A quick scan of the guests told Maven that, in uniform at least, he was the most junior officer there, a fact that made him uncomfortable. His discomfort was made worse when he spied a Major, five years younger than him whose inability to command had been no barrier to advancement. The officer's face was set in the same permanent chinless grin he remembered from before. Maven recalled the man's habit of braying in an annoying fashion when the drink took hold. Maven struggled to recall his name then got it: Wingate. That was it, from old money in Warwickshire. The Major caught Maven's stare and seemed equally displeased. Wingate turned away.

The men and women had separated early on in the evening and it was difficult to keep an eye on Kathrine as she circulated. He noticed that none of her conversations seemed to last beyond the briefest of pleasantries before she moved on to the next group. Usually, it would be her interlocutors who moved away to circulate. After three hours of uninspiring small talk and two visits to the buffet table, Maven was more than ready to leave. Even the colourful Lord Mazarine had proved to offer limited entertainment. His military service had been curtailed by a wound sustained in England and the failure to make it into the conflict on the continent weighed on his conscience and he made Maven awkward with his requests for war stories. Maven had decided early on that he would drink no more than the polite minimum but the absence of non-alcoholic drinks meant he was thirsty as well as bored. His continual observation of Lady Cooper gave rise to more than one vulgar comment and the senior officers labelled him as a man in love. Kathrine, for her part, went the whole evening without once catching his eye.

As the drink took hold of the room, the mood relaxed and the groups began to mingle. Maven watched her across the room. She was engaged in earnest conversation with a tall, handsome man. The gentleman was smartly dressed and carried himself with authority and confidence. The stranger did not match the description Kathrine had provided of Audley and Maven relaxed. Still, she seemed to be tense and there were no smiles. It was the sort of exchange one might observe between a couple who had known each other for several years and had grown sufficiently comfortable in each others presence to discard the polite smiles that accompanied drawing room conversations. Then Maven felt someone alongside him and turned to see it was Mazarine, his cheeks a rosy hue now from the wine. Maven's heart sank at the thought of further military talk but, instead, he said, "I never thought I'd see those two in polite conversation."

"How so?"

"Let's just say he was a little put out by her choice of husband."

"General Cooper?"

Mazarine was rather drunk now and he leaned closer to Maven.

"I should have thought he had more on his mind that what Lady Kathrine was getting up to these days. Frankly, I am surprised he had the nerve to turn up at all."

"Who is he?"

"You mean you don't know, old chap? That's Henry St John."

"Bolingbroke?" Maven recognised the name from its regular appearances in the Daily Record.

"Indeed. Just when we all thought he had been banished for good, back he comes to taunt us again. He'll never learn," chuckled Mazarine, "he really is yesterday's man. Still it must be killing him to have to stand there talking with her."

Before Maven could ask why, the braying Major Wingate decided he could no longer resist the temptation to engage Maven in conversation, his earlier reticence driven away now by an excess of Bordeaux wine and cognac. Mazarine moved away as soon as he saw him heading in their direction. Maven, suddenly exposed, decided on a tactical retreat and drifted to the side of the room where he stood by the bookcases pretending to recognise the names of the authors.

"Didn't have you down for a literary man, old chap," said Wingate to Maven's shoulder, only a slight slurring betraying the considerable amount of alcohol he had consumed.

"Just browsing, Major. Us half-pay officers have plenty of time on our hands. Reading helps to pass the time, don't you think?"

"I wouldn't know. I have plenty to keep me occupied in the city," he replied, a little too loudly, leaning forward to examine Maven's uniform more closely. Wingate took the cuff of Maven's coat between thumb and forefinger and tutted. The material was worn and its condition did not reflect well on its owner.

"Still wearing the General's cast offs then," he said, looking across the room at Kathrine. Maven snatched his sleeve away.

"Steady there, Maven, I think you will find I outrank you now."

"Promotions are easier to come by if you simply have to hand over the cash, Wingate. Besides, we are both civilians now so your rank gives you no advantage."

Wingate stepped closer to Maven and, in a lower voice, said, "Don't knock the system too much, Maven. We all know the Duke has seen you right."

Wingate looked at Kathrine.

"They say she has some history and that she's a little feisty. Too hot for Bolingbroke as well. Too hot for you too, I shouldn't wonder."

"It's not what you think."

"I think it is, Captain. Your eyes have been on her all night. The other thing they say is that she no longer has a use for men, if you follow."

"Unlike you, Major, or is that just a scurrilous rumour as well?"

Maven knew that he should not have said it. Pride, combined with the copious amount of drink led Wingate to take loud and dramatic offence at the insult. The drunken officer stepped back and made to withdraw his sword but was restrained by a strong male hand that rested on his forearm and persuaded him to leave the weapon sheathed. Wingate shrugged the man aside and came at Maven with his fists clenched. His aim was true but there was little strength in the blow, which caught Maven on the chin. Maven reacted with the instinct he had learned growing up on the London streets. One blow, straight to the centre of Wingate's face was enough to send the assailant to the floor in a crumpled heap. There was a scream from one of the ladies as Maven stood, somewhat embarrassed, rubbing his knuckles.

Maven felt the presence of someone alongside him.

"That was rather unnecessary, Captain," said Bolingbroke. "You and I have much to discuss. We should arrange to meet in more propitious circumstances."

Kathrine was by Maven's side within seconds.

"Come along, Captain I think it is time we were going," she said and then, as an aside to him, "for pity's sake, can you not confine your brawling to the officers' mess?"

She excused them from Bolingbroke's presence and guided them to the front door, where Lord and Lady Mazarine were already busy seeing off other guests. Behind them, Wingate, unsteady on his feet and with blood coursing from his nose, was being ushered from the room in the opposite direction, the same companion doing his best to avoid the stares that followed them.

To Maven's back, Wingate shouted, "Commoners have no business calling themselves officers. You, sir, couldn't even afford the damned uniform. If it were not for the benevolence of your betters you would be standing there naked. And you are still dipping into Cooper's estate, I see."

This last comment brought gasps of astonishment from some of the ladies. Maven looked at Kathrine and saw only a withering look of contempt for Wingate. She was unharmed by his slanders. Wingate's associate pulled him away from the scene and back into the drawing room where he could do no further harm but the young Major broker free and had to stop his own momentum by grabbing Maven's shoulder.

"You're own your own now, commoner. Marlborough won't be there to fight your corner, nor Cooper," and then, as his aide tried once again to guide him away he leaned forward and added, "She belongs to Audley and Bolingbroke. Don't get in their way. Your life is worth nothing to them."

In the corner of his vision Maven saw Bolingbroke gesture to Wingate's aide, keen to bring the exchange to a halt. Maven ignored the three of them and turned towards the door. He was relieved to find the coach waiting in front of the house. Maven opened the door of the coach himself. While Kathrine received the sympathies of the hostess, Mazarine wandered out to commiserate with Maven.

"Take no notice at all, Captain. They can all be fine officers in peacetime, eh? I know who I'd rather be in battle with. Sturdy blow, by the way. Good show!"

He shook Maven by the hand. It still hurt.

"What can you tell me of Lord Audley?" asked Maven.

"An absolute rake, sir. A drunk and a gambler who is damned close to losing his birthright. Far too quarrelsome for my liking. He and Bolingbroke are mixed up with all sorts of seditious nonsense. Wingate may be a fool but his advice is sound. Be careful, Captain."

Kathrine skipped past and leapt into the coach without the need for Maven's assistance. He swung in after her and Hammond had them away at the double. Mazarine waved at them as the carriage retreated.

In the entrance hall another couple had gathered their coats and were awaiting their own coach. Gideon Crouch and his wife had enjoyed a most pleasant evening and passed a few minutes thanking their host and hostess for their delightful hospitality. As he adjusted the angle of his awkward frame and shook Mazarine by the hand, Crouch leaned his thin face forwards and enquired after the tall gentleman escorting Lady Kathrine.

"Captain Luke Maven, late of the Duke of Marlborough's office and one of the finest soldiers who ever served this country, sir," replied Mazarine.

"Really?" said Crouch, nodding, "then why was the young Major insulting his honour so?"

"Breeding and upbringing, Mr. Crouch, breeding and upbringing."

Crouch thought for a moment.

"Really? Maven's or Wingate's?"

Henry St John Bolingbroke hurried away from the Mazarines' Chelsea drawing. If the roads were clear he estimated he would arrive at his destination in less than half an hour. Only rarely did his temper rise to the surface and then it was a wonder to behold as his enemies caved in around him. He was vexed now, as he always was, by that intransigent woman. He had struggled to maintain his decorum and it was as if she chided him deliberately. However hard he tried he could not shake her from his thoughts but at least she took his mind off the conversation he was about to have. An occasional foray into London's social life still presented the opportunity for some discreet liaisons and, provided he was untroubled by footpads he would be able to use this evening's party as cover for his true purpose of crossing the river.

He arrived in St James's on time. The darkness was almost total and there was no other movement in the Square. The coach stopped in front of the club and Bolingbroke let himself down and swung the carriage door shut. He did not have to break stride to enter. The servants had the door open as soon as the coach drew to a halt. The thin, angular Colonel, bowing and smiling, met Bolingbroke, who smiled, hiding his opinion that the Colonel was a fool whose brain had been weakened by a fondness for port and a proximity to gunpowder.

"My Lord, it is a pleasure to see you again."

"Is he here?" replied Bolingbroke.

"Indeed, sir. Please walk this way."

The Colonel took Bolingbroke upstairs and along a narrow corridor. He knocked on a door marked "Private" and entered without waiting for a response. He ushered Bolingbroke inside and withdrew, closing the door behind him. A gentleman sat alone in a wing-backed armchair annoying the fire with a poker and causing sparks to leap out at his feet. He turned when his visitor arrived and Bolingbroke greeted him with a warm smile.

"Now then, Edward. It is time you and I had a little chat."

Audley was a short man and his build was slight and he seemed lost in the large armchair. His complexion betrayed the generous quantities of wine he had drunk that evening and despite his relative youth the red spiders' webs about his cheeks and nose indicated his fondness for claret. He had trouble focusing on his guest.

"And what would you like to chat about?" he replied, his soft accent slurring a little. Bolingbroke sat down in the chair facing Audley. His arrival had been expected and there was a second glass, which the host filled with wine. Audley made a show of holding the full glass out toward the fire so he could examine its contents.

"The usual good claret, Harry. Don't look so glum."

Audley handed him the glass and they sat in silence for a minute. Then Bolingbroke placed his glass on the table and leaned forward.

"Edward, I hear that some people have been helping themselves to the supply line."

"Have they indeed?"

"These are delicate times, Edward. It is not good to have Jacobite spies found dead in the woods."

"I should have thought the authorities would be rather pleased at such a turn of events. One less to worry about, eh?"

"Summersby and two of your men met him at Deptford. The port is awash with spies and they were falling over themselves to scuttle back to Westminster with their damnable information. What on earth was he thinking? What on earth were you thinking?"

"He was thinking, Harry, that the funds would be stolen once they reached the north of the country so he might as well put them to good use down here. Just for once we might be in a position to make some genuine preparations instead of indulging in the pretence that stands in the way of real change. He has my full support."

"You have heard that Bishop Atterbury desires to postpone any rebellion?"

"Of course. He has made sure that all of Parliament is aware of the whispering. That is all the more reason we should ensure that the funding finds its way to a safe place."

Bolingbroke twisted the glass in his hand.

"I think it would be wise if we were to avoid meeting again, I think. At least for a few months."

"Then you, sir, are a coward."

Audley waited for a reaction he knew would not be forthcoming.

"You see, Harry I am right. I insult your honour and you do nothing to defend it. Damn you, man. I am in no position to wait for your laborious plotting!"

Bolingbroke leaned forward.

"I saw Kathrine this evening. She has a new man."

5

Maven woke with the dawn and the birdsong. His lodgings in the roof space of the Hatton Garden house were small and the ceiling was low, so that standing upright had to be reserved for when he left the room. He lay on his cot and stared into space. The pewter trinket box lay open beside him and its contents were arranged on the bed. He fingered the silver necklace and polished its locket with the soft cloth he kept for this purpose and allowed his thoughts to take him to a different place. His mind wandered to the events of the previous evening. After their ignominious departure from Chelsea he and Kathrine had ridden back to Hatton Garden in an awkward silence. At one point on the Oxford Road he had punctured the silence and offered to walk but she would not hear of it, the reputation of the area's bandits, real or imagined, being the deciding factor.

Only when they had arrived at her home did she initiate a conversation. "Do you understand, now?" she had said. They sat once again in the drawing room beneath the painting of General Cooper and throughout their exchange she stole glances at the great man. Sarah had placed on the table between them a tray with a bottle of claret and two glasses and they quaffed a glass while the conversation continued.

"It was nothing, just an idle threat from an idle man."

"But don't you see? Audley has told his cronies of his intentions. The whole world knows."

"He's ruined your prospects for other men, you mean?"

"Quite."

"But you don't want another man."

"That is not at all the point, Captain, as well you know."

He did not know, but ventured on. "But you said that a woman with her own income has no need to support a man and submit to his wishes, or something like that, as I recall."

"Reputation, Captain. My reputation is all. If people are gossiping about me and sniggering behind my back then I might just as well move away from London and live as a country spinster."

Maven felt awkward and kept his own counsel. Sarah was summoned and instructed to light the way to her lady's bedroom. They left Maven alone to finish the wine and find his own way to the attic.

Now, as he leaned on his elbow and turned to look out of the window toward the hills west of London he weighed up his options. He liked the lady. In so many ways she was like Ruth and he saw in the widow many of the qualities he recognised from his late wife: more money, of course, but in her personality and spirit Lady Kathrine was the sort of woman that Maven admired. She was sensible enough to recognize the realities of her situation and brave enough to take a stand against becoming a mere chattel. And yet. There was a look in her eye, a glance and an expression that spoke of secrets that she would prefer to keep hidden.

He wondered whether Kathrine would send him on his way after the events of last night. She was frightened of this man, which was ridiculous, he decided, especially if Audley was one of Wingate's set. They were braying young gentlemen desperately clinging to the old ways. Maven decided that merely protecting Kathrine was no longer an option for she would remain a prisoner forever at the mercy of the aristocrat Audley. No, he thought, he should find Audley and encourage him on his way.

Sarah rapped on his door and called his name, her unpolished London tones so at odds with the accent of her mistress.

"Message, for you, Captain. 'E says it's urgent."

"I'll be down in just a few seconds," he called back.

She stomped down the stairs in her boots, her passage punctuated with grumbled complaints about the state of her feet and the steepness of the stairs. Maven dressed and succeeded, for the first time since he had taken up temporary residence, in not knocking his head on the roof beams. He stowed the trinket box and went downstairs to investigate. It was from Trescothick, at The Star. The Cornishman had scribbled something barely legible on a scrap of paper and grabbed a boy off the street to run it over. The boy had waited impatiently for a reply and then, tiring of his duty and being wary of the unfamiliar neighbourhood, had darted back to the grimy streets of his usual daytime existence.

Kathrine had not yet appeared.

"She might be having one of her 'eadaches. Don't suppose we'll see 'er until this afternoon."

Maven grabbed a hunk of bread from the kitchen table and tipped a little milk from the jug into a china cup and sniffed at it. The milk had been stored outside overnight to keep it cool and remained just the right side of sour. He poured some more and drained the cup. He took his leave and Sarah admonished him for not sitting at the table to finish his breakfast. He decided to walk. It was a dry morning and he made good progress. He made his way southwest, crossing Lincolns Inn by the diagonal footpath where he tipped his hat to return the salute of an old soldier. As he reached the corner of the field he went onto alert for the constable and rather than go directly to the tavern via Long Acre he followed the crowd and turned south to the fruit and vegetable market.

Trading was in full swing and a healthy crowd jostled as it sought out the goods on offer. It was noisy here as the costers competed to attract the attentions of shoppers, many of them, judging by their dress, from the better quality households that had sprung up on the outskirts of what remained an insalubrious area. Servants shopping for their masters' tables, he thought. A young slip of a baker's boy manoeuvred through the throng holding a basket filled with loaves on his head, drawing the mocking attentions of the stallholders, two of whom competed to knock the bread out of the basket by throwing apples and pears. The boy blushed and quickened his pace but his efforts did not spare him from being the focus of much laughter among the crowd.

The variety of smells that wafted on the air aroused in Maven the widest range of emotions. The stench of dead animal flesh, however freshly killed, revived too many memories of battles past but at least meat was in the minority in Covent Garden. He quickened his pace and was soon past the butcher. Then the perfume of spices landed from the east and sweet fruits just in from the west improved the atmosphere considerably. Stalls were laden with pineapples, lemons, limes, oranges and pomegranates. He slowed so he could imbibe the pleasant fragrances. Every once in a while he caught the whiff of nutmeg and the thing they called All

Spice. A stray dog ran across his path, chasing what looked like a black rat but the presence of the animals was a common enough sight here and did not interrupt the commerce. Suddenly, a costermonger caught Maven's eye and shouted above the din, "'Ere y'are guv'nor. Taste one o' these. Beautiful they are. New in this mornin' from Kent. Late pickings."

The stallholder tossed over a small red apple and Maven caught it at chest height. It was fresh and ripe. He took a bite and was pleased with the result. Maven nodded his thanks to the fruiterer and handed over a coin in return for a bag of the apples. He continued through the throng then turned north and reached the edge of the market. Sitting propped against a wall was a small child, a girl in what was once a white smock, which was now grey. The garment was torn at the hem and armholes. The whites of her eyes shone out through the grime of her face. She was no more than eight years old and yet there was so little in her expression. No hope, for sure, and no fear, but a contempt for the people who passed by without noticing her. Maven made eye contact and she held his gaze. He tossed her an apple, which she failed to hold, the red ball spinning away from her on the filthy ground. She rolled across the dirt and retrieved it, rubbed it against her smock and set about its consumption hungrily. Maven smiled but received no emotion in return.

He turned north onto James Street, crossed Long Acre and entered a narrow passage on the left that led to The Star's discreet rear access. Maven's attention was alerted by a noise, which sounded like a fight. Two men were shouting. Maven stopped and stood in the shadows. He heard a horse whinnying, as if in a state of some alarm. Then, the assembly hove forth through the side gate and into the yard – two men and, surreally, in this confined area, a large grey horse in some distress, its forelegs kicking high. The men were doing their best to restrain the beast, which bore full tack, including an expensive leather saddle. Maven paused to observe the show, taking a backward step so as not to be swept into the melee. The first of the men, a round, ruddy-faced individual was Trescothick himself, doing his best to appear in control. He had a hold of the reins and was attempting to force the animal to a standstill. Given that the beast was nearly twice his height and considerably heavier, it was a battle he was unlikely to win. Instead, the horse dragged him across the yard in whichever direction it decided. The second man, a smaller, thinner fellow with short grey-white hair was Peck, who was usually to be found clearing the empty tankards or otherwise cleaning up after the topers. His presence seemed to be doing nothing except antagonising the beast and, after a near miss that saw him stuck between the horse and the tavern wall, he slipped inside to safety. Trescothick gave up the fight and released the reins. The horse took full opportunity to exploit its freedom and galloped around the small yard three times before realising that it was trapped. The older man bent double and the monk's patch at his crown shone directly at Maven. Trescothick wheezed then hawked and spat on the ground. He brought himself upright, cursing all the while under his breath.

The horse, meanwhile, had found its way to Maven and the apples he was holding. Maven knew nothing about horses and, as usual when he was in the presence of animals, adopted guesswork as the best way forward. He stroked the horse on its nose, tapped it on its neck and murmured some words to establish that he presented no threat. The horse took a proffered apple without hesitation and snorted its thanks. Trescothick stared at the animal from about twenty yards away. He walked across to Maven, giving the horse a wide berth on the way.

"About bleddy time," he said, still struggling for breath.

"And good morning to you, too, Tresco. I came as soon as I got the message." Maven offered an apple to his friend.

"We've had the militia here," he said between bites, spraying Maven with small droplets of apple juice and flecks of the white flesh.

"Looking for me?"

"Aye, who else would concern 'em?"

"To do with that business the other night?"

"No, no. None of that. That whiffling idiot went and got himself run over by a wagon. He's laid up proper and won't be troubling no one for a while. These was proper militia. Three of 'em come up from Westminster last night. I had to show 'em your empty room to prove you weren't 'ere. Stroppy so-and-sos they was."

"Then they left?"

"Aye. Gave me an order first, mind. Lieutenant, he was. Says I was to let 'em know where you was."

Trescothick finished the apple, core and all, then continued.

"I told him, when he's got as much blood on his red coat as I 'ave on mine then I'll take orders from 'im. In the meantime, no bleddy toy soldier is going to be ordering me about in me own pub."

"But you still sent me a note, though."

"Course, I did. You might be in trouble. And when you's in trouble tis always fun seeing you get out of it, sir."

"Well, Tresco, I'm glad I can be of assistance. How on earth did you know where I was?"

"Well, you might be the best there is at skirmishing in Flanders villages but here in the city you has become a civilian. When you left here the other morning I sent one of the boys after that coach to see where you went. Them things don't travel too quick, do they? Even so, he was mighty pleased you didn't get carted off to the country, sir. Big new house up in Hatton Garden, I hear. Who's the wench?"

"Do you remember General Cooper?"

"Aye, mad sod. Bit too brave for his own good, that one."

"Lady Kathrine Cooper is his widow."

"I 'eard she were a tart. What she want with you then?" Before Maven could answer, Trescothick continued, "Oh, there's one thing I has to give you. That militia Lieutenant left you a letter. It's inside. Come and 'ave a drink while I fetches it.

The Hanoverian knew he was taking a risk by visiting in daylight but, he reasoned, he had nothing to hide from anyone who might observe his comings and goings. The Elector's wishes were of a higher importance to any local gossip that might be ignited. Dressed in his customary black outfit, Herr Bothmer had become well known about the town and, he thought to himself, he did rather enjoy the London experience. It was so much livelier than Hanover. The sedan carriers had done their best to unsettle him on the journey and had rocked him to and fro until he felt his breakfast might reappear and he had conveyed his displeasure by rapping on the coachwork and growling his complaints at them. Despite the discomfort, Bothmer rather enjoyed the way the men shouted at other road users to make way for an important gentleman. Then they arrived and no sooner had they stopped than they had dropped him to the ground with a spine-jarring bump. He allowed himself a second or two to settle then climbed out of the chair and looked up at the sky. It was cloudy but did not seem to threaten rain, though there may be a shower later. He congratulated himself on how quickly he had developed the English obsession with the weather.

"Wait here for me."

The lead chair carrier nodded to him, sullen but grateful for the respite, for it was some distance from St James's Palace and the foreigner was no light weight. Bothmer paused and looked up at the house. It was as grand as he expected for a gentleman of status and he granted his approval with a nod. He stepped up to the front door and tapped the brass knocker that was fashioned in the shape of a lion's head. The servant who answered was surly and silent and Bothmer made a mental note to convey his thoughts to the master of the house. The hallway was cold, bare and gloomy, illuminated only by the daylight that followed from the front door. Bothmer's footsteps echoed on the polished wood as he made his way to the rear of the house. At the end of the corridor, the servant stood aside and showed the visitor into the reception room. This was more like it, he thought. How very English. There was a red leather settee, a cumbersome affair that dominated the room, and two smaller armchairs. A fire roared and the room was stifling. The chimney needed to be swept for there hung in the air a haze of grey smoke. A large desk stood in front of a pair of doors that led into a small courtyard. The host looked up from his papers.

"Herr Bothmer. Do please take a seat. I thank you for coming so soon."

"Nonsense. It is I who should be thanking you for your time, sir. You have something for me?"

"I regret that what you seek, sir, has been destroyed."

"So they say, Mr Audley, so they say. But I wonder if we cannot take steps to be sure. Bring me the man who says he destroyed it. I shall decide if he tells the truth."

6

The letter instructed Maven to wait outside the Whitehall office of Mr Gideon Crouch, secretary to the Duke of Shrewsbury. Maven had assumed that he would be searching in Tuthill Street for a grand building, or at least an obvious location for the Lord Treasurer. Unfortunately, what he found before him were some undistinguished, rather plain houses, each with similar entrances and none with any signage that might help the casual visitor. Still, he reasoned, he was early and had, at least, given himself time to observe whether he might be the victim of a trap. He circled the area, walking up King Street as far as Bow Street then wheeled back so as to flush out anyone who might have been following. There was nobody as far as he could make out. So intent was Maven in looking at what was happening behind him and across the street that he only just avoided cannoning into Gideon Crouch, who stood before him and cleared his throat in a gesture of reproach. The taller man just managed to stop his forward motion, which would surely have knocked Crouch to the ground.

"Captain Maven?" asked the twisted, wiry man whose odd expression suggested his contorted body was causing him chronic pain. Maven recalled seeing him at the Mazarine house the previous evening, although they had not been introduced.

"Mr Crouch? I didn't expect you to meet me on the street, sir."

"No, indeed," replied Crouch, looking up at Maven with his neck at such an angle that it caused his body to buckle rather alarmingly. They exchanged half-hearted bows.

"Follow me, we shall be going to the offices of the Duke of Shrewsbury," said Crouch and set off at a pace away from Parliament and into the open area known as The Sanctuary. Maven paused for a second to allow the information to permeate.

There were few people around and Crouch made good progress, leading Maven back into Tuthill Street, where the smaller man stopped without notice. He whirled around, his beaky face seeking out something that might annoy or worry him. Finding neither he darted through a green front door that had been opened from within by a servant. Maven wasted no time in stepping inside the house behind his host.

The hallway was lit with candles, which served their purpose of lighting the way but provided no additional illumination so that the pictures that adorned the walls remained a mystery to Maven as he swooped past in pursuit of Crouch, who had galloped ahead. Crouch executed a right hand turn into a small library that at least allowed the daylight in through a single tall window. The musty smell of old books pervaded the atmosphere. Maven stood in the centre of the room, his neck craning to take in the floor to ceiling storage of reading material. The bindings on several of the shelves suggested the books were of a great age. Crouch busied himself by lighting more candles, a task that seemed unnecessary until the little man drew the heavy red velvet curtain and shut out the daylight.

"Sit, please Captain, do take a seat. There is no need to stand."

Maven considered the options and selected a simple wooden chair that was on his side of a dark oak desk that dominated the end of the room nearest the curtains. On the other side of the desk was a heavier chair, upholstered with maroon leather, a piece of furniture that sang out that its use was for the owner rather than his guests. As he expected, Crouch took the grand seat. The clerk had conjured from nowhere a notepad and one of the new fangled fountain pens.

"Now, then," said Crouch, "where shall we begin? Captain, we have, you might say, something of a situation on our hands. The Duke may join us presently but he has been detained by parliamentary business and has asked me to deputise. I regret that today may not turn out to be the day that you meet him."

Maven wondered why Crouch required a pen. Evidently, so did Crouch for he replaced the writing implement on the desk and leaned back in the chair. Maven shifted awkwardly.

"Force of habit," said Crouch, glancing in the direction of the pen and then began a dance with his hands, at once leaning forward and resting his elbows on the table, then sitting back and folding his hands in his lap. Then he jumped up from the chair, peered around the curtain and examined the solitary window, checking first that it was closed by rattling it then looking through it into the narrow alley. Crouch returned to his chair and cleared his throat. Crouch leaned forward and spoke in a low voice.

"We find ourselves in a most busy period. Yes, busy indeed, with much to-ing and fro-ing by politicians, clerks and various representatives. It is, frankly, something of a task to keep up with it all. However, since the Duke and I are, so to speak, new to the job, I use my relative inexperience as an excuse and I shall continue to do so for as long as I am allowed to get away with it!"

With this, the clerk guffawed, surprising his guest not only with the joke but also with the peculiar, strangulated laugh that emanated from his mouth. Maven joined him with a smile, so as not to appear rude. His knowledge of politics was limited to what he read in the Daily Record, so Maven elected to keep his own counsel. He hoped, though, that his host would hurry up and get to the point.

"Captain, thank you for coming to see us at such short notice. We are very much obliged by your attentions. The Duke is with the Captain-General at Marlborough House otherwise I am sure he would be here to have this conversation with you himself. Now then, to the point. There are, perhaps, no more than two hundred gentlemen at Westminster who could be said to exert control over this fine country. Their opinions and decisions shape the nation, so to speak, and it is wise to understand who is dealing with whom. And why. One of those gentlemen is causing a degree of vexation. Edward Audley, Lord Audley of Waltham appears, as it were, to have joined the ranks of the Jacobite tendency. He has been missing for some while and we should very much like to locate him. I gather your erm, friend, Lady Cooper faces a similar challenge."

"Her problems are of a rather more personal nature than yours, Mr Crouch."

"Quite so, yes."

Maven thought for a moment.

"Could he be dead? It is not unusual, sir, that when an otherwise respectable gentleman goes missing it is the case that he has, how might one say, over-indulged and passed on. His location would be a secret known only to his victualler or certain ladies of his acquaintance."

"Hm, straight to the point, sir. His death would indeed be a pleasurable thought. However, although Lady Kathrine would also no doubt be cheered by Audley's passing, our situation is not so straightforward. We have explored just such an avenue and found it to be barren."

Maven thought the pause indicated that Crouch recalled having to explore the various aristocratic fleshpots, access to which would normally have been denied him. Crouch then brought himself back to the task in hand.

"Audley is, one might say, something of a difficult, rather quarrelsome customer and one whose actions are unpredictable. At a time when we seek to bring together the various factions of our Parliament, Audley is one of a decreasing number who clings to, shall we say, the old ways. He refuses to accept that a new broom is about to commence sweeping."

"Society understands him to be a Tory. He makes no secret of it." said Maven.

"Yes he is a Tory, but I hope you do not construe the word Tory as an insult, Captain. Our Parliament depends on a wide range of opinions to derive the results it seeks for the country. Inevitably, some of the opinions one hears are disagreeable; indeed they are often not even sensible. Despite Audley's extreme tendencies you should not fall into the trap of believing all Tories to be seditious Jacobites. Nor, for that matter, should you accept at face value the opinion that all Whig gentlemen are money-grabbing anti-Papists.

"So, we find ourselves missing Audley, who has made no secret of his liking for the court of the Pretender. Frankly, his interests are better served by them as his stock is largely worthless in the City. As is the way with these things, he has gone missing at a time when we would most like to know where he goes and who he sees. Now then, I can in all honesty say that we hope he has absconded once and for all and is now gainfully occupied at the court of the Pretender, scheming without effect. However, I fear that the true state of affairs may not be so simple and I would like to be sure of his whereabouts in advance of the Coronation."

Crouch leaned forward again and lowered his voice still further so that Maven could barely hear him.

"Captain, the feminine troubles of Lady Cooper are of no concern to me, though she will no doubt ensure they continue to be of interest to you. Audley, on the other hand generates a very grave peril, a peril that should worry every gentleman in the land. The

Duke and the Captain-General believe with some justification that Audley means to dispose of the new King."

Crouch paused while his news was received and Maven fidgeted in the uncomfortable chair, relieved they were finally getting to the point.

"Captain, your challenge is to find and retrieve Lord Audley. The Captain-General has no doubt you will flush him out for the Lady so the additional burden of presenting him to me should not present too much of a challenge for you. We believe him to still be in London, being hidden by accomplices."

"There are over half a million people in this city."

"Most of them cannot be mistaken for aristocrats, though. Nonetheless it is a good point and one that I had considered. I believe that Audley does not work alone, rather that he is the senior man in a small clique."

"Do you have any idea who the other gentlemen might be?"

Crouch pondered the question, resting his elbows on the desk and raising his hands to face in a prayer-like pose, tapping his fingertips against his nose.

"One has to be very careful about making unfounded allegations, Captain, as an unblemished reputation is usually a gentleman's greatest asset. I would not wish to be seen to be enquiring too closely into Lady Kathrine's delicate matters but may I suggest you look close to home for the answer?"

"Your letter was written on the notepaper of the Lord Treasurer. Is Shrewsbury part of this arrangement?"

"Indeed he is, Captain. Like Marlborough he has the interests of the country at heart."

Crouch leaned forward and stared at Maven.

"I had though my news that our King was in mortal danger might stir you more than it has. May we rely upon you? The Captain-General speaks highly of you and it is not my place to disagree. Will you help us?"

"Mr Crouch, I am no politician but my reading of the newspapers suggests that Audley and his cronies have nowhere to go but to the Pretender's side. The mob wants a protestant succession which means Audley will be out of favour quite soon. And you have confirmed that is a state he can ill afford."

"Then you know he has the motive as well as the means. He must not be given the opportunity. He poses a very real threat Maven."

"Is that it? Any further instructions?"

Crouch paused, thought for a second and then said, "For what it is worth I do have a list of addresses where Audley can be found from time to time. Some of them are among the more reputable establishments in the capital but, given his plunging reputation, you are unlikely to find him there. Try the clubs that have a lower status. His residence is on the list, though, and you may find some clues there, I suppose."

Crouch stood and Maven followed his lead.

"Oh, just one last thing, Captain. I stress that on no account is any of your work to be attributed to the Duke of Shrewsbury," he paused for effect and then went on, "or to me. You will understand the reasons, I am sure. As far as the outside world is concerned you are working for Lady Kathrine."

"Mr Crouch, please tell me truthfully, is she in danger or does the Lady bring distress upon herself?"

Crouch pondered the question.

"Audley is a loose cannon. If he believes himself to have been slighted by her rejection he will take action, of that I am sure."

"And has he been slighted?"

"Lady Cooper has behaved with impeccable good sense. The trouble with respect and status is that the man who most values it tends to be the man who least deserves it. In his eyes she has wounded him and that is all that matters. He has nothing to lose by harming her."

Gideon Crouch stood and, with a subtle lifting of his right hand, suggested Maven might like to do the same. Both men moved toward the door. As they left the room Maven asked, "Why is it necessary to exercise so much secrecy? Would it not be simpler to turn the militia out to find him?"

"Indeed it would, Captain, if circumstances were normal, but I regret they are not."

Maven's puzzled expression prompted the clerk to continue.

"I wonder whether you recall the case of Sir William Perkins?"

In response to Maven's blank expression, Crouch added, "The Turnham Green Plot. Surely you recall?

Maven recalled the name but not the circumstances.

"You would have been quite young at the time. It was, my goodness, eighteen years ago. Perkins and others made a quite pathetic attempt at regicide and were, of course, apprehended. Perkins' house was found to be full to the brim with weapons of all kinds."

Maven recollected that there had been a great excitement when Perkins' head had been exhibited on a spike at Temple Bar.

"I still don't see the problem," said Maven, "just have the man arrested, search his house and let justice take its course. What could be simpler?"

The look on Crouch's face bordered on the patronising and, had it tipped been any more condescending Maven might well have hit him.

"My dear Captain, Audley isn't acting alone and we haven't found the arsenal. Moreover, we may well have overreacted for there are several known Jacobites, Bishop Atterbury for instance, who have solemnly declared that there is no plot. If we turn to the blunt instrument of the militia the whole town will think there is definitely something afoot and the real culprits, if there are any, will slip away while the mob goes on the rampage. There are already bonfires burning across the country and if the King isn't crowned soon fire will turn into riot and riot will become ... well I need not go on. The spirit of rebellion is alive and well in the hearts of many Englishmen and, let's face it, a combination of excessive drink and misplaced patriotism only ever leads to trouble. It's not exactly what the new King wants to be greeted with when he steps out of the Abbey. So no, Captain, there shall be no action that might lead to civil war. Marlborough and Shrewsbury have immense wisdom in these matters. Discretion is the way that has been chosen and discretion is the way it shall be."

"I thought you people employed an army of spies to do this sort of thing. Surely you have someone better suited than me to do the work?"

"On this occasion it has been decided that we require the services of someone ... outside the circle. Your acquaintance with the Lady is fortuitous but makes you an ideal candidate. "

"And Shrewsbury? When will I meet ...?"

"All in good time, Captain, and when the Duke decides it is appropriate."

With that, Crouch guided Maven to the door, which was again opened for him by the servant who nodded graciously as he departed then closed the door silently, leaving Maven standing in the street.

7

That evening, Maven dined in Hatton Garden with Kathrine. Her invitation had been pinned on the kitchen door and, for good measure, delivered verbally by a belligerent Sarah, who had made it clear how she felt about staff dining at the same table as the mistress. Despite the new fashion for dining late, the Cooper household maintained the tradition of eating at six unless there were guests. As Maven did not count as a guest the meal was arranged early. The light wardrobe he carried with him meant there was no choice but to dress in the same attire he had worn to Chelsea and he was more self-conscious now of the quality of his uniform following the insults Wingate had levelled at him. He waited for her in the dining room on the first floor, checking his reflection in the looking glass and pulling the coat about so that it might fit him a little better. He sat on one of the chairs and then stood and went to look out of the window, fidgeting all the while with his cuffs. Like the rest of her house the dining room was tastefully and expensively furnished. The oval table was not too big and sat in the centre of the room. A matching cabinet against the wall brimmed with silverware and a vase of fresh flowers.

There was a quiet knock and the door opened. Sarah came in with a candle to light the room. She took the opportunity to appraise him with a critical eye.

"Very dashing, sir, I'd say. I bet you've broken a lady's heart once or twice. I'm just bringing a bit of light before it gets too dark in here, don't you mind me. Then again perhaps if we waits in the dark you might be walkin' about and find yourself accidentally upon an ample lady, eh?" and with this she cackled playfully, "and then where would we be?"

Maven smiled and replied, "Sarah, I should like nothing better to oblige you but I am sure Lady Kathrine would be aggrieved to see the servants flirting so."

The door opened again and Sarah's giggling was replaced by a serious frown. Kathrine had arrived ten minutes after the appointed time and without an apology. Maven thought she looked stunning. She wore a dark blue gown with white gloves and her hair was worn up with delicate ringlets tumbling down by each ear. She wore no jewellery and her pale shoulders and neck were the better for it. Her face glowed and the candlelight highlighted her high cheekbones. He bowed a greeting and she returned with a graceful curtsey, her smile genuine and warm.

"Captain, do please sit down," she said, guiding him to one of the places set for dinner. They were seated opposite each other but not at the heads of the table. Instead, the positioning was intimate, with only a small floral table decoration between them. Sarah withdrew then returned a moment later clattering a silver tureen onto the table. Kathrine nodded to Sarah and the housekeeper served the soup, a broth-like concoction with pieces of potato and peas in it. Once the first course had been served and the tureen safely returned to the sideboard, Sarah seated herself on a chair near the door. Decorum was to be maintained.

"Tell me about your day, Captain. Is there anything to report?"

Maven had debated all day whether or not he should share the full details with her.

"No progress as yet."

There was a pause before she answered, "Is that it? You were out for, what, seven hours. Do you have nothing at all to tell me?" Her tone did not match the directness of the question and he sensed she was struggling to mask her fear behind a cloak of authority and politeness. They sipped red wine with their soup, the silence awkward, both of them finding it difficult to summon conversation. Maven told her about Trescothick, as much to drown the sound of cutlery against crockery as to convey any information. Then he regretted his reference to the army.

"Tell me about your service. When you were with my husband."

"I would rather not"

"And I would rather you did, sir."

"There really isn't much to tell."

"Now, Captain, I know that isn't true. Tell me, why did you join?"

He thought brief and his mind wandered back ten years to a chance meeting in a Cheapside alehouse. The recruiting officers knew where to find the poor wretches who could be enjoined into the service of their country and they knew to time their assaults to coincide with the hour when landlords were throwing the drinkers into the street to find their way home.

"I had nothing better to do, I suppose."

"No trade? No family to stand in the way of your patriotic duty?"

He paused. "No, no family."

"Tell me."

She looked him in the eye and he was powerless. She smiled gently and he relaxed, feeling as though he had known her for years. "I lost my parents in a fire. My father had not put out all the candles before he slept. I think he was a little the worse for drink, put his arm out for something and upset the light. It was a small house and the fire spread rapidly."

"I'm sorry. Where you there?

"No."

"And that left you alone?"

"My two sisters died young. Neither made it beyond childhood. But I was no orphan. I was married by then," said Maven and immediately regretted introducing Ruth into the conversation.

"And your wife?"

"I lost her a few months later. There was nothing to be done."

"I'm so very sorry."

There was silence between them then and Maven searched in vain for some topic that would lighten the mood. They finished their soup and Sarah removed the shallow dishes and replaced them with clean plates for the meat course. She served large roughly hewn pieces of lamb and placed a dish of potatoes between them She topped up the wine glasses. This time she did not return to her seat but tended the fire, then left the room. If there had been an instruction from her mistress then it had evaded Maven.

"Hugh pitied many of the men in his regiment. He wondered how awful their lives must have been for them to want to exchange them for the hell of war."

"Most joined for the money. That and the free grog. Some for the chance to murder legally."

"Not you though?"

It was more of a statement than a question. Maven was not given to self awareness but could not help himself.

"It was either the army or throw myself in the River. Same outcome usually."

He admonished himself for letting her unlock his thoughts, especially now that she looked at him with pity.

The meal finished, they sat alone and faced each other across the table. She said, "Do you think I am a bad person?"

"Why?"

"For refusing to submit to convention."

"If submitting to convention means giving your inheritance to a bully who threatens you because he cannot get his own way then, no I do not."

"Do you think all women should marry?"

"Not if they do not want to."

"But it is expected."

"You won't marry because you have already made up your mind and you do not seem the sort of woman would easily change it. Besides, the General would never forgive you."

"Tell me about your wife."

"I would rather not."

"Are you still in love Captain? Do you miss her?"

"Yes," he said, "I do."

With this he felt somehow unburdened for it was a question he had never been asked.

"Then, "she replied, "We have something in common."

They sat in silence and finished the last of the wine. Presently, she said, "Will you light the way to my room?"

"Of course. Before that I should like to know about Mr Bolingbroke. What is he to you?"

"He is a memory. Part of my past."

"Not of your future?"

"You need not worry yourself about him."

He stood and took the lamp from the sideboard, taking care to cup his hand around the flame. He blew out the remaining candles so they were left with the single light source, which threw their shadows across the room. He led her up the stairs to the landing and waited outside her door. They stood facing each other in the gloom and she reached out a hand to touch his chest, stopped herself then took the candle from him and went into her room, leaving him alone in the darkness.

In Whitehall, three gentlemen gathered. To be more precise, two gentlemen had gathered and a clerk had listened at the door in case he should miss out on any developments of what was, according to the Duke, a delicate situation. It had been agreed by the gentlemen that they would eat separately beforehand and then meet for conversation later in the evening. Crouch had been pleased at his suggestion since it had avoided the embarrassing situation of deciding what meal to serve. The household's knowledge of what foreigners considered appropriate fare was lacklustre, and the clerk had fretted for several hours that there might be a diplomatic incident of some kind if the menu insulted the guest. This evening he had needed to serve only the best brandy. The drink had been well received. Herr Bothmer was clearly a man of some taste, after all.

"Crouch!"

The summons took him by surprise and he beetled about in the vestibule, returning to his desk to retrieve his pen and paper before bursting into the Duke's study. He bowed and assessed whether or not their guest was in a relaxed mood. It was one of those rare occasions when the clerk was unable to deduce the state of play for their guest was not someone who displayed his emotions readily. Bothmer's stern face implied impatience, his body suggested otherwise, for he had relaxed deep into the large armchair and sat with his feet apart twirling the brandy glass playfully.

"Sir?"

"Herr Bothmer enquires after Matthew Webb," said Shrewsbury, "What news do you have?"

Shrewsbury knew very well what news he had since they had discussed it earlier but Crouch knew his employer well enough to understand his grasp of etiquette: it was a servant's duty to deliver news.

"There has been a development, sir. The courier came ashore as planned and was met. He had expected a safe passage and he left Deptford with them. Needless to say he did not reach the North."

Bothmer rested his glass on the table.

"May I meet the courier?"

"I regret that will not be possible, sir. The traitor met his death. I gather our man was unable to spare him, though he would have done so had he not been watched closely."

"What did he bring ashore. More money?"

"Yes, sir, a considerable quantity of gold. As much as a man can reasonably carry about his person without attracting undue attention."

"Audley robbed him?"

"Yes, sir."

"Their actions appear to represent a change in the process, Mr Talbot. It concurs with the gossip we have been hearing that Audley is increasingly frustrated by the actions of his Jacobite friends."

"Or lack of action, perhaps?"

"Quite so. Has he taken the initiative? What do you think the gold will be used for?"

"The usual things," replied Shrewsbury, "Only with Audley being rather more zealous than his friends we may find that this particular shipment does actually find its way to the quartermasters."

Bothmer turned to face Shrewsbury.

"He must be stopped Mr Talbot."

"We have the matter in hand."

"Your man is useful to keep up our sleeves, yes?" continued the German and Bothmer laughed at his use of the idiom. He picked up his glass and drained it then held it suggestively in the hope that he might be granted a refill. Crouch edged forward with the bottle and obliged. Bothmer waited for Crouch to withdraw and close the doors before he continued.

"He is a good man, no?"

Shrewsbury seemed non-plussed.

"Your servant, Mr Crouch, he can be trusted?"

Outside in the ante-room, Crouch beamed, waiting for the ringing endorsement from is master.

"As much as any of them can, I suppose."

Crouch reeled back from the door so that he almost missed the resumption of the conversation. Bothmer leaned forward and steepled his hands, resting his elbows on his knees.

"There is a letter. A packet of letters to be precise. You know of them?"

"Go on."

"It is said that these letters were the Queen's most valued personal possession, that she slept with them under her pillow each night."

"Yes, I know of them. They have aroused concern and amusement in equal measure Herr Bothmer. However, no one apart from Bolingbroke seems ever to have seen these items. You know how rumour can spread around court. It gathers pace like a forest fire."

"Indeed. But I am assured that the letters do exist."

Shrewsbury was taken aback by the certainty in the visitor's tone.

"You know what the letters contain?"

"I know what the rumours suggest," replied the Duke.

"Mr Talbot, if it is true that the Queen intended to change her mind and let it be known that her preference was for James Stuart to succeed her then such a revelation would cause many problems."

"Undoubtedly, sir. But such a thing is impossible and the Queen knew it to be so. The Act of Succession, for one thing."

"My messengers bring me news of unrest in the country. It seems Englishmen cannot resist the lure of violence. Even those who cannot understand the difference between Protestantism and Catholicism seem to enjoy setting fire to their towns and villages in the name of one cause or the other. Do the people sense something is amiss?"

"No, Herr Bothmer, if these letters existed then I would have heard of them. Heavens, man, I would have seen them. And if I had not then Marlborough would."

"We need to be sure Mr Talbot. If they are a matter of fact then I need to have them. I should very much like your assistance with this task."

"Sir, I cannot find something that does not exist. That is surely a fool's errand. We may search and search for ever and still not give you satisfaction."

"The King would like reassurance that the letters do not exist. How you provide it I shall leave to your imagination."

During the night Maven lay on his cot and stared at the ceiling. Any thoughts he may have had about walking away and leaving the Lady to the mercy of Audley were gone now. He had spent the night sleeping fitfully, his semi-consciousness dominated by thoughts of Wingate, five years previously, inspecting his troops before the hostilities at Malplaquet. Maven and Trescothick had returned from the forest with a small reconnaissance party that had had to draw upon its light infantry expertise when they had happened upon a small band of French deserters. The honour of the French had outweighed their desire to surrender and in the resultant skirmish all of the enemy soldiers had died. Tired, grimy and weighed down with enemy weapons, Maven and his small band had watched as Wingate's men lined up in the square, the better to instill panic in the enemy as the massed redcoats advanced at a march. They watched as Wingate, braying and immature, implored his men into battle and observed how those grizzled, battle-hardened veterans looked upon the young boy with contempt, so that Wingate lost his temper and struck a man, then struck him again when he still failed to do as he was ordered and wipe that surly look off his face. That so many of those good men perished and Wingate survived to be promoted raised Maven's ire. The anger was made worse because he had never been able to explain to the widows of fallen comrades why their husbands or sons would never return, nor could he explain what their deaths had achieved. Wingate, that reedy aristocrat who was more terrified of battle than any of his men, had stood and shouted until his weak little voice could take no more and had sunk into a rasping incoherence instead of the strident rallying call for which he searched.

Maven turned in the bed, hoping to rid himself of this demon and only found a brief period of respite before he was troubled by a dream of Lady Kathrine Cooper, running toward him in a pure white dress, smiling, her arms reaching out to him and her eyes shining, then the white of her gown staining red with blood; just slightly at first, a small thin slick of red below her breasts and she ran towards him but never reached him. He saw that the wound was about her heart and the crimson stain spread out across the stomach. As she ran to him, her smile faded and her eyes began to implore him to help. And then she fell at his feet and he saw the sword in her back, run all the way through her. Its silver hilt was a crucifix. As she fell he saw a man standing some distance behind her, like the pathetic and inept Wingate only taller, stronger and smiling cruelly, standing firm on the ground, his feet apart, pleased with work he had just done. Then the woman on the ground was not Lady Kathrine Cooper but a French peasant girl. Suddenly, alongside the officer appeared a phalanx of redcoats, some with flintlock rifles and others with muskets, smiling along with their captain, then laughing, rocking with the humour of it all, pointing at Maven, an upstart officer with no breeding and the peasant girl who had dared challenge the authority of her conquerors. Then the girl was screaming and banging his boots with her fists as she lay dying on the floor until her anger receded and her hands could move no more. He woke with a start, as he always did at this point, breathless, his shirt wringing wet. He sat bolt upright. It had been a long time since he had had the dream but its return was inevitable as soon as he had set foot in this house. He knew that trying to sleep was futile and he spent the rest of the night staring out of his window into the darkness.

As soon as the sun began to rise he got up and washed, found a clean shirt in his bag and went downstairs before the household had roused itself. He took a small loaf from the kitchen and was leaving by the back door when he heard the leaden-footed Sarah descending the stairs in her usual noisy manner. He pretended not to hear her call as he closed the door. It was cold and the smoke from the fires of the houses and businesses of the metropolis was only just beginning to wend its way into the atmosphere. The usual fug of London soot had not yet formed and he watched the weak sun dart in and out of light clouds but would be obscured within the hour. He walked to Covent Garden, the better to plan his actions. He needed Trescothick to have had a good night and he hoped the old Sergeant had not succumbed to the temptation of a lock-in and an opportunity to relieve his punters of their lucre. He needed him to be awake and alert, his son also.

He reached the tavern as George was folding back the wooden shutters that protected the premises from the vagaries of Long Acre in the night. Any establishment containing grog and tobacco was fair game to the rooks and ne'er-do-wells. George smiled as he saw Maven striding up the street and he stepped forward to greet his visitor with a handshake rather than a bow. Physically, George was the same man his father had been twenty years ago: the height, the weight, the attitude and nuances of speech, the accent less pronounced but the mannerisms were there. In twenty years' time the son would be a double for the father, and this was a good thing because the world needed more men like Trescothick.

"Hullo, Captain, not used to seeing you about this early in the morning."

The younger Trescothick was short and broad-shouldered. Duties that included lifting and rolling barrels of ale about the place and ejecting drunken and unwanted visitors from the tavern ensured that he stayed strong and hard. George still had his naturally fair hair pulled away from his face and tied at the back with a black bow, a source of constant derision and fun for his father but the opening of many a conversation with attractive women for George, whose habit when he thought no-one was looking was to preen himself in the glass like a Drury Lane actor preparing for opening night. His round face still had the smoothness of the boy about it yet his eyes betrayed the secrets of the London streets. Nonetheless, his father had remarked more than once how relieved he was that at least his boy had been spared the horrors of the battlefield.

The old man had saved his booty judicious and the tavern had been purchased with an eye on George's future. Trescothick had served the country enough for the pair of them, he said. George carried with him a nagging fear that he had somehow missed out on something. The older men had the unspoken allegiance of those who had shared something so dreadful that they dared not discuss it for fear of awakening memories best left buried. And it was this curiosity that Maven wanted to harness.

"Is your father around?"

"In the tap room, Captain."

Maven trooped in through the front door, bending his neck to avoid striking his head on the low beams.

"Tresco!"

"Down 'ere!" came the reply and Maven went over to the trapdoor that led to the cellar. There was a lightweight wooden ladder that Maven had never dared try, although it seemed to have borne the weight of the Trescothicks without ill effect. He clambered down, the wood flexing under his bulk.

"Go orn, man, she won't hurt you"

Trescothick stood waiting for Maven with a candle. As the big man got one foot on firm ground the Sergeant turned away quickly and disappeared into a recess beyond where the barrels were stored. He returned with a magnum of claret.

"Had the bleddy militia man back again. What exactly you bin doin'?"

"I need your help Tresco."

"Aye, figured that."

Trescothick walked past him and climbed the ladder. It barely held his considerable weight. Maven flashed a petulant look at his back and followed.

"I needs you to tell me, sir. Is it anything illegal?"

"Tresco, really, I thought you knew me better than that."

"Tell me."

"You're serious."

"Aye, am that. Now tell me."

"No, it is not illegal," but then he hesitated for, in truth, he could not be entirely certain.

"Sure?"

"We're working for Marlborough again. In a manner of speaking. And I'd like to borrow George."

Trescothick harrumphed, unimpressed by the mention of his former employer.

"Why do you want the boy? Not that he'd object, of course, but if he's to be involved in summat then I should be pleased to know what it is."

George walked towards them with a tray of cold meat, large enough that it needed both his hands to hold it.

"Cook says this has to be gone by lunch or it'll kill someone. Looks alright to me, so if you're feeling lucky dig in before I chuck it out for the dogs."

His father was relieved to change the subject.

"Get away with yer, boy. Tis good for another day at least."

"George, I need your help," interrupted Maven.

"How so, Captain?"

Maven explained what he wanted and George turned to his father for approval who was slow to respond.

"Tis the Captain-General's work," said the older man finally, "so you be sure and do it well."

8

Maven and George followed the trail suggested by Gideon Crouch. The Hatton Garden household possessed just one map and the late General had purchased it some five years before, resulting in its detail being less than helpful. It was, Maven decided, better than relying on his and George's memory as to where the various streets might be found and, more importantly, who owned which house. They had sat at the kitchen table poring over the details and constructed a plan for their day. Gideon Crouch had given them the address of Audley's London home and also suggested The Blackbird Club, from which the errant Lord had famously been ejected earlier in the year, allegedly for cheating at cards.

Kathrine allowed them the use of her coach on the understanding that they undertook no activity that frightened the horses and George engaged Peck, the Tavern's pot man as driver-cum-footman. He was a scrawny fellow with a complexion like the skin of a lemon. His shoulders drooped and he wore a perpetual hang-dog expression. His lack of a uniform and surly manner detracted considerably from the effect George had hoped for.

Peck's driving performance had given the lie to his assertion that he was an accomplished coachman and on the journey across town he had had two narrow escapes, drawing the sort of foul-mouthed abuse from other drivers that Maven had not heard since he was in the army. Now they found themselves waiting to turn right into Albermarle Street, where Audley made his London home. Peck waited for a heavily laden eastbound wagon to trundle past and then turned across in the gap of the traffic. The tall terrace was smart and uniform in its design. The General's map was of good quality and seemed to be accurate. Each of the houses was correctly recorded and the map helpfully gave the name of each owner. They drove past the Audley house and paused fifty yards away at the corner of Stafford Street, where the two passengers disembarked and walked back to the house. They sent Peck on to turn the coach around and promised him plenty of time to execute the manoeuvre.

George had in his hand a parcel, wrapped in brown paper at the kitchen table that morning. He had addressed the parcel to Lord Audley using a pen that had once belonged to the General. The pen was now safely nestled in his inside pocket on the off chance, he said, that he might require further use of the clever instrument. There being no obvious place for tradesmen to knock, the pair of unlikely deliverymen strode up to the front door and George tapped on the door. A servant, a wiry man whose facial features were pinched to the point of meanness answered the door. His nose was long and thin and his eyes were an icy blue that matched his frock coat. He stared at them.

"Parcel for ...," George looked down at the label, " ...Audley."

"Lord Audley is not here. Leave it with me and I will see that he gets it."

"We have instructions that we may deliver only to the addressee. In person."

"His Lordship does not receive tradesmen. In any case, he is not here."

"Do you know when might be back?"

"His Lordship is away from London, I am afraid, and he will return when business matters permit him to do so."

"And you've no idea when that might be?" interjected Maven a little too aggressively.

The servant paused, affronted by Maven's tone.

"None whatsoever. Are you sure I cannot accept the package on his ... what on earth do you think you are doing?" Maven had slipped a few steps away from the conversation and was now peering through the window into the drawing room. He had expected to find the usual aristocratic trimmings, soft furnishings, paintings, perhaps an urn and certainly a table or two. Instead, the room was bare, completely stripped in a manner consistent with the occupant having moved house.

"Doesn't look like he's got much to come back to."

"And what business would it be of yours?"

"If he has nothing to come back to then maybe he isn't coming back."

"I believe our conversation to be at an end, sir. Good Day. "

As the servant stepped back inside the house and made to close the door, George stepped forward.

"Hang on a minute. Don't be so hasty. We have a little problem, see. Me and my colleague don't get paid unless we delivers this package and gets a receipt from his Lordship. From one working man to another, so to speak, you couldn't give us a little clue as to where we might find him, could you?"

The sing song lilt of the west country brogue found servant in a more even spirit than Maven's pugnacious London tones and he seemed to mellow a little.

"His Lordship is not here. He has not been here for several weeks and I know not of when is likely to return. His staff have, on the instructions of his solicitor, left his employ."

Warming to the role, George sidled up to the man.

"Don't tell me, you sold all his furniture and took the money in lieu of wages. Good for you, sir!"

"We did nothing of the sort!"

"His Lordship's obviously got money problems, though, judging by that empty room, there."

The servant slammed the door. Maven and George wandered towards the main road clutching their parcel.

"Told you it wouldn't work," said George.

"If finding Audley had been as easy as knocking on his front door then he would have already been seized and they wouldn't need the likes of us to find him."

"Fair enough. At least we know he ain't got any cash and if an aristocrat is reduced to selling the family silver he must be in some serious trouble. What's next on the list?"

"The club."

"How do you suggest we deal with them? No point waltzing up to the front door there, sir. We'll get sent packing well and truly."

It was Mother McGrath's usual practice to protect the identities of her gentlemen callers by receiving their coaches only at the reverse of her Southampton Street house, preferably after dark. Outside the street was busy and the daylight was broad. She was not pleased. It created problems when they did things like this. This one, especially, was well known. He might even be the most famous man in all of London. It only took someone in the street to recognise him and the grubby reporters would be hanging around the front door bothering the girls. More to the point, she thought, her other gentlemen would be frightened away. They took such chances, these foolish men. She hurled a tot of rum down her throat to steady her nerves.

In the room in the attic the one they called Claudette had woken at first light. In truth, she had been so terrified of her assignment that she had not dared go to sleep. Instead, the eighteen year old had lain awake for six hours listening to her lord and master's snoring. One day, the bawd had said soon after she had collected Claudette from the Norwich coach, one of the Lords would be so taken with her he would sweep her away and she would be a kept woman. The handsome man who lay in the bed was indeed taken with her but, like the others, he had shown no sign of installing her in a house of her own. She lay in the bed next to him and stared at the ceiling while his deep contented breathing caused the bed to rock gently.

Downstairs, Mother McGrath was as nervous as she had ever been in the ten years she had spent in the capital. She ran a decent house, she thought, clean enough for the great and the good to give it patronage but it worried her so when the gentlemen flaunted the rules. She paced about the ground floor peering discreetly through the windows for signs of unusual activity. No, she thought, she did not like daylight at all.

The journey from Albermarle Street to the Blackbird Club was a short one, taking them across Portugal Street and into James Street. Ahead of them loomed St James's Palace, the residence of the new King and his standard fluttered in the stiff breeze. They made a circuit of the square and located the club premises, a magnificent white stone building. Maven rapped on the coachwork and called for Peck to stop. They sent Peck back into the Square. George led the way to the rear of the house into a covered entry, which opened onto a large yard, empty now but with space aplenty for coaches and stabling around the perimeter. The owner of the property had expended rather less on decoration here than he had on its frontage. From this vantage, the large house was plain and functional. The bricks were of a varied and dubious source, being of odd sizes and fashioned into a straight wall only by the constructive use of mortar. It was clear, also, that the best efforts of the servants in cleaning the place were concentrated on the areas seen by the members, for the floor of the yard contained a generous share of horse manure, even though no horses appeared to be present in the stabling. In the corner, a strong arm's throwing distance from the door was a pile of cooking debris, potato peelings and the less edible parts of root vegetables. Alongside were several large wooden boxes that on closer inspection contained empty wine bottles. Maven's arrival disturbed a large brown rat and the animal scurried for cover.

"Not much different from The Star, this place," said George.

"They may be a little more choosy in who they allow through the door."

"Don't you let me dad hear you saying that."

Maven knocked on the door. It was a half-glazed affair and the white paint had chipped off where it had been repeatedly kicked open and closed over the years. The door was unfastened and opened inwards with the only the slightest pressure. Maven leaned his head in and looked about.

"Hello! Anybody here?"

Taking no reply as an invitation to enter, they went in and got their bearings. They found themselves standing on the flagstone floor of a dimly lit kitchen. Iron pots and pans as well as quantities of empty wine bottles and a multitude of unwashed glasses littered each surface. They glanced at each other, shrugged and went through the narrow doorway to their left that led into a darker, narrow passage, at the end of which was another door. George went to try it. This one was firmly closed. As George turned the doorknob, his hand was thrown off by an equivalent turn from the other side and the door opened towards them. They were met by a short, barrel-chested man who filled the doorway.

"Who the bloody hell are you?"

George pretended not to be fazed.

"George Trescothick, sir, and this is Captain Maven, reporting for duty."

The short man nodded his head toward the kitchen, indicating that a retreat was called for.

"We can talk in there."

In the better light of the kitchen their host looked them up and down and his expression betrayed no clue that he might be impressed with what he found. For a small man he presented an impressive sight. Barely five feet two inches tall, the way he carried himself added inches to his height and his ramrod straight back demonstrated that formality came as standard. His pate shone like his black leather shoes and his dark bushy eyebrows had merged into a continuous fringe that guarded a mean and piercing stare. His black stockings and breeches were spotless and fit perfectly, setting off a shirt whiter than any that either of them had seen outside of a gentleman's outfitters. He wore the shirt open at the throat and the sleeves were rolled to the elbow. The thickness of his neck and forearms told them that, short though he may be, the gentleman was not to be tangled with.

"So?" he barked.

"We are reporting for work, sir. Cleaning, polishing," George looked towards the pots, "washing up and such like."

Maven's pulse raced and he was powerless to prevent George's enthusiasm from driving him forward.

"You've come up from the west country to do the washing up?"

"No sir, of course we haven't, sir. Only we are at something of a loose end on account of our most recent employer finding himself in straightened circumstances. Would you be a military man yourself?"

"That I would. All of us here are from the service. The members like it that way."

"Ah, it would suit us perfectly. I do miss the army."

"I'd wager you are a liar in that respect young man. There's few would exchange a warm bed and hot food for the life we led over there. You, big man, you carry yourself like an officer.

"Captain Luke Maven," said Maven, offering a bow that was not returned, "if we have come at an inopportune moment we shall leave you in peace –"

"Pardon me if I don't salute you sir," interrupted their host, "there was too many made up to Captain that was never merited. No more than killers most of 'em that never bought their commissions. You'll forgive me if I say your mode of dress suggests you are not a man of means."

"Too true, too true. I didn't catch your name and rank, sir."

"That's because I never gave it to you. And there is no need for the sir business neither. Corporal Dench is the name, batman to Colonel John Summersby. The Colonel understands army discipline, which is more than I can say for many of the members. Now you're wanting work you say?"

"Indeed we are."

Like a practised interrogator, Dench turned and faced George and stared hard at the youngster.

"And who is this employer who has dispensed with your services?"

The question took George by surprise but he knew that he needed to answer it promptly if their pretence were to continue. George lowered his voice, reasoning that the name he was about to supply might elicit some sort of negative response.

"Lord Audley, Corporal."

The response it prompted was one of dumbfounded silence and a long cold stare from the batman. Maven checked the door and made ready to run. He would explain the elementary mistake to George when they got outside. Right after he had slapped him.

"Is this some kind of joke?" he boomed.

"No joke at all, Corporal," interjected Maven, deciding to adopt an exit strategy, "my Lord suggested that as he was no longer able to support our employment on his Essex estate we might find success here. It seems he was wrong."

The change of location from London to the countryside seemed to wrong foot the suspicious batman.

"You'd do well not to show your faces here again. I'll tell you this for no other reason than we were brothers in arms, captain. Audley is a wrong 'un. He owes thousands all over the shop, especially here. You'll know what a one he is for the gaming tables but maybe you're not aware of how often and how much he loses."

"We had heard the rumours," ventured Maven.

"The trouble with your employer, if you don't mind me saying so, is that he is always working on some big scheme or other that is going to make his fortune and another fortune for all the club members that invest along with him. He's got a nerve sending the pair of you in here looking for work."

"They lost money?"

"The members? Oh, they got their money. But it came back on the turn of a card rather than in the form of dividends. So you might say there was no real harm done. Mind you that's nothing to do with me."

"Now, corporal, are you sure that we cannot find gainful employment here for a few days?" asked George.

"I don't believe I made you an offer, young man."

Dench looked at Maven.

"This one doesn't look like he was ever in the army, captain. There's a look about a man who has seen battle. I can see it in the eyes. And I don't see it with this young 'un."

"Indeed not, sir. I served with his father, a good man, honest and brave."

"He'll be in a minority then."

George shifted uneasily, not at all pleased to be discussed by the two men while he remained in the room.

"We have among our members some Gentlemen who would be pleased to be served by a young man such as this. I would need to check with the Colonel before I offered you any sort of terms, mind, especially given your background. You'll be wanting rooms as well, no doubt? References would obviously be a problem. Why don't you come back this evening when I have had a chance to talk to the Colonel. You ever waited at table?"

George struggled momentarily to come up with a response that maintained the subterfuge and then recovered himself just in time.

"Y-yes, sir. I served Lord Audley above stairs for about a year, sir. When he was in the country."

"Well, all right. Both of you be here tonight at six. "

Claudette sat up and eased herself quietly off the edge of the bed and slipped her delicate hand into the pockets of the coat that hung on the back of the door. Her client opened a sleepy eye to see what she might be doing then smiled and lay in silence watching while she completed her task. His manhood stirred and he considered the opportunity then decided that he would not use her again. When he was sure she had found what she searched for he called her to him and when she turned to face him she wore on her face a look of terror. The gentleman was perturbed that she thought him capable of some atrocity. He gave her two guineas and told her that the money was for her. He would pay the bawd as usual on his way out, as usual and the old hag was not to know of his generosity.

She was excused so that he could dress. Outside the room she withdrew the bundle of letters from her bodice and looked at them. The paper was heavy and cream coloured and it bore a heavy red wax seal. Her reading was barely that of a child and she did not attempt more than the title. She trembled at the thought of what might happen to her when he discovered they were missing.

She went downstairs to find Mother McGrath. The house was quiet and there was none of the music, the laughter of the clients and the giggling and girlish screams that gave the hours of darkness their life. It was as if, in the daylight, the house wallowed in its own post-coital guilt and felt the remorse that would never be shown by its visitors. The bawd turned from the front window and gave Claudette a frosty welcome.

"Well?"

"Well what?"

"Did you please him?"

Claudette sneered.

"He didn't need a lot of pleasuring ma'am. Just a few seconds. Then he was straight off to sleep like a lamb. Easiest guinea I ever earned."

There was a running battle for money between Claudette and her employer and the girl never wasted an opportunity to remind the bawd that she knew precisely how much of her earnings was stopped for "rent".

"Watch your mouth you little tart. I shall see you out on the street if you don't behave yourself."

Mother McGrath moved closer to Claudette and the girl felt the stale breath of the older woman on her cheek. Though the bawd insisted on high standards of cleanliness for her girls she maintained no such rules for herself and she stank like an open sewer.

"Did you find it?"

"Find what?"

"Don't play your saucy games with me, whore. You know damn well what. Hand it over."

"Cost ya!"

"Give it here. You don't know what you're involved with. Hand it over girl, if you know what's good for yer."

Claudette held the papers in her hand and waved them in front of Mother McGrath.

"What's it all about then? Seems a lot of fuss over a few bits of paper."

"Ain't ours to know," she said, snatching them away. "Just give 'em here and lets get 'em off the premises."

9

Maven presented himself at six o'clock as ordered. George, now sporting a hackney driver's tunic and a black tricorn hat had dropped him in Piccadilly then took the coach into St James's Square to wait for the return journey. Maven went to the back entrance, which at this later hour was busier than it had been earlier. He found Corporal Dench resplendent in a black frock coat and lace stock striding about the place dispensing orders to his small team.

Dench looked up, "Wondered if you'd turn up. Where's the pretty boy?"

"He's found himself some other work."

"I hope I didn't frighten the boy away."

Maven stared back.

"You'd better get started on the ironware," said Dench finally and then busied himself in the far corner of the kitchen harassing a boy who was arranging glasses on a tray.

In the Kings Head Tavern south of the river near Lambeth Wells, William Taylor settled down to another evening of drink and entertainment. The courier evidently brought more gold than the Colonel was expecting, as the payment he left for Taylor had been more generous than usual. Since then Taylor had been drinking steadily to celebrate his good fortune. Moreover, he had been paid twice for his work and the first toast he had drunk had been to the health of Matthew Webb, a fine gentleman and, as it turned out, a true patriot and not the Jacobite swine he had first feared him to be. Exactly as Mr Webb had predicted, Taylor had received a visit from a mysterious, nervous individual with a beaky nose and what may have been a hump on his back. Taylor was less concerned about the visitor's physical appearance when he had handed over a full ten guineas in return for the papers Taylor had removed from the courier's pocket when he had dragged the poor wretch's body into the woods.

It was Taylor's philosophy that money was a commodity best enjoyed as soon as possible before some blackguard thief stole it. So William Taylor had spent his week visiting old friends, alehouse keepers, smokers and gamblers and now that the funds were largely spent he had made his way to the Kings Head to conclude the day's amusements in the best traditions of the London rake he imagined himself to be. Those thereabouts knew well enough to leave him alone. Taylor was a fighter with influential friends and more than one fellow had crossed him in the past only to regret it later in the dark streets when he was set upon and left battered in the mud.

The public part of the Kings Head was a single ground floor room with a low ceiling. A candle on each of the tables provided a poor light. A miserable tapster kept his customers at bay with ribald insults and rapid service. He was a short, fat man with no neck and a tendency to point his chin at the floor. The pub was crowded with chandlers, gardeners and other working men. Many were enjoying a smoke, and of those that did, most used the shared clay pipes provided by their grumpy host. The venomous cloud of smoke hung heavily above the steady hum of conversation. Taylor called for more beer to quench his thirst and a jug of good red wine. His effusive tone suggested to all thereabouts that he was with funds and meant to enjoy himself this evening. When the girl brought his drink he pulled her towards him and whispered in her ear, taking the opportunity to grope her thigh with his free hand. Soon, Taylor was joined by two buxom women. Now he sat on the bench, red in the face grinning smugly and his new friends smiled benignly at his every utterance.

Presently, one of the wenches rose, went to the barrels and spoke quietly to the landlord who shuffled aside to allow her through and up the stairs to the living quarters and the spare room that was reserved for special guests. Soon she was joined by her colleague and then Taylor, who collected two more jugs of red wine from the landlord as he staggered through, smiling lasciviously.

"Awright?"

The voice came from a boy, barely old enough to be employed, who stood alongside Maven.

"Welsby. Jack Welsby. How d'you do?"

"Pleased to meet you," said Maven.

"First day?"

"Yes."

"They give the new boys all the best jobs. Wanna drink?"

Without waiting for an answer, Welsby reached across and grabbed a silver claret jug and poured two glasses of red wine.

"Get that down ya."

Welsby raised his glass.

"Cheers."

It was the best wine that Maven had ever tasted, better than the "good stuff" Trescothick kept hidden in The Star and certainly the equal of the grog that Marlborough shared with his officers. Welsby appeared to read Maven's thoughts.

"French. The buggers up there," he gestured to the ceiling, "would never admit it but they'll have this 'cos it's better than the Portuguese stuff. Don't blame 'em meself. Can't beat a decent drop of claret, eh?"

Maven drained the glass and, fortified by the alcohol, remembered why he was there.

"What are they like here, the members?"

"Bastards," said Welsby, the answer considerably more forthright than Maven had anticipated and his shocked expression invited the boy to provide more of an explanation.

"If it was possible, they would like you and me to be invisible. They wanna be served but they don't wanna be reminded that there are people like us in the building. They know we see everything and we hear everything. And they don't like it one little bit."

Welsby warmed to his theme.

"It seems to me that a London gentleman on the up does not want to be reminded of the mob on account that he knows that there but for the grace of God goes he, so to speak, whereas your genuine aristocrat with a big family fortune and all the rest of it is secure in the knowledge that he will always be above the mob. Ergo, we gets more respect from the proper aristo than we does from the newly wealthy. The trouble is, in this club we don't have many genuine old money types left. It's mostly new money."

"New money?"

"City boys, merchants, traders and what have you."

Maven was about to ask how Audley fitted in when Welsby swept his question aside. Welsby's hand made a downward sweeping curve as he explained, "And meeting the new money on the way down again are their Lordships who need, shall we say, a helping hand."

"A helping hand?"

"They are your younger brothers, the disinherited, the one's who didn't get the family house when the old man shuffled off. Sometimes just them who are clinging onto the old ways like England is their birthright. They tend to be the nastiest, George, very nasty indeed some of them. They've gotta be devilish cunning, pretending they've got money and influence whilst at the same time having nothing to spend."

"I suppose it must be difficult for them."

"Don't waste your sympathy on 'em. They sure as hell wouldn't think twice about you, mate, that's for sure."

"And what do their Lordships do here?"

"Oh, they play their cards, they read the papers and they drink their wine. And then ..." Welsby leaned towards Maven and dropped his voice to a whisper, "... some of them indulge in certain private functions. There's a couple of special rooms set aside and the Corporal sees to it that the members are not disturbed. You'll see. Some time during the evening there'll be carriages drawing up and a few ladies will appear. They come through the back way here, naturally. Couldn't have them coming in through the front door, could we? It wouldn't be proper."

In the Square, the light had gone completely. The breeze had turned into a cold wind and brought with it a chill that made George wish he were wearing a heavier coat. Although St James's was one of the better lit districts of London, the Square itself had no illumination apart from the moon and the watchman's torch. Twice now, he had been approached by the elderly man brandishing and asked to move on. The first time Maven had said simply that he was waiting for someone; the second had required some more imagination to convince the attendant that he was not a vagrant. George was reassured by the rather gentle way in which he was spoken to. That, and the fact that the man worked alone, suggested that night time visitors to the Square were unlikely to become the victims of crime.

Still, the darkness was disconcerting and he looked continually for signs of unwanted activity.

The Square was busy with carriages coming and going. Aside from the Blackbird Club there was the East India Club and at least two smaller establishments. Members arrived and departed regularly, their coaches dropping them in front of their chosen venue then clattering away, some to return at some appointed hour and others to wait nearby until summoned. This latter group congregated at the eastern end of the square where the drivers chatted and fussed over their horses. A driver who was especially popular seemed to have the pleasure of driving a new carriage and his fellows were carrying out a thorough analysis of the vehicle. Maven wondered how the men kept warm on their winter nights of waiting when he suddenly got the answer. From out of a narrow passage that ran alongside the East India Club, one of the men brought a brazier, a black bin-like thing with two wheels and two legs, which he wheeled towards the group. George watched as they got the fire going, tinder sticks and thicker lumps of wood suddenly appearing from the stowage areas of two of the coaches. The men stood around the brazier and warmed their hands and the conversation was punctuated by jokes at which the company laughed heartily. George pulled his coat about him, moved nearer to the Blackbird Club and continued with his surreptitious watch.

A matter of minutes later there arrived a smart chaise, which waited outside the club until the front door was opened. Only then did its tall occupant descend from the vehicle, opening and then slamming shut the carriage door himself. It took no more than four long strides to traverse the distance between the chaise and the door and, within seconds, the front door was once again closed and the source of light extinguished. Had Maven spied the coach rather than George he would have recognised that it was Bolingbroke who entered the club. The chaise rattled past, briefly illuminated by the watchman's lantern, and the elderly man had to step out of the way to avoid being run down. George settled back onto his bench.

As soon as Bolingbroke's chaise was clear of the Square a second coach pulled up outside the front door but even though the front door of the establishment opened no one stepped out of the vehicle. Instead, the liveried servant looked out as if to verify who it was that had arrived then signalled for the driver to move on. The horses were coaxed forward and turned the corner, pausing in the darkness at the mouth of the alley that led to the rear of the club. Only then did the passengers, a man and a woman, alight.

Inside the club, the evening was unfolding much the way Mr Welsby had suggested. Just after nine, a short, slim gentleman strode briskly through the kitchen, Dench escorted the man upstairs and slammed the inner door shut behind him. Then a fashionably dressed young woman, giggling and merry from drink had tumbled in and sat down at the large table in the centre of the room. Corporal Dench was in attendance again, removing her light jacket and stowing it in the small cloakroom. Maven, his sleeves rolled to the elbow, had almost completed the scrubbing of the pots and turned to place the final item, a large black skillet, on the rack to dry. He found himself face to face with the woman. She was undernourished and her lively brown eyes seemed at odds with her pale and sickly complexion. He put her age at no more than eighteen but her manner suggested she had had sufficient experiences to last her a lifetime. Her teeth were poor and she hid them by a tight lipped grimace. She appraised the Maven expertly. Maven had never doubted about his attraction to women and had proved his desirability many times. This, though, was the first time a woman had made him feel like livestock: in the space of two seconds she satisfied herself that his good looks did not outweigh the limited opportunity he presented to enrich her purse. The effect on his self-esteem could not have been more pronounced had she mocked the size of his manhood loudly in a city taproom.

Dench checked his fob watch and then nodded to the young woman like a stage manager calling the star to the stage. She swept imperiously from the room in his wake and Maven stared at her back.

The evening wore on and it was clear that Maven would not be invited to serve the gentlemen upstairs. Instead, his role was to wash up and to add bottles and glasses to trays for the uniformed service to take to the upper floors. Occasionally, the Corporal would return to the kitchen to keep an eye on proceedings but, for the most part, Maven was left alone with the occasional return of Welsby to keep him company.   Presently, the young woman reappeared, flinging open the door and striding in imperiously.

"Easy night, tonight my darling," and then wide-eyed in response to Maven's mystified look, "I gets to keep me drawers on!"

She helped herself to a bottle of the "good French stuff" and decanted it with some skill into a priceless piece of crystal. Dench, it seemed, knew better than to tussle with her and he left her to do as she pleased. Maven discovered that she chose to go by the name of Claudette. The small talk continued until, the first bottle downed, Claudette opened a second. Maven ventured a question.

"How come you're not upstairs?"

The drink had taken hold rather sooner than he would have imagined for someone as practised at the consumption of wine as she seemed to be. She leaned across the table, giggled childishly and breathed alcohol fumes in his face.

"Well, y'see, I works when they wants me and I drinks when they don't. Suits me either way. Actually," she slurred, "I prefers the drinking, cos with the other I might catch cold … or something!"
Her laugh was desperate and failed to mask her sadness.

"Look my love, I come here with his lordship. Sometimes he wants me and sometimes he don't. I gets paid either way so it's all right by me."

"Which lordship is this?"

"Never you mind."

It took Claudette about twenty minutes to kill another bottle of the French wine. Maven spent the time washing a handful of glasses that had found their way downstairs. It seemed like a slack night, although none of the other servants, including the chatty Mr Welsby chose to remain in the kitchen with them.

"Bloody lord this and bloody lord that," slurred Claudette suddenly breaking the silence, "they think they bloody own me. Trouble is I think they might be right. And in the absence of any passing actor-managers I think they're probably all I've got. But, trust me, it ain't much of a career. When him and his mates wants to have a private chat he goes into one of the boudoirs, see. I make a show of slipping in there with him and then I leave him alone, come down the back stairs and sit in here. His fellow, or sometimes fellows if there is more than one, are waiting in the room next door and they goes into see him. When the old man has gone I gets the nod from the Corporal and then we gets to go home. Easy money in anyone's book, except when his lordship fancies a bit of the other."

"But what do they do?" asked Maven.

"That, my love, is not for us to know."

Then suddenly at a louder volume to greet the arrival of Dench, "perhaps they are buggerandos who spend the evening examining each others privities, eh Corporal?"

Dench blushed. Claudette's smile suggested another direct hit in a long and bloody battle between the pair. He found whatever it was he was searching for and left rapidly.

While Maven assembled clues at the Blackbird Club and George shivered in St James's Square, the landlord of the Kings Head received a deposition from the militia led by a keen young officer who had been genuinely disappointed at the signing of the Treaty. As he saw it, that single action denied him the opportunity to serve his country. Lieutenant Maddox looked five years younger than he really was and his pale complexion had a feminine delicacy about it that led to a great deal of ribald banter at his expense. That he was also possessed of slim hips and a reedy voice merely gave his persecutors more ammunition.

The Kings Head remained busy but less full than earlier. Many of the clientele had drunk their fill and had either gone home or passed out in the street nearby. A group of eight uniformed soldiers was outside, waiting for Maddox to give the order to enter, which he did once he had concluded his brief conversation with the landlord. The plan had been to approach as quietly as possible, which in the circumstances proved to be difficult to the point of impossible, this being a district that was a stranger to the rule of law. Therefore, the entrance of a group of armed redcoats caused the assembled persons to pause their conversations and to check that they were not the object of the militia's intentions.

The soldiers marched through the room in short order and went straight upstairs to the private room. The Lieutenant reasoned that since it was not possible to run up the wooden stairs in silence they would need to ascend quickly in order to maintain the element of surprise. Maddox nodded to the Corporal at the head of the column who kicked down the flimsy door. The landlord looked on, shocked, since he was standing by with a key. The object of their search lay comatose in the middle of a large, dishevelled bed between his naked female companions. The presence of soldiers caused the women to squeal and leap quickly from the bed, gather together their clothes and dress themselves. Their requests that the soldiers might at least look the other way were ignored and only encouraged the men at the rear of the column to push forward in order to get a better look.

Taylor did not wake at all throughout the episode, the effects of a week's more or less continuous drinking having rendered him unconscious, which pleased Maddox greatly. He ordered two of his men to tie the man firmly about the wrists and the ankles and then two more to drag him down the stairs and outside to the waiting wagon. Once his men were clear of the room he turned to the women and brought from his pocket two small leather purses, which he handed over with a small bow in each case. Then he walked smartly down the stairs, slipped a similar purse into the discreetly positioned hand of the landlord and left the tavern.

In St James's Square, George was stirred from his worsening temper by a party of gentlemen leaving the East India Club. He yawned and removed his watch from his pocket in an attempt to see what the time was. He held the timepiece up high in front of him to catch the moonlight and illuminate the dial. Suddenly, he sprang to his feet as Maven emerged from the shadows at the corner of the Square, having stayed hidden while the revellers passed him by.

"Over here," he hissed, waving his arms to attract Maven's attention.

Maven saw him and increased his pace, striding toward the boy at just about the same time the watchman entered the Square on the far side. Maven grabbed George's arm and led him away to the south in the direction of Pall Mall.

"Are you all right, Captain? Tell me you weren't found out," asked George breathlessly.

"Not at all, George. It seems I have secured you a permanent job. You can return tomorrow and take my place."

10

The following morning at The Star, Maven sat again at the big wooden bench-table by the fire and sipped reluctantly at his drink while he warmed himself. His request this morning for tea rather than beer had been greeted in much the same way as if he had appeared for breakfast wearing one of Kathrine's gowns and had resulted in the Sergeant checking his officer's brow for signs of a fever.

"You has to start the day with beer, Captain, tis the way of things. I is worried that fancy woman is giving you airs and graces."

"You worry unnecessarily, Tresco. I need to keep a clear head, that is all. There are things going on here that I cannot begin to understand."

Presently, George appeared looking even more pleased with himself than was usually the case. He carried a wooden platter more often used for the transportation of joints of meat about the place. On this occasion it bore a shallow white china dish with steam drifting in wisps from its surface. He set the tray down on the table and stood back a step, the better to admire his handiwork. Maven looked at the dish and then to George.

"Coffee," said George.

"Indeed."

"Taste it, sir, go on."

Maven peered into the dish and considered the black steaming liquid that had about it a look of beef broth. Not only did it not look like coffee but it smelled only faintly of the richness of roasted beans. One would need a great many dishes before the aroma of the Jerusalem or Garroways was recreated.

"The price of this stuff is enormous, sir. We can double our profit by selling dishes of this alongside the ale. We can still sell the sotweed as well and we don't have the problem of throwing out the drunken so-and-sos when they've had too much grog and get a bit punchy. Tis a civilized victual."

Maven looked into the dish again then looked up at George quizzically.

"And you followed the instructions in making up the drink?"

"Of course."

"I am not so sure, George. I wonder what fates will befall you if you serve this dreadful concoction to a paying customer."

Trescothick senior snorted loudly and marched out from the kitchen.

"I told him, I told him I did. These fancy ideas is all very well but you got to do it right or you'll be a laughing stock."

George, his eyes, like saucers, stared at his father, betrayed and amazed at the older man's nerve in shifting the blame so. Maven roared with laughter and slapped the table with an open palm.

"Tresco, you are priceless!"

The three of them had been concentrating on the coffee dish and had not seen the Lieutenant enter through the main door. He stood alone just inside the doorway, waiting for an opportunity to interrupt the reverie, feet apart and his hands neatly folded behind his back. He cleared his throat weakly and the trio turned to look in his direction.

"Aye up. Here's the bleddy toy soldier again."

Lieutenant Robert Maddox of the Honourable Artillery Company stepped forward and blushed and could find no riposte to the mockery of the old Sergeant, though he at least tried to exert his authority.

"Thank you landlord, we'll have a bit less of that, if you please. Would you be Captain Maven?"

"Depends who's asking."

"Your King is who is asking, sir, and were it not for your senior rank I would consider teaching you a lesson in respect."

"Lieutenant, I fear you have earned all the respect you are going to get for the moment. What can I do for you?" replied Maven.

"So you are Maven?" asked Maddox, suddenly in awe, a state of mind that was enhanced by Maven standing to greet him and making him feel as small as the adolescent he so recently was.

"You have another note?"

"No, sir, not a note but an instruction from Westminster. You are to come as soon as you may. Your," he looked around to check who might be listening before continuing, "your benefactor wishes to share information with you. It is of the utmost importance."

Maven sighed, disappointed that he would have to postpone his return to Hatton Garden.

He rode with Maddox in a carriage that bore all the hallmarks of having been cast off by a gentleman who had moved onto better things and decided to perform some civic service by donating his old transport to the London-based regiment. The manner in which the driver handled both the vehicle and the pair of horses that pulled them suggested the coach would not be long for this world. It was a bumpy and uncomfortable journey down St Martins Lane, through the morning chaos that was Charing Cross before they halted outside Admiralty House, where the white stone reflected the autumn sunlight. Maddox put his head out of the window and clarified his instruction to the driver. They swung right and clattered through the Horse Guards Parade. Their driver whipped up the horses to a fearful pace and sped across the parade ground and into St James's Park.

The journey ended at walking pace as the horses ambled alongside the back of St James's Palace. Maddox swung open the door and jumped down rather dramatically, leaving Maven alone with the coach rolling forwards at walking pace. He faced the back of the coach and could not see the exchange that took place ahead of them. He could only just hear the indistinct greeting and the muffled whisperings that followed and, on alert, turned to look out of the window. As he did so, the driver brought the coach to a complete stop and the carriage bounced uncomfortably on its worn springs. Lieutenant Maddox and two other redcoats stood by, each facing away from two gentlemen. One was Gideon Crouch, hunched and untidy, his powdered wig slightly askew on his head. He had a stick in his hand, on which he rested his hand gently. It was clear that Crouch's companion was the senior of the pair and by some considerable margin. He stood tall and erect, a handsome specimen, whose blue coat fit him perfectly. In his left hand he also held a stick but had no need of its support. In his right he held a large white handkerchief, in much the same way as a dandy might keep a perfumed cloth within reach to protect his delicate nose from the noxious odours of the street. The use of this cloth became apparent when the gentleman began a coughing fit as loud as it was violent, causing one of his protecting officers to turn and check whether his master required assistance.

Crouch looked up at Maven.

"Stay there, Captain."

The pair climbed into the carriage without any formal introductions. The two gentlemen faced him, squashed together on the bench seat.

"Your grace, this is Captain Maven, whom we have discussed."

"It is a pleasure to meet you Captain. We have heard a great deal about you from some very respectable people."

"Don't believe all you hear."

"Maven, in case you re not aware, this gentleman is Mr Charles Talbot, the Duke of Shrewsbury. A little deference might not go amiss."

The Duke leaned forward and raised his stick. The silver tip headed directly towards Maven's right temple and, instinctively, he leaned to the left in an avoiding manouevre. The weapon struck the wood of the coach a double rap, at which the vehicle started forward with a jerk and the Duke fell back into his seat, partly crushing the arm of his clerk. Maven noted that the Duke had sight in only one eye and, as a result, looked into the space beyond Maven's shoulder as he addressed him.

"Thank you Crouch," said Shrewsbury, "I am sure the Captain would have addressed me correctly had I introduced myself. The fault is mine, sir. Now Captain, my clerk has already outlined the nature of a certain problem we have at the moment and I regret that I was unable to attend that meeting. It is a rather pressing time as I am sure you can imagine and we have a great deal of business that requires our attention. My priority, naturally, is to deal with this blessed coronation. If we can get that away without a disaster then we should all be mighty pleased. Eh Crouch?"

The Duke's attempt at a turn in his seat to face the clerk was thwarted by the lack of space. He grunted his disapproval.

"Quite so, sir. Now, Captain, may we enquire what progress you have made in finding our friend?"

"Progress? You have barely supplied the instructions."

"Time enough to make your rounds, though. Did I not provide you with a list of suitable addresses?"

"You did, sir. I had envisaged some more time to deliver my response."

"Captain, our urgency is driven by our nervous disposition," interrupted Shrewsbury, "But, do please indulge us. What say you?"

"Audley has left his London home, sir, and it appears from what we saw that he has little intention of returning in the near future."

"That much we already knew, Maven," interjected Crouch.

"And," continued Maven, "we are told that he has not been seen at his club for some weeks, has been removed from its membership list ..."

"You hesitate, Captain."

"I cannot be sure whether we have the full picture from that establishment. Their loyalties are to their members, but we shall continue to keep a close watch there."

"You say we, Captain," asked Crouch, "Who is we?"

"I have some help at my disposal."

"I should like you to share with me who that help is, Captain."

"I would prefer not to."

"If your help amounts to that overfed Sergeant I think we might attempt to find you someone a little more suitable from the Guards."

"We are performing the task well enough as we are, Mr Crouch. You need not trouble yourself."

"Is that it, then? You have nothing else to say?" Crouch was becoming increasingly agitated.

The coach drew to a halt outside the house where Maven had first met the clerk.

"Come along Crouch. You as well, Maven. Let us go inside. It has to be more comfortable than this infernal contraption." Shrewsbury leapt from his seat and flung open the door, twisting himself through the aperture in an easy movement. Crouch followed smartly and, from the pavement, called back to Maven, "Come along, man, what are you waiting for?"

Maven did not rouse himself overly quickly, but took care to exit the carriage with dignity, checking the quality of the ground before committing to his exit. Crouch had already scuttled into the house and the door stood open and inviting and the face of the servant peered around to see where the guest might be.

They re-convened in the small library and, there being only the two chairs, they all stood. Once again the heavy velvet curtain had been drawn and the candles emitted their dim light. It was the Duke who spoke.

"Captain, we may have another piece of information for you to explore. A man was taken into custody last night on my orders. I believe he may know something of the whereabouts of the scoundrel we seek. He is an associate of Audley and is well known to us. His name is Taylor. He is a ne'er-do-well of some kind in the yards over at Lambeth."

Maven noticed the exchange of glances between Shrewsbury and his employee.

"And he is an associate of Audley?"

"Surprising as it may seem, yes he is," replied Shrewsbury. "Not only that but he has a reputation as a fighting man, an absolute rapscallion of the worst kind. Audley has spoken for him and spared him justice in the past. He carries out certain tasks for Audley when the scoundrel would prefer not to get his hands dirty."

"Where is he?"

"Right now, he is kicking his heels in the Southwark Compter, though I would have preferred him to be at Artillery House. I have made arrangements for you to see him there. Given the delicacy of the matter I would rather not have him in any of the usual places and we certainly don't want him anywhere near Westminster. Make sure you keep one of the guards with you, though, he's a nasty one."

The Duke picked up his pen and dipped it into the ink well. He began to write a note on the top sheet of the stack that sat before him. They waited, the silence punctuated only by the scraping of the nib on the paper.

"There. That is your authority. Crouch, have Lieutenant Maddox accompany the Captain. He knows well enough where the blackguard can be found since it was his initiative that put him there."

11

Maddox rode ahead and agreed to meet Maven in Southwark later in the morning. Feeling nervous and exposed, Maven walked back towards St Margarets with his head down and pondered the new information while he considered the best way to get to Southwark, over on the southern side of the river. He barely noticed the people around him. Nonetheless, as he re-entered The Sanctuary and passed the Gatehouse, his peripheral vision picked up a man loitering against the wall of the Abbey, almost, but not quite, blending in with his surroundings. The instinct that had kept him alive for so long in the war kicked in again and, though he could not describe the feeling rationally, he knew that the man was wrong. Perhaps it was something about his black coat, too heavy for this time of year and too clean to belong to a man of the street; perhaps it was the hat, slightly too wide of brim and almost purpose built for obscuring the face. Maven continued walking, his stride unbroken, then, at the corner of Bow Street, turned sharply left and ducked into the shadows of an alley, arousing the suspicion of a washerwoman who quickly returned to her business when he scowled at her. Maven watched his follower falter and glance around. The man hesitated, wondering whether or not he should proceed. The decision made, the pursuer turned and walked down the centre of Bow Street, past the alley where Maven was concealed. Once the man had gone thirty yards ahead, Maven left his hiding place and followed. Suddenly, there was no human presence in the street save for the two men and when the stranger turned, having accepted his quarry was lost, he found himself face to face with the tall officer. The man hesitated just a second too long before turning to run. Maven had already hit his full speed by the time the man had gathered his footing and it took just a few long strides before he was caught. Maven twisted the stranger's arm behind his back then forced him into the narrow passageway by the Cocke Inn. A pot man in the inn spied the two men tumbling into the narrow space, made as if to intervene then thought better of it and disappeared into the building on a suddenly pressing errand.

Maven let the man's hat fall to the floor, revealing the stranger's identity. His face was that of a boy. Despite his relatively slight physique, the force necessary to restrain the youth was considerable and Maven delivered two sharp blows to the face with his free hand and applied a dead leg in order to quieten him.

"Keep still, shut up and you won't get hurt. Tell me your name then I need to ask you just two questions. You will answer them truthfully and I will allow you to go. That is the arrangement and there is no negotiation to be done. Do you understand?"

The man uttered an oath and Maven punched him again, this time in the solar plexus, drawing breath from his victim.

"Don't make this more difficult than it needs to be. Tell me who you are."

He paused briefly for the reply then, with nothing forthcoming, he twisted the man's arm up his back, causing him to cry out in pain and then shout, "All right! God damn it, leave my arm alone before you break the damn thing. Francis Jess is my name."

The accent was not at all what Maven expected, from Scotland rather than London and that of a man newly arrived in the capital. Maven relaxed his grip and allowed his prisoner to catch his breath.

"You sound like a stranger to these streets, Mr Jess. What kind of fool sends a man to walk the streets of a strange city, eh?" To emphasise that he required a reply, Maven recommenced the arm twist as he finished the question.

"All right, all right. I'll tell ye. Just stop hurtin' me, will ye?" After a brief pause, Jess continued, "I'm just to follow ye then report back and tell a gentleman where you've been. That is all, sir."

"I want a name, man."

"I cannae tell you, sir."

"Can't or won't?"

Maven felt his temper rising and struggled to control it. Maven had unwittingly resumed the arm twist. It had the desired effect, though.

"I don't know his name", Jess paused reasoning whether he should be more afraid of Maven or of his employer, then made his choice, "… he is a wealthy gentleman, sir, but I swear I do not know his name."

"Thank you. Wasn't that easy?"

He released the grip slightly.

"Now, Mr Scotchman, please tell me where I can find the good gentleman."

"I don't know where he is."

Maven did not have to work hard to summon the aggression again.

"Do you think I am some kind of fool? How were you proposing to share your information with him?"

Jess began to tremble, at the end of his tether now, the combined fears of his betrayed employer, a situation out of his control and a belligerent Englishman seemingly hell bent on killing him rushed upon him and brought tears that coursed down his face. He sobbed uncontrollably and sagged in Maven's grip. Maven could barely make out what he was saying.

"He said, sir, that he would find me, sir, at my lodgings. This evening."

Maven released his grip completely and said slowly, almost as if he were speaking to an upset child, "And tell me, my friend, where would your lodgings be?"

The knowledge transferred, Maven was relieved that the Scot had not been billeted in the City where the number of inns was considerable and the chances of finding the right one no easy task, even for a local. The Scot had been billeted across the Bridge and on the main road as well, an easy location for a newcomer to locate. Any fear Maven had about the younger man was gone now and the pair relaxed, the battle over. Maven wondered what to do with the wretch, considered leaving him where he was and then thought better of it.

"Do you have money?" he asked.

"A little," replied Jess, which was likely, since there was a possibility of having to take cabs if he had done his job properly.

"Then I suggest you take a hackney to the wharves in the Pool and barter for a passage home. Try one of the Newcastle coal barges and you might even get some paid employment. Go home, man. This is no place for you."

The young man's face was filthy now and he looked at Maven like a son might look at a father. Maven lifted Jess to his feet and looked him in the eye. Maven had dealt with prisoners who were beaten, injured and, in many cases, barely alive, but in their eyes there had been anger, a desire to cause harm to this Englishman who had dared to inflict upon them an emasculating defeat. In those situations it was remarkably easy to treat the prisoner with dignity as to do so merely added to his humiliation. With this one there was nothing, no challenge at all, just abject surrender.

"My God, man, you are no soldier. If you are killed here your mother will never again hear of you. Go home, for God's sake." Jess rose to his feet.

"You go first," said Maven, "on no account should you follow me or try to find me. And if I hear of you trying to contact your employer I will find you and shoot you. Is that clear?"

He pushed Jess out of the alley and into Bow Street, following a discreet distance behind. Too late, he realised the youngster had left his black hat in the alley and Maven reached down to pick it up. When they reached King Street he saw the Scot try and fail to persuade a cab to take him to his destination. Then, once a few minutes had elapsed and he had gathered his wits about him he was able to convince another driver that he had funds enough to pay the fare. Maven turned the hat in his hands and rubbed his knuckles, sore from the violence, and wondered how he should approach Audley, a potentially more formidable enemy than Shrewsbury and Crouch seemed to understand. Maven watched the cab disappear north up King Street then followed it on foot until it was out of sight, by which time he had almost reached the hackneys standing at Charing Cross.

Three coaches resplendent, at least from a distance, in the regulation yellow livery stood waiting at the stand. The jarveys in their blue coats were standing at the side of the line gossiping while a waterman tended to the thirsts of their horses. Maven asked to be taken to Puddle Dock where he knew there would be plenty of ferries to take him across to Southwark. The oldest of the trio broke off from his conversation reluctantly and nodded to the foremost carriage. Maven stepped to the door and opened it as the ostler barged past and water from the bucket destined for the horses splashed his boots. Presently, whatever story was being told reached its conclusion and Maven heard the three drivers laugh together. The jarvey stepped up onto the running board so that his moon face filled the window and confirmed the destination with a mocking, "Right you are, sir."

They pulled away from the stand and Maven was thrown back against the hard wood of the carriage. They passed Aldwych then the traffic and pedestrians impeded their progress and they paused by Temple Bar. Maven looked out of the window at the vehicles travelling in the opposite direction, a mixture of wagons and dog carts, mostly, filled with sacks of who knows what, evidence of the trade that pulsed through the city's veins. Yet, for all of the modernising that had come about since the beginning of the century, there remained many of the old ways. He could see on the street the underclass that was being left behind as London's fortunes raced ahead. The poor wretches mooched listlessly from one shadow to the next, fending for themselves and begging for scraps or cast offs. Perhaps they were among the increasing number for whom the parishes offered no comfort, their charitable resources exhausted by the demand. As they blended into the drabness of the city these shadow people became indistinguishable from its buildings. Were they to become part of the fabric? They were ever present, a ballast to the city, he thought. The carriage jolted forwards and shook Maven from his thoughts. He would interrogate this man, Taylor and persuade him to offer up Audley's whereabouts. One way or the other he would finish this soon.

Last night, Lieutenant Robert Maddox of the Honourable Artillery Company had elected not to take his prisoner directly to the armoury as instructed. Instead, he chose to make use of the Southwark Compter and the narrow street outside this small but busy building was where he and Maven now found themselves, the bright morning doing nothing to improve the dirty, foetid scene that lay before them. The front door of the compter was guarded by two redcoats and an undertaker's carriage was parked a few yards away, its rear doors opened in anticipation. The undertaker, a gaunt, sluggish man whose personality and pallor were ideally suited to his occupation, fussed gently as he waited for his boys to retrieve the corpse from the tiny gaol. The gaoler sat on the floor, morose, his head in his hands. He had apologised to Maddox on several occasions and, when Maven arrived, he did so again. Try as he might, he could summon up no recollection of the gentleman who had visited the previous night.

William Taylor's violent demeanour had proved too much for the Lieutenant and he had put into Southwark rather than risk travelling across the bridge and through the city. Awoken from his drunken torpor and invigorated by the oxygen of the London air, Taylor had thrashed around with his arms and legs, such that the part-time force had quickly run out of ideas of how to restrain him. The wagon they were using to transport the felon still sat outside the compter and bore the wounds of his attacks, not to mention his blood where he had hurled the chains against the inside of the flimsy wooden vehicle, dragging his limbs into painful and repeated contact in his manic desire to escape. The wagon had rocked from side to side. His passion struck fear into the horses and caused them to rear up and there was a great risk of the whole equipage turning over.

At the time, the decision was sensible and the consequences could not have been foreseen. So the Lieutenant stopped without considering that even someone with Taylor's brute strength and stamina would have to give up at some point. They had, with a great deal of difficulty, moved him from the wagon into the gaol and secured his chains to the iron brackets on the wall as best they could. This still left him with around a yard or so of free movement in which he flailed about like a baited bear, swearing and cursing as only an old soldier could. This had set off the three other wretched prisoners who, drunk or senseless had begun their own caterwauling and complaining.

Maddox agreed to return in the morning to collect his prisoner in the hope that Taylor's anger might be tempered by sobriety. The upset caused to the gaoler was assuaged with the usual remedy of some coins changing hands and the officer and his men had stood in the near darkness wondering where they could find a drink to calm their nerves. A suitable venue identified, the group piled into the premises. None of them saw the figure that had followed them from Lambeth Wells.

The slim gentleman, dressed in a dark frock coat, had aroused no suspicion from those on the street despite looking rather too smart for his surroundings. He waited until the soldiers were clear of the area and approached the front door of the compter, reasoning that to allow the warder to drift back into a lazy doze only to be woken again would not serve his cause well. He knocked at the heavy door loudly with the brass tip of his cane and received no response. He was in the process of knocking a second time when the Judas hole slid open.

"Ain't no need for that, sir. Little bit of patience wouldn't go amiss."

The beady eyes of the gaoler did their best to analyse who it was that was calling and was surprised to find a solitary gentleman.

"You alone, sir? No prisoner for me?"

"No warder, I do not have anyone for you. Rather you have someone for me."

The tone of voice was superior and intended to brook no dissent.

"I can't let you in sir. Not without good reason."

"You have one of my clients in there and it is a matter of urgency that I see him."

"Ain't no-one in here but a bunch of drunks, sir."

"That may well be true, warder, but he is still entitled to legal representation."

"Now then sir, you know's as well as I do that there's no such right no matter who they is. They is all asleep now. Tis best you come back in the morning. You may see him then."

With perfect timing, Taylor recommenced his noisy protests, raising such a hideous din that the other prisoners joined him.

"I think you will find, warder, that Mr Taylor seems to have awoken. I am sure if you allow me to visit with him I will be able to calm him. He will be best served by not annoying you and I should like to tell him so myself. I have some compensation for you, sir."

It was a longstanding grumble of the gaoler that the diminutive gaol caused him no end of financial trouble. Firstly because the prisoners were not in there for very long before being released or shipped off to Newgate he was unable to amass more than a few coppers for supplying food and drink and, secondly, it had room for only half a dozen souls. The gaoler thus convinced of the gentleman's good intentions, stepped back to draw the heavy bolt. He opened the door just enough to enable the visitor to slide through sideways and then slammed it shut behind him. The gaoler led the man down a short, dark corridor that dripped dampness and as they approached the door of the cell the noise level increased, the foul and abusive vocabulary promising damnation to all and sundry, but especially the militia men and the treacherous landlord. They paused outside the door and the warder produced a heavy bunch of keys.

"Does you want me to come inside with you, sir?"

"My client is entitled to some privacy."

"I was thinking more of your safety, sir."

The gentleman paused.

"Very well, leave the door slightly open and go back to your desk. I shan't need to release him from his confinement. If I need you I will call."

The arrangement satisfied the gaoler, who unlocked the cell door. Such was the noise emanating from within that the prisoner was unaware of his visitor until the door had opened and the gentleman had entered. The shouting ceased immediately while Taylor peered through the gloom and tried to make out who stood before him silhouetted in the weak moonlight. . The gentleman put his finger to his lips in a gesture of silence. Suddenly, Taylor recognised who it was that stood before him. His temper vanished and was replaced by a stark fear. He reversed across the filthy floor so that his back was pressed firmly against the damp wall.

"You. H-how did you get in here? W-what do you want?"

The stranger did not answer. Instead he unsheathed his sword and, twisting his wrist so that the cold blade pointed directly at Taylor, he leaned forward. The point pressed slightly against his throat and the light from outside reflected off the steel with a silver blue tint. Leaning forward so the sword pressed against Taylor's skin, he whispered, "You were given clear instructions. Stay quiet and stay out of sight. We could not have made it easier for you. Instead you have drawn attention to yourself with your debauchery and drunkenness. Worse than that, you have been seen conversing with gentlemen who plot against us."

"I-I am sorry, sir. I have b-been betrayed, sir. Please, I am sorry."

As he tried to push himself forward to beg his forgiveness Taylor found the steel point unyielding, so that his own forward momentum caused the tip to pierce the skin at his throat and a small trickle of blood ran onto his sternum.

"You are a liability. Unreliable, treacherous and dangerous. You give me no choice."

The stranger pushed the point home further, drawing more blood and his victim's eyes bulged at the combination of the pain and the terror at what was happening. His fear was so great that he did not attempt to scream until his larynx was broken and then it was too late. The stranger withdrew the sword and, without pausing, plunged it through his victim's heart, a symbolic and dramatic gesture worthy of a matador. The restraining chains rattled, taking Taylor's weight as he fell forward. The stranger withdrew the sword and breathed in audibly, as if to emphasise his dominance then calmly wiped the sword on his victim's breeches and sheathed the weapon.

The visitor paused for a few seconds to collect himself and the left the cell, pulling the heavy door closed behind him. The gaoler was pleased that the lawyer, if that is what he was, had calmed his client. He was looking forward to a peaceful night and was on the verge of nodding off when the visitor walked towards him from the gloom. The gaoler leapt to his feet and scampered to the front door.

"He's calm now is he, sir?"

The thin man avoided eye contact.

"He understands that he must not bother you again but I suggest you leave him alone to be sure. Those chains will ensure he goes nowhere. I shall return in the morning to see he is treated properly by the militia."

"Right you are sir, right you are."

The stranger stepped into the street and felt the rush of air behind him as the heavy door slammed shut, then heard the heavy drawbolt slide into place, locking the warder inside with his prisoners.

Now, as Maven and Maddox stood together in the street, the morning air was polluted by the foul odours that permeated the open door of the compter. Maven's first instinct was to interview the other prisoners but they had all been unreliable in their own ways and it had been a waste of time. None had seen anything of the intruder and all were so wrapped up in their own troubles that he doubted they could have described their own mothers.

"Don't blame yourself, Lieutenant. You could not have expected this outcome, I am sure."

Maddox was humiliated by his error and desperate to atone for his omission. Maven made a suggestion.

12

Later that evening after cursing the name of Maddox, Maven sat in the darkest corner of The Christopher and seethed inwardly at the incompetence of the Honourable Artillery Company. In an attempt to gain something positive from their disastrous day, Maven had decided to arrive in Borough High Street early and camp out in the tavern to await the arrival of Mr Jess's employer. So it was that Maven occupied the optimum viewing position, in the corner facing into the tap room with a clear view of the doors to the front and the rear. Seated just inside the front door ready to block an unsanctioned escape was Sergeant Trescothick, nursing a tankard of ale, under strict instructions to remain sober for the evening, an order that the Sergeant intended to carry out to the letter.

The final member of the trio was the one Maven was most concerned about. There was no chance at all that Maven or Trescothick could pass themselves off as the young Scot, with or without the wide brimmed hat. So Maven had suggested to Maddox that he might redeem himself by joining them on the jaunt south of the river. Maven's first choice would have been George but he had been keen to take Maven's place washing pots at the Blackbird Club. Maven had gone over the instructions several times, just to make sure he understood what he was getting into and George had taken himself off to St James's looking forward to an evening of conversation with Claudette.

Maddox, now dressed in civilian clothes, sat near the barrels with his back to the door, black hat on head and in conversation with the serving maid, whose attention had wandered quickly to the handsome young stranger. He was only slightly broader than Jess but otherwise there was enough resemblance from the back that Audley, if that is who was due, would be well inside the tavern before he realised his error. No suspicions had been aroused. But there was no Audley either.

Visibility was limited and the light from the busy road was diminishing now that the sun had sunk below the roofs of the buildings opposite. The torches that the landlord had recently lit failed to meet the challenge with the result that the corners of the room were in near darkness. The trio believed, not unreasonably, that a peer of the realm would stick out here like a choirboy in a Turnmill Street brothel. The plan was for Maven and Trescothick to approach from different directions, ensnare him in a pincer movement and escort him outside before he had a chance to react. But an hour later they were still waiting and exchanging furtive glances with each other. After another hour passed, along with a further four rounds of drinks, Maven's stomach acids gnawed at him. He sensed an ambush and a glance at Trescothick suggested the old campaigner thought the same. It was time, he decided, to take the initiative. When the landlord brought over the refill for his tankard he caught the man by the wrist and beckoned him to lean forward so that the question was not broadcast to the entire room.

"I have an appointment with somebody, a young Scotchman known as Francis Jess. Would you know him?"

"No, sir, can't say as I do."

"He has a room here. I believe he stayed last night."

The landlord did a good job of pretending he had no idea what Maven was talking about. Maven did an equally good job of glancing round the room and settling on Maddox.

"Not unlike that gentleman."

Maven primed the landlord's memory with more money than was necessary to cover the cost of the drink.

"Well, now you comes to mention it, sir, I do recall something. He dined here last night and the night before."

"Is he here now?"

"I've not seen him today, no, but then guests come and go without my knowledge. They use the side door."

The landlord struggled to prevent a sly grin creeping onto his face.

"So he could be in his room?"

"Aye, could be."

That would be another reason for choosing the Christopher. If Jess could come and go then so could Audley. The landlord slipped away. As Maven rose and went after him, his broad shoulders clattered into a line of tin mugs that hung on the wall behind and two of them fell to the stone flags prompting several of the topers to turn and stare. Maven, angry now, caught the landlord on the shoulder.

"Which room was Jess's?"

"Sir?"

"The gentleman I enquired of a few seconds ago. Which of your rooms did he rent?"

"I'm not rightly sure if I can tell you sir. Our guests like their privacy."

"I bet they do. So how about I go upstairs and knock down each door until I find him? How many preachers and wagtails do you think I'll disturb before the task is done?"

Maven rose to his full height. The low ceiling made him seem freakishly tall and he towered above the innkeeper by a foot. The tapster decided that discretion was to be called for. He beckoned Maven to follow him to a tatty dresser and collected a large cloth-backed book, opened it and ran his finger down a list until he found the name.

"Seventeen."

"Thank you, it's much appreciated."

"Only his name's not Jess. It's Webb."

Maven paused for a second to consider the news. Next to them, the maid leaned forward towards Maddox with her elbows on the table, gazing into the eyes of her new found beau, whose own gaze was settled none too subtly on the young woman's cleavage. Maven elbowed Maddox discreetly and leaned down to speak, loudly enough for the barmaid to hear as well.

"Lose your friend, we've got work to do."

Maven stepped away and out the front door, passing Trescothick, who rose and followed. The pair stood on the street and waited, where they were joined a matter of seconds later by the sheepish Lieutenant. Trescothick was the first to speak.

"Enjoying yourself, there, boy?"

There was no reply.

"Keep your brains in your hat, not your trousers," said the Cornishman mysteriously. Maven took over and said, "There's another door that guests can use to go to their rooms without passing through here. Audley will have gone directly upstairs to avoid drawing attention to himself."

Maven led the pair down the side of the inn. The stench betrayed the use that most of the clientele made of the alley and Trescothick muttered under his breath about Maven owing him a new pair of boots. The side door opened easily and they let themselves in. The small hallway was in darkness and the stairs directly ahead were lit halfway up by a solitary candle.

"Stay here Lieutenant. Shout if anyone tries to follow us in."

Maven fingered the pistol that was stowed in his belt then changed his mind and removed the short knife from his boot. He led the way, signalling with his hand that they should be as quiet as possible. At the top of the stairs they paused, once again in near darkness, the only lamp being midway down the long corridor. There was just enough light that they could make out the numbers on the doors if they got close enough. There were eight rooms each side of the corridor and one at the end with the number seventeen stencilled on it. Anyone approaching would have to walk the length of the corridor and be in the sights of the occupant all the way. We are completely exposed, he thought. There were two choices: withdraw and find another way in or charge ahead quickly. Given that the element of surprise had been lost he decided on a tactical withdrawal and turned to tell Trescothick. Suddenly, the door to number seventeen opened and out tumbled a giggling young woman dressed only in a white shift that was open to her navel. As she stumbled towards them along the narrow corridor she tied its laces to better cover her large breasts. She yelped loudly when she saw them then giggled again, covered her chest with both hands and tripped along the corridor, cutting them a saucy glance as she turned into room five, slamming the door behind her.

Maven ran to the end of the corridor and pushed open the door to number seventeen. The room was empty and the moonlight bathed it in a blue pallor. As he had suspected there was a window, open, and on the wall behind the bed was a string that passed down the wall and through the floor. Trescothick's broad form appeared in the doorway.

"It's an alarm system," explained Maven, "if the place is ever raided the landlord rings the bell and chappy can make his escape at one end of the inn while his pursuers are floundering about climbing the stairs at the other."

"What about the girl?"

"Go and talk to her Tresco. My guess is she's too drunk for you to get any sense out of her but see what she says anyway."

Maven walked across to the open window. The drop to the ground was about the same as it had been in Covent Garden. The yard was in darkness and Maven was about to turn back inside when he caught a faint movement in the shadows.

"You down there. Show yourself!"

Nothing stirred.

"I said show yourself, dammit. Come on, I haven't got all night!

Maven put his knife away and withdrew his pistol as the figure of a man appeared in the space beneath the window, lit only by the light from the moon.

"Been a long time, Luke. You're last on the scene as usual. Not much changes, eh? Do you want to come down and talk about it? Might be easier than me shinning up the wall."

Trescothick returned and joined Maven, peering past him to the scene in the yard.

"What the bloody hell...?"

"Careful with that gun, Captain," continued the voice. The stranger stepped forward and looked up at Maven, who could just make out a patch over the man's left eye.

"You don't want to go and hurt someone."

"Don't tempt me," said Maven quietly and then to the stranger, a resigned tone in his voice, "meet us in the ale house. We'll be right down."

They collected Maddox on the way and, much to his evident delight took him back into the tap room where he reacquainted himself with the maid. Maven and Trescothick sat down at the table in the corner, where Captain Robert Lancaster was already seated and ordering tankards of ale for the three of them. Lancaster occupied his seat like he was the proprietor, feet wide apart and leaning back against the wall, the front legs of the stool off the ground. Lancaster was as tall as Maven but thinner. He wore a malodorous black periwig and had several days growth of beard. His skin suggested he had spent many days on the road. But it was the patch over his eye that gave Lancaster his most menacing feature while the look in his good eye was one of studied malevolence. The girl upstairs has a forgiving nature, thought Maven.

"I'd heard you were circulating, Luke. Care to share with me what you've been up to?"

"I think it's you who should be doing the explaining."

The bitterness between the pair was palpable but only Trescothick knew the reasons. This was not the occasion to be dragging up the mutual antipathy. The Sergeant steeled himself to come between the officers if the situation got out of hand but kept his own counsel for the moment. Lancaster leaned forward and rested his elbows on the table, the legs of the stool scraping on the flagstone floor.

"Look, this is serious. You can't possibly know what you've got yourself involved in."

"So explain it to me."

Lancaster looked at Trescothick.

"You're looking all right Sergeant, life treating you justly? Plenty of padding round the belly, I see."

Trescothick nodded graciously.

"Can't complain. Plenty worse off than me."

Lancaster looked across at Maddox, chatting to the maid.

"Who's the pretty boy?"

"Never you mind who he is." replied Maven.

Lancaster's good eye rested upon the Lieutenant for just a second or two longer than was necessary.

"One for the ladies, it seems. Don't go relying on him in a skirmish, Luke."

"I won't. Now, will you tell us what you are doing here?"

Lancaster pondered his options and made his decision.

"I'm going to work on the basis that Luke Maven would only ever be on the side of the good and the gracious, so I'll trust you."

He took a long drag of his ale and continued, his voice now so low they could barely hear him and had to lean forward to catch his words. The landlord grinned at the overt conspiracy.

"I'll wager you were here searching for someone."

"An idiot could have worked that out."

"And that someone would have been Edward Audley?"

They both nodded their assent.

"Trouble is, Luke, you missed him. So did I, as a matter of fact, and I'm not overly pleased about it. He has been staying here for the last two nights. He and a young Scotchman."

"Francis Jess."

"You know him?"

"We bumped into each other."

"This afternoon was it?" he paused for an answer that did not come, "Thought so. Young Master Jess came straight here and warned his master off. The pair of them have disappeared. God alone knows what the consequences will be."

Maven elected to go on the offensive.

"So why are you still here? When you found out Audley was missing why didn't you follow?"

"No point. He'll be miles away by now. The landlord, fine gent that he is, couldn't get word to me in time so when I arrived, I decided to stick around for some relaxation."

"Old habits die hard."

"You met her on the landing, I think. A sweet, obliging young thing. Anyway, it seemed sensible to see who else turned up. Audley was obviously running away from someone. And now we know who."

"Why did you jump out of the window?"

"I needed to be sure you weren't going to burst in on me with your guns blazing. These are dangerous times and Audley has a lot of enemies. I didn't want to be the victim of mistaken identity."

The landlord refreshed their drinks, pouring ale from a large metal jug.

"You gents need anything else? A smoke maybe?"

"Bugger off," said Lancaster in a not entirely good natured way.

The landlord scuttled away.

"You haven't improved your way with people."

"He's heard worse."

"I still think you owe us some explanation," said Maven, bringing his chair in towards the table to try and get the huddle going again.

"Maven, it's not often we agree but I fear this is one of those rare occasions. We are caught up in the same game and you've got in my way."

"Your way?"

"Yes, Maven, my way. My game, my rules, my way."

"But we have instructions from..." he paused, unsure whether to continue but before he could decide Lancaster got there first.

"Instructions from the highest authority? From the Government?"

"Well, yes..."

"But what is the Government? Who is the power in this land? This is not the army Maven. It was easy then. We fought for Marlborough and Prince Eugene. They gave the orders and we followed. But this is a different battlefield and the enemy isn't dressed like a French dragoon. There is no Marshal Tallard to be outflanked; in this war it is not clear who is the enemy."

"You make it sound very dramatic," interjected Trescothick.

"Because it is, Tresco. Dramatic is exactly what it is. If anything, that description is understated. These days men fight for money and for power and they form their allegiances secretly, behind closed doors in St James's and the City. There are no uniforms to tell the sides apart."

Lancaster threw himself back on the stool and leaned against the wall again, allowing his words to sink in.

"Are you sure you want to fight in this war Maven?"

This cashiered officer, whose opinions Maven despised and whose acts of atrocity had festered in his memory in the years since they had last met had accurately summed up Maven's own opinion of the peace. He wrestled with conflicting emotions.

"I am a soldier. I follow orders."

Lancaster banged the stool down hard, scraping the legs on the stone again.

"Whose orders, eh? Tell me that. Tell me who is really in charge of this God-forsaken country."

"Why don't you tell me? Whose orders do you follow?"

"Shrewsbury."

Maven's surprise could not be masked.

"Surely not," he said, "why would Shrewsbury pitch the two of us against each other?"

"You are Shrewsbury's man as well?" Lancaster was as incredulous as Maven.

Before they could continue, their attentions were diverted by activity in the area around Maddox. Another young man was standing to Maddox's left and a second man, taller and wider and looking like the older brother, stood to Maddox's right. It seemed that the younger of the two had taken offence at the attention the Lieutenant had lavished upon the maid throughout the evening. The trio eased back in their chairs and waited for the scene to unfold. They suspected the young officer did not share their experience of pub fighting and they wondered how Maddox would acquit himself.

The routine started in much the same way as these matters usually begin. Brother number one tapped Maddox on the shoulder to gain his attention and enquire what he thought he was doing talking to his sweetheart. Maddox feigned innocence. At this point, various options presented themselves to the wronged beau. This was the Christopher, an inn on Borough High Street that was frequented by dockers and boatmen. A diplomatic solution was never really an option here and the shoulder tapping and parleying was simply a precursor to the obligatory fisticuffs. Maddox dealt politely with the initial provocation and resisted the urge to respond to a shove from brother number two. Around them was an expectant air, the locals waiting not only to see what the stranger would do but also what would be the actions of the other men, conspiring secretly in the corner and, for that reason alone, already the source of much suspicion among the regulars. Maven's heart beat a little faster and surreptitiously he took in his surroundings, considering how best to get the three of them out of there in one piece. Lancaster could take of himself. Maddox turned in his seat, looking for Maven but saw only Trescothick and Lancaster grinning back at him. He turned back to the table and took a final sip from his tankard then surprised his audience.

Maddox swung the tankard full into the face of the shorter brother, contorting the container and causing the barmaid to scream in alarm. His victim fell to the floor clutching his face in his hands, groaning in agony; a trickle of blood appeared through his fingers. The second assailant, his attention diverted by the screaming barmaid missed Maddox turning towards him and, as a result, was pole-axed by a sharp blow to the stomach followed by one to the face with the distorted tankard. He joined his brother in a crumpled heap on the floor, clutching his wounds. Maven braced himself for reinforcements, for the brothers must surely have friends in the room who would come to their aid (they always did, in his experience). Instead, with all eyes in the crowded room trained now on Maddox, the young officer looked left then right and, satisfied that there were to be no more combatants, turned to face the maid. Instead of the welcoming feminine smile that he expected he received an indignant female fist, square in the centre of his face. He cried out in alarm and bent double, clutching his nose, which now poured with blood. The landlord, sensing that enough was enough, took her away by the arm and Maven breathed a sigh of relief, relaxing now that the entertainment had turned out be no more than a bit of harmless fun. Trescothick rocked back and forth with laughter both at the officer's expense and also at the landlord, who now struggled to prevent his aggrieved employee from inflicting further violence.

"You've a mite to learn 'bout the fairer sex, m'boy!" cried Trescothick, his portly frame trembling with hilarity, which was infectious and most of the other drinkers decided that the time was right to enjoy a laugh at the three men and their various injuries. Maddox, his pride dented, replaced the misshapen mug on the table and stole a final glance at the young woman, bemused as to why she should attack him yet impressed by the force with which she had done so. He turned to face her for a final time and, despite himself, smiled at her, the cracks between his teeth stained with the blood that still poured from his nose.

The noise settled down to the same hum of conversation that had gone before. Trescothick was about to stand and offer Maddox some genuine sympathy when he was startled by Maven's voice, sharp now and jarring against the jollity that had just gone before.

"Where is he?"

Trescothick turned to face the Captain.

"Lancaster, where did he go?"

The stool, which had so recently supported Lancaster, was empty and his mug sat half full on the table. Maven offered the same question to the room.

"Where did he go?"

There were no takers and it seemed not one of the two dozen or so men had seen where the one eyed stranger had gone. Gone he had, though and, for a second, Maven was at a loss. He gathered his thoughts quickly and ordered Maddox and Trescothick outside at the double. Trescothick took some parting from the remainder of his ale and brought up the rear still supping as he walked. He was intercepted by the landlord at the door who relieved him of the now empty tankard. Maven took the opportunity to round back and meet the landlord.

"Does he come here often, the one with the eye patch?"

"No sir, don't believe he does. First time in tonight, I'd say."

Maven spat on the floor in disgust and left the saloon to join his colleagues outside.

George Trescothick wended his way back to Covent Garden uncertainly. He and Mr Welsby had helped themselves to a bottle of good burgundy wine and had gloried in its quality so much they had taken another. The toping had provided George with some compensation, for Claudette had appeared at the club again but had been whisked away after a few minutes of flirtation.

George retained enough of his wits to stay in the centre of the lit streets and avoided his shortcuts, all of which made it easier for the thin man who followed at a discreet distance to keep an eye on the youngster.

13

The disappointments of the previous evening riled Maven and as he sat on the small wooden bench outside the back door in Hatton Garden he turned the events over in his mind. The country's most senior minister had been distracted, he thought. According to the newspapers, Shrewsbury did not particularly want to hold the office of Lord Treasurer and the man was clearly unwell. The fact remained that the Duke had decided to invest time in a meeting with a former officer who was operating outside all the normal channels. Moreover, he had been sufficiently concerned about William Taylor that he had ordered the normally reliable HAC to keep him in custody. He should, he thought, have asked more questions. He would do so next time. He wondered what secrets had died with Taylor, what the wretch had known that had made his life untenable and, crucially, who exactly had done for the man. Finally, and this was the thought that grieved him most of all, he could not make sense of the return of someone who he had hoped never to set eyes on again. The crimes Lancaster had perpetrated in the name of war sickened Maven almost as much as his memories of how the General had turned away and allowed the evil to continue unchecked until even he could stand it no more. That Lancaster, such a contemptible and dishonest excuse for an officer, had surfaced again was a deeply unpleasant surprise. That Lancaster might also be employed by Shrewsbury on the same errand was even more difficult to stomach.

Kathrine called his name from the kitchen. He stood and let her know where he was.

"I thought we might take a stroll," she said.

"Now?"

His irascible response caused her to flash a reproachful look at him.

"Yes. That's unless you have something of greater importance with which to occupy your time?"

He could think of nothing other than his dislike of perambulating, of being on show. She did not wait for a reply.

"Hammond is waiting outside with the coach. Shall we take a turn?"

"Is that wise?"

"Maven, he hasn't tried to come near me since you've been around and I don't suppose he would start anything in a public place."

"There is no sense in waving it in his face though, is there?"

"I'm sorry?"

"Don't ... tease the man."

"Oh. So I am to be a prisoner? A non-person?"

"If you like."

"I don't think I do like, thank you very much."

The pause was awkward. Right now he could not have cared less if she had skipped round St James's Square shouting virulent abuse for all of Audley's many friends to hear. It might flush the blackguard out. He simply was not in the mood to make idle conversation. Then she smiled.

"We shall go north. No-one of any note shall see us and I shall be invisible and quite safe but at least I shall be out of the house and enjoying some air. It won't be long before winter is upon us and the apothecaries shall have me locked in for the good of my health. Besides, it offers an excellent opportunity for you to meet Matthew Webb."

"Audley's accomplice?"

"Hardly."

"But I thought ..."

"Matthew has placed some distance between himself and Audley. Much like every other gentleman London as far as I can see."

She turned and left him standing in the yard.

They journeyed to the New River Head in silence, uphill all the way, turning left off the Islington Road and stepping down from the coach when they reached the New Tunbridge Wells. The area had become something of a leisure destination and despite it being a weekday several couples strolled on the pathways that dissected the fields. Ahead of them the water works stood like a windmill shorn of its sails, a conical stone tower built from bricks of London clay surrounded by wooden fencing, broken where the local urchins had created places to scramble through in search of mischief and salvage. Aside from instructions to her footman, Kathrine had uttered no words at all since she had turned away from Maven at the house. Maven enjoyed silence and was happy to keep his own counsel. During the dark times he had gone for days without uttering a sound. He knew he could hold out for longer than her.

They had a choice of pathways. One led them to the circular walkway beyond the works, a fenced gravel path that was home to the intimate couples that circumnavigated slowly, oblivious to everyone around them while they exchanged giggling small talk. The second choice led down the side of the works and across the field to Merlin's Cave, a country tavern that had about it the air of a city toping den. Its fake roguery attracted the middling sort who could indulge in the pretence of dangerous living, safe in their knowledge that they were far enough from the city to not come to any real harm. Maven strode out for the tavern, knowing she would follow. Seated on the ground just off the path was an old man, a pathetic specimen who held out a filthy hat in the hope of some charity. Maven reached into his pocket and tossed in a coin. He heard her calling him.

"Wait. For goodness sake!"

She shuffled after him and caught up.

"Will you tell me truthfully whether you have made progress?"

"Progress?"

"In catching Audley."

"If a man doesn't want to be found it is remarkably easy to hide himself in a city. And he must be good at it, for there a lot of people who would like to find him besides me."

"Such as?"

"The debt collectors, we think, and his fellow members at the Blackbird Club. There are all sorts after him and they are hiring the worst kind of men to do the hunting."

"Like you?"

"Thank you ma'am. Anything else you would like to know?"

She did not reply.

They walked on for a while and he paused to observe how the land rolled gently down to the metropolis. He could see the great dome of St Pauls and admired Wren's work, marvelling at its presence on the horizon. From a distance behind them a woman laughed and the happy sound carried to them on the breeze. Kathrine paused to consider the view with him.

"Why do you despise me so?"

Maven looked at her.

"Is it because I am an independent woman, made rich from my late husband's bequest? Perhaps I am a threat?"

"To me?"

"To any man."

"No."

"No what?"

"No, I am not threatened by you but then I am not entirely sure what you mean."

"Do I subvert the normal way of living? A single woman has value, Maven. Normally she is the subject of a bargain and bought from her parents, to become chattel once she marries, whereas a widow with money has no need to marry. Not for financial reasons at least. For decorum perhaps. Is that why you dislike me?"

"There are some gentlemen who would be worried in case too many of your gender wake up and realise the truth of what you have just said. They will reason that if you are not serving their needs or indulging in some harmless pastime then you shall become bored and look for things to do. You might even start reading the wrong sort of books."

"Oh but I read the wrong sort of books already. I seek them out."

"Then you must expect that many gentlemen will be frightened of you."

"Not all of them?"

"Some of them."

"Are you? Frightened of me?"

"No."

"Why is that?"

"I am happy for you to have your freedom. I don't want to own you."

They walked on and reached the tavern and Kathrine decided she would rather sit outside. Maven turned a full circle slowly, looking at the people around them, probing for signs of suspicion, for anyone who looked out of place, looking for the mysterious Matthew Webb. As was his habit, Maven selected the chair that gave him the best view and ensured he did not have his back turned to newcomers. The innkeeper, a swarthy, pockmarked individual with only three fingers remaining on his left hand, treated them with polite suspicion. The tapster was unable to find the right pigeonhole for the tall, dark man who had about him the air of a guards officer but on closer inspection resembled a footpad. Maven flashed him a sharp, irritated look and the man turned away smartly.

Kathrine placed a gloved hand on his for a few seconds.

"Will you tell me about the debt you owed to Hugh?"

"I thought you already knew."

"No, at least not in detail. I should like to know."

Yesterday he would have said no and meant it but the appearance of Lancaster had changed his mind. Without understanding why, he felt the need to unburden himself. The tapster returned with their drinks and made a great show of serving them. When he had departed Maven continued.

"Your husband saved my life. Not in the obvious way that might happen in battle but he stood up for me when my word was challenged. It was all too rare and it cost him greatly to do so."

"But he saved your life?"

"Ma'am, there are other men searching for Audley who are best avoided. I met one last night, Robert Lancaster. It was from him that that the General saved me."

Maven settled into his chair and cradled his glass of small beer.

"Lancaster and I are both Captains. Unlike him, I had been promoted from the ranks."

"Most officers buy their commissions, I would imagine."

"Quite. I was the upstart and Lancaster took offence. He hated that I was Marlborough's man. In truth so did several others but he was the only one who let it be known that he found my presence inappropriate. He decided that I was too honest."

"Honesty was a rare commodity also?"

"Like many of his colleagues, he was over there for reasons other than fighting the enemy. He created a successful business that ferried the payage, the valuable stuff at least, back to England. Silver plate, jewellery and what have you. Not that he was the only one, of course, for armies are expected to live off the land and forage for whatever they can. But he took more than was necessary and instead of handing it over to the prize agents he smuggled it away. Always, he went too far."

"Thieves like to be left alone I should have thought."

"Thievery can be overlooked. After all, this country seems to thrive on it. But Lancaster also developed a successful career as a pander for his fellow officers. He had a way of procuring the prettiest girls and then would let it be known that he was happy to turn a blind eye to the practices of his colleagues. It would be impolite to describe those practices, madam. Then he had quite literally to turn a blind eye when one of his own girls turned on him with a poker straight from the fire. He should have died from the injuries but he has the strongest will and he clung on to life. He went looking for her. The General had ordered him not to but his pride was damaged and it was if he were possessed by the devil. I made the mistake of trying to enforce the General's order but he would not listen. The girl in question, Clothilde her name was, was a favourite of the Captain-General."

"Of Marlborough?"

"Why not? He is a soldier, after all. In any case, Lancaster saw an opportunity to settle two scores in one. He brought her to my quarters and while his henchman kept me under guard he … he had his way with her. Quite brutally. Then he took my sword and ran her through. I managed to break free but in my struggle to get away from his man, I knocked over a lamp and set the place alight. In the meantime, one of them had raised enough of a rumpus to wake the whole village. General Cooper saw them running away. Then he came and helped me to drag the girl from the tent."

"Did she survive?"

Maven shook his head.

"Lancaster and his cohorts concocted a story between them that had me murdering Clothilde. All quite ridiculous but in the army honour is a strange thing. Without your husband I should have perished for no one else stood up and spoke for me in front of the Captain-General."

"Nobody at all came forward to defend your name?"

"As I have said, Lancaster was not alone in his resentment."

"What happened to him?"

"For the rape and murder? Nothing at all. That is how it is. But General Cooper was watching him and it was only a question of time before Lancaster transgressed again. He was cashiered. And now he has returned, searching for Audley and proving once again that there is no God."

"Please, don't say that."

She placed her hand on his again.

"Thank you for telling me. I think I should like to release you from your obligation."

"Why?"

"What you have described should not have been the subject of a debt, surely? So, if you wish, you are free to go. I shall not hold you here against your wishes."

They finished their drinks and she asked him to order a second round.

"Is it possible that you might provide an introduction to the Duke of Marlborough?"

"For you?"

"No, for Matthew."

Maven frowned quizzically.

"Why would the Captain-General want to meet your brother in law?"

"He has something that Marlborough needs. I have no idea what it might be, but he is in desperate trouble. Audley is out of control."

"But that will put you in even more trouble with Audley."

"Indeed it would but I must act or my sister too will know what it means to be widowed."

"And Webb needs a woman to help him out of the corner?" said Maven with disdain.

"Oh, Maven, you do not know him. Matthew means well enough but he seems to become attached to the wrong people."

Maven felt comfortable in her presence would have been happy to stay there all day if she let him. It had been more than ten years since he had shared his thoughts with a woman so openly. She looked into the distance towards the skyline of London and he looked at the outline of her face against the blue sky. He thought how beautiful she was. During their third drink she screwed up her eyes and seemed to be looking at something.

"Oh my goodness."

"What?"

"Over there. Those two men."

She pointed to the narrow road that led past the burying fields to Clerkenwell, where two men stood engaged in earnest conversation. They had just stepped down from a coach and the vehicle waited by them. They were dressed well as far as he could see from this distance, sporting wigs and tricorn hats and their standing poses reflected the confidence of the upper classes. Their conversation, though muted from where Maven sat, was not amicable and one of the men was raising his voice, his mood emphasized by the lifting of his stick, the silver tip directed at his adversary the better to make his point.

"The man on the right."

"The one losing his temper?"

"It's him. That is Audley."

"How sure are you?"

"As sure as anyone could be, even from this distance. Yes it is him, his dress, his pose. I am sure that is the scoundrel."

Maven stood and his intention was to go after Audley but Kathrine gripped his hand and restrained him. At the same time, his conversation evidently concluded, Audley and his companion parted. The stranger turned and walked towards them while Audley climbed into his coach, which departed in the direction of London.

"Let him go. You'll never catch him."

Maven sat down and waited for the second man to approach them. The man was the servant he and George had encountered at Audley's house. He strutted past the tavern as if the establishment and its customers did not exist. His attention was diverted by the presence of the beggar who still held his scruffy felt hat in front of him. The servant ignored the wretch even when the beggar dropped to his knees and cried out for alms. As he strode past, the servant turned and spat on the man then poked at him viciously with his cane. Maven tracked the servant as he walked north to the buildings where a hackney cab waited, its yellow coachwork glinting in the autumn sun. When the visitor was far enough away that any movement in front of the inn would not disturb him Maven stood.

"It isn't safe to stay here. I suspect they have followed Matthew."

"If Mr Webb is here."

"He will be here somewhere. Matthew would not put me in harms way. There will be a reason he has not showed himself."

"You are safe enough. We are a fair way from the path."

"I shouldn't like to see him if he should walk back this way," she said, indicating Audley's companion.

"Do you know the servant?"

"Yes," she said and her dislike was evident for a chill passed between them briefly. "Yes I do know him. His name is Pinchbeck, Ezra Pinchbeck. He is probably Audley's most loyal man. Be careful, Maven."

Kathrine stood and they walked to the side of the road. He waited with her until Hammond was in front of the tavern then escorted her down the path to the coach. Then he walked left through the trees and got as close as he could to Pinchbeck. A gentleman had stepped down from the hackney and, as he conversed with Pinchbeck looked left and right and Maven thought he was advertising to anyone with an ounce of sense that he was up to no good. Dressed as well as Audley and his servant, the new man was taller than Pinchbeck but just as thin. His clothes hung off him and his eyes were sunk into his head like he was troubled with illness and had not slept since the robbing and murder of the courier in Camberwell, now a week ago. His white lace neckerchief was either new or recently starched, for it shone out and deflected attention from his troubled and pale face. The tree line ended too far from the roadside and Maven was unable to move close enough to hear any of their conversation. The actions, though, were those of a trade. From inside his coat Pinchbeck produced a heavy bag. He showed it off but did not hand it over, the proof of its existence having been established. Pinchbeck nodded to the cab driver, strode to the door and climbed in. There was a pause while the other man decided whether or not to join him, but with Pinchbeck in the hackney and the door waiting open for him, he was left with little choice and he clambered up and slammed the door shut behind him.

Maven watched the jarvey, a thickset unshaven man with dark stubble and dirty black hat. He had on a black cloak but it was not the regulation uniform. Nothing happened for thirty seconds then Maven heard a knock from inside the coach, presumably from Pinchbeck's cane. The jarvey cracked the horses into life and the cab moved off with a jerk. It bumped and slid south towards the city down Bridewell Walk, travelling too fast for the road.

Hammond had parked Kathrine's carriage by the works' buildings, about a hundred yards across the grass. Maven ran towards them and hoisted himself into the vehicle then called on Hammond to move forward and before he could shut the door behind him the coach was off. The field in front of the Merlin's Cave tavern formed a triangle and the road would have intersected Pinchbeck's cab just south of the tavern had it been travelling at a more sedate pace but the hackney was now well ahead of them and rattling down the hill. Maven settled himself with his back to the driver and opened the communication vent.

"Don't get too close and don't do anything dangerous. They mustn't suspect they are being followed."

There was little danger of getting too close, for the cab was hurtling down the slope towards the capital at a strong pace and they struggled to keep up. Maven knew the area. Once they were past the burying ground they would reach the twisting streets of Clerkenwell and would be forced to slow down.

"Easy there, Hammond. We'll catch up with them soon enough!"

Kathrine clung on to the grab handle with both hands as the coach bounced over the uneven road. She slid about the seat but stared straight ahead and was clearly troubled.

"Maven..."

"What?"

"The man we saw ..."

"Audley's servant?"

"No, the other one. The one in the hackney cab."

"What of him? Do you know who he is?"

"That was Matthew."

Maven paused to allow her information to settle in but he had been sure enough already of who it was he had been looking at.

"Did he see you?" he asked.

"He must surely have recognised the coach."

They continued to travel too quickly and he turned to shout at Hammond and tell him to stop. She reached out a hand and prevented him.

"Let's follow them as far as we can. Please don't abandon him."

As they got closer to the City the road narrowed and houses crowded in on them on either side. Hammond allowed a man pushing a barrow to move between them and the cab and they slowed to walking pace through Clerkenwell Green then stopped completely at Turnmill Street. The Fleet Ditch stank even this far north of the Thames and Kathrine raised a perfumed handkerchief to her nose. Maven's stomach turned and his sixth sense that had guided him through Flanders screamed that the Lady was in danger here.

"I'll go the rest of the way on my own," he said, "have Hammond take you home. I will see you there."

"You can't go alone. I want to come with you."

"Not down here. It's barely safe enough for me. Go home. I will meet you there."

With that, Maven jumped down from the carriage and closed the door silently behind him, pausing to repeat his instruction to Hammond. Ahead, he could see the reason for the hold up. A drover was herding cattle toward Smithfield market and the animals, sensing their fate, were reluctant to go forward. He walked back to the carriage, stepped onto the running board and peered in through the window, startling Kathrine.

"They are stuck in the traffic further down near the market. Nothing is moving. If they've come down this way then they must be near to where they are headed otherwise they would have gone around the outside."

"But I want to come with you. Matthew looked troubled."

"You would have to walk through the market ma'am and that is unthinkable. Please go home.

Hammond turned to him and cleared his throat.

"They are getting down, sir."

Maven allowed himself one brief glance at her brown eyes and she reached out a gloved hand to touch his. Though her touch was light he felt for the briefest of moments that her reaction had been somehow contractual rather than emotional. He jumped down, span round and joined the slipstream of a man carrying a large basket of fruit on his head. Maven mingled in the crowd that pressed its way down the street, competing with the throng that was attempting to move itself north. The two men in front looked utterly out of place and their manner of dress marked them out as targets for the Smithfield regulars. Within seconds they were accosted by a beggar and then by a pedlar who attempted unsuccessfully to sell them some of the rags he had on a tray in front of him.

The stench of polluted water from the Ditch was replaced now with the smell of a thousand farmyards, physical evidence of which was everywhere underfoot. Occasionally, a woman would pass with a nosegay or a scented handkerchief pressed to her face but, mostly, the locals were oblivious to the pungent air and went about their business in ignorance of the noxious odours. Pinchbeck and Webb were closer to the market now. The noise increased in volume. The lowing of cattle was punctuated by the occasional clanging of a cowbell and their distress set off the sheep that were already penned at the market. Maven saw the pair reach the junction, where the drover's cattle were being held until space could be found for them in the pens. The countryman had allowed his herd to walk too far and it now blocked the junction with St John Street. No vehicles could move and there was scarcely room for the foot traffic to get by. The crowd was restless. Some, angered and impatient, shouted at the drover while others laughed at the fun of it.

Drunk, of course, uproariously so for this time of the morning, Barren Nell was an infamous whore who had long since ceased to provide value to any passing traveler foolish enough to succumb to her charms. Pinchbeck was clearly not familiar with the area else he would, like his acquaintance, have avoided her, for the woman was a permanent fixture perched on the edge of the stone horse trough on the corner of St John Street.

"'Ere y'are m'loves. Grab 'old a summa this!"

Webb skirted round the back of the crowd but Pinchbeck's path took him directly in front of her and before he realised his fate he had gone too far to turn back and find another way. The locals were watching the show and to retreat would have invited scorn and ridicule. A gentleman was, after all, expected to defend his honour. As he approached her she stood, uncertainly at first, and then staggered towards him, a stone jar in her hand containing her gin ration for the day. She held the jar close to her body in case it should somehow escape her. Pinchbeck did not break stride, but shoved her aside imperiously with his cane and tried to continue his journey. He found his way blocked, for Nell was no small lady and she had the ability to handle objections in a forthright manner.

"Madam, move aside and allow me past!"

Nell handed her precious gin jar to a market trader in blood soaked overalls. Her ravaged face cracked a smile, revealing the black stumps that passed for teeth and her bulbous red nose seemed to swell in sympathy. She stood squarely in front of her victim then tore open her bodice to reveal her ample bosom.

"It's all yours my darling. Whaddya say? Threepence and a decent meal."

She roared with laughter and the crowd about her joined in.

Pinchbeck could think of nothing to say and he blushed like a teenager. Around him, the market men laughed and passed crude comments that insulted not only Nell, who was well used to it, but Pinchbeck's manhood. The servant cringed and looked for Webb, wishing he could be anywhere but here. Nell returned for her second assault.

"Don't you want me, lover? What's wrong wiv me?" and then to her audience, she shouted, "He's not man enough for me, is 'e? Give us back me gin then!"

"Madam, please, allow me to pass. I command you."

Pinchbeck's instruction lacked authority and betrayed his weakness.

"You ain't gonna disappoint old Nell are you darling?"

She waved her little finger at him in a gesture that needed no explaining to the crowd, who roared with laughter again. Maven watched the show from the corner of the street, hidden in the doorway of a bakery where the smell of fresh warm bread was just about winning the battle against the stench of livestock. He grinned at Pinchbeck's discomfort but made sure he kept an eye on Webb, who was edging away and looking up St John Street. Maven looked for accomplices but saw no one else who might be an acquaintance of Pinchbeck.

Pinchbeck stepped aside smartly and wheeled past the whore, who swigged greedily from her gin jar. She bowed deeply to the crowd and her huge breasts swung loose. The show over, she fastened her bodice and staggered back to her perch on the trough, cackling at the fun of it all. Pinchbeck, head down and red in the face, scowled with anger as he met his companion and they continued their journey. Webb's humble smile did nothing to appease him. The pair squeezed past the unsettled cattle, crossed Long Lane and went into the market itself. Maven followed at a discreet distance.

The open space was sub-divided into a multitude of pens of various sizes, most of which seemed to be over-filled with livestock. The pens to the right were for cattle and those to the left for sheep. Some small goats skipped about at the feet of the crowd, their pens too loose to retain them. Pinchbeck led them through the centre of the market towards the great dome that loomed beyond the hospital of St Bartholomew. They turned sharp left and evaded a dogcart that was speeding across the square laden with a side of beef. They stopped and Pinchbeck looked about him. Maven guessed they were checking to see whether anyone followed them. He continued until he reached the far side of the open space, stopping when he reached the white stone of the hospital. He saw them enter Cloth Fair and doubled back to catch up. It was a narrow street with the church of St Bartholomew the Great on one side. On the other were timber houses that had slipped on their shallow foundations and hung over the thoroughfare. Unlike the area north of the market, Cloth Fair was free of traffic and there were few people. Maven almost got too close. He had assumed they were heading for the Hand and Shears but a few yards before the tavern, the pair paused outside one of the houses in the row directly opposite the entrance to the churchyard. To Maven's surprise it was Webb who indicated to Pinchbeck that they had reached their destination. Pinchbeck nodded and they went inside. Maven cut into the churchyard and took shelter behind the largest gravestone he could find. The ground was uneven and the stones betrayed the effects of constant disturbance, presenting an untidy and unkempt line like a peasant's teeth. He moved nearer to the door of the church and by looking between the v of two stones that sat at alarming angles he could see the house quite clearly. Webb and Pinchbeck gave no clue that the house was occupied.

Maven was disturbed by a sound behind him and took it to be the church warden or perhaps even the preacher and he turned, ready with an excuse to explain his presence. Maven paused and looked into the man's face. After the shock of seeing Lancaster for the first time in years, he was unprepared to once again come face to face with a second gentleman from his army days.

"No, not you as well," he said and before he could stand the man smiled malevolently and hit him hard on the head with a wooden club. Maven crumpled into a heap and lay unconscious against the cold gravestone.

*

Audley pulled his fob watch from his pocket and checked the time. He had two hours to make the meeting and was determined not to be late, for he knew how his host valued punctuality. He would make what could only be a brief stop. Audley's driver jumped down from the carriage and banged on the front door repeatedly with his fist until it swung open.

"Alright, alright, give it a rest will you?" snarled the bawd. The servant turned away and opened the carriage door. Audley stepped down smartly and skipped quickly into the hallway of the brothel then closed the front door himself. Her bodice was stained with food and ale.

"You needn't have made an effort for me, Mrs McGrath."

"Shove it up yer arse. Sir."

Audley ignored the abuse and smiled at her in his most condescending manner.

"Will you bring Claudette to me, madam," it was an instruction rather than a question.

"She ain't 'ere."

"She was told to wait. Did she not follow the plan?"

"Plan? What plan?"

He stepped towards her and made to grab her but then changed his mind as the smell she gave off repulsed him.

"Bolingbroke was here was he not?"

"Aye, slept the night an' all, the bugger. With him and you skulking around in the shadows like footpads you shall be the death of me, sir. You shall certainly be the death of my business."

"Stop your whining, woman. Did she lift the papers?"

"Aye."

"Hand them over. Come on, woman."

"What are they worth?"

His temper could not be contained and he stepped forward and slapped her across the face.

"Damn you, you worn out fricatrice. Stop playing with me and hand over the goods. We have already concluded our negotiations. Give them to me now."

She nursed the wound with her grubby hand and looked at him with contempt.

"You shall die of the pox, sir."

He had his hand on the hilt of his sword but he did not draw the weapon. Instead he grabbed her by the throat and forced her back against the wall.

"The papers are worth far more than your life could ever amount to. You can save yourself by giving them to me now. The alternative is that I have this foul den torn to pieces until I locate them."

He released her and wiped his hand on the curtain. Mother McGrath went to the smart, new bow-fronted cabinet that was her most recent purchase and slid open an exquisitely crafted drawer. Audley stepped forward and snatched the papers from her and examined first the broken seal and then the contents.

"You are to forget you ever saw these," he said.

"Where's my money?" snarled the bawd.

"All in good time. There shall be time enough to - "

His attention was fully diverted by the words on the page and once he realised he had been deceived he scanned ahead, as if to make sure that he had not been mistaken. What he read was not a passage describing the late Queen's true wishes for the succession but a list of noblemen with Jacobite leanings and near the top of the alphabetical list just below Atterbury was his own name. Mother McGrath had seen Audley in his temper but this was the first time she had seen any man's ire boil so incandescently. Audley screwed the papers in his fist and hurled them to the floor.

"What has he done?" he screamed, "Do you know what he has done?" and before she could answer he struck her hard across the face and the force of his blow sent her to the floor.

By the time he arrived at St James's Palace, Audley had collected his thoughts and when he stepped down to be greeted by Bothmer's manservant it was as if the visitor were an old friend come to share luncheon. Bothmer kept his visitor waiting for ten minutes and Audley wondered whether it would be impolite to help himself to a chicken leg from the table. Then Bothmer burst in through a door that led from a quiet corridor. The visit was to be discreet.

"Mr Audley, good morning. How lovely to see you again. Please, sit, let us be informal."

Bothmer sat down heavily on his chair and leaned back, very much the proprietor of the meeting.

"So, what do you have for me?"

"I regret, sir, that I come empty handed, at least for now. It seems that our friend may not, after all, be in possession of the items you seek."

Bothmer inhaled deeply and pursed his lips. He rested his large hands on his knees and leaned forward.

"Well, that does rather damage our arrangement, no?"

"You are already assured of my loyalty, sir."

"Your word is of less value than you might imagine."

"But I have - "

Bothmer slammed his open palm down hard on the table.

"Do not be so simple as to think that the matter can end here! You, sir, are in considerable trouble and you are nowhere close to being out of it. I want those letters! What are you to do about it?"

Audley paused and did his best to remain outwardly calm while his heart raced. He looked at the guards who blocked the way to the exit. They were of the battalion that had travelled from Hanover with the elector. He wondered if they spoke English. Probably not.

"An answer, sir, if you please. Do not forget that I already have enough evidence to hang you."

"I shall need some time. I will see to it that the letters will be in your possession before the coronation."

"Mr Audley, if those letters are not safely in my possession before the King is crowned then I shall have you hanged. You need to be very clear about that."

14

Maven awoke to find a man standing next to him, dressed in black, and he started, propelled by the fear that this was his attacker watching over him. The young curate stepped back in alarm.

"Woah! I am sorry if I startled you, sir. The Reverend Chilcott has gone to fetch the chirurgeon."

"There's ... no need."

Maven's head hurt and it throbbed above the temple where he had been hit. He rubbed it with the palm of his hand. There was a large bump and what felt like dried blood had coursed down his face. Trying to rise, he was unsteady on his feet and had to reach out for a gravestone to steady his weight. He looked at the clock on the spire but struggled to focus on the Roman numerals.

"Come into the church."

The curate led the way and beckoned for Maven to follow. Maven stayed where he was. He patted down his coat and found, to his great surprise, that his purse was still there and that it contained the same number of coins it had this morning. Discreetly, he felt for the weapon inside his boot and was relieved to find that this, also, had remained undisturbed.

"Who lives in that house?"

"Which one?"

"The house directly in front of the gate, there."

"It belongs to the church, sir. It is used by the wardens occasionally, but mostly it is reserved for visiting clergy who would rather not use the tavern."

"Who is using it now?"

"Now? Why nobody, sir. The house has been empty for weeks, although we are expecting several visitors for the coronation and they will lodge there."

"But there were men there this morning."

"I am sorry, sir. You must have been mistaken. Would you like to come in out of the air? I can arrange for something to eat."

Maven's balance was returning now and he stood without the aid of the stone support. He set off uncertainly in the opposite direction, anxious to investigate the house. The curate followed nervously, as much to protect the property of the church as to watch over Maven's health. The frontage of the house appeared to have sunk into the ground and the upper storey leaned forward at such an angle that Maven could have rested his head on it. The height of the front door was significantly lower than it would have been when the house was newly built and he had to bend down to get close to it. He gave the iron handle a good shove and then forced his full weight against the wood without dislodging it.

"I say, I really don't think you should be ..."

"Who has the key?"

"No, sir, I am afraid I cannot ..."

At that moment, the curate was relieved to see two men turn the corner. One wore an untidy grey wig and the uniform of a preacher and was accompanied by a short, rotund man who carried a vast bag of the size that might be used by a workman for his tools, except that this container was made of dark red leather and had a brass clasp. The preacher looked older than he truly was. Although possessed of a wide girth he had in his eyes a resigned and careless look and the expression of one who had been disappointed in the outcome of his career, perhaps passed over unjustly for a bishopric. The voice of the Reverend Henry Chilcott boomed out.

"What in heaven's name is going on here?"

The curate shrank in the presence of his superior.

"I tried to restrain him but he would not be stopped, sir."

"Who the devil are you, sir and what do you think you are doing?"

Maven looked at the man but did not answer. Then the surgeon stepped forward. He had clearly left home in a hurry for though he carried his instrument bag he was without his wig and his head was shaved, quite recently judging from the razor cuts that decorated his scalp. He had bushy white whiskers that meandered down his jaw and stopped just short of his mouth.

"Nasty bump you have there, my man. I'd lay down a while if I were you, perhaps let me take a look at it."

"Who lives here?" asked Maven.

"I don't see what business it is of yours, my man ..."

"I followed two men here earlier today. A third man struck me about the head. I have met him before and I can assure you he is no man of God. Now will you please tell me, who lives here?"

Reverend Chilcott shuffled forward and stood directly in front of Maven. He did not make eye contact.

"The property is empty, Mr ..."

Maven paused for the briefest of moments.

"Lancaster."

There was no reaction.

"Mr. Lancaster, the property is unoccupied at present."

"There were men here today."

"Then they must have purloined the key from the warden for there is no obvious damage to the door as you can see. But the warden is a careful man. He would not lend the key to just anyone."

Reverend Chilcott rummaged inside his coat and, as he held the garment open, they could all see that its lining was torn and dirty. His hand surfaced with a metal ring about three inches in diameter on which were half a dozen keys. He held the keys up close to his eyes and made a great show of choosing the correct one. The surgeon grew frustrated that he would not be called into action. He placed his bag on the ground and folded his arms.

Behind them, in the doorway of the Hand and Shears, a boy leaned against the brickwork and, when he was sure that the group was about to gain entry to the house he darted away in search of the constable, just as he had been told.

The key was quite small for such a thick door but the mechanism turned easily and Chilcott pushed the door open. Inside it was dark and cold, there being no way for the October sun to have penetrated the hallway. Chilcott leaned in.

"Hello! Is there anybody there?" His loud voice carried to every corner of the house. Maven listened carefully, as much for the sound of someone escaping through a back door as for a verbal response but nothing stirred. He bent his head down and stepped inside and was struck by how chilly he felt. No fire had been lit here for a while and there was dampness in the air. The front door opened directly onto a small parlour, the only furniture being two rude wooden chairs either side of the stone fireplace. He stepped inside. The room at the back was a kitchen, with a stove and a table and several chairs, one of which had been upended, like its occupant had been surprised and had left in a hurry. A stone jar stood on the table, its cork stopper alongside. Maven bent to the jar and caught the scent of gin. The three men had followed him in.

"It's not holy water, vicar."

He turned then and went upstairs and the treads creaked and bent under his weight. The banister was unsound and, had he leant on it, it would certainly have given way. There was a landing and the same two room arrangement, although the bedrooms had doors, both of which were closed. He went to the front room and pushed open the door. It swung easily to reveal a bed, bare to the mattress with a tidy pile of blankets stacked upon it, a small wardrobe and a tiny three-legged stool painted a vivid red. The floor sloped alarmingly and the ill-fitting window provided an interesting if somewhat disconcerting view of the street. The three men had not followed him but he could hear their murmured conversation. Maven moved up the slope to the back of the house and tried the door of the second bedroom. He pushed gently and caught the faint whiff of something familiar. He stood in the doorway and looked at the wall opposite and saw what he was afraid would greet him.

"Reverend! I need you here."

He turned and stepped away in shock. Leaning against the wall, sitting on the floor, with each hand nailed to the wooden crossbeam was a body. Maven recognised Matthew Webb as the thin, worried man he had followed from the New River Head. His throat had been cut and the blood had soaked his white neckerchief so that the whole of his front was stained dark brown.

Reverend Chilcott appeared. He looked inquisitively at Maven then shifted his attention to the floor. What colour there was in his face drained from it immediately.

"Oh my life …"

"Who is he?"

"How can this possibly have happened?"

"Please tell me who he is. Do you know him?"

"N-no. He is a stranger, sir."

Maven stood and thought. The murder of Matthew Webb coming so soon after the death of William Taylor struck deep within him. He was suddenly consumed with the fear that Kathrine was in danger. His early thoughts that Audley was nothing more than a gentleman with dubious connections and a few money worries had been swept away in less than a day.

Then the surgeon joined them and there was barely room for them all in the small room. Maven sensed the men were staring at him, waiting for him to take the lead. He had seen enough bodies to deduce for himself that the death had occurred soon after his arrival for the corpse was almost cold, but he wanted to give the surgeon something to do that did not involve wondering who the tall stranger in their midst might be.

"How long has he been dead?" asked Maven. The surgeon poked and prodded the body and dipped his finger in the man's blood without reassuring anyone that he knew what he was doing.

"You say you were here before midday? I'd wager he was killed quite soon after. The blood is quite dry and has soaked into the floor. The smell also suggests death occurred several hours ago. We should fetch the constable. We shall need an undertaker as well."

"Indeed," said Chilcott, grateful for any excuse to leave the room, "we shall do both of those things. Mr. Lancaster, perhaps you and I might continue our conversation downstairs?"

They descended the staircase one at a time, neither of them trusting the woodwork to bear the weight of the both of them simultaneously. They stood in the street, and whilst the air was far from fresh it at least released them from the smell of death that filled the upper floor of the house.

"Mr Lancaster, it is a strange trade you follow that leads to you being assaulted in churchyards and discovering dead bodies. Whom is it that you represent, sir?"

Maven looked up and saw a gentleman enter the eastern end of Cloth Fair. He took him to be the constable. The curate was nowhere to be seen, which meant someone else had alerted him. Quickly, Maven turned to Chilcott.

"Do you know Lord Audley?"

Chilcott paused, wrongfooted by the question.

"No, I can't say as I do. Should I? Is he important?"

Maven turned away from him and made towards the market. Chilcott called after him, "I say! I think you should stay and explain yourself to the constable, Mr. Lancaster!"

Maven heard the thumping of the constable's feet on the damp ground as he ran to catch him. He had a pistol in his hand. Maven looked back and knew that if he kept the distance between them to at least thirty feet he would be safe for the weapon was hopelessly inaccurate at that distance. Then it seemed as though the constable drew the same conclusion for he gave up the chase and called after him.

"It's no use running, Maven. We know where you lodge. Give yourself up now!"

The traders of the meat market were early risers and did most of their business before their fellow Londoners woke, which meant that by this time of day Smithfield was quiet and there were fewer people on the street now. There were still plenty of animals occupying the pens, many having only recently arrived, driven down from their fields in the home counties, while the thin and the sickly and the otherwise unsold remained for tomorrow when they would doubtless fetch less than it had cost the farmer to raise them. The drovers crammed their animals into the pens and took turns to watch over them. Having got the beasts as far as they had without being troubled by thieves they would not stand aside meekly and allow themselves to be robbed before they could obtain their fair value at the tomorrow's market. They sat about, perched on the fences of the pens and eyed Maven suspiciously as he walked among them and crossed the market. At this time of day there was a lull, a quietness that hung over the area before the nocturnal activities started up just as soon as it was dark enough to obscure the identities of the ladies and gentleman who indulged in a different kind of meat market.

Maven slipped down the side of the hospital then crossed into Cock Lane. The sun was obscured by heavy grey clouds and his head hurt and he was more upset than he would allow about the sight of Matthew Webb's body hanging on the wall, slaughtered for a reason he had yet to fathom. The trade had gone wrong, that was clear enough, but was his death the result of a reluctance to part with a bag of cash? It seemed an unnecessarily elaborate murder if money was its motive. Perhaps Webb had not kept his side of the bargain. Audley was involved, though, and he had seen it himself this morning. Perhaps, he thought, Audley had taken the opportunity to make some sort of demonstration and had lured him here. It had been a trap, perhaps, and Maven had walked right into it.

London was brutal, the most dangerous, infested, rathole of a place in the Kingdom but murder, proper cold blooded murder, as distinct from the death that arose from brawling, was still mercifully rare. People of all kinds would be robbed, burgled and cheated before the night was out but it was usually only drink and fists and misplaced pride that took the wretches away from this world. He thought of Kathrine and quickened his pace. He reached the Holborn Bridge and looked over the parapet at the stinking Fleet below him. Theoretically navigable to this point, it was a brave or foolish boatman that tried to reach the bridge. Until the tide rose and swept away the remains the Fleet would be home to the unwanted offal disposed here by the Smithfield butchers, the presence of which in turn summoned the rats, who competed with the dark eyed poor, the men, women and children whose only hope of sustenance was to pick what they could from the unsanitary debris. Around them was piled all the effluent of human life from the courtyards either side of the ditch that teemed with too many people. Holborn Bridge was not a place to dwell.

By the time he reached Hatton Garden Maven was running, such was his fear that some evil had been done to her. He rapped on the front door vigorously and repeatedly, causing Sarah to reprimand him severely when she finally reached the front of the house. He burst in and went straight to the front drawing room and, finding it empty, went to the kitchen, where he could hear the voice of Sergeant Trescothick telling one of his interminable good-natured stories of Cornish life. Maven entered the kitchen breathlessly, flinging back the door. The chatter stopped and he found Trescothick sitting with George and Kathrine. On the table was a large jar of ale and three glasses, all of which contained the amber liquid. They were all looking at him, at the bump on his forehead, which had now bruised alarmingly, at the blood on his face and his shirt and his boots and at the look of sheer terror on his face. Kathrine raised her hand to her mouth. He stared at her.

"You have to get away from here. As soon as possible, it is too dangerous for you in London."

They forced him upstairs to bed and in his pained and dishevelled state he had complied but only once he had extracted promises from Trescothick to remain in the house overnight. Maven spent an uncomfortable and painful night in the attic room convinced that the constable was part of some wider conspiracy that would see them all carted off to Newgate. He ran the situation through his mind over and over and before long the present had mingled with the past so that his fear was no longer of mercenaries and murder victims but of battles past, of blood and slaughter, drumming and shouting, screaming and pleading, gunshots and booming artillery fire. All the while, drifting in and out of the background were his thoughts of Ruth, the image of her face faint now. Her brown hair blew long and free and the strong breeze pinned back her white smock against the outline of her breasts. She smiled at him and her right hand beckoned, the fingers at once outstretched and then curling gently, slowly toward her. In his dream he felt himself walking to the vision of Ruth, stepping over bodies, ignoring the plaintiff cries for mercy that always drifted across the field of battle when the killing was done. He walked to her, her arms now outstretched to welcome him, her smile broader with each step he took. Then, as he got nearer the volume and frequency of cannon and musket fire increased but it was not Ruth but Matthew Webb who smiled and called Maven towards him.

He woke abruptly and stared up at the ceiling. The faint light of dawn was breaking through the window. He felt the cold air on his bare skin. He had thrown back the blankets during the night when the heat of his dreams had made him sweat, as they always did. He moved his head from side to side and there was no pain. He reached up to touch his temple with his hand and found the bump was still there and was tender to the touch but not as large as it had been the night before.

15

Had events gone to plan then Maven need never have known.

Despite his assurances to the Captain that he would remain in the house, George left Hatton Garden with his father. Kathrine had insisted they take a hackney and there had been no argument when she handed over more than enough money to cover the journey. Trescothick senior left the cab in Covent Garden, and was replaced as a passenger by the ever obliging potman, Peck, who travelled with George to St James's Square. There, George had got down and sent Peck back to Hatton Garden in the hackney to keep watch on Kathrine. Peck was instructed to remain alert and vigilant for the whole night and was not to leave the kitchen unless the mistress rang for him or Maven awoke from his slumber. Peck, duly washed and tidied in honour of his elevated role, followed his instructions to the letter until about three o'clock when he dozed off. Sarah found him at the kitchen table resting his head on his folded arms. Her anger raised, she struck Peck a blow across the back of his head with the bristled-end of the house broom and cursed the ineptitude of the men who were supposed to be protecting them.

George arrived at the Blackbird Club in time to begin his evening shift. He presented himself to Corporal Dench at the back door and was assigned to cleaning duties. George removed his jacket and rolled up his sleeves. He set about the handful of glasses and crockery that had accumulated from the lunchtime session.

"Many members in today, Corporal?"

"What's it to you if there was?"

"Just making conversation."

"Well don't. And leave the women alone and all. What you do in your own time is your own business but I don't want any familiar ways while you're in here. And don't go believing none of her stories, neither. Trouble with her having a lot of time on her hands is that her imagination runs riot. That one makes up all sorts of fancy tales. The members here are important and they move in circles, you understand, circles?"

"Move in circles, yes Corporal."

"And it is not for us to understand why they do it. And it certainly has nothing to do with a tuppenny ha'penny whore, so don't you forget it."

With that, Dench sniffed to reinforce his point and left the room. George continued with his chores, slowly so as to keep himself busy for as long as possible. Just as he was giving up on having company he was joined by Mr Welsby, who darted silently across the flagstones and was at his side before the door slammed shut behind him.

"You wanna watch him when he's like this. The old codger gets punchy a bit too easy. He may be a short 'un but I've seen him set about blokes and leave 'em bleeding on the floor if he's a mind to. You don't seem the sparring kind, George. Best stay out of his way."

"What about Claudette?"

"What about her?"

"Is she due to visit tonight?"

"How should I know? If they send for her then she comes. If not she stays at 'ome. Ain't know rhyme or reason to it. And you'd do well to not ask too many questions, George. It ain't good practice, especially when Dench is in a mood."

Welsby arranged a bottle of French wine and two glasses on a silver tray and threw a white cotton napkin over his forearm.

"Mr. George," said Welsby in faux-refined tones, "would you kindly get the door for me sir? I seem to have slammed it shut on me way in."

"Right you are Mr. Welsby."

George wiped his wet hands on a dry cloth and laid the cloth over his own forearm, bowed to Welsby and then walked slowly, with his head in the air, to the door, "Please walk this way, sir."

He folded his left arm across his chest, marched to the door and opened it. Welsby passed through and as George was about to release the handle and let the door close he heard Dench clomping down the stairs with two men following behind him. Welsby had to wait for them to pass, which allowed George some cover while he observed their actions. Dench led the first man to the door of a storage room across the passage, which he unlocked with one of the keys on his belt. The passageway was narrow and, even when Welsby had departed, the space was confined enough for the second guest to wait on the stairs, out of George's eye line. The man he could see did not look remotely like he might be a club member. He was unkempt and wore a scruffy coat and dirty boots. He had on a tricorn black hat that he wore without a wig. George kept the door ajar and observed through the narrow crack. The man had a swarthy, unshaven face and the dark shadow failed to hide a vicious scar that ran down his left cheek. The poor light in the passage served to render his dark eyes very sinister indeed. Had George been able to see the second man he would have noticed that he was slightly taller and carried himself in an upright fashion, more like a gentleman. Like his colleague, this man was unshaven and his hands were quite dirty. His most distinguishing mark, though, was the red velvet eye patch.

There was a bang as the back door swung open. George stepped away smartly. The noise had been loud enough to disturb Dench and Scarface and caused them to look his way. He was back in the centre of the kitchen in three strides but before he could speak the door was open again and Dench had burst through. He stopped when he saw who it was. Ezra Pinchbeck held Claudette with her arm firmly behind her back.

"Keep your noise down. I don't want the members disturbed."
Pinchbeck threw Claudette into a chair at the big table. She sighed through puffed cheeks.

"Bleedin' horrible day then I've gotta put up with him roughin' me up," she said, indicating the thin manservant with an insolent raised eyebrow. "Be a darling and get us a drink, George."

Pinchbeck stared at George but said nothing. George looked at Dench, who paused for a second, nodded faintly then turned and left the room. Pinchbeck smiled at George.

"Have you found him yet?"
George was terrified in his silence.

"Audley? Have you found him?"

"N-no, sir."

"Good luck in your search," said Pinchbeck, taking a chair at the far end of the table. "Fetch the lady a drink."

As he retrieved a bottle from the cabinet near the door the door to the storage room slammed shut and keys rattled as it was locked again. The murmur of the voices was too low to make out what was said and the three pairs of boots tramped noisily back up the staircase. She was watching him.

"Come on George, darling. Girl could die of thirst waiting for you."

He placed the bottle and a glass in front of her and caught the waft of stale alcohol on her breath. The door flung open and Welsby presented himself in a foul temper.

"If they don't want me to see nothing then they shouldn't bring the bastards in 'ere."

They looked at him in silence.

"Two blokes. You must have seen 'em George. Half-pay officers turned into footpads. Right pair they are. Got no business soiling the hall carpet with their boots."

"Who are they?"

"Never seen 'em before me old mate, but I knows bother when I sees it. You don't come by scars like that one had without knowing where to find trouble. And talking of trouble ..." Welsby cast a lascivious glance at Claudette. At that moment Pinchbeck adjusted his pose slightly and it was as if he had been invisible up to that point. Welsby froze.

"What trouble do you expect?" asked Pinchbeck.

"N-nothing. Nothing at all, sir."

"Good. There will be no trouble then."

"No, sir."

Pinchbeck stepped forward and stared hard at Welsby.

"Give it a rest you little weasel," said Claudette.

George looked at them quizzically and got the stranded feeling that comes from being left out of a joke or a story that ought to be common knowledge.

"News travels fast, Claudie, it's gonna ..."

"I said shut it!"

"Has she told you George, has she?"

"Told me what?"

"Looks like our friend has been a naughty girl."

Claudette stood and grabbed the wine bottle by its neck. Her eyes shone with undiluted fury and a blue vein on her temple pulsated.

"Put it down, my dear," said Pinchbeck.

Welsby froze as if he knew there had been a change in the thin man's mood. Claudette did as she was told. Welsby weighed his options. He span for the door but he was not quick enough and Pinchbeck was there before him. There was a flash of shining metal and Welsby screamed in agony and rolled onto the floor clutching his hand.

"What the bloody hell are you doing you savage? He's killed me George.   He's bloody killed me! I'm gonna bleed to death!"

Death was an unlikely outcome unless he bathed the wound with river water but, even so, Welsby was in some distress and reeled away to the far side of the room, grabbing a fresh white napkin and wrapping it around his injury. George looked at Pinchbeck who was cleaning his weapon on a piece of cloth. Despite the regular parade of alcohol-fuelled altercations at The Star, it was the first time George had ever seen pure hatred in someone's eyes and he feared the new arrival was going to go after Welsby and finish the job. Welsby was rescued by the return of Dench, who had heard the crash of glass against the wall.

"What the devil is happening here?"

"It's him," cried Welsby, sheltering now in the corner, "he's trying to kill me."

The balance of power between Dench and Pinchbeck was clear in a moment and the Corporal looked down at Welsby.

"No doubt you attacked him first. I've a good mind to put you in front of the magistrate."

"But you won't though will ya? Too bleedin' scared o' what I might say. I know too much, old man. You can't touch me."

"If you had any sense you'd keep quiet," said Pinchbeck. "Very soon you'll be worth more to us dead."

Welsby returned to the table and sat down. He rested his hand on the wooden surface and peeled back the blood-soaked napkin.

"Go and pour some water over that," said Dench, "George, go and help him. Use the boiled stuff, not the muck that's been standing there all day."

Welsby returned to the sink and stood by the metal pail while George splashed water over his injured hand. George leaned closer and, pinching thumb and forefinger together, began to remove specs of dirt from the victim's hand. With each tug Welsby winced and cursed under his breath.

Dench prepared a tray with a fresh bottle and three glasses and he eyed Claudette, as if daring her to touch it. Fear replaced her fury now, her eyes sunk back into her head and her shoulders slumped. Welsby had a good look at the wound, Dench also, and they agreed that George had made a good job of its repair. He almost dismissed it casually as a skill gained after years of practice in a lively London tavern before stopping himself at the last second.

Dench had been glancing anxiously at the timepiece on the shelf above the fire since he had returned to investigate the disturbance. When there was a loud knock on the back door it was clear he had been expecting it.

"Look away and find something to do."
George and Welsby stood, turned their backs to the door and busied themselves at the sink. Claudette remained where she was, staring into space. Dench approached the door and opened it slightly, checking that the shadow he could see through the glass in the door was the gentleman he had been expecting. Once he had confirmed this was the case, he opened the door widely, the man entered and Dench closed the door smartly behind him. George contrived to position himself so he could see who had joined them. The visitor wore a dark blue coat with black stockings and his black leather shoes sported polished brass buckles. He had a full black periwig and a wide-brimmed hat that shaded the upper half of his face. The lower half was masked by a woollen scarf that he had pulled up over his mouth and nose. He did not pause, gave no sign that he had noticed there was anybody else in the kitchen, then strode briskly across the kitchen without waiting for Dench to guide him. He was light of foot and barring one creak of the stairs he ascended in silence. Dench fussed around nervously.

"Take those drinks upstairs to the green room, come on man, move yourself."

Mr. Welsby tried and then failed to pick up the tray with his injured hand.

"Not you, you idiot."

He turned to George.

"You've been promoted, boy. Top floor, furthest from the landing, you can't miss it. It has a green door."

George's heartbeat accelerated. Claudette caught his eye and her look betrayed a deep sense of unease. Something was going to happen to her this evening. She knew it but she was powerless to stop it, unable to run, utterly resigned to her fate. Dench moved to the door and held it open. George rolled down his sleeves in an effort to smarten himself up.

"Leave 'em, just go as you are. Don't loiter."

"Go with him," said Pinchbeck. "We don't want him making a run for it."

Briskly, George swept up the tray, grabbed a clean white napkin and threw the cloth over his arm. As he passed Dench, the Corporal's stone face cracked slightly to reveal a smirk, a look that in Covent Garden would have spoken of gangs and tricks and traps for the unwary but here in the dignified surroundings of a gentleman's club was interpreted as mere pleasure at a servant's discomfort. Dench followed him up the stairs. At the ground floor the bare wood gave way to carpet, a thick dark red pile worn down by the foot traffic from the front door to the ground floor rooms. The doors were propped open, revealing in each chamber an arrangement of armchairs, settees and tables. A small number of gentlemen of various ages and sizes lounged and conversed amid light clouds of tobacco smoke, warmed by open log fires.

He turned onto the main staircase, the red carpet continued up to the first of the three floors above him. He walked more slowly now. The columns of the balustrade were painted white, quite recently he judged, looking at the way the paint shone and reflected the candlelight that bore down from the wall at regular intervals. The handrail was stained the colour of oak, a light brown that matched the occasional furniture in the hallway and on the first floor landing. The staircase bent ninety degrees ahead of him and there were a further six steps until he reached the first floor. Ahead of him, looking directly down the stairs was a portrait, one of many that adorned the walls. George was too preoccupied to pause and read the nameplate but, had he done so, he would have seen that the picture was a fine representation of Viscount Bolingbroke and the artist had done an excellent job of retaining St John's youthful good looks.

Finally, George reached the top landing and stopped to get his bearings. To his right was the front of the house and, by the window that overlooked the Square, a further set of stairs. His breathing had become shallow and rapid. He settled himself, took a deep breath and exhaled slowly then stepped forward into the corridor. The dull murmur of whispered conversation from the downstairs salon had receded into silence and his pulse throbbed in his ears. The final door on the left was unique in that its upper section had been replaced by a padded green panel in the centre of which was a brass plate bearing the word "Private". He stood outside the door unsure of where to knock. No sound came from within. He tapped lightly on the frame and waited.

"Come!"

He took a deep breath and reached down to the handle, pushing the brass lever and releasing the door. He took one step inside and, with a deft movement, turned and sealed the entrance. He turned again to face the room, which was too large for the three men that occupied the space. There were cabinets and upright dining chairs around the perimeter and a group of padded armchairs pushed together to form a group around the fire. In the seat facing him was the stranger, who had now removed his hat and scarf. He was slightly built but handsome, about thirty years old and the clean lines of his face and the quality of his wig suggested he might be a member of the aristocracy. He stared back at George and considered the youth who stood before him. A second man sat in the chair facing the fire. He leaned forward and turned towards George. It was Scarface and the light did nothing to improve his features. The pink flesh of his wound dominated the dark shadow of his complexion like a bolt of lightning. On the table there was a jug of ale, warming in front of the fire and Scarface held a mug of the liquid in his hand. He moved the jug along the table to create more space.

"Put that down over here." He spoke like he looked.

George stepped forward and slipped between the chairs, bending to place the tray on the table. As George brought himself back to an upright position, he felt the boot of the third man tap his ankle gently and he pulled away instinctively, stiffened and froze. Lancaster smiled wickedly, like he was about to enjoy some sport.

"What's your name, son?"

George's throat suddenly dried and he could not speak.

"Cat got your tongue? You were asked a question, boy. It deserves an answer. Who are you and what are you doing here?"

"I - I am working here, that's all, sir."

To his relief, Dench's arrival halted the conversation. He came in not through the green door but through some sort of secret arrangement in the wooden panelling. He checked the room then reached behind him for Claudette and thrust her into the room. Scarface ignored the new arrivals and stared malevolently at George.

"Tell us where you used to work before you came here, boy."

George said nothing.

"Corporal Dench, you tell us. Seems the boy has forgotten 'ow to use 'is voice."

Dench smirked.

"I believe, gentlemen, that Master George was previously in the employ of Lord Edward Audley."

The explanation was greeted with laughter from the two ruffians and with an expression of pensive annoyance from the gentleman ahead of him, who now spoke for the first time.

"How is it, young man, that you claim to have been in the employ of the Audley household when I, your supposed employer, sit before you having never set eyes upon you at any time in my entire life?"

"I-I can explain…"

"I am sure you can but I regret we do not have time for your stories. They will serve only to annoy me. My understanding is that you approached the house recently looking for me. Suddenly you pitch up here. There is a pattern emerging, would you agree?"

Dench had wheeled around the room holding firmly to his prisoner and now stood between George and the door. There was no clear escape route either to the green door or to the wooden panel that sat ajar just beyond Audley, which left only the two windows that overlooked the yard. They were shielded by blue velvet curtains that were closed and hung from ceiling to floor. In any case, George recalled that the windows were heavy, sash affairs and that even if he could get to them they would not be easy to open. He resolved to run for the door as soon as he got the opportunity.

Audley continued.

"Tell me of Captain Maven. Who is he and why does he seek me?"

"He - he has been hired t-to look after ..."

"Go on."

"To look after Lady Cooper, sir."

"As a bodyguard?"

"You might say so sir."

"Hired by whom?"

"By her sir."

"Not by another gentleman?"

"No, sir."

Audley reached forward and filled a glass with some of the wine George had brought up. His hand was very pale and it was delicate and feminine. It had about it a slight tremor which caused the neck of the bottle to tremble against the wine glass. He eased back in his chair and sipped the wine.

"Indeed. Now this is what I find so surprising. You see, in my world, a bodyguard defends his charge from attack, stays with her when she goes out, protects the house after dark, that sort of thing. So why is it that we find Captain Maven searching for me in the Borough, visiting my house and following my manservant to Smithfield. That is not what I would describe as being a bodyguard. Do you see my point, George?"

"Y-yes, sir"

"Where is Maven now?"

"He is in Hatton Garden, sir."

"Recovering from his exertions no doubt. How are his wounds?"

Scarface leaned forward to address George and smiled, revealing blackened and misshapen stumps where his teeth should have been.

"Perhaps I should have hit 'im a bit harder."

"Lieutenant Barclay knows Maven from the war," said Audley, "as does Captain Lancaster. It does not suit us to have someone such as Maven becoming involved in our affairs.

Protecting the harlot is one thing, George, but I fear you are not sharing the full story of Maven's involvement with us. I should like you to think for a while. I believe you know Claudette."

Barclay stood and pushed back his armchair, creating a space in front of the fire on the patterned rug. Dench pushed the girl forward. She had shrunk from the brazen, lively young woman of the previous night into a petrified young animal. Audley stood, walked towards her and continued his commentary.

"Claudette, as you can probably guess, is a stage name, there being nothing French about this particular tart. She is, though, a fine actress and very willing and able to follow direction. She has played many parts for me, every time without shame or complaint. Her talents are legendary, aren't they my dear?"

Audley walked around the girl, stroking her face and her neck.

"But the trouble with actresses, George, is that one can never tell when they are playing themselves and when they are playing some other character. Often, they are confused and are themselves unable to tell the difference. This, I fear, is where we find ourselves with the lovely Claudette."

Audley nodded to the Lieutenant and sat down. Barclay withdrew his sword from its scabbard and flourished the weapon with a twist of his wrist. He took a short step forward and rested the sharp point at Claudette's throat. She raised her face and looked directly at him, as if this were the fate she always knew would be hers, tilting her head slightly in a gesture of insolence. Barclay used the sword to tear at her dress and the strands of light blue cotton fell away to reveal the pale white skin of her shoulders. Dench stepped forward and went behind her, grabbed at the dress and tore it open, caught the damaged material before it fell to the ground then threw it on the fire. It smouldered and smoked before catching, and all of them were drawn involuntarily to the yellow flames that flickered as the dress was destroyed. She stood before them in her white shift, her legs bare from the knees down, reddening from the heat of the fire. Her black boots were clumsy and out of place. Audley looked at her with contempt. He was not excited by seeing her dressed as she was. They all knew he had seen her quite naked. He had used her many times.

"My dear, you have taken from the Viscount a personal possession. I know you took it so do not lie and deceive me. Someone of your class looks upon theft as a daily occurrence. Thievery defines you. It is the way of things. You made a choice to steal them. Why would you do that?"

The half-pay officer re-sheathed his weapon and George sighed inwardly with relief. Then Barclay stepped forward and punched the girl hard in the stomach, causing her to collapse to the floor, clutching herself in agony. The tears started, silently at first and then with gentle sobs. Audley turned to George.

"You see, George, some people can be trusted and some cannot. Has she passed this package to you?"

Suddenly George's pulse raced and he felt his stomach turn. There was a taste of bile in his throat.

"N-no sir. I don't know what you are talking about."

"And I sense that you are telling the truth. Your honesty may one day prove to be your undoing but today it has saved you."

He turned to Claudette, now curled in the foetal position before him.

"Did you give the letters to the bawd?"

Claudette did not look up but mumbled to the floor.

"Damn you, you bastard."

"It is a sad state when the harridan is more trustworthy than you, my dear." He looked at George. "She will tell us the truth soon enough and it will be her choice how long it takes and how much it hurts before she does so. How long do you think she will last, George?"

Audley did not wait for him to answer but got up and walked to the girl and stood over her. With the toe of his shoe he eased her face up to look at his.

"The papers, Claudette. I need them. They have no value to you. You took them from the traitor Bolingbroke and now I want them."

He crouched down and took her chin in his right hand. He whispered.

"We are friends, Claudette, and I do not want to hurt you. But if you give me no choice…"

"I don't know what you're talking about."

"You lie."

"I ain't lying."

"Do not mock me with your insolence. You spent the night with Bolingbroke. That filthy shit-caked whore who panders your charms told you to take the letters. You had enough opportunity, for God's sake."

"I took 'em and I give 'em to Mother, I swear. She has everything I took."

Audley's temper was released now. He stepped closer to her and dragged her by her hair to a seated position.

"Tell me the truth bitch or so help me - "

"If you kill me, you - "

"What? What will you do? You are nothing. In the eyes of the law you do not even exist. This is not a situation in which you hold the upper hand. As Master George would explain if we allowed him to ..."

All eyes in the room turned to George. He had no words to express what he felt.

"P-please don't hurt her, sir. Tell him Claudette. If you know, just tell him."

Audley turned again to the girl and looked into her eyes with what in other circumstances would have passed for a genuine fondness. He stood and walked to the window and turned aside the heavy curtain just sufficiently to see out.

"Help her remember, Lieutenant."

Barclay rose quickly and stood above her. He bent forward and tore off the shift, tossing it aside so that it landed just in front of George. She lay naked, curled up tight again to shield herself. Her back and shoulders were the purest white, utterly unblemished and George could make out the ridges of her spine. Barclay grabbed her feet and removed her boots. Audley had his back to her, feigning a dislike of violence. Barclay pulled her feet and turned her round, stretching her legs so they hovered near the fire.

"No!" It was George, shocked at what he was witnessing.
Audley, to the curtain, said, "You see, my dear, George understands. He knows that you are likely to be hurt. Do please stop this nonsense and tell me."

Claudette trembled and looked like she was now incapable of reasoned thought. Barclay pulled her closer to the fire. He held her foot over the fierce heat of the glowing coals. Barclay's demeanour suggested he was happier she had not divulged her secrets. George turned away and did not see exactly what Barclay did next.

She screamed.

It was a scream that released a lifetime of terror. It was a scream of all-consuming fear. Barclay pulled her away from the fire and let her go. She returned to the foetal position and clutched her foot, which was scorched red and throbbed with agony. She sobbed uncontrollably, gasping for air but struggling to find a way for it to reach her lungs. George went forward and crouched down next to her. They let him.

"For God's sake, girl, tell them what you know."

She ignored him and the sobbing continued. Audley turned back into the room as George stood and stepped away again.

"Tell me who has the letters. Who have you given them to?"

Claudette sobbed noisily. Audley nodded to Barclay. Roughly, Barclay gripped her swelling left foot and jerked her toward the fire a second time. He allowed his free hand to stroke the inside of her thigh. This time he did not wait but plunged her foot directly towards the heat.

"All right!"

Barclay lifted her foot away.

"All right. Just stop. Please just leave me alone and I'll tell you."

Audley nodded and, with a degree of reluctance, Barclay released his grip. She coiled up again. She spoke in a whisper, barely audible and the peer bent down, almost tenderly, to hear her.

"He has 'em back, the gentleman."

"Bolingbroke?"

"He caught me trying to take 'em. I told him I was after money and he give me some papers and a guinea. But he took back these other papers, whatever they are and he put 'em in his pocket. Told me to forget I'd ever seen 'em. Satisfied?"

Incredibly, Audley stroked her now, gently on her shoulder and as she sobbed she reached out for him. He held her hand in his.

"Dench, bring her some clean clothes," he said gently.

George wondered where they might locate women's clothing in this entirely masculine environment but Dench showed no hesitation. He left through the green door and it crossed George's mind that the opportunity to escape was upon him. He was not quick enough. Lancaster, who had remained silent throughout, wearing the inane grin of one who found the proceedings thoroughly entertaining, stood and took George by the arm.

"Come, George, sit. It is too soon to think about leaving us." He sat within a few feet of Claudette. Audley left her alone and collected his hat, coat and scarf. He paused by the secret door and spoke to George.

"This Captain Maven. Is he a man of honour?"

"Y-yes, I would say he is, sir."

"So, when he discovers you have over-reached yourself and been taken as our guest he will come and find you?"

George nodded. He hoped he was right. Audley leaned over him and spoke quietly.

"Do as you are told and you will come to no harm. You will be taken from here and we will leave word with your father that you are safe. If you do anything to put yourself in danger it will be your fault, not mine. On Saturday the German oaf is due to be crowned. Sometime between now and then the course of history will be changed and I do not want Shrewsbury's hired hand getting in my way. It will be far better for all of us if he is out in the countryside searching for you."

Lancaster laughed and said, "Maven was always more concerned for the peasants than he was for the officers. He'll come searching all right."

George and Claudette were shackled to the inside of a covered wagon, a solid affair that smelled like it had recently been in use by an undertaker and had been washed down superficially before being sold on. They were bound by hands and feet with canvas strips, khaki in colour. Each was gagged with the same material and it tasted earthy and damp. Claudette's tears had stopped soon after Dench returned with clothing for her to wear. It was, by any measure, a better set of clothes than the attire she had worn earlier in the evening. Although she had been mightily put out while Lancaster and Barclay had watched her dress, her discomfort was short-lived and George had even spied her sneaking a look at her own reflection as they left the salon and made their way down the back stairs to the kitchen.

It had taken George very little time to run through his limited list of options. He was faced with three armed men, at least two of whom seemed not only capable of murder but who also listed torture among their chosen pursuits. He had earlier, for the first time, since he was a small child felt the warm rush of blood to his face and the burning in his throat as the tears welled within him. He knew that only ridicule would follow if they saw him crying and he had forced himself to maintain his dignity. They had been made to wait in the wagon for several hours and the October night was cold and windy. Their captors had given no thought to blankets so the young couple huddled together for warmth and George felt the strength of her presence, a maternal powerful strength that somehow reassured him.

"Was that the truth you told him?"

"No, but he wanted to hear something and that was the best I could do."

"How did you know he would believe you?"

"I'm not sure he does. Don't forget, I've seen him at his most ..." she paused and searched for the word, "vulnerable. He wasn't ever gonna kill me. Not tonight at any rate."

"So who has these letters?"

"I took what he had. Obviously that wasn't what they were after."

The wooden sides of the van did not quite meet the roof and, whilst this made their night a cold one, it enabled them to see when the dawn was breaking. It was at this time that they heard two horses being walked across the yard and hitched to the wagon. Then the vehicle rocked on its dilapidated springs as first one man, then another climbed aboard the box and urged the horses forward.

16

Events failed to go to plan the night before and they spiralled out of control the following morning. Trescothick presented himself at Hatton Garden in a state of high alarm with the news that George was missing. Unconcerned that his son had not found his way home by one o'clock when he put the lamps out, Trescothick had locked up and turned in. Then, as dawn broke, he was roused from his sleep by a fearful racket at the main door of the tavern. He descended the stairs with the intention of rebuking his son, his ire increasing with each step that he took. By the time he had fought his way through the dimness, the banging on the door had ceased and he had no need to unbolt it. On the floor, slipped through the draughty gap, was a letter, a thick, cream thing, unsealed. He unfolded the single piece of notepaper and read the few words that had been written on it.

Now it was Maven's turn to be woken and Trescothick rapped noisily on the front door. Sarah was first to the scene of the disturbance she had looked through the spy hole to see who was making such a din.

"Keep your noise down, tapster," she shouted, "and behave yourself else you should wake up the whole street with your din."
She had barely begun to open the door when he burst in.

"Get 'im up! Go and wake 'im. Bleddy idiot. I told him this would 'appen."

"What the devil has got into you, sir? Don't you know what time it is?"

"'Course I knows what bleddy time it is, woman. Go and fetch the Captain. I need him 'ere now."

"He's asleep, sir. He's probably still unwell after yesterday."

"I don't care, woman, go and fetch –"

He looked up to see Maven descending the stairs, tucking his shirt into his breeches. Trescothick, suddenly lost for words, waved a piece of paper at him and Maven snatched it away irritably.

The boy is being cared for in the country. Do not try to find him.
Tell Maven to remain in Hatton Garden with the woman until
Sunday, when the boy shall be returned to you unharmed.

The note was unsigned but had been written by someone who had been educated well for the handwriting flowed beautifully and there were none of the spelling mistakes that were common even among ladies and gentlemen of the court. They sat at the kitchen table. Peck stationed himself sheepishly at the far end, as far from Sarah and her broom as he could get. Sarah fed them all with bread and tea and then went to fetch her mistress, as instructed.

"This is your bleddy fault, Maven. If you hadn't got him involved ..."

Maven yawned and read the note again.

"He's got no experience, aside from a few punch ups. How's he gonna get himself out of this?"

"I seem to recall asking him to stay here last night. If he had done as he was told ..."

"He was trying to help you, playing the hero 'cos he thought you'd be impressed. You know how he looks up to you. He was trying to get information on his bleddy lordship. If you ask me this is nothing to do with us. Bleddy aristocracy should sort their own problems – "

They were joined by Lady Kathrine, who ignored the tirade with good grace. She sat down at the table while the three men greeted her arrival by standing and executing small bows. Maven showed her the note.

"Mr. Trescothick, this is all my doing and I am so very sorry. I should have been firmer in telling George to stay here. Captain, what do you advise? The letter suggests that if we sit and wait then George will be returned to us. Surely that is the best course?"

"If that were the case then we would not have been given a clue as to his whereabouts. In fact, we would not have been given a note at all. No, the writer intends for us to take action."

"So, you will go and find him?"

"Possibly."

"What the bleddy hell you gonna do then? Just leave 'im there?"

"It's a trap, Tresco, and a pretty obvious one at that. While we gallop off to look for George they will expect us to leave Lady Kathrine unguarded or," he looked across at Peck, "in the protection of someone else. George could be anywhere within a day's ride of London. Let's just take things one step at a time. We shall go to the Blackbird Club and see if we can establish what has happened. Mr. Peck, can you be trusted to mind the tavern?"

Peck was suddenly an interested party.

"Can he 'ell as like! Bleddy place can stay shut. Buggers can sup some place else for a few days."

By the time Maven and Trescothick arrived in St James's Square, the wagon was in open country and the spires of London were some way behind it, lost in the grey haze of drizzle that covered the capital. Out here the air was fresher, still cold but the perpetual staleness of humanity, of poverty, industry and close confinement that hung over the London streets had gone. George was awake. He stared at Claudette, amazed she could sleep as the vehicle swayed left and right on its springs and pitched wildly each time it struck a pothole in the uneven road.

Maven and Trescothick left Peck with the carriage in the Square and went to the corner where the coaching entrance met King Street. There was a delivery in progress. A cream coloured open wagon was parked in the courtyard of the Club and the horse, a tall, black, elderly beast, stared at them malevolently. The animal made neither sound nor movement as they walked past on either side. The vehicle carried a generous supply of fruit and vegetables stacked in boxes, each one with a paper docket to indicate its destination. The greengrocer had dropped the rear flap and had perched himself on the edge, where he sat idling away the time by smoking a clay pipe. Trescothick followed Maven to the door of the club, which was shut up tight. The greengrocer called to their backs.

"No one around!"

It was a farmer's accent.

"How come? Shouldn't they be serving breakfast or something?" asked Trescothick.

"Aye, should and all. Don't seem to be no one there, though."

Trescothick looked at Maven. No words needed to be exchanged. Instead, Trescothick ambled over to the greengrocer to continue the conversation at a more discreet volume. Shielded behind the sergeant's broad shoulders Maven set about the lock on the door with a sturdy length of iron that he had concealed beneath his jacket. The lock was a strong and heavy, stronger, it seemed, than the door that it was designed to protect. Maven applied the jemmy and levered it into his body. The wood splintered as he rocked the iron tool back and forth and then the door swung freely. The greengrocer looked on in alarm.

"Gambling debt," said Maven.

The kitchen was much the same as it had been when George had been called upon to make his delivery upstairs. Welsby had absconded as soon as it was safe to do so and the spilled blood stained the flags. Trescothick remained in the kitchen and kept an eye on the door. Maven made his way through the narrow doorway that led to the foot of the stairs. He walked in George's footsteps, past the storage rooms then up the wooden stairs to the red carpet with the deep pile. His stride was long and he moved purposefully, checking all the while for the presence of other people. The place was empty. He opened a door and found himself in the dining room, large and with a high white ceiling stained yellow by tobacco. Candle wax had settled in mounds under the lamps and there were dirty plates, uncleared from the previous evening. Glasses were uncollected and ashtrays unemptied. A stale smell of last night's alcohol lingered. He went upstairs and tried each room in turn. Each was much the same as the other: three of them had armchairs, tables and a fireplace. The rest were bedrooms. None of them appeared to have been used the previous night. Finally, he reached the top floor and walked down the corridor to the room with the green door and the sign that said "Private". The door was locked. He stepped back as far as he could in the narrow space then kicked at the wood just above the handle. Just as the kitchen door had yielded easily so did this one, the material splintered and the lock fell to the floor as the door swung back wildly. The room differed from the others only in the respect that it had been occupied and someone had taken the trouble to lock it after departing. He paused and looked around. The chairs had been rearranged, the table had been left at an awkward angle and a rug that pretended to be Persian had been rucked up and left in an untidy state. A dark green wine bottle lay on its side by one of the chairs. By the fire were pieces of white material. Other, similar pieces had been burned, tossed onto the fire then abandoned to their fate. In amongst the remains of white cotton were pieces of blue cloth, charred around the edges.

There was nobody here. The Blackbird Club seemed to be the only club in London without any members. He returned to the basement to find Trescothick sitting at the table facing the outer door eating an apple noisily. The delivery man had decided he had better things to do and had departed, leaving three boxes of greenery by the step. Trescothick had a large blue book open on the table before him. It looked to Maven like a ledger. There was a list of names down the left hand side and, at various intervals, sums of money had been inserted in columns across the page.

"These are the members. Some interesting names, 'ere. Lord this and Viscount that."

"Audley?"

"Aye. Paid up his fees an' all. At least that's what it says 'ere."

Maven tookhold of the jemmy and went back out to the small space at the foot of the stairs. There were two doors, painted white. Each had a black iron drawbolt with a complicated and heavy locking mechanism. He studied the door on the left. This was not a room that could be entered accidentally nor was it ever likely to be kicked open. He took the tool and inserted it by the door jam. The wood began to splinter but the metal lock held firm. He tried again, forcing the iron slightly further in. He levered with all his strength, his arms and shoulders at full stretch. His teeth clenched tight and the tendons in his neck stood proud. There was no further movement to the door.

"You's wasting your time with that, boy!"

Maven turned to see Trescothick standing in the doorway smiling. The Sergeant waited a few seconds so he could maximize Maven's annoyance then held up a bunch of keys, the same keys that had been used by Corporal Dench the night before. A breathless Maven beckoned Trescothick to him with a nod of his head. The Sergeant was sorting through the bunch for a suitable key. He chose well and the black iron slipped into the lock and turned easily in his chubby hand. Trescothick pushed the door and turned back to the kitchen to retrieve a light. Maven looked inside but could see nothing but darkness beyond the first few feet.

Trescothick returned with a lamp, handed it to Maven then returned to his sentry duty in the kitchen. The room was non-descript, a simple storage area about twelve feet square, a blank whitewashed wall at the far end and whatever was stored either side of the room secured by dusty hessian sacking. The only entrance was from the inside of the house. There was no delivery hatch to the yard, not even a grating for air. Not the sort of place one would want to be kept prisoner, he thought, and yet he was breathing easily enough. It was damp and the straw underfoot felt wet through his boots. He peeled away some of the sacking at the far end of the room. Maven could not believe his eyes.
"Tresco!"

Maven stepped forward, the better to look at the cache that was now revealed. One side of the room was lined with flintlock rifles, each one wrapped in sackcloth, the better to protect it from the dampness. Maven tried to count and lost interest at twenty, for there must have been three times as many. Trescothick joined him and on the other side of the room lifted into view some heavy cases. He popped the clasp on the first of these and lifted the lid. The heavy wood knocked against the wall with a satisfying thud. The box contained a pair of pistols, a make unfamiliar to Maven but possibly French. The delicate metalwork around the priming mechanism confirmed his suspicion.

They stood in silence, this pair who had between them seen and heard a thousand times as many weapons in action. Maven was unsure what he felt. He was not impressed, that was for sure, for this collection of arms was sufficient to see its owner sent to Newgate for a long duration while the authorities decided what to do with him. Had George stumbled across the cache?

"Bleddy French. Bleddy papists. There is goin' to be an invasion one of these fine days and when it happens I should wager this lot'd be a part of it."

"I expect there's more in the room next door. And where, I wonder, are the ammunition and the powder? They've surely not been sleeping on top of a bomb?"

"They ain't that stupid. The gear must be split up. It'll be nearby, though. You'd want to be able to bring it all together quick. Tell you what, be 'andy for our old lot, wouldn't it? Those of 'em still in London. What do you say? A hundred blokes, all fightin' men, ready to defend the city, armed and with plenty of metal to cut down the traitors. How about we shift it?"

Maven looked at the Sergeant with disdain.

"What's this all about Tresco?"

"You read the papers, Captain. There's gossip about. They say the new King don't even speak English. Hates us and hates our land. If the papists want the Pretender instead then this'd be a fine time to do it, wouldn't you say?"

"You spend too much time listening to drunken old fools who have nothing better to talk about."

"These people look serious enough to me. And what's more, my boy has got himself mixed up in it. We 'as to find him Maven."

They took the ledger and returned to The Star. Most of the names were unfamiliar but, occasionally, Maven recognised one from the newspaper. The only thing they had in common was their sympathy for the Pretender. The club's secretary, Colonel Summersby, had allocated himself the prime place in the ledger, membership number one and, like a child might adorn a new book gifted to it at Christmas, had also written his name and address on the first page. Alongside each member's entry there was a shortened address. Audley's was not given as Albermarle Street but, instead described a country residence in the same area as Summersby. Matthew Webb's address was in the same location. They agreed that it seemed a sensible place to continue their search. Maven continued to pore over the book.

"What you searching for, Captain. You been through that five times or more."

"Hardly Tresco."

Then he found it.

"Here we are. I was searching for the wrong name."

"How so?"

"I was looking for Viscount Bolingbroke but he is here under his given name."

"Which is?"

"Henry St John. Perhaps he was trying to be discreet."

"But you saw his picture on the wall."

"Indeed. Discretion didn't get the better of his pride, it seems."

It had been more than five years since they had gone into battle together. The Captain-General had sent them on a reconnaissance jaunt through a Flanders forest with the more reliable elements of the light infantry. Their instruction was to get as close as they could to the enemy, note its strength and location then return to Marlborough with the sort of information he had come to rely on from his best scouting party. But Trescothick had struggled and, though his mind was as lively as ever, his body had failed him. They had been discovered, had come under fire and lost two men. It had been the final time for the old Cornish soldier who insisted on taking the blame for slowing them all down. Now Maven felt the trepidation in the air as they prepared for a journey into a homeland they did not know. Trescothick could not join him and they both knew it.

The older man made it easier than Maven expected. The memory of the forest near Malplaquet had remained with him and the veteran made his decision without referring to the Captain. Trescothick disappeared upstairs for several minutes then returned bearing a canvas kit bag, filled with clean clothes and assorted provisions. From a stash that must be held somewhere in the bowels of the tavern, Trescothick had procured two pistols, a box of ammunition and a savage, serrated hunting knife. He moved silently, there being no need for words. Maven knew how much this hurt him and stayed quiet in case he upset the man he respected more than any other.

"I want 'im back unharmed. Whatever else happens, he's all I got. You know that?" Trescothick spoke to a place beyond Maven for he could not meet his eyes. Then he turned his back and began to tidy his tavern, searching out items to wash or wipe clean like a hunting dog might search for rabbit holes in a green field. Then he was gone, out into the living area to be alone with his thoughts, perhaps to pray, as Maven had seen the old man pray before battle, for the safety of his men; mumbled prayers, infested with obscenities, but the prayers of one who cared.

The two gentlemen shared a bottle of claret, though Bothmer was disinclined to quaff it with quite the same enthusiasm as his visitor. He had made a commitment to the Elector that these papers would be found and destroyed and Audley had, thus far, provided nothing but disappointment. Bothmer twisted the glass in his hands. The visitor had been here an hour and they had shared small talk and fine wine. Bothmer was bored and frustrated.

"There is nothing to be done except approach the traitor directly, no?" asked Bothmer.

"You plan to ask Bolingbroke for the letters?"

"Why not? If I make it clear that his life depends upon them being handed over then surely that will remove any choice he has in the matter."

"Those papers are the only items protecting his liberty. If he hands them over you shall escort him to the Tower. At least that is what he believes."

Bothmer knew that Audley was right.

"Then I must reassure him."

"He despises you, sir. It makes a weak foundation for trust."

They sat in silence. Bothmer left his wine untouched while Audley drained and then replenished his glass. Bothmer shifted uncomfortably, anxious that Audley should leave soon. He had not yet learned the subtlety the English had of easing an unwanted guest from the house without causing offence. He stood.

"I have decided! I shall visit upon Bolingbroke and we shall compromise."

Audley took the hint and helped himself to a generous farewell swig from his glass. He stood and made himself comfortable by stretching his clothes back into shape.

"Good luck, Herr Bothmer. You shall need it."

"Your job is not done, Mr Audley, so do not believe it so. Remember, the letters were only part of our arrangement."

Audley stepped forward, as if to remonstrate with his host.

"You can take him whenever you wish to do so. I cannot see what use you have for me, sir."

Audley's reaction was more forthright than he had intended and it caused the soldier in the corner of the room to stir into life. Bothmer defused the situation by taking Audley's hand, as if to shake it. He clasped it firmly between both his own hands.

"Do you think me a savage, Mr. Audley? Evidence is what is required for justice and evidence is what we shall have. Now, one step at a time, yes? You have failed in the first part of your assignment and I am giving you an opportunity to atone for your errors. After all is done it may you who spends his final days in the Tower, no? You may choose, sir: it is you or Bolingbroke. One of you must hang. "

17

Maven swung his kitbag over his shoulder and set out for Hatton Garden. Long Acre was busy and he pushed through the crowd. The light rain soaked his face and occasionally stung his bare skin when it was caught by the cold wind. He wondered where all these people came from, what they were doing. London had become a thronging mass of humanity in the last few years and all was chaos. London now was noise, crowds, impatience and anger. He hated crowds. He pushed on and got to the Oxford Road where the tumult thinned. To his left, Broad St Giles's appeared benign but the small huddles of scruffy, conspiratorial men indicated its malice. It was not a place to linger. Behind him he heard two men conversing in strong, rough Irish accents, bemoaning their lack of work. He turned right, towards Holborn and was pleased when they took the opposite direction. When the street opened out he had space to pick up some speed and he stepped forward with enthusiasm. He wanted to see her, needed to see her. For the first time in more than a decade his need to be in the presence of a woman represented an urge more powerful than he could control. He wondered what she would be wearing this morning, whether her hair would be covered or not. Then he forced himself to focus on the task ahead and he made his plans.

It was easier here to see who it was that followed him. When he left the tavern he had picked up on a small man, too clean for Covent Garden. They were good, he thought, whoever they were, for by the time he had reached St Giles the small man had been replaced by a young woman dressed in the drab browns and dark greens that made for perfect street camouflage but she too was out of place. Poverty has a look that cannot be adopted at short notice and the damage done to the human spirit by living day to day on scraps and handouts created a look in the eye, an expression that was unmistakable. He thought it strange that they continued the pursuit when it was quite obvious where he was going. They could have broken off and picked him up again at Hatton Garden.

He turned left. Parked outside her house was a black coach similar to the vehicles he had seen in St James's. It faced away from him and he could see the outline of its driver's head and shoulders. He quickened his pace again and when he was level with the house he crossed and approached the carriage.

"Excuse me. Who does this coach belong to?"

The driver was startled from his daydream and proved unwilling to engage. Maven drew himself up and adopted the tone he reserved for surly and uncooperative enlisted men.

"I asked you a question, man. Tell me who is the owner of this coach."

But the man was not to be forced into compliance and he met the question with silence and a contemptible look. He rolled a ball of spittle around his mouth and then launched it, sending it into the ground just short of Maven's boot. Maven tried again.

"What business do you have here?"

The man looked down at him.

"My master shall tell ye if he's a mind to. Ain't my pleasure to do so, sir."

Maven accepted defeat and stepped around the pair of horses to knock on the front door. Sarah let him in. He slipped off his heavy coat and threw it with the kitbag into the corner by the front door. She showed him into the drawing room immediately.

"Come along, sir, m'lady said she wishes you to join them if you was to come back this morning."

"Who does she have with her Sarah?"

"She shall tell you herself sir, I'm sure, if she's inclined."

He smiled to himself. The discretion of the servant class would forever protect its masters. He entered and Sarah closed the door behind him. The visitor stood to greet him. It was Bolingbroke. Somehow in the small room he was taller and more handsome and he seemed younger at close quarters than he had across the room in Chelsea. He bowed and Maven returned the gesture.

"Kathrine has been telling me all about you. I should like to thank you for the assistance you are providing."

"I am not sure my assistance has yet solved the problem, though, my lord."

Kathrine spoke for the first time.

"Come, let us not concern ourselves with these formalities. Do please sit, both of you. We have wine. Ale if you prefer?"

He felt the barb.

"Wine is perfectly acceptable, ma'am." replied Maven.

Bolingbroke stared at him briefly.

"You are a soldier, I understand?"

"I am."

"An officer. You served with some honour."

"So they say."

"What keeps you busy now?"

"I drift."

"You drift? What sort of answer is that? You have no profession?"

"I am a soldier, sir. That is my profession."

"Ah, yes and no doubt you hold me in contempt for daring to arrange the peace. Well you need not expect me to apologise for I do not intend to give you that pleasure. Is it not the fate of soldiers to die in battle? Some might have it that by ending the hostilities I have saved your life. Doubtless, you shall not deign to thank me."

"There were too many that lost their lives on both sides. Peace shall always be the better choice, sir, and I bear you no malice," replied Maven though his response carried more hostility than he had intended.

There was a flicker across Kathrine's eyes, as if a thought had occurred to her. Her guests looked to her but all she said was, "Come now, gentlemen. Whilst I cannot expect you to be firm friends there is no place for aggression in this room."

"My dear, I have endured resentment from every rank of the army from the Captain-General downwards. I shall allow Maven his opinion with good grace." He turned to Maven, "But Captain, you must understand that the war was draining our economy. Trade is better for the country than continual battle. God wants us to persevere, to invest and to reap the rewards of peaceful endeavour. Are you familiar with the parable of the talents?"

Maven was not. He had not picked up a bible since Ruth's funeral.

"I regret, sir, that I may have given the impression that I bear you some personal resentment. I do not."

"Thank you Maven, then we shall cease this war talk and move onto something much more important. You are familiar, I believe, with the threat that hangs over Lady Kathrine?"

"Audley? Yes, I understand the danger."

"I gather the threat has widened. He has taken an associate of yours?"

"It would seem so."

"If there is anything I can do to assist I should consider it an honour if you would ask."

"You could tell me sir, about the Blackbird Club. I could not help but notice your portrait adorns its wall."

Bolingbroke looked at him for a moment.

"It is a gentlemen's club, similar to the East India. We gather to smoke and to wager. Not unlike the mess hall, I would suppose."

"The members are of a certain political persuasion?"

"Tories to a man, Maven."

"And is that all they are?"

"I am not sure I am pleased with your tone."

"No sir, I am sure you are not."

Bolingbroke placed his glass on the table and stood. He walked to the window and looked out.

"I should like very much to take Lady Kathrine to Battersea for her safety but I regret that decorum prevents me from doing so. It would damage her reputation terribly."

Maven looked at Kathrine. He thought he saw an apology in her eyes.

"I already have somewhere in mind," he said.

"Good. If you tell me where, I shall have my people stand guard."

"Would these be the same people that have followed me from Covent Garden this morning?"

The hesitation gave him away.

"I don't know what you are talking about. I am not in the habit of indulging in matters of subterfuge, Captain."

"Thank you for your offer, my lord, but we shall be fine."

The two men stared at each other for a moment and Bolingbroke surrendered, hurt by the insolence but unwilling to take action to deal with it. He excused himself and Kathrine called for Sarah to see him out. They stood at the window and watched the carriage turn in the street and head back towards Holborn. Maven returned to his chair and sat down only to leap up again when he realised that Kathrine had remained standing.

"Tell me about him."

"You already know of him, Maven. He was a good friend to Hugh. We dined at Golden Square several times and he offered his support when Hugh died."

Maven leaned forward and caught her by the wrist then dragged her to towards him.

"Ow, you're hurting me. Stop it."

"If I am to help you I need to know the truth. Your attitude in his presence suggests a good deal more familiarity than a friendship with your husband. What is he to you?"

"Let go."

"Not until you tell me the truth. Do he and Audley fight over you? Is that it?"

"He is married, sir. How dare you suggest such a thing?"

He released her wrist and she caressed it with her left hand. It was red and he had been rougher than he had intended. She flung herself down in the chair opposite. Here it comes, he thought. Her look was that of a temptress, playing with him. Eventually, she said, "I should like to dispense with your services, Captain. Viscount Bolingbroke shall provide for me, I am sure. He has people."

"People like Audley, you mean. Their club is not what it appears and I should like to know what secrets they share. So, I am sure, would the Captain-General."

"Marlborough? What on earth has he to do with it?"

"He loves this country ma'am. He will serve the new King as well as he served the late Queen. He hates traitors and more than anything else in the world he despises your friend Bolingbroke. If you are involved in his plotting then I fear you will hang. You will destroy your husband's reputation. I should like you to think on it and when I return we shall deal with the question of your safety."

"You were leaving anyway?"

"George Trescothick is missing and it is my fault. You will be perfectly safe here. The Viscount has people."

Maven cursed Peck for it seemed the pot man had procured the largest horse he could find, a bay stallion named Prospero that stood sixteen hands high. It was a heavy, sullen beast and represented a challenge for all but the most experienced of riders. Prospero picked up Maven's trepidation immediately and was as difficult as an intransigent donkey until they were well beyond Islington. Maven was neither a natural or confident horseman and he did not relish a journey that would take him most of the day. Though the rain had eased it had left the roads wet and muddy. Despite the conditions, he maintained a fierce pace and passed through the villages of Hoxton and Hackney without stopping. By the time he reached Clapton, Prospero was steaming. At the Royal Oak he stopped for a lunch of bread and lamb shank and the horse was relieved to be watered and rubbed down by an obliging ostler, who introduced himself as Makepeace Matthews. The ostler was an under-nourished boy of no more than seventeen and he had a harelip that made his speech close to unintelligible. Maven had to lean close to learn that there were no more inns this side of the marsh, a journey of several miles. He would have damaged the horse had he not stopped when he did.

The Royal Oak was a working man's tavern that had no pretensions to becoming a coaching inn despite being on a route to the capital. The floor appeared to have remained unswept since the Queen's coronation and the low ceilings and dirty windows lent the interior a dark and mysterious air. Maven was the only customer. The landlord was a surly individual and the powder burns on his hands gave away his former occupation. Maven deflected the questioning of the tapster by fobbing him off with a story about going to Essex to look for work. Despite the chilly welcome, the food was good and he was replete by the time he came to leave. Outside in the wide street, Makepeace Matthews held Prospero's reins proudly. He had fed and watered the horse and brushed him diligently. As Maven approached, Matthews beckoned him closer with his hand. The landlord stood in the doorway behind Maven.

"Take no notice of his chatter, sir. He's simple."

The boy was telling him that the river was high now and more rain was due. All the paths other than the main road would be dangerous and impassable. Notwithstanding that the boy seemed to be concerned more for the safety of the horse than for its rider, Maven tossed him a coin and Makepeace Matthews was grateful, snaffling it away into an inside pocket before anyone should see.

The boy was right about the river, which had risen above its banks and soaked the plain. There were various pathways leading off to the north and south, some of them quite well used. There was a single bridge to negotiate and he approached with caution in case it had been damaged by the water. The stone was of a sound construction, though, and rose sufficiently above the river to allow safe clearance. Although the bridge itself was dry the rest of the road had succumbed to the rising water and it was hard going. The wet clay soil sucked the hooves of the horse down and tired the animal soon after their restart. They passed an abandoned wagon, stuck fast in the mud. The huge grey sky loomed overhead and threatened more rain and the smell of the wet marsh rose to assault his nostrils. Apart from an occasional distant bird nothing bar the tall grass stirred in the vast expanse.

The villages on the far side of the marsh were drab and wet and their inhabitants were indoors. The slippery mud on the road surface was almost orange as the clay showed itself at the surface. It was not until he reached Snaresbrook that he saw human activity again, a farm labourer to judge by his dress who was returning home with a bundle of twigs. It made for a pathetic sight and Maven wondered how long it would be before the bundle would be dry enough to burn.

At this higher level, the road had dried but Prospero's hooves were caked in heavy mud. Maven jumped down and walked the horse into the large pond opposite the village then sat on a roughly hewn wooden bench and wiped the hooves down with his hands. At the top of the village he turned left for Woodford and, although the road climbed steadily, they made good progress. He was tired from the journey but he forced his mind to remain alert for he was close to his destination. He hoped they had guessed correctly. The ledger book, which was stowed in his kit bag, had given Summersby's address as Hereford House, Woodford. At first, he had not linked this information with the home of Kathrine's sister until he had seen in the book that Mr. Matthew Webb resided at the old cottage in Woodford Wells. The first six names on the membership list were listed as living in this area. Most importantly, Audley had given his address as Prospect House. It was too much of a coincidence that all three of them should live in the same village.

Coming towards him at regular intervals were parties of travellers, some in coaches and many on foot. They were all in good spirit, on their way to the capital to celebrate the coronation. Without exception each party acknowledged the tall stranger travelling in the opposite direction. One group engaged him in conversation, suggesting jocularly that he might be heading in the wrong direction and, in return, he had warned them to stay on the main road for the marsh road would be impassable for coaches. Otherwise, the travellers were content to exchange a friendly nod or a wave of the hand.

Maven rested the horse at the King William Inn and had the stable boy check Prospero's hooves. The boy washed the horse down while Maven went inside and supped a glass of small beer and rested his aching flanks. He chose the inn because it sat on the main road at a busy junction and seemed to be favoured by travellers and traders who passed through, rather than by locals. He drank in silence, cursing inwardly his poor equestrian ability. The landlord was busy installing a group of three gentlemen into rooms upstairs and they were congratulating each other on getting through the forest without being assaulted by robbers. He gathered that there were other travellers due here before nightfall, with the result that there were no rooms to be had for a stranger heading north. Disappointed, Maven returned to the yard where he found the boy still busy with Prospero.

"He's a beauty, sir."

"Thank you. A little temperamental, perhaps."

"Aye, best ones always are, sir."

Maven gave the boy tuppence when a penny would have been ample.

"Tell me, do you know of a Matthew Webb?"

"Can't say as I do sir."

It was an honest denial.

"What about Colonel Summersby?"

The boy hesitated, though he attempted a recovery.

"No, sir, not him neither."

"Sure?"

"Yes, sir."

Maven looked around the yard. There was no one else within earshot and they were far enough from the windows to not be overheard.

"I'd like to leave the horse here overnight if I may. Will you take care of him for me? Take him out in the morning for a loosening up?"

The boy had not relaxed his grip on Prospero and was grateful to be given the opportunity.

"'Course, sir, I'd love to. You can leave him 'ere. Are you staying?"

"No, there is no room. I shall walk up a little way and take my chances."

"No problem, sir, there are one or two places in the village and there's always plenty of room here for a fine horse like this."

"Now tell me about Summersby."

The boy looked around the yard then took Prospero by his bridle and walked him out to the entrance. Maven strode alongside and was careful to remain silent until they had passed the open window of the inn.

"'s not a name that strangers asks about that often, sir."

"I'm asking now. What do you know of him?"

"He's got the big house up by the common. Thinks he's an important man. Hereford House, you won't miss it."

"He's the landowner?"

"He'd like to be. It's Mr. Child what owns the manor, decent bloke he is. He's building a school. You'll have heard of him I'm sure, they tell me he's in the newspaper."

Maven recognised the name of Childs but he wanted to hear it from the boy.

"His father owns the East India Company."

Child senior was certainly the head of the East India and he would have dearly loved to own it but, in reality, he controlled the company for a long list of private investors. The family was undoubtedly wealthy and owned land in some abundance.

"And Summersby? How does he fit in?"

"He's an officer, obviously. But really, he's a businessman of sorts. I'm not sure he has much to do with Mr. Child other than he pays him rent. They aren't what you'd call friends, not as far as people round here can tell."

There was a coach trundling down the main road from the north and Maven guessed that it bore more travellers for the coronation.

"Looks like you have work to do, you'd best get on. I'll be back in the morning for the horse. Take good care of him. And you're sure about Matthew Webb?"

"Yes, sir. Do you know whereabouts he lives?"

"The old cottage in Woodford Wells."

"Could be anywhere, sir, there's a fair few cottages. You could try Mr. Rogers. It's a way, though, up by the Wells. There's a sign on the main road for his house."

The travellers were upon them, their voices audible over the noise of the coach as it turned into the yard. The boy wheeled round and followed it, leading Prospero towards the stabling block.

Out on the main road Makepeace Matthews ducked silently in and out of the trees, staying far enough back from the road so as not to be seen. He knew the marsh well and had taken the north path, which was wet but passable. The further he went the more nervous the boy became for he was outside of his home territory. He had waited outside the village and curled himself up tightly behind a clump of bracken and settled himself in for the night. Maven's reappearance took him by surprise and, like he had been told, he followed the stranger to see where he might go next.

Maven hauled his kitbag over his shoulder and walked on northwards, taking care to stay by the side of the road where the ground was firmer, and found himself facing a meandering caravan of pedestrians all heading south. Passers by tipped their hats to him and were generally friendly but nobody stopped or entered into conversation for it was late and they were keen to reach the safety of the next inn. He soon passed a second tavern, the White Hart, on his left and saw a small building he took to be the constable's residence, for they were commonly to found alongside or even inside taverns this far out. Opposite was the cage, the home most villages kept for lawbreakers and other miscreants until a passing magistrate could deal them with. Next-door was the church of St Mary's and behind was a grand house signed as Woodford Hall. There was money here, he thought, and the houses looked as though they were owned by

191

gentlemen who had found some recent success in the city but did not wish to move too far from the source of their wealth.

Slightly further on, he came upon a large house set back from the road on the left hand side and untroubled by any near neighbours. It was a large affair in the modern style, freshly painted in the palest yellow with a front door of bright blue. The shining white window frames advertised its recent redecoration. A discreet sign by the door bore the name Hereford House. A milestone suggested it was eight miles to London. Maven thought it seemed further, especially after his struggles through the mud. Anxious not to be seen loitering in front of the house he moved on and walked through an avenue of oak trees and made for the next inn, which he could see about a quarter of a mile ahead.

The Castle & Two Brewers was a solid, square building of timber that had mostly retained its shape, though the flank wall nearest him had blown. He went in and looked around. Mercifully free of London-bound coach parties, the saloon was quiet. Maven supped on a glass of ale and asked after Mr. Rogers. A chubby elderly man with white wiry hair and a farmworker's skin tone overheard Maven's conversation with the landlord and beckoned him over. The man called himself Godfrey. For the price of a refill Maven got his information. He chanced his arm with a supplementary question.

"Would you know of a Mr. Webb?"

"Webb, you say?"

"He may have rented a cottage?"

"Rogers does have tenants in his cottage but he ain't the only one fancies himself as a landlord, mind. If it is him then he's got a cheek charging 'em rent for it if you ask me. Darned place is fallin' down round their ears I shouldn't wonder. What would you be wantin' with them?"

"I must deliver a message to them, from a relative."

"Nice young couple they are. Got a nipper. I sees her about in the village a bit but him, what did you say his name was? Matthew? Don't really see him much. He must go off to London, like so many of 'em round here."

Mr. Rogers lived in a surprisingly modest stone house near to the Wells. The house was at the end of a narrow lane that struck out through the trees to the west of the main road. Maven was glad the boy at the King's Head had told him to look out for the sign for the forest was dense here and the house nestled among thickly planted trees and was invisible from the road. Behind the house were the dense woods that rose to cover Higham Hill.

He stepped back, called out and looked around, hoping to find someone who might help him. Nobody came so he approached the front door and rapped loudly, again without success. Then, approaching the house using the lane that Maven had followed there came a buggy drawn by a pony that was too small for the task in hand. There was only the one occupant, a tall, stocky, ruddy-faced man whose silver whiskers blended with his dusty white peruke. He wore a scarlet tunic that from a distance might have suggested a military uniform. The driving of the buggy had evidently caused him to expend as much effort as it had the pony and the man wheezed as he jumped out.

"How do you do sir? Who might you be?"

Maven judged the man to be twenty years or so older than himself. The gentleman had the palest skin and the whiteness of his skin drew attention to his rodent-like eyes. It seemed that everything about him was either red or white.

"I am fine, sir, thank you . You are Mr Rogers?"

The man nodded and raised a hand to his mouth to stifle a wheezing cough.

Maven offered a deep bow to his host. With considerable effort the gentleman lowered his bulk into a bow from which there was some doubt that he might arise again. Maven was relieved when his host found himself once again in the upright position.

"My name is Maven. Lady Kathrine Cooper asked me to ride up and meet with you. She is Mrs Webb's sister."

"Come, we cannot stand out here all day. Get yourself inside, sir, and we shall discuss it over some tea. Bacon!"

In the absence of any other human being within what seemed like several miles, Maven was unsure whether his host called for a servant or was demonstrating some other eccentricity. Rogers took Maven inside the house, continuing to shout for Bacon all the while until the servant, an elderly stooping gentleman with hair as white as his master's wig, presented himself as if by coincidence, oblivious to all the calling. He was promptly despatched outside to see to the pony and thence to return to supply Maven with some refreshment. These instructions were delivered with sufficient hand signals to enable Rogers to make himself understood, the old servant being completely deaf.

Left alone in the bare and chilly drawing room, Maven dumped his kitbag on the floor beside him and looked around at the shelves lined with a sparse selection of books bound mostly with dark blue or black cloth. The room was host to just one painting, hung on the far wall, of a woman of ample bosom and average beauty and he judged the lady to be the former Mrs Rogers, gone now he decided, as the cold house lacked any evidence of a female presence. Rogers joined him after a minute or so, during which there had been more shouting. He brought with him the tea that he had ordered from the ancient servant. They discussed what Rogers described as the peculiar goings on at the Webb house, the lease for which, it transpired, was up for sale. Rogers was concerned that Maven might be interested in making an offer.

"I find there is no shortage of interested parties, Captain. Life in the city seems to be one long round of trading success. Were I a few years younger you know I believe I would join the young bucks myself and add some livres to my own small and dwindling fortune. You know that hereabouts we have several directors of the Bank of England. And Mr Child himself owns not only the manor of Woodford but also of Wanstead. We are honoured, most certainly."

"As it is," continued the host, suddenly changing direction and leaning towards his guest, "one hears of the most odd things. These people move out here, lavish heaven knows how much money on their properties and invite the most hideous types to socialise with them at their ... gatherings. Mind you, the ladies do tend towards the, how shall we say, attractive side, what!"

"Would I be right in saying you do not grace these parties with your own presence, Mr Rogers."

"Sir, I do not. Perish the very thought and I am mightily relieved that I do not generally receive invitations to do so."

"And, Mr and Mrs Webb, do they feature in this social whirl?"

"You know, I believe they do. Mr Webb enjoys the company of city types. They stick together, do they not?"

"And what of Colonel Summersby, is he an acquaintance?"

Rogers was silent and his small red eyes stared at Maven.

"I shouldn't have thought so. Now you mentioned that you were here on an errand for Mrs Webb's sister? "

As their tea was finished and Rogers seemed to have lost his appetite for conversation, they went, at Maven's suggestion, to visit the cottage. They elected to walk on the basis that it was less than a mile and because Maven could not face the thought of being responsible for Rogers' pony being once again pressed into a service for which it was not suited. They crossed the main road, having waited for yet more London bound travellers to pass by, and ambled down another narrow lane.

The cottage was not as Godfrey had described. Either the Webbs had invested in its repair or the landlord had been shamed into spending money, for the small house was tidy and sound, just the sort of place a young city trader might choose as a discreet country residence before he invested in a larger house. Maven looked around and saw only forest. He heard nothing but birdsong and the wind doing its best to remove the leaves from the trees. The cottage was quite deserted.

Rogers waited outside while Maven entered the property, calling out in case anyone was home. He visited each of the downstairs rooms and then poked around under the stairs. Memories of Smithfield found their way into his mind.

"Rogers!" he called, "whose is this trunk?"

Rogers leaned his pale face through the front door.

"Ah yes, Captain. The trunk belongs to Mrs Webb."

The box contained a bundle of the sort of papers every household accumulated over the years. An occasional letter was addressed to Elizabeth from her sister, sent from Hatton Garden on lilac paper. Nothing interesting was present in the trunk now, although Maven judged that someone had turned over the papers not long ago. Maven left Rogers by the front door and explored the rest of the house. He strode up the narrow staircase quickly, the better to get it over with, though, in truth, he felt nothing was amiss here. So it was, for he searched each of the two upstairs rooms and found nothing to concern him. Hidden in the woods like it was, the house was such an ideal location to hide a prisoner and he was disappointed not to have found George here. He went round again, more slowly this time, looking closely at the floor and the furniture.

In the downstairs kitchen parlour the fire was out. He let his hand hover over the dead embers and found, to his surprise, that they gave off a gentle warmth. He retraced his steps and found himself again in the upstairs room that overlooked the back garden. It was bare, aside from a bed that had not been slept in for a good while and a wardrobe, which was empty. He crouched down and looked closely at the bare wooden floorboards. The surface was scratched, like a heavy object had been dragged repeatedly across the boards. He pushed the bed aside and it moved easily. One of the boards sat slightly proud of its neighbours. Maven prised the wood up with his fingernails. It gave easily. He slipped his free hand into the narrow gap and explored the space under the floor. As he was about to withdraw, his fingers brushed against some paper.

18

As stables went it was quite luxurious. Horses certainly had a better existence in the country than in the city, thought George. He and Claudette were cold but at least they were able to huddle under a thick blanket. He had followed their progress through the gaps in the wooden coachwork of the undertaker's wagon. They had stopped just once when they pulled off the road and into a forest clearing. A loaf had been hurled in the back door and a stone jar of ale slammed onto the wooden floor. They were both famished. George let Claudette have first go at both the food and the drink. She had thought about eating all of it then changed her mind. George had looked around for an escape route but his captors had kept him bound to the vehicle.

This morning, he looked out through the gaps between the wooden planks of the stable. They were close to a big house. It was white and had a fine garden with trees. Men walked about the place and there was the occasional laugh or a shout but mostly they seemed to be getting on with some kind of work. Claudette had said if they were going to be killed they would have done it by now and he decided she was right. They were to be held as some kind of ransom, though who would pay to release the likes of them George had no idea. He hoped they would bring them some more food soon.

By the time Maven had searched the garden and the lane it was late afternoon, and Maven told Rogers it was too late to begin the return journey, the roads between Woodford and the City being too dangerous after dark. Instead, he resolved to stay locally and return to London in the morning. The old man's offer of a bed in his cold and ramshackle home was made from obligation rather than hospitality and Maven declined, politely insisting he did not want to put his host to any more trouble. In truth, Maven wanted to get into the warm confines of a local inn and find out some more about Mr and Mrs Webb and their friends.

Rogers recommended the Bald Stag, a coaching inn a mile north on Bucket Hill and they parted company. Maven arrived at five o'clock, chilly from the walk through the forest and found that many of the overnight residents had already settled in. The tavern was an imposing, two-storey construction in the Tudor style, surrounded by woods. The milestone by its front door indicated he was now ten miles from London. The saloon was sectioned off into rooms, seemingly to give the locals some privacy from the travellers. Each room had a strong fire going and the whole place felt warm and busy. He could lose himself in here quite easily, he thought. The serving staff, mostly young women, bustled about delivering plates of food, jugs of ale and bottles of wine to customers who had elected for their own protection not to travel any further on the road that evening. Crime, or at least the fear of it, certainly paid for the innkeepers of Epping Forest. Maven settled in the room where he found the landlord chatting to a group of locals. All working men, they were lounging on the wooden benches or leaning over tables in conversation. A game of chess was in progress and one man, who may have been a blacksmith from his apparel, bowed his face close to a newspaper that had been clamped between two battens of wood and traced words with his forefinger. Maven nodded to the landlord and every face in the small room turned in his direction. He put it down to his being the same height as the ceiling. They seemed the sort of crowd that would find it uproariously funny if he knocked his head on a beam.

Maven took himself to the only remaining table. He caught the landlord's eye and ordered a jug of ale and a plate of a cold meat and bread.

"By yourself, sir?"

Maven nodded.

"You might find yourself a bit more comfortable in one of the other bars, sir. Can get a little rough round the edges for some on this side," said the landlord, addressing the second half of the sentence as much to the other drinkers as to Maven. They seemed to take it as a compliment.

"These gentlemen look to be good company. I shall be fine here, I think. Is there any chance of a room?"

The tapster retired to give the food order to the kitchen. He returned a few seconds later with a key, attached to which was a large wooden block with the number four chiselled out and, for good measure, painted over in black so that there was no danger of a traveller forgetting his room or, indeed, neglecting to return the key. The rate quoted by the landlord was optimistic, topping even that charged in the City but there did not seem to be much competition about and they both knew that room rates increased as it grew darker.

Maven reckoned it would take about ten minutes. In fact, it took seven. A middle-aged man, dark and unshaven, sauntered over and, without waiting to be asked, sat down at the table, scraping the stool on the stone floor and banging his tankard down just hard enough to make his presence felt.

"Not seen you here before."

"No."

"What's your business?"

"Just travelling through."

"On foot?"

"Yes."

Maven paused and then decided to wade straight in.

"Do you know a Mr Matthew Webb?"

Maven could not get the picture of Webb out his mind.

The man regarded him with some suspicion and said, "What'd you want to know about 'im for?"

"Many reasons. Why don't we start with where he is? And his wife."

"Ah, word gets round a bit quick. You up from London?"

"Mrs Webb's family is concerned for her safety. Would anyone here be able to help?"

The man leaned forward and extended his right arm to reveal a hand that had dirt caked in each crease and under each fingernail. He smiled.

"The name is Osgood, Salem Osgood. And whether I can help you depends."

Maven paused to consider the man's not so subtle request.

"They will pay," answered Maven, "not much, I am afraid, but all they can afford, if the help is worthwhile."

The man paused while a young woman brought Maven's supper to the table. Maven was struck by her resemblance to Kathrine. She had dark curly hair and her hazel eyes were full of life.

199

A good deal less sophistication than the mistress of Hatton garden but rather more mischief, he decided. Her cheekbones were high and her smile generous. She bent down to lay the tray on the table, revealing her ample cleavage to him. She looked him in the eye and smiled the sort of smile a stranger miles from home might find difficult to resist. Osgood took the opportunity to give the woman a playful slap on the backside.

"Leave me alone you ugly old brute."

"Only a bit of fun Molly. How about a refill?" he said, waving his tankard in front of her.

"Get it yourself, you know where the barrel is."

She flashed Maven another smile as she turned away. Her white dress was cut low across her shoulders and every lascivious eye in the room rested its gaze on the rise and fall of her breasts. At Osgood's beckoning, the landlord appeared, a goblet of wine in his hand, which he handed to Maven. He sat down without being invited.

"He wants to know about the Webb house," said Osgood.

The look from the landlord was fleeting but sufficient to reveal his concerns. Maven leaned forward and tried to adopt an encouraging expression.

"It is very important. They may be in danger. Can you tell me something about them?"

The landlord thought about the question but it was Osgood who leapt into the silence.

"Mr and Mrs Webb moved up from London a while back with their little kiddie. A boy, I think. But an alehouse ain't the sort of place Webb would be seen. I don't think she would let him, for a start. They pretended they was more the sort for house parties with the middling sort, the ones who've made a few pounds in London and moved out here; merchants and bankers and the like."

"Pretended?"

"Aye, she forgot there's plenty round here with long memories and longer tongues."

"People knew her, you mean?"

"Aye."

"And she was a danger to them?"

"Hell, no. But people don't like airs and graces in previously humble folk and they could see right through her. She kept herself out of the way and that suited all parties."

Maven changed direction. "These other people, the middling sort, can you give me any names? Someone I might call upon tomorrow? I have met Mr Rogers. He is their landlord, I believe."

"Aye, miserable old skinflint, that one. We don't see 'im in here neither."

The two men looked at each other, a note of caution in their mutual glance.

"Look, sir. I don't know who you are but you strikes me as a fair sort. You would be an officer, would I be right?

Maven did not reply.

"Young Lizzie has got herself attached to some trouble. Webb is mixed up with some people who have a very nasty side, sir, very nasty indeed."

"And would this group have included Colonel Summersby?"

The two men exchanged another glance, "Yes," said Osgood, "but you don't want to be spending too much time with that one."

"How so?"

"He don't take kindly to visitors, sir. Has been known to shoot 'em. Shoots 'em on sight he does."

"Rogers seems to know him."

"Knows of him, I'd say. Them two won't ever be friends."

"Anyone else I might approach?"

"They kept themselves to themselves. Mostly their visitors come up from London," said the landlord, "that's why we figure you is the sort of bloke that needs to know. Sometimes, you see, these visitors was foreigners. They'd arrive late, after dark sometimes then they'd be away again when they thought no one was around to see 'em leave. Summat odd there, sir, wouldn't you say?"

"Because they arrived at strange hours or because they were foreign? Look, there is someone else I need to find, while I am here. A colleague came up on the same search, yesterday, and I would like to meet up with him. I couldn't find him at the other inns down in the village."

Maven described George but knew there was a good chance that they had not brought him this far north.

"Don't recall anyone such as that, sir, and there ain't been no blether," said Osgood. Maven knew he was telling the truth. There would be a network of casual observers that was only too pleased to enliven its dull days by gossiping about the comings and goings of strangers. The conversation petered out and the landlord excused himself and walked to the adjacent room to hurl abuse at a slothful pot man. A few minutes later Osgood took his leave, slipping out of the back door to the yard where a coach and four with yet more travellers had just arrived.

Maven only realised how hungry he was when he started to plough his way through the meal. He finished it quickly and washed it down with the ale. It was good beer and good bread and he slipped into a relaxed comfort, warmed by the fire. For no reason he could think of, he felt safe here. He thought of George and made his plan for the following day. He decided on an early start and to use the cover of the last of the darkness. The ride up from London was now beginning to take its toll on his energy levels. He picked up his kitbag and decided to see what delights room four had to offer. He ordered a jug of ale from the pretty waitress they called Molly and asked for the drink to be brought to his room. He smiled and allowed his look to linger for a second or longer than was necessary. She graced him with a small curtsey and a smile in return and he knew he would have company later.

Room four was much the same as any other room to be found in an English coaching inn. There was a large wooden bed with a small table on each side and a wardrobe stained the same dark shade, not classic furniture but solid and built to last. There was a single chair, badly upholstered with a pink material that might previously have seen service as part of a dress. On an occasional table under a looking glass were a white porcelain basin and a towel that had once been white but had faded to grey with countless washes. Maven walked to the window. He was at the front of the building and overlooked the London road. The sun had fallen below the tree line of the forest and set a glow of faint orange in the distance. The habit of sleeping at sunset and rising at dawn was ingrained in country dwellers. He decided there would be little or no movement on the road until morning. He sat on the bed and removed his boots. The mattress was lumpy. He whiled away some time checking his pistols, playing with the firing mechanism and blowing dust from the pan.

Then he took the papers he had found at the Webb house from inside his jacket. There was no writing on the outside but there was a wax seal, red like every other seal had ever seen except it was smaller and more delicate than the heavy wax embossing they would use to seal orders. In the gloom he could not make out the Latin inscription. He held the letter in his hand and bounced it lightly on his palm. Had Matthew Webb died for this? Someone had obviously hidden it and nobody hid things under floorboards unless they had value. He was about to read what was inside when there was a knock on the door. He hurriedly stowed the letter in his kitbag. It was the landlord with his ale. Maven was disappointed not to find the serving girl, Molly standing before him.

"You asked after the Colonel, sir," mumbled the landlord.

"I'm sorry?"

The landlord came in and closed the door.

"They say there is somethin' afoot at his house. Men arriving in the night, wagons going backwards and forwards, that sort of thing. Be discreet sir. He won't thank me if I'm known to have said anything to a stranger. You know where the house is?"

Maven nodded and the landlord made to withdraw. The coins that Maven offered by way of thanks were returned and the landlord shuffled closer to Maven as he explained in a soft voice, "No, sir. There's mischief stirring and I'd wager you are about to help us a lot more than you know. Remember, people has long memories."

Once the landlord had departed Maven poured himself a large glass of ale and sat on the bed. He thought of George and where he might be, and then he thought of the coronation on Saturday, just two days away. All sorts of theories raced through his mind. He settled on Audley trying to kill the King then needing to get away, probably to France, and needing a shield of some kind in order to get him to the coast. But he would need a shield more valuable than a tapster's son. It made no sense. No, he thought, George has been taken to lure me here and in that aim they have succeeded. Hereford House held the key. George was there, he was sure of it.

Maven was a way from the drink taking hold and it was a good feeling to be resting on the cusp, warmed, fed and as relaxed as he could be, knowing that George was held prisoner. He considered going down to Hereford House now but decided the darkness would not help him any. George would have to sit tight. He lay back on the bed and thought of Ruth and the feelings that had stirred within him when the waitress had smiled earlier. He asked his wife to forgive him as he was his way in these cases. He sat up and reached for the jug to pour another glass then changed his mind, took a deep breath and paused while the familiar feelings of resentment and frustration welled up from within. He could never tell when the darkness would come but it was usually prompted by his memories of Ruth and the anger he felt about losing her, about losing the only woman he had ever truly cared for. He hurled the glass at the far wall, watching as it splintered into tiny fragments. He leaned forward with his head in his hands and suddenly there was tension in his gut and a fear that had not come upon him since Malplaquet. His hands trembled and he forced himself to regain control by walking around the room. He had a picture in his mind of Lady Kathrine Cooper, smiling at him. Then there was the body in Smithfield again. And then there was the face of Nathaniel Barclay in the churchyard, hideously scarred and as ugly as ever, leaning forward to hit him. Barclay and Lancaster working together, but surely not for Shrewsbury. Surely not. He threw himself onto the bed and tried unsuccessfully to sleep.

He tried to summon up his memories of Ruth and if they would not come then he would revert to what he always did on these dark nights and he would drink until sleep took over and all the pictures and memories left him. He reached for his bag and took out the pewter box, flipped open the lid and spilled the contents onto the mattress beside him. Her necklace, its semi-precious red stones, polished smoother by his near constant attention, the silver locket with the single lock of her dark hair and the square of white cotton he had torn from her dress as they took her away to lay in peace with the child she had wanted so desperately to give him. Her screams echoed from the depths of his mind and grew louder and louder until there was silence and the silence was not filled with a baby's cry but the sobbing of a broken woman. And he had stood outside her door, pacing, helpless. As he had done so often before he lay on the bed and arranged her things around him and summoned up these painful memories and part of him was sorry that he was not with her now, though he had given God enough opportunities to take him.

A while later a light knock at the door woke him. He looked around to find the room in complete darkness. There was another knock, slightly firmer this time and the door opened. It was Molly, smiling, carrying a tray, her curly dark hair bouncing on her shoulders as she walked towards him with the tray and her resemblance to Kathrine caused Maven to wonder if he still might be dreaming.

"I brought you some wine."

And two glasses. She placed the bottle of wine and the glasses on the table and then closed the door. He sat up to thank her but she walked to him and placed her forefinger on his lips. From her sackcloth apron she pulled two candles that she fixed into the china dishes on the bedside tables and lit them. Maven watched her graceful movements and heard the gentle rustle of her skirts. Then she went to the windows and drew the curtains. The candlelight caused shadows to dance on the bare walls. She stood before him and paused.

"Don't get too many handsome strangers through here," she said then lifted her white chemise over her head and the candles flickered. She wore a white bodice that laced at the front and its tightness pushed her breasts over the top. The poor light gave the suggestion that her shoulders were a creamy Mediterranean brown rather than the milky pallor that daylight would betray. She untied her apron and her skirt at the same time, allowed them to fall to the floor and stepped out of them, naked from her waist down. Maven at first fought against the temptation but the availability of the pretty stranger overwhelmed him and he conceded. If he did not concentrate too much on her voice and the just-too-much flesh around her hips he could pretend he was with Ruth. He leaned forward and unlaced the bodice enough for her to wriggle out of it. She leaned forward and kissed him and let his hands move over her naked body. They went to bed and time slipped away.

Maven woke several hours later, the candles burned down now to less than half their height and the dishes full of spent wax. He lay on his back and Molly lay with her head on his chest, her left leg across him. She was warm and her skin was soft, her shallow breaths barely causing her to move at all. He closed his eyes and imagined that he was with Ruth and felt her dark hair resting on his chest. There were times when he had to work very hard to bring to mind the subtlety of her beauty and the ten years that had passed quite often meant that his memory failed him and he became annoyed with himself. Tonight, though he remembered her so clearly he could reach out and hold her again. He drifted back into sleep.

As he slipped in and out of his dream it was not the face of his long departed wife that looked up at him but that of Kathrine. He stroked her dark hair and she rolled onto him and rocked back and forth. He looked into her beautiful eyes and he kissed her. Her lips were moist and they welcomed him. She moaned and trembled. He moved his hand to her neck and, in his subconscious state, recalled the wound there and he awoke suddenly to find it was the tavern girl upon him and he sighed, not so much with disappointment but rather with guilt. He looked at her and wondered whether she could read his mind, whether she could feel the absence of compassion. He wondered how many other passing strangers there had been. Plenty, he thought.

The suddenly he woke with a start just a minute later, as the wooden door crashed back against the wall. The girl sat up and screamed and held the bedclothes to her chest. Striding into the room was a tall man with a blue greatcoat, open to reveal a sword and pistol in his waistband. And he wore a patch over his left eye.

"Get out from under that woman, Maven, we have to leave!"

"What the …"

"Now! There is no time to explain."

"Tell me what …"

"I'll tell you when we're on the road and not before. Now get your clothes and come with me. You, girly, stay here and don't go raising any alarms."

"There'll be no need," said Maven swinging his legs out of the bed, "not with all the noise you're making. The whole inn will be awake wondering what the devil is going on."

Lancaster was drunk, and the alcohol fumes wafted across to the couple. The three of them paused, waiting to see who would make the first move. Lancaster was gazing at Molly, waiting for her to reach for her clothes but she was not giving him the pleasure of seeing her naked. Nor, for that matter, was Maven.

"Get out!"

Lancaster leered at Molly with his good eye and smiled. Then he belched, turned on his heel and left the room. She looked at him and her eyes begged him not to go.

"Do you know him?" he asked and she replied with a gentle, unconvincing shake of the head.

19

Maven threw back the front door of the inn and strode out into the cold night air. He wondered what the time was and the best he could do was that it was late enough to have cleared the inn of its customers. The heavy door slammed shut behind him trapping the lingering warmth of the sleeping tavern inside and he felt the cold breeze on his face. As his eyes became more accustomed to the darkness, Maven identified the tall figure astride a large horse on the far side of the road. Maven had dressed quickly but had also taken the time to remove the pistol from his bag and stow it in his waistband.

"I hope you've got a good reason for this, Lancaster."

"Get a move on, damn you. We have to get away from here."

Maven sauntered across the road and Lancaster edged his mount forward, the percussion of the hooves on the road breaking the silence of the night.

"Come on, swing yourself up here. The animal is strong enough to take the pair of us."

"Damn your eyes, Lancaster. On these roads in the dark the beast will be lame within a half mile. I'll walk. And so should you."

Lancaster kicked his mount and set off at a trot and left Maven to stride behind him. The trees on either side of the highway rocked back and forth gently in the autumn breeze and threw dappled blue shadows across the road in front of them. Lancaster reined in the horse, swung himself down and waited for Maven to catch up. They walked on together. The stillness of the pitch black forest was punctuated by the occasional animal going about its nocturnal business and the heavy breathing and sporadic snorting of Lancaster's horse. They could barely see each other when the moonlight shrank behind the clouds and their footfalls were punctuated by splashes as their boots found the puddles of rainwater.

"Did you follow me from London?" asked Lancaster

"Why would I do that?"

"We're both seeking the same information. I'm not pleased Maven, I'll share that with you for free. First you barge into the Christopher and scare off Audley and his cohorts and now you come up here and draw attention to yourself by swiving the staff. If you're going to play with us you are going to have to start learning the rules."

"This is not a game. And rules? That would be a first for you, wouldn't it?"

"Look, if we don't co-operate we shall both wind up in the graveyard. I have information that may help you and I daresay you have some that will help me. Now tell me why you're here."

"I'm the one who was dragged out of his warm bed in the middle of the night. I think I have a right to an answer first. "

They walked in silence for five minutes, neither willing to lose face by conceding and then, much to Maven's surprise, Lancaster spoke up.

"You are in mortal danger, Maven. Caused, I might say, by your less than circumspect approach. You cannot expect to walk into a nest of vipers such as that place," he said, jerking his thumb back over his shoulder, "and ask questions of men who have far more to lose than you would ever know."

Maven was impressed: his former colleague was working hard to carry off his subterfuge, if subterfuge it was. There followed another silence during which they tramped on down the main road. Maven racked his brain for what he might know that would interest Lancaster or, more to the point, what Lancaster thought he might know. Maven spoke first.

"You make an unlikely guardian."

"Trust me, it's not through choice. At any other time I'd have left you there to fight your own skirmish, but the gentleman I work for thinks you possess valuable information and that, sir, seals your safety. At least for the timebeing."

"Ah, and so we get to the truth."

"Maven you don't know the half of what you're –"

Lancaster failed to complete his sentence, as he was interrupted by an arrow bursting out of the darkness behind them and thudding into a tree, passing near enough that the feathered flights disturbed the air around them.

"Get down!" shouted Maven.

They ran to opposite sides of the road and crouched in the undergrowth and their silhouettes disappeared into the darkness of the forest. Lancaster's horse, left stranded in the middle of the path became nervous and then spirited, sensing that some foe or other was near but unable to see or hear it clearly.

"Where did it come from?" called Maven in a stage whisper.

"Behind us."

Maven rolled across the road and joined Lancaster in a shallow ditch.

"I don't like to say I told you so, Maven ..."

"Whoever is out there was aiming at you," replied Maven, "I can't see anyone on the road. They must be in the trees, which is where we should be. Come on."

"They should inter you in Bedlam for your madness. We'll be lost within five minutes."

Maven squinted into the middle distance and got his bearings.

"I was hereabouts this morning. I reckon we'll find a house about a quarter of mile that way," he said, indicating towards the southeast.

"Would that be where your sweetheart's sister lived?"

"Still does, unless you know something I don't."

"And you reckon you can get us there in this darkness?"

"Do we have a choice?"

Lancaster lifted himself up slightly and withdrew his pistol from his waistband.

"Put that away, man, you'll not get a clear shot at anyone in the woods."

"Won't do any harm to try, I'd say."

Lancaster rolled onto the road trying to catch the reins of his horse.

"Leave it," hissed Maven as a second arrow thudded into the ground a few yards short of the prone Lancaster, who abandoned the horse and rolled back into the ditch.

"Come on, this way," said Maven and set off in the direction in which he hoped to find the Webb house.

They went in silence, taking a meandering route and staying ten yards or so apart, which was about how far they could see in the densely covered forest. Maven had a vague flashback to the woods around the village of Blenheim ten years ago. On that occasion, he was the one doing the tracking, following an assassin intent on locating the Captain-General himself. If they can see us and can get a clear shot in, we're done for, he thought. Whoever the bowman was, he was experienced enough to know not to bother taking aim among the trees. The probability of hitting anything was reduced to nothing more than an off chance, even in daylight, so a moving target in darkness was no sport at all.

The ground was uneven and every few yards one of them tripped over a bare root or had their way impeded by a fallen tree. Each could hear the other's heavy breathing and Maven felt his pulse racing with the effort of the run. There was no path that he could discern and the going was heavy. He cursed when he caught his hand on a thorn bush and felt the skin lacerate. Then, after about ten minutes of scrambling through the dense forest floor, Maven hissed, "there's a clearing over there. The house is just across the way, I'm sure of it."

They met up and sat together on the edge of the glade, both breathing deeply. This was the Webb house he was sure, though it was obscured by the dark woods behind it. He caught Lancaster's arm and pulled him back as he was about to set off across the clearing.

"No! Go round the edge. Keep the forest behind you and stay low, then you won't make yourself a target. I'd wager there is only the one bowman. If we split up and take separate routes he won't be able to hit the pair of us."

Maven took the anti-clockwise route around the circle and found himself on the edge of the lane that serviced the house. Lancaster got around the far side of the house and crouched by the front door. He raised his arm and beckoned to Maven, who took a breath and rolled across the lane, landing in the bushes beside the house. As he did so, a loud boom from a rifle echoed around the trees. With no clue as to where the bullet might have gone he muttered a quick prayer. No pain. No blood. Maven brought himself up into a crouch and threw himself against the front door, knowing it would present no challenge. Lancaster followed him inside and slammed the door shut behind them.

"Upstairs, Maven, we'll get better view of who is firing on us."

"You mean you don't know?"

"Not exactly, no."

Maven allowed Lancaster to go upstairs first then dragged the heavy wooden trunk out from under the stairs and jammed it inside the front door. Then he took a broom from the kitchen and wedged it between the trunk and the bottom stair. It would not hold against any but the gentlest shove but at least they would have some warning if anyone tried to gain entry. He recalled from his visit this morning that there had been an ancient rifle hanging on the wall of the kitchen. He grabbed it, made a cursory tour of the downstairs to check that each window was securely fastened and went upstairs to join Lancaster.

"We're sitting ducks," said Lancaster, his breathing rasping and heavy and condensing in the cold air.

"Maybe, maybe not. Depends if our friend wants to identify himself. Arrows and bullets can't get through the stone walls so provided we stay out of sight I'd suggest the advantage lies with us."

"It's a siege, Maven. We'll never get out."

"We've got the rest of the night to think of a way, though."

They made an unattractive pair. Maven had snagged his coat on a branch when he was scrambling through the undergrowth and the front pocket hung loose. His face was dirty and the thorns had cut his hands like a barber's blade. In avoiding the rifle shot when they were close to the house he had rolled into a bush of firethorn and had drawn blood above his eye. Lancaster sat in the furthest corner of the room, his breathing heavy. His boots looked like they may have been the same pair he had worn at his discharge. They were filthy and worn to the uppers; the bare skin of his hands and face was grimy, more so than Maven's surface dirt, suggesting that it had been some time since the half-pay officer had visited a bath. The eye patch was the man's trademark and even this was a ragged specimen. They agreed to take it in turns to sleep, three hours on and three hours off. Lancaster did not dissent when Maven suggested he would like the first watch. As watches went, it was a bore. An occasional glance out of the window presented nothing but darkness and the tops of trees silhouetted against the night sky, bending slightly in the wind. He watched as the wind chased the clouds across the sky.

Whoever had shot at them had not come any closer to the house. The open window and Maven's keen hearing ensured that he would have heard anyone approach. Instead, the only noises had been the scrabbling of what turned out to be a fox and the occasional hooting of an owl a way off in the trees. The wind had not let up and it was getting colder in the house. He wondered which of them had made the journey here first. Travelling up this morning, Maven had watched closely and, though he had seen Makepeace, the strange boy from the inn, darting in and out of the trees in his stead, even the most cursory backward glance would have picked up this untidy specimen.

After three hours, the light had improved and dawn was struggling to make its appearance. Maven must have dozed for he was surprised when he looked out of the window and could see for some distance across the clearing and into the woods. Several rabbits scampered about in the open space and the few birds that had not yet flown south were chirping, so much so that Lancaster stirred. Maven wondered how the man could sleep so easily in such uncomfortable conditions. A soldier's ability, he decided, to snatch a few hours shut-eye if you didn't know when the next opportunity might arise. As quietly as he could, Maven stood and stretched, silently cursing the dampness of the floor, which had seeped into his bones. Lancaster lay hunched under a blanket in the corner while Maven stretched. Leaving Lancaster to sleep on, Maven went downstairs carrying the heavy rifle, tiptoeing so that his boots did not clatter on the wood as they had done earlier and he used only the edge of each tread so that it did not creak and betray his departure. He paused on the bottom stair and checked that the trunk remained wedged against the front door before he went all the way to the bottom. In the kitchen he unfastened the shutters on the window that opened out onto the back of the house, pushed open the window and stuck his head out. There was no sound at all. If we're being watched, they will be looking at the front door, he thought. He threw the rifle out and let it drop into the bushes then clambered out and closed the window behind him as best he could.

He set off through the undergrowth, making a wide circle until he was parallel with the narrow lane. He made for the main road as soon as he could, hoping that the early starters would have risen with the dawn and set out for London already. The forest was not immune to daylight footpads but a robbery was unlikely, and, as he expected there were coaches and groups of pedestrians abroad already. The walk to Hereford House took him through the straggle of houses that was Woodford Wells and he moved urgently and remained vigilant. It was a little over a mile to the house and he left the road before he reached it and looped round to the back. The house dominated its surroundings and if there were lookouts alert in the upper floor he would very likely have been seen despite confining himself to the dense undergrowth. The garden was surrounded by a stone wall about six feet high but the enclosure extended no more than fifty yards from the house. He walked to the furthest corner and levered himself up. He rested his elbows on the top of the wall and looked around. He was screened from the house by an apple tree and several tall bushes. The back of the house was quiet and there were no doors or windows open. There were two carriages parked at the side, in front of a stable block. He spread his hands on the brick wall, pushed himself up and clambered over. He fell to the ground on the other side and his pistol jabbed him in the ribs as he landed.

Suddenly a door to the side of the house opened and a groom carrying two buckets crossed behind the carriages to the outbuildings, whistling as he went. The buckets clanged together and if anyone slept in the house their rest would have been disturbed for sure. Maven edged closer to the stable block, sticking close to the wall and keeping the thick bushes in front of him. When he reached the edge of his cover he paused. He had a good view of the side and rear of the house here and an escape route back over the wall if he was quick enough. He waited until the groom had returned to the house then he eased himself further along until he was level with the stable. From here he could look back down the garden, which had been landscaped in the modern fashion, no doubt at some expense, for the manicured lawn gave on to a fine array of shrubs and perennials that were dying back for winter. He took a deep breath and scampered round to the front of the stable and slipped in through the door. There were four stalls on each side but only three were occupied. Each of the horses stood and stared at the stranger and he guessed they must be hungry and awaited their feed. Maven made his way to the back of the block, checking each of the empty stalls. In the last one he found what he was searching for.

The return of the groom disturbed him. He now carried a refilled bucket in each hand. The servant had to place his load on the ground to turn and close the door to the house, which gave Maven the opportunity to throw himself into an empty stall, where he landed on a bed of dry straw then rolled out of sight to where he could spy on the groom without being seen. He wore a dark leather apron that almost reached to his boots and his hands were grubby with the dirt that comes from years of working outdoors with animals. He stooped with the effort of carrying the feed and he whistled to himself then spoke in turn to each horse as he filled its trough. There was a good deal of petting and rubbing of noses as each horse in turn snaffled an apple. Presently, the groom completed his chores and extended his task by sharing with the horses his thoughts on the day ahead, which seemed to consist of nothing more than some exercise on the common and the polishing of brasses. He left the stable block still whistling and the empty metal buckets tolled with each step he took.

Maven got up and rubbed off the loose straw then went into the box opposite. George Trescothick lay there, gagged and bound at his hands and feet, his eyes wide open, terrified by the situation in which he found himself. Alongside him, tethered in the same way, was a young woman. Maven was unsure where he had seen her before. Then he recalled that she had been at the Blackbird Club the night he had been there. Her eyes seemed empty of life, as if she were resigned to being blown along on the breeze to reach whatever outcome fate determined for her. Maven dropped to his knees and set about releasing George, beginning with the rough canvas gag, then untied his hands. George sputtered for breath and rubbed at his neck and throat where the material had chafed him.

"Captain, thank God you are here."

Maven raised a finger to his lips and George dropped his voice to a whisper.

"You were absolutely right about the club. Something big is planned, sir. This is Claudette. She, erm, works at the Blackbird

Club, sir," then, sensing that Maven already knew this he added, "she has a burn to her foot, sir. They tortured her."

The bandage wrapped around Claudette's left foot was dirty where she had walked on it and the material had begun to unwind. She looked at him, imploring him to get to her restraints as soon as he could.

"There is something happening today, sir. There is loads of activity, all sorts of people were coming and going last night."

Maven freed George's restraints and turned his attention to Claudette. Like George, she rubbed her throat but she had nothing to say. Instead she stared at Maven and seemed to be considering whether his presence increased or decreased her chances of survival.

"What happened to your foot?"

"Burned it. An accident."

She turned away from him then and it was clear the conversation was ended. George looked hard at her, surprised by her reticence. Then he turned to Maven.

"Captain, I think Audley might be here. The bloke who owns this house has been flying about like a dervish ever since we got here, shouting orders and chasing his servants about. There's a bunch of them going down to London. They mean to cause some mischief."

"We need to get you away from here as quickly as we can."

Maven looked at Claudette.

"Can you walk?"

Claudette stood and tried a few steps. No, she could not walk.

"I'll carry her, sir."

"We have miles to go, George, too far even for you. I have my eye on that carriage there. Can you hitch two of these horses to it?"

"Yes, but it will take a while. The blokes in there will see us soon enough."

Then George nodded to the house and Maven turned. Standing directly in front of him, framed by the doorway, was a man, a stranger, tall and upright with an angular chin and a long nose. Aged about fifty years old, he wore a cream wig and white lace cuffs protruded from the sleeves of his coat.

"Colonel Mark Summersby, sir. Welcome, though I do not believe I issued you an invitation."

He bowed. The accent was polished and his words were clipped. "Captain Luke Maven, sir, I have been looking forward to meeting you."

From the shadows behind the General emerged a second man, the short but very upright Corporal Dench, pigeon-chested as ever, and carrying a pistol, which he levelled at Maven. Dench jerked his head upwards a couple of times and Maven took the hint, raising his hands to head height.

"Are you going to shoot me, Corporal?"

"Might do, if you don't behave yourself. Hand over your weapons. Do it slow and don't muck me about."

Maven reached down slowly with his right hand and withdrew the pistol from his waistband then threw it towards Dench. It clattered onto the hard ground and rested with its barrel pointing directly at Summersby, who bent down and picked it up. Maven weighed up the chances of disarming Dench and taking out the older man and thought they were better than evens. Summersby had struggled to get down and retrieve the gun. He presented no challenge at all. Then Maven sensed the presence of someone behind him. He stole the briefest of glances over his right shoulder, where a rear door to the stable block was swinging open and a tall figure had entered.

"Best hand over the knife as well, Luke. We don't want anyone getting hurt do we?" said Lancaster, who had withdrawn his own pistol and was now pointing it at Maven's head. Maven spat on the ground in disgust. As slowly as he dared, Maven drew the knife from his boot and held it by the handle in front of him, daring Dench to lean forward and take it.

"Don't even think about it, Maven," said Lancaster who had seen the move before and his warning saved Maven's life, for he would have shot him in the back without a second's hesitation. Dench stepped forward, took the knife and hurled it to the ground outside. Maven turned to face him.

"What was all that business with the bows and arrows?"

On cue, a dark haired man stood in the doorway, dressed, if anything, even worse than Lancaster. A vicious pink scar ran the length of the right side of his face, twisting his features into a permanent sneer.

"I should have known," said Maven, "if you find one stinking rat there's normally a second close by."

"Nice to see you again, Maven," said Lieutenant Nathaniel Barclay, who raised his hand as if he were about to salute and then converted the respectful gesture into a v-sign instead.

Summersby's disdain for the ragged half-pay officers was evident but he ignored Barclay and addressed Maven directly.

"The whole nation knows Marlborough has nailed his colours to the Hanoverian's mast but if he has sent one of his finest up here then we must have him rattled. Does he believe we plan to do away with the foreigner?"

"I have no idea what you mean, sir."

"Oh come on, Maven, don't take me for a fool. What on earth are doing trying to track down Edward Audley and staking out the Blackbird for if it isn't at Marlborough's bidding?"

Maven remained silent.

"So that is it, then. Well I fear the Captain-General should have sent more than a single officer to face this challenge, Maven."

"Do you?" asked Maven.

"Do I what?"

"Plan to do away with the King."

"What do you think?"

"It is regicide, sir. You'll be hung drawn and quartered. You and your accomplices," he added taking in Lancaster and Barclay with a swift glance.

"Not if we install the true King, Maven. He waits in France for the signal and shall come immediately."

"You seem very confident."

"I have every reason to be. Our task is very necessary. If we allow the Elector to succeed Her Majesty then it shall be the end of the monarchy as we know it. The country will be run by merchants and lawyers and the King shall become nothing more than a side issue. Surely you can see that?"

"I can see that you have a great deal to lose if you have backed the wrong horse, sir."

"It is not about personal interests."

"Really? Bring Audley in here and let me hear him say that."

20

The Captain-General had never lost the habit of rising early. A soldier's habit he called it. With him for breakfast this morning were Shrewsbury and the Elector's man, Bothmer. He watched as the guests slurped noisily from dishes of coffee and tucked into a leg of beef that was left over from a Marlborough House dinner the previous evening. The Duke sat back in his sturdy dining chair with his arms folded and his legs apart. Shrewsbury's eye complaint gave him an untrustworthy appearance for he appeared to look beyond Marlborough whenever he addressed him, and although he had grown used to it, Marlborough still had to force himself to remember that the Lord Treasurer was an ally.

"Tell me how Maven got himself mixed up in this mess."

Shrewsbury, for his part, had never got used to Marlborough's directness. He put it down to his soldier's ways and reasoned that such a tone was inevitable if one occupied the status as England's foremost commander. A tone that brooked no dissent must be necessary if one is to send hundreds of men to their deaths. Bothmer stopped chewing and looked at Shrewsbury. He was also interested.

"It seems that Lady Cooper acted on her own initiative. Her late husband had some sort of arrangement with Maven that she might call upon him if she needed assistance."

"Hugh Cooper chose well. Maven has a weakness for damsels in distress."

Bothmer cleared his throat gently so he might announce his entrance to the conversation. He had not yet derived the measure of their host despite meeting him several times. The Elector would entertain no criticism of Marlborough and considered him a most formidable ally. In Bothmer's eyes, though, the Captain-General was downright threatening if one found oneself on the wrong side of his argument. Bothmer spoke. His voice was weaker than usual.

"Does he interfere with our arrangement?"

"That depends, Herr Bothmer."

"How does it depend, sir?"

"Maven has a way of locating the moral high ground. He must have some internal barometer that does it for him and in my experience the man is always right. If he believes his personal mission is of greater importance than yours then he will best you."

"But surely our mission is of greater importance than anything with which he might be tasked?"

"He measures himself against a different moral code, Bothmer. If Maven decides the widow needs his protection then protection is what she will receive and I would counsel against getting in his way. Unless she threatens the King, of course, and then the due precedence of things must prevail."

"He is a good soldier?"

"One of my finest and bravest. Lucky as well."

"Lucky?"

"Some men just have the habit. He's a fierce brawler, as good a scrapper as any man who ever served under me but even the fighters need good fortune from time to time."

"Perhaps he has a guardian angel," smiled Shrewsbury but his humour was not reciprocated. Marlborough harrumphed his impatience.

"Come! Reassure me. Will George Lewis still be King come Monday?"

The directness of the question surprised them and Bothmer caught his breath and fought the urge to splutter coffee. He failed and spots of the dark brew spattered down his white shirt.

"Oh come on man, there is no point in pussy footing about. If there is a plot against the King then it shall be stopped. Root out the damned ringleaders and hang 'em. It'll discourage the rest."

"The plot, sir, is stopped, of that we are assured," explained Shrewsbury.

"Then what the devil is all this tomfoolery with Audley?"

"Audley has agreed to help us with certain matters."

"Bolingbroke? And you trust the blackguard?"

"I believe we do, sir."

"Mm. More than I would venture. His record is not a good one."

Bothmer leaned forward.

"He has agreed to bring us the ringleader."

"We already know who the damnable ringleader is!"

Bothmer rocked back into his chair. He crossed his legs involuntarily. Shrewsbury leapt into the silence.

"But, your grace, we live in a civilised society. Evidence must be obtained and the appropriate judicial process must be followed."

"Hm. Justice is a good deal more straightforward in the army. So what does Audley want in return?"

"His freedom."

"Not enough. If he walks away then he is a marked man. He will know that. What else does he want? He has debts all over the town, I hear."

"Quite so. He would like us to deal with those. And he wants the woman. And a free passage to the colonies."

"Cooper's widow? Ah, I see," said Marlborough and looked briefly into the middle distance, "I'm not surprised she objects to being part of this bargain. She's a feisty one and clever with it. Audley is an idiot if he thinks he can take her voluntarily. Moreover, she has hired herself the best protector in the land."

"We thought you might speak to him, sir," suggested Bothmer.

"Not a chance."

The guests looked at the Captain-General in a matching state of shock. Marlborough was the centre of his guests' attention, where he loved to be and he made them wait for his explanation while he helped himself to a refill of coffee.

"If either of you had served as a senior officer you would know that there is a time to give orders and a time to remain quiet. If we were trying to whip Marshal Tallard's arse then Maven would follow every order I issued. To the letter. But his contract is with the widow. Granted, he would find a way to disobey me with honour but he would not follow my instruction and my authority would be undermined. No gentlemen, on this occasion I shall not issue an order but I will warn you that Maven is a man you want on your side. Allow him to help you."

"But, sir, we have the power of the state with us."

"I think you will find he doesn't much care. He spent ten years putting himself in situations where he might get his head blown off and he walked away unscathed every time. There is not much you two can do to frighten him."

Shrewsbury tried to recover something from their meeting.

"Whilst I respect your opinion, sir, I wonder if I might request a favour?"

Marlborough looked at him enquiringly.

"I should find it most helpful if you would refrain from advising Captain Maven of our intentions with Bolingbroke. After all, we would not want him to ... take a moral stance, shall we say."

"Very well, but I shall not betray one of my finest officers, Charles. Nor shall I dishonour Cooper's widow. But then I shouldn't need to if you follow the plan properly. I have to say, though, that all this plotting discomfits me. If you make a mistake then the consequences are too dreadful to mention. Can you not just arrest Audley and have done with it? Bolingbroke and the rest of them will be disgraced by association."

Bothmer was beginning to tire of the line adopted by their host.

"They are already disgraced, sir, but we need them to be caught red-handed if their punishment is to fit the crime."

Maven's curiosity got the better of him and he allowed himself a brief look through the planks in the stable wall by leaning back and turning his head. A wagon arrived, and the gravel of the driveway hissed like the incoming waves on the shore. The vehicle stopped and the groom went briskly to see to the horses. Some conversation took place, mumbled, confirming that the journey had been uneventful. He gathered that whatever was in the wagon had been collected from several nearby locations. The men tried to reverse it into the yard by the side of the house. The groom held the horse by its bridle and its driver was struggling to turn the wagon. The driver was the young Scot from Westminster, Francis Jess.

Lancaster shoved Maven in the back and he walked forward, following Summersby to the gravel drive in front of the house while Dench stayed with George and Claudette. Men scurried back and forth busily carrying sacks and boxes. It struck him that the servants were dressed the same way, like a makeshift militia, but these were not redcoats. They were mostly clothed in shades of brown and their attire was made of heavy sack-like material.

A gentleman came out of the front door of the house and walked towards them. He had on the same blue coat that he had worn in Islington, his wig was powdered and combed and every inch of his being sang out that he was the senior man. Audley went among the men and greeted them, a tap on the arm here and a nod of the head here, but without exception each of them received a friendly word. He ended up at Summersby and, pointedly ignoring Maven, put his arm gently around the taller man's shoulder. They walked away so that Maven could not hear what was said, though he was undoubtedly the subject of their conversation. The pair made a wide circle of the drive and then walked back towards him.

They stopped by the wagon and Summersby had one of the men roll back the canvas sheet. There were barrels, about twelve of them, each separated from the other by rolls of sacking. They looked like kegs of ale but it was the cushioning between each one that gave away the true nature of the contents. Did these drivers know what they carried? Did they know what effect a loose spark might have? Somebody did, for the purpose of the wadding, packed in tightly, was to stop the barrels of gunpowder rubbing against each other and igniting the whole payload.

The canvas was off completely now and the ropes hung loose at each corner. There was movement from the stable block and two of the men hauled Claudette between them, the wisp of a girl was barely able to walk, so that they had to carry her while she hopped on her right foot and trailed her left uselessly. Audley nodded to confirm his order and the men dragged their prisoner to the wagon. They lifted Claudette onto the barrels and forced her to lie on her back across the uneven load. She was a dead weight and utterly submissive. They tied the ropes from the cart around each of her wrists and ankles and as they knocked her injured foot she let out a yell of pain. They had her tied down tightly, spread-eagled across the front half of the load, her legs and arms stretched as far they would go.

The men who had tied Claudette now turned their attention to the younger Trescothick, who proved reluctant to comply at first but became more docile after he was struck across the face with an open hand. They tied him firmly to the rear of the wagon. There was a minor hold up while Audley and Summersby conferred, the latter suggesting that the prisoners ought to be gagged, and there was a halt to proceedings while the groom was despatched to the stable for the material that Maven had so recently released.

Barclay led Maven to the house and took him to a drawing room on the ground floor. Dench appeared and pulled a set of wooden shutters closed, temporarily plunging the room into darkness until Barclay lit a candle then used this to light a second lamp. Audley sat behind a desk, his back to the window. He stared directly at Maven and his blue eyes made for a piercing stare.

"What are we to make of you, Captain?"

"Sorry?"

"We have never met, as far as I can tell. And yet I hear your name in all sorts of surprising places. You have a fine reputation, it would seem. And now, I find you interfering with our preparations. Nonetheless, it is an honour to meet such a great man in person." Audley leaned back in his chair and steepled his hands.

"Contrary to what you might think of me, I am a gentleman and a patriot and the work that you see here is in the interests of our great country, much the same as yours was in the war. My rule is that I do no harm to any man unless he has done me a disservice. Have you done me a disservice Maven?"

"Not as far as I am aware but give me time. How had William Taylor crossed you?"

"That reprobate cheated me then had the temerity to brag about it in public."

"There is a legal process for that sort of thing. Another gentleman might have paid to have the thief indicted and then looked on while he swung at Tyburn."

"I merely hastened the inevitable. Taylor's demise is no loss to society."

"And young George and his friend out there?"

"Your acquaintance is also a dishonest man, Captain. He passed himself off as my servant, albeit at your behest. You should by now be feeling some pang of guilt. Am I right?"

"Then it is I who should be strapped to a wagonload of powder, not the boy."

Audley paused and looked out of the window, as if to check that George remained shackled to the wagon.

"I have a task that I need you to undertake. You have met Mr St. John?"

Maven remained silent.

"I would appreciate an answer when I ask you a question. Viscount Bolingbroke. You know him, I think? Unlike him, I am a man of my word, and when I am instructed by a higher authority to undertake a mission I seek to complete it even though it may be at some cost to my reputation. I think in that respect you and I have something in common, if your reputation is to be believed."

Maven ignored him. "You are reputed to be part of a Jacobite plot, sir."

If Maven was hoping to inflame the man's temper he was mistaken.

"Jacobite, Hanoverian, Whig, Tory. What, in the end, is the difference? Let us be perfectly honest with each other Maven. Those who aspire to high office are primarily interested in obtaining power for themselves and those who have secured power are primarily interested in retaining it. Walpole, Stanhope and their Whig cronies have courted the Elector well for he has chosen to overlook their treacherous natures and they stand to prosper when the prizes are distributed. For the good of our country there is only one way that outcome can be stopped."

"So you plan to kill the King? All that will do is get you hanged. Or do you pretend to assume the monarch's role yourself?"

This time Audley exploded with rage.

"Do not mock me with your feigned ignorance. You know very well that there are at least fifty others with a stronger claim on the throne than an offensive little foreigner. For heaven's sake, even the late Queen herself did not want that odious upstart to succeed her. His presence here is nothing but political expediency designed to bring the Whigs to power."

"So you would have the Pretender returned from Bar-le-Duc?"

"At least he has a proven blood line."

"And his religion?"

"Pah! What is religion but control of the populace after all? Catholic, Protestant. I hardly see the Pope invading these shores do you? What I do see are the fires that have burned across the nation these last few weeks. The fires that tell us the people are seriously questioning "King" George. If James were to row ashore today then I know who would be receiving the crown tomorrow and it would not be a German who has had a dozen years to learn our language yet still fails to make himself understood."

Before he could continue the argument they were disturbed by the return of Corporal Dench, bearing a silver tray with a bottle of wine and a glass. The Corporal sneered at Maven as Audley continued.

"A sensible decision for you would be to follow my orders. Then you shall be released with your friends there," he said, nodding toward the window.

"If you murder the King what will happen? Should you not wait for the French to land before you take action?"

"If we wait for the French we shall forever be a pawn in some shabby little intrigue. Action from this side of the channel is the only way. Removing the Elector will force Louis' hand and he shall have no choice but to provide the support he has so long promised."

Maven was out of his depth and decided he had nothing further to add. Audley apparently drew the same conclusion.

"Maven, I urge you to see sense. Shrewsbury has sent you to head off our plans and you have failed. Sadly for you and your employer, I shall be proceeding with the action and you are no longer in a position to stop me. You do have a choice, though."

"A choice?"

"You have met Kathrine, Lady Cooper, a woman who has promised herself to me."

"I think not –"

"A woman who has promised herself to me! Yes, indeed, of her own free will, sir. She would not thank me for telling you but our marriage was proposed and accepted a long time ago. When you see her again I suggest you ask her to tell you her story. She has led an interesting life. No, Maven, the lady is not in a position to withdraw. There is a contract in place and we shall be married."

Audley fixed him with a stare. He had the most penetrating eyes Maven had ever seen.

"And my choice is what?"

"Come along, Captain. Surely you can predict the task I am about to set you. Do it well."

"My life depends on it?"

"Good heavens no, Captain. I would not presume to expect you to put yourself above that of a lady, even a common whore. You are a man of honour, are you not? No, if you fail to deliver Kathrine to me then your young friends out there will remain strapped to the powder. Even after it is ignited. The coronation is tomorrow morning, sir. I wish to be married while the German's body is still warm. After the wedding we shall blow him to pieces. By then you and your acquaintances will be many miles from London, if you have any sense."

21

"What, may I ask, is this?"

Henry St John Bolingbroke brandished a small piece of material at Shrewsbury, who took it from his guest and examined it closely.

"It appears to be the coronation favour. It has the union arms on it. Here, see?" said Shrewsbury, handing it back.

"Yes, I can very well see, Charles, but why on earth would you approve this ridiculous motto? King George, our defender from Pope and Pretender. Really, sir, I should have thought you would know better."

"It strikes the appropriate chord. I was rather pleased with it to tell you the truth."

"It represents an incitement to riot."

"Nonsense. It merely panders to the populist tone. Nothing wrong with a little national pride. Besides which, I have heard that the pinning on of the colour as a breast knot gives rise to all sorts of flirtatious opportunities with the ladies. I am surprised you have not discovered this yourself."

"I am beginning to wonder if you have not lost sight of the gravity of your office. Have you not received the reports from the country? Norwich, York, Worcester to name just a few. More or less everywhere, in fact, where the eyes of the people are not clouded with the stinking smoke of this diabolical city."

"We have been through this, more than once. You moved too soon in your enthusiasm for action. Stirred up feelings. In Audley, for example. Now there is a gentleman who has run out of control. He believes the French are about to invade us yet Louis has long since accepted the legitimacy of the Elector. For now, at least, the French represent no threat to this country. You knew of this as soon as Peterborough returned with the signed agreement. You should have guarded against the tendency to rely on the wishful thinking of zealots who reside impatiently in Lorraine. No, Harry, your actions have put the King I danger and it is a situation entirely of your own making."

"And so we are to stand aside and let this foreigner usurp the throne of our great country?"

They paused while Shrewsbury coughed into his handkerchief.

"The deed is done, sir."

"And what is to become of me?"

"You made yourself an enemy of Marlborough and the Hanoverians when you forced the Treaty, though if you could find a neutral observer they would no doubt agree your reasons were laudable. But whilst you advanced England's cause you hurt Hanover. I expect the King will repay that ill favour as soon as he can. What is it that you are most fearful of, Harry? The loss of your status? I fear you must reconcile yourself to that fact, as, in the end, must all your cohorts, for your status is lost already. Will you flee?"

"Where on earth shall I go? France? No, I shall throw myself upon a statesman's mercy."

"You will end up in the Tower if Marlborough has any say in the matter. Nonetheless, I am sure the Elector recognises repentance when he sees it, even if he does need to have our correspondence translated into French before he understands it."

"Yes, there is a certain irony in the King of England being unable to speak this island's language," said Bolingbroke, grinning and then continued, "I hope you shall be fine bedfellows. You know his people are already drafting an Act that will allow him to leave these shores and return home? It is unthinkable. Never before has the monarch been allowed to desert the country."

"It does not seem entirely unreasonable in the circumstances. He is a Hanoverian. Should he not be permitted to return and see his family once in a while?"

"His dearest wife, you mean? I should not have thought she is his reason for returning to Hanover. His contempt for her is well known. He would not dare to use that poor woman as an excuse to change the laws of our nation."

"Perhaps you ought to think of his absence as an opportunity to fan the flames of discontent. If, as you say, there is a will in the country to restore the bloodline then what is another year?

One might look upon his coronation as a call to arms for those who have yet to declare."

Gideon Crouch entered the room after the most perfunctory of knocks. He paused at Bolingbroke's shoulder, raised his hand delicately to his mouth and cleared his throat. Crouch was aware of the depths to which Bolingbroke's reputation had plummeted and it was acknowledged among the administrative class that the Viscount merited no respect at all now. Shrewsbury summoned Crouch across with an impatient wave of his hand and the clerk slid around to the far side of the desk. He bent down close to his employer's ear and whispered discreetly. Bolingbroke fidgeted uncomfortably in his seat, unaccustomed to being left out of important conversations. The Duke waved his clerk away. The message delivered, Crouch straightened up and left the room, casting a casual and less than respectful glance in the guest's direction.

"He is a mite too clever for his own good, that one," said Bolingbroke.

"He has been a loyal servant for many years, sir. His presence is an asset not a liability, which is more than I can say for most of the unreliable rapscallions who demand cash from the nation in exchange for their dubious information."

Bolingbroke began to stand and excuse himself but the Duke bade him remain where he was.

"Stay, at least for a while yet. Crouch brings news that you need to hear. It would seem that your friend remains active. They are gathered in Essex."

"Audley retains a fondness for the county."

"Don't be coy, Henry. You know what he plans. He was supposed to have been stopped."

"Audley and his tiny militia are no threat to anyone. So he robs a few Jacobites. I wouldn't have thought that bothered you overmuch."

"Henry, you should have ended this nonsense by now. Audley does not understand the subtlety of the situation and I fear he believes he still has your support. Does he?"

"You know very well he does not. I have made it perfectly clear that he no longer enjoys either my patronage or protection."

"I should like you to meet with him again. The coronation is tomorrow and his continued freedom makes me nervous. I should prefer it if Audley were to be persuaded to remain out of London. You are the only one he will listen to. The groups that were riding from Worcester and from Norwich have been apprehended. Their leaders are in custody. He is utterly isolated now."

"Then why do you not complete the job and have Audley arrested as well? Then you can be reassured of the King's safety once and for all?"

"Come, Henry, you are a master diplomat. You know very well that would be a clarion call to Lorraine. It is not a trap I intend to fall into. Arresting a few unknown merchants from the shires is one thing but a peer of the realm? I think not. No, Audley must withdraw his threat voluntarily. I should like him to speak out publicly against the others. Go to him. Appeal to his better nature. He is a gentleman, after all."

"And if that fails?"

"Offer him money," smiled Shrewsbury, "he is a little short at the moment."

After Bolingbroke had departed, Shrewsbury summoned Crouch to return.

"You surprised me with your news, Crouch. I had not thought the clerks would have finished their work so quickly."

"We entrusted the task to our very best man, sir," smirked Crouch.

"Quite. Do you have the translation?"
Crouch retrieved from his pocket the original papers that William Taylor had brought them. The bundle had now doubled in size, enhanced by a translation from French into English.

"And the scribe? He can be trusted?"

"He knows this is a matter of national importance, sir. I would guarantee his silence with my own life."

The Duke paused then got the message.

"Thank you Crouch. Am I mentioned?"

"No, sir, you are not mentioned in the translation. However, the Viscount is featured, quite extensively."

"Is there any ambiguity?"

"Not now."

"Then his fate is sealed. Put the English version in the safe, Crouch. We shall most probably not require it but it will be useful to retain. The gentlemen at Lloyds Coffee House call it insurance, I believe."

"Quite so, sir. And the French version?"

Shrewsbury took the original French language papers from Crouch and turned to face the fire, thought for a second then threw the letters into the flames.

22

Audley remained inside the house while Maven was escorted back to the wagon. He was shackled about the wrists and left in the care of Summersby and Dench, and the latter took great pleasure in prodding Maven in the kidneys with a baton whenever he required him to move, which was often. There was a great deal of movement as men went this way and that preparing, it seemed, for battle. Audley had surrounded himself with some experienced officers and they knew how to lay in supplies for a campaign for it was not just weapons and ammunitions that passed before him but food and drink and clean clothes and blankets, and Maven saw what appeared to be a set of surgeon's instruments that clanged noisily in a black case. This is what happens, he thought, when you allow an army to disband in an unruly manner.

While Maven stood, his captors took the opportunity to rest their legs. Summersby sat upright on a wooden chest observing proceedings. Dench, uncharacteristically, lounged on a sack of grain that had been dumped alongside a number of others by the entrance to the stable. Maven stood there for perhaps twenty minutes and could feel his legs tiring. Then the sudden appearance of Audley had the company active. Men scurried back and forth, horses were brought forward, saddled and Audley's tiny army made itself ready for the journey. The driver assigned to the wagon stepped up on his board with trepidation and stole a nervous glance at the cargo. Then Maven felt the warmth of a horse alongside him and Audley leaned down.

"It is eight miles from here to London, Captain."

Maven did not answer.

"Don't expect to ride, unless you fancy your chances on the powder wagon."

"I'll walk. Why don't you untie the boy? He bears you no ill will."

"We will hand him back to your task is complete. Kathrine will see you return and you will tell her the boy is safely back with his family. How impressed she will be. Then you will advise her that she has been mistaken, that I am not the beast she pretends and that she should commit to the marriage as she has promised."

"You do not know her very well."

"I know her very well indeed, Maven. She pretends to be an independent lady of means but she is a whore. All her deportment is learned and not yet perfected. Everyone in London knows where she came from."

"And that means she must marry you?"

"She is promised to me. Besides, no other man will have her. That is how it works."

"She will no more accept my opinion than she would yours."

"That may not be a problem. All you have to do is detain her in her home. I shall take her from there."

"Kidnap her?"

"The boy's life for hers. It is not an unreasonable arrangement for you. It is not as if she is going to die. His fate, on the other hand, is sealed if you fail to honour your side of the bargain."

Then Audley's attention was diverted by something on the far side of the yard. He wheeled around and was gone.

Dench busied himself with his preparations, darted into the stable and returned astride one of the horses. He prodded Maven with the baton again and told him to wait alongside the wagon. George was terrified, his eyes were wide and his brow ran wet with perspiration. His whole body trembled.

"Relax as best you can, George. I will get you out."

Lancaster rode around to face Maven.

"The corporal and I have loaded pistols and we shall be quite pleased to use 'em. You will find that I am neither as obliging nor as patient as the guv'nor."

"That business in Smithfield. Was it you or the servant who was responsible?"

"Mr Pinchbeck? Ah but there is a man who takes pride in his work. That fellow Webb resisted somewhat as I recall and Barclay needed to help him finish the job. He did not take his punishment well. I wonder how you might behave in the same situation, Captain. I do very much hope you shall give us cause to find out."

They waited by the front gate of Hereford House while Audley and a detachment of four riders departed and made brisk progress down the main road in the direction of the city. Then the wagon lurched forward, the horses struggling under its heavy weight. It would be slow progress and they would be lucky to be in the city by nightfall, thought Maven. Walking behind the wagon Makepeace Matthews, the odd boy from the Royal Oak, turned and smiled his twisted smile at their captive.

Maven estimated that it was about a mile to the Queens Head where he had left Prospero and although the bonds around his wrists were tight and uncomfortable he decided he could survive for the half hour or so that it would take them to get there. Once their guard was down he would make his escape.

They waited for the wagons and the troops to set off and followed closely in their wake. Lancaster and Dench flanked him and, as he expected their attentions began to wane within a quarter of a mile. His confidence, however, was misplaced, for as they reached the White Hart Lancaster and Dench stopped their mounts and allowed the convoy to go forward without them. At its rear rode Nathaniel Barclay and the three of them watched as his dark outline faded into the distance, his black hat resting on his head at a jaunty angle. Lancaster jumped down and tied his mount on the sturdy bar that had been erected outside the tavern for that purpose. He entered the tavern and then returned a few seconds later with a burly, middle-aged man whose grubby breeches were tied around the waist with string. The newcomer was a beast of a man and his forearms were thick and coated in a dark mane. He had a nose that had been broken several times but there was a good deal about his demeanour that suggested he had never suffered defeat in a tavern brawl, though many had tried. Lancaster smirked.

"This is the constable, Maven, so you'd better behave yourself."

"Why should I be concerned? I've done nothing wrong."

"What a short memory you have, sir. Trespassing, breaking and entering, burglary. I don't recall that you settled your account at the Bald Stag. And I reckon that wench you were swiving will be claiming rape before the day is out. Nothing wrong, sir? They'll throw the book at you come the next assize."

Lancaster turned to the constable.

"Colonel Summersby has asked that this man be locked up for the safety of the parish. Mind you take care with him, though, for he is the very worst kind. A half-pay officer without gainful employment. He seems to have forgotten that the war is over," and for Maven's benefit, he continued, "'tis all very well raping and pillaging on a continental field but when you come back to your own land you are expected to behave yourself, sir."

"What about the deal? What about Kathrine?"

"Leave her to me, Maven. As far as Audley is concerned, you tried to escape and we had to shoot you. You gave us no choice." He began untying the horse. "Good luck with British justice."

The constable seized Maven by the hands and dragged him across the road. He offered no resistance and soon they were facing the cage, the door of which hung open in readiness. The constable spoke with a countryside burr.

"Get yourself in there, zur and you behave now."

A hard shove in the back sent Maven into his confinement and he rolled to the wet floor.

"I'd wager there'll be someone along some time later with some scraps for you to feast on, zur. Usually is."

Maven understood perfectly what lay in store for him as the day wore on. It was common practice for the local populace to bring stale and rotten food to hurl at the men who found themselves locked up in a village cage. Strangers especially were treated to a pelting. This particular cell offered all the temptation a villager could wish for since it was open to the elements on all sides and even the roof was nothing but bars. He looked up at the grey clouds that threatened more rain. The constable waddled back towards the tavern where, no doubt, there was a large and complimentary breakfast waiting for him. Maven felt the packet of paper in his pocket. Lancaster, incompetent as ever, had failed to search him.

The view across Golden Square was one of a perfect autumn, he thought. The leaves on the trees had turned but not yet fallen. Golden, indeed, and a sight of some beauty, he thought.

Bolingbroke stood in the doorway and examined the gathering clouds with a critical eye. He had a long way to travel and needed to return to London by nightfall. His black coach waited by the front door and his father stood by the vehicle checking with the driver the route he would take.

"Harry, are you sure about this?"

Bolingbroke was not at all sure but his decision had been made and he was not about to reveal any sign of weakness to his father.

"Father, it is the final step. I need to be sure that Audley is stopped. If he proceeds as planned then he shall bring me down."

"And no one else can do this?"

"No one else will be able to get close enough to him."

"I should like you to take some people with you. For your safety."

"No, father, I must go alone. It is a question of trust. Besides, I have Wentworth, here," he said, indicating the driver, "and he is armed and strong enough to protect us both. Please do not worry about me. I shall be back later this evening."

He climbed into the coach and closed the door.

"There is a more important aspect, you know," said his father, "for if you are delayed on your return and you miss the coronation it will be taken as a snub. If you insult the King it will increase the resolve of those who would see you exiled. Is this not a trap that Shrewsbury has laid for you?"

"Of course it is a trap but I have no way of preventing an outrage unless I go and see Audley myself. Rest assured that if I am delayed I shall seek a safe passage to the continent directly!"

It rained heavily for about an hour and then drizzled steadily for another two before finally stopping. Maven sat in an ever increasing puddle and leaned against the iron bars of the cell. He stared miserably at the White Hart tavern. Contrary to his expectations nobody had pelted him with fruit and nobody had sworn or spat at him. In fact, he had been completely ignored as the village went about its business. Anger fomented within him. He had earlier kicked against the strong iron and tried to release his bonds by rubbing the rope against the metal but he gave up quite soon when progress was non-existent. He fretted about George and he fretted about the treachery of his former colleague. Then the constable appeared again, tumbling out of the front door of the White Hart in a state of some drunkenness. He staggered over to the cage and made a great show of walking around and examining Maven from all four sides.

"Y'alright, zur?"

Maven nodded.

"Tis stopped rainin' so you should cheer up a bit. Don't you be goin' nowhere, now. I shall be back later to zee 'ow you are."

Then he roared with laughter and wandered off, slipping occasionally in the wet mud.

About half an hour later Maven saw Mr Rogers appear, once again in the cart pulled by the pony that was too small for the task. To make matters worse, he had a passenger. As they drew to a halt, Rogers puffed out his pink cheeks in a great show of exertion. The passenger eased himself out of the trap and jogged over to the cage, splashing in the puddles of rainwater that lay upon the grass. It was Salem Osgood, from the Bald Stag. He grabbed the bars with both hands and looked down on the hunched figure.

"Now, sir, you didn't strike me as the criminal sort."

Maven looked up at Osgood. If he had come to heap more misery upon him then Maven hoped that he would get on with it.

"They say Summersby had you chucked in 'ere."

Maven nodded.

"That bumblin' idiot in the pub don't know any better than to do what the Colonel tells 'im. I reckons we needs to get you out of there before you die o' the vapours."

Osgood's intention encouraged Maven to stir.

"You were at the inn, Osgood. One of the charges laid against me is rape, for heaven's sake. What does the girl say?"

"Molly? I shouldn't take no notice of what she says, sir. She does favours for the Colonel. Word is that he paid her to look after you last night. Famous for it she is. Don't you worry none about 'er."

Maven's relief was tempered by the assault on his pride.

"And the landlord? What about the bill?"

"Twas 'im that sent me down 'ere. Pay 'im next time you pass through, sir."

It all seemed too good to be true.

"Do you have the key to this thing?" asked Maven.

"No, sir, that I do not. But there'll be a spare one in the tavern there. You just wait patiently while old Rogers fetches it."

Maven's would be rescuer had indeed disappeared.

"Mr Osgood, how are you to know that I can be trusted?"

"Two reasons, sir. One is that the one eyed scally that was supposed to pay Molly kept the guinea for 'imself and that makes 'im a wrong 'un 's far as we is all concerned."

"And the second?"

"The bastard is ridin' my 'orse, sir."

The same boy who had proved so friendly on his arrival was again in attendance at the King William but this time there was no conversation. Maven ran into the yard and demanded Prospero be prepared as quickly as possible. He begged forgiveness that he had no money to pay the boy but had to get on the road quickly. Maven clambered up onto the huge beast without elegance and turned to thank the boy. Most of the traffic headed towards London. There were vehicles that carried whole families and the mood was joyous and celebratory. Maven dug his heels deep into Prospero's flanks to speed him past the singing and the laughter. Thickening grey clouds had once again stolen upon him and more rain threatened. At the Spread Eagle Inn the road forked right to the marsh, to the way he had come up and the north eastern approach to the city. A drier, higher road lay straight ahead. In terms of mileage it was a longer route to go south through Mile End New Town. He imagined Audley and Summersby discussing their options at this very spot. Then Maven kicked Prospero and span to the right, to the marsh, reasoning that if the insurgents had gone the other way he would steal some time on them and if they had been foolish enough to take this road he would doubtless find them marooned in the waterlogged expanse.

The rain started again as he left the village of Whipps Cross and the river valley opened out in front of him. It was a light rain carried by the wind and it stung his face and froze his knuckles and made him wish he had gloves on. He had to screw up his eyes to see ahead. Around him, all was silent and, aside from the same wading birds he had passed on the way up, he was quite alone for no one, not even the knowledgeable locals would venture out this way when the ground was so wet. He rode on slowly and allowed the enormous animal to take care with its footing. The wet clay sat just a few inches thick on top of a hard, compacted layer of earth and the surface was treacherous. Prospero slipped and slid and Maven, never a confident horseman at the best of times, decided in the end to get down and lead his mount on foot.

As he reached almost the exact centre of the open ground the rain got heavier, the wind dropped and the squalls became stair rods. He felt the ice-cold wetness go right through his coat and shirt and run down his back in rivulets. His breeches offered no resistance and where his coat hung open the material was sodden and stuck to his thighs. Yet more water trickled down into his boots. He plodded on relentlessly, making little headway. Then he saw it and his spirits rose. Just off the track, laying in the mud and soaked through with rain was a black tricorn hat, seemingly discarded, perhaps caught by a gust of wind and lifted off its owner's head or perhaps left there as some sort of sign. He stopped and picked it up. In truth, it was much like any other black hat but he knew instinctively that this had been worn by George Trescothick when he had been strapped to the cart. He looked around. Cart tracks and hoof prints were being washed away by the force of the downpour but faintly, just barely visible on the surface of the unmade road, there was evidence that a cart, possibly a heavy wagon, had left the road, for the track at the very edge of the marsh was that of a single wheel. About ten yards ahead the parallel set of wheels rejoined the track and the tufts of wet grass there lay flatter than their neighbours, as if something heavy had lain upon them. Had the youngster had the good sense to drop his hat to the ground when no one was looking? Maven hoped so, for the alternative scenario he had in his mind was too much to bear. As if the gods were rewarding him for his outlook, the rain eased at that moment and had stopped completely by the time he had walked the few yards to collect Prospero's reins. Maven turned, slipped on the wet orange mud then regained his balance and strode toward London with greater purpose, shrugging off the tiredness and the fear that had enveloped him while he had been in the cage.

23

When the caravan reached the village of Hackney Lieutenant Maddox raised his right arm to bring the procession to a halt. He had eschewed the earlier offer of a guide. The young officer knew the road well and the presence of thirty six armed men in three wagons was a reliable guarantee for his safety. They pulled out of the Artillery Ground and lumbered slowly past the plague pit and onto Old Street and St Agnes le Clare. Boredom set in within a few minutes and the men began their singing to pass the time, a low murmuring at first, which settled into the usual repertoire of battle tunes and ribald rhymes. He tried his best to learn the words that wafted out of the covered wagons but his heart wasn't in it and as hard as he tried he could not see the attraction.

The tiny village, a ribbon of dwellings and huts either side of the muddy road, was asleep at this hour, or at least it appeared to be. They turned onto the Ware Road and went north and he looked all the while at the weather that threatened to roll over them from the west. He had promised them a break and some ale and when they came upon what looked like a suitable establishment he raised his hand. The ruddy face of a corporal peered hopefully out of the first wagon. Maddox nodded at him and the corporal returned to the men.

"Get yerselves out. Come on, there's grog abaht!"

Metal studded boots scraped on bare wood as they clattered down, dragging their rifles behind them. Maddox dismounted and tied the horse on the post outside the alehouse. He went inside to seek out the landlord. Presently, he returned, having calmed the tapster with payment and a promise of good behaviour.

"So, where are we headed, sir?" asked a young private.

"Clapton," replied Maddox, "the village on the edge of the Lea Marsh."

"Are we arrestin' someone?"

"You shall find out soon enough. Now sup, for I cannot guarantee when you shall see your next meal."

The mood changed when they left the tavern and restarted the journey. The road ahead of them cleared as villagers dived into their properties fearing the presence of a recruiting team. Maddox led from the front and did his best to pretend that they were not spied on from every window even though he felt the eyes upon him. In the wagons, the singing was replaced by whispered conversations. Maddox was glad he had installed a corporal in each vehicle to stem the worst excesses of the men's imagination.

In the distance he could see the village. He wheeled his horse around and trotted back to the rearmost wagon, bringing it to a halt. The men filed out and lined up in a vaguely organised manner and then, their orders received, fanned out to guard the road and discourage anyone from following the other two wagons, which lumbered on towards Clapton. Maddox left them to their duty and galloped after the rest of the company, grateful to expend some of the nervous energy that had been building within him. On the edge of the village he ordered them all out and sent the wagons away filled with the women and children who chose to be taken to a place of safety. Not everyone trusted the red uniforms with their household possessions, however, and Maddox had to agree that those who wished could remain behind as long as they stayed off the street and away from their windows. He had primed his pistol to reinforce his authority and his self-confidence swelled with every utterance.

The redcoats spread out and found hiding places behind barrels, in doorways and alleyways and in sheds and parlours. Maddox stationed himself in a house that looked directly down the High Street and onto the bleak and chilly marsh where he could make out the dark shapes in the distance. Beside him sat his Sergeant chewing on a clay pipe, waiting for the officer to give the order.

*

Colonel Summersby left his caravan behind and rode ahead to the village of Clapton and found it deserted. Maddox watched as he crossed the bridge and walked his horse up and down the quiet street then paused outside the Royal Oak. The group that Audley had promised would meet them here was not present and Summersby had cursed aloud, a soldier's instinct for disaster alerted.

"We shall continue alone," counselled Audley when Summersby had returned.

"Is that wise?"

"What other choice do we have? I have not hauled this load across such devilish terrain only to abandon the cargo to a bunch of peasants. And we certainly do not want to take it back. No, Colonel, we shall proceed. We still have a task to perform. Have the men put into the Oak as we planned. They are expecting us here and it will be good to start early in the morning with the men refreshed."

Audley sat imperiously on his mount and observed his adjutant with a pained expression while he roused the men. Summersby trotted around the straggling company and told them all what had happened, confessing that their fears had been realised. Summersby had not lost his touch for leadership, however, and his method of imparting the bad news had the effect of galvanising the men, stirring within them the bloody minded spirit of battles past when they had been let down and hopelessly outnumbered and yet had delivered victory and had taken the prizes they believed they had so richly deserved. Dench took up the challenge and went around the men on foot, cajoling and threatening and demanding. Though there was no enemy in sight they would meet one soon enough, he told them.

"Our great country needs you like it has never needed you before. The rest of the bloody cowards are too scared to come here and fight with you, so it's down to you lads, down to your sorry souls. Dig deep, dig deeper than you ever have before, boys, for tomorrow you will make history and your names shall be writ large on monuments. What say you?"

"Aye!" shouted twenty men in unison but Dench had the first stirrings within him that this was already a lost cause and in his belly he knew that this ragged little army would be no match for whatever the authorities chose to put in its way. The Corporal looked for Lancaster and Barclay, as sorry a pair of officers that ever graced a battlefield, he believed, but they were all he had. While Dench waited for them to give their orders the disreputable couple spoke with Audley, sitting astride their horses twenty yards away.

Alone, out of their earshot was the mysterious servant, Pinchbeck, on board a grey mount that twitched nervously. He glanced with disdain at each of member of the motley crew that had been assembled to serve his master's wishes. There was lively and enthusiastic talk among the men of a thirst quencher at the pub. They knew their only hope now was to stir up trouble at every village they passed and to add to their ranks small numbers of fighting men so that when they reached St James's they would present a formidable force, the sort of riotous assembly for which England was famous.

George and Claudette were bound to each other. She glanced at him and despite their misery and their fear George saw, for the first time, that she no longer buried her humanity beneath a defensive cloak of aggression. Though he could not find the words to describe how he felt, he knew that both their lives had changed for ever, whatever the outcome might be. The subtle change in Claudette's eyes and the softening of her look told him that she knew it too. She shivered and he was desperate to reach out for her. When the wagon had slid off the road into the saturated ground he had thought at first that she would end up crushed under the load but somehow the vehicle had remained upright, albeit at a precarious angle. The men had been ordered to untie them and then he had been forced to help them take the cargo off, leaving the wagon light enough to push back onto the narrow road. It had been no easy task, for the left side had sunk so low into the mire that it had to be hauled out and it had taken all of their number to bodily lift the thing up and heave it forward. His reward had been to help reload the wagon but at least she was spared the punishment of being strapped to the lethal consignment. As she walked alongside the wagon, the bandage had departed and her wound had become dirty and cold. She dragged her injured foot behind her and must have been in excruciating pain but she hid it, for her pride would deny her enemy the satisfaction of seeing her suffer.

Half a mile behind them, Maven stomped across the sodden ground dragging the reins of the reluctant Prospero, anxious to reach the other side of the morass before darkness or the heavens decided to pour down upon him again. His thighs hurt and he had a pain in his side where he had expended so much effort without replacing it with food. Then, in the fading light, he saw the feint outline of the wagon and small black dots of men fussing around it. He slowed his pace and, instinctively, crouched lower in case they should see him. Distant memories stirred within him.

Maddox fretted about the company. It was all they could round up at such short notice and he wished the Duke had given him the order sooner since there were better men left behind. His heart raced at the thought of the skirmish he was about to start and the risks of failure that such a fight brought with it. They would be shooting a Colonel, for heaven's sake.

He planned to wait for all the mercenaries to be locked into the Royal Oak before they moved in for the capture. The redcoats remained well hidden. Maddox had breathed a sigh of relief that none of his men had gone for glory and opened fire. That none of the villagers had opened a window on the upper floors to which they had been confined impressed him even more. Hiding in a small white cottage and peering through the small panes of glass, Maddox watched as the enemy hove into view. He was disappointed at how dishevelled and disorganised they appeared. Then Audley and Colonel Summersby had ridden up and down the village searching for something and seemed not to find it. They rode back to their men. He watched as Audley, Summersby and Lancaster conversed but they were too far away to hear what was said. The Lieutenant looked at the Sergeant and the Sergeant shrugged his shoulders in a should-we-shouldn't-we go and get them gesture. Maddox shook his head. Orders were orders.

They turned when the black coach clattered noisily into the village from the London Road and Maddox sighed inwardly, relieved that the corporal he had stationed on the road had done as he was told and allowed it through. Its wheels rattled and splashed across the ground, spraying muddy rainwater about. It paused in the centre of the village while its driver looked around, unsettled by the absence of people. Then the front door to the Royal Oak opened and the landlord's hand beckoned the coach forward. Do as you were told, tapster, don't lose your nerve, thought the officer. The driver snapped the reins gently and the coach eased into the courtyard of the inn. A boy ran out and grabbed the reins to hold the horses steady. There was a lull as the redcoats waited for the occupant to step down. Nothing stirred for thirty seconds then the coach door opened and a gentleman leaned out and stepped down gingerly, looking about him. He trod lightly across the muddy ground and slipped into the inn by the side door. Maddox tensed. This was it. Had Audley's crowd seen the arrival?

Audley concluded his conversation with a grim-faced Captain Lancaster. Audley cursed volubly and voiced his disappointment that their allies had not materialised at the appointed time and place. He could not help feeling a secret regard for the Viscount, for Bolingbroke had said repeatedly that his influence was greater than his own. He had promised Audley that he would end up raging against the establishment alone and he had been right, after all.

Audley pursed his lips. They would wait overnight in this forsaken village and advance on London in the morning. As he was about to confirm the order they all heard the coach rattle into the village and turned to watch its progress.

"The coach is a good one for this road," said Lancaster.

"Let it be for a few minutes," said Audley, "There shall be no harm in making him wait, if its occupant is who I believe it to be."

Audley's mount shivered and stepped sideways, seemingly unnerved by something but it was Audley's unease that the animal had sensed. He wheeled the beast away and the other two followed him back to the men. Audley sat imperiously on his mount and observed his adjutant with a pained expression. Lancaster rode about and got the men formed up to cross the bridge. Much to the delight of the men he confirmed they would indeed stop overnight in the Royal Oak. It was an unlikely looking safe house but he assured them they would be fed and be given a warm bed. Four advance riders went over first, Lancaster, Barclay, Summersby and the Colonel's aide, who had seen some service and who could be trusted to hold his nerve. They went one at a time and the last of them shouted back that the wagon would get across but there would not be much room on either side. The gradient was quite steep here as the land climbed away from the river. Maddox watched them come. The perfect place for an ambush, he thought. Men travelling up hill move slowly. Moreover, men trapped in a narrow space have nowhere to go except forwards or back toward their companions. Maddox watched Lancaster glance across to Lieutenant Barclay and the look told him that the mercenary shared his opinion.

Though they planned to wait until the enemy was safely inside the inn, the Sergeant had them ready in seconds, just in case. He hissed, "Load up and get your bayonets ready!" and the vicious metal objects, sharpened in expectation, were slotted onto the ends of the weapons. As they had practised and drilled over and over to the point of boredom, each man reached for the paper-wrapper and tore off the bullet with his teeth. Even those that had seen action before had never got used to the salty, foul tasting powder that leaked onto the tongue and there was a great deal of discreet spitting. Maddox watched the youngest soldier, a boy of no more than fifteen, slight and under-nourished. He struggled to open the musket's frizzen and Maddox fought against the temptation to stride over and help him, especially when he caught the Sergeant's withering glance. Suddenly the boy got the knack and in a moment had dropped a pinch of powder onto the pan and resealed the frizzen. They waited for him and on the nod from the Sergeant the company rested the brass butts of their weapons on the ground and poured the remainder of their powder down the barrel. Each of them leaned over the end of the weapon and spat in the bullet. They withdrew the brass tipped metal rods from their hoops and rammed the ball and the powder together firmly in the breech. It took only seconds and they were upright and facing front again. In the silence, a small boy poked his face out of a window and Maddox hissed at him to get himself hidden.

"Front ranks kneel or get yer heads blown off!" whispered the Sergeant suppressing his urge to shout the order with all the venom and force he could muster. But this was battle at close quarters, a genuine skirmish with the lightest of infantry, and there was a need for silence. He whispered the order. Maddox winced as their boots clattered on the surface. Two lines of redcoats spread loosely across the road at the top of the village hidden in gaps between houses and behind barrels and carts. The front rank dropped to one knee as they were instructed while the row behind them took aim.

The driver of the wagon was too anxious to get his vehicle across the bridge and did not line it up squarely. The hub of the axle on the right side jammed against the parapet of the bridge and the wagon had to be eased back so as to avoid damaging the wheel. It was growing darker and the chilly evening was beginning to creep across the marsh. Dench shouted at them to hurry. The tired and bedraggled company squeezed past the stricken wagon one at a time and began to trek slowly into the village. The only sound was the splashing of hooves and boots in the puddles. The men walked in a strung out line. It was an effort for them to get up the slope.

No one, least of the all the youngster, was quite sure how it happened, but he fumbled with his musket and it went off sending a ball towards the bridge, where it struck Barclay in the upper arm and the shock made his horse rear up, clawing at the air with its hooves.

"Forward! Quick as you can!"

This was Lancaster, shouting as loud as he could at his three colleagues. He leaned across and grabbed at the reins of Barclay's mount and did his best to settle the mare. Barclay recovered his composure and seized control. Then as redcoats appeared around them he and Lancaster were off, leaving their colleagues confused and alone. They hurtled through the redcoats that emerged from their hiding places and scattered them left and right. The wagon was trapped on the bridge and Audley was sheltered behind it with a handful of his men. The Sergeant looked at Maddox and Maddox had half a second to make the right call. His plans to offer the rebels an honourable surrender were forgotten in the heat of the battle and the humiliation of two riders charging through his line.

"Fire, damn you!"

The front row had had the good sense to stay low and from where they now stood their colleagues let go a volley over their heads, cutting down the second pair of riders and the driver of the wagon. Summersby was hit in the chest and slid ungracefully from his mount and hit the ground with blood pouring from his wound. His aide fared no better but somehow twisted in the saddle and caught his boot in the stirrup so that his panicking horse dragged him through the village. Audley's pathetic infantry was not only taken by surprise but, trapped by the wagon, they had nowhere to go except into the wet marsh or the river itself. Eight balls fired and eight hit a target, an incredible result. The rebels scattered left and right in a disorderly chaos. Dench waved his pistol around and tried to restore order but his shouts were in vain and went unheard.

"Front rank stand! Fire! Second rank reload!" ordered Maddox.

A second volley cut down another six of Audley's men, his best men, the few that had recognised the danger early enough and had tried to load their weapons. None of them succeeded. The redcoats re-loaded, fired and then broke up to go in search of the stragglers who had run back to the bridge and along the riverbank. They fixed their bayonets eagerly.

Tied to the wagon, George heard but did not see the musket fire and his initial relief that there was a solid object between them and the gunfire evaporated when he remembered what cargo the wagon carried. He looked around the side of the vehicle and saw that all was panic. Riders wheeled around, trying to find a way out of the melee and the men that had been so threatening earlier ran like children. The second volley was ruthless but, in truth, George knew that even he could have succeeded in hitting that target. The screams as men were struck were sickening and he ducked his head back in, his heart racing. Next to him, Claudette trembled. They fell to the ground and George set about undoing their damp canvas bonds.

"If they hit the powder then we're done for, little darlin'. We have to get ourselves away from here."

The straps were bound tightly, though, and even when she tore at them with her teeth they were not to be budged. George heaved at the wagon but force alone could not free them and she told him to stop for fear that he would break his wrists in trying. They crawled as far away from the back of the wagon as the canvas would allow them and sat there while the remnants of the mob regrouped around them.

In the fading light, Maven saw a flash and a sharp crack of a musket echoed all around. Distant memories stirred within him and he somehow expected the musket fire to be followed by ground-shaking cannons. He turned and leapt upon Prospero, kicked the beast into life and galloped towards the action, instinct winning out over self-preservation.

Prospero hurtled toward the clouds of smoke without fear, teeth bared as he charged forward, spattering wet mud into the air, urged on by his rider who could see now that the group defending the village had all the best cards. They were up a slope, had the cover of solid buildings and their enemy was trapped in a narrow pass. Moreover, he could see also that a wagon had cut off their retreat. Maven pulled Prospero up when he saw a mounted figure behind the wagon. It was Audley. His horse was frightened by the noise and, blind to the source of the confusion, it had become alarmed. Suddenly the rider gave up trying to find a way past the wagon and turned away from the fight, riding towards Maven at a gallop.

Audley rushed towards him and he held in his outstretched right hand a pistol. Unarmed, Maven had no choice but to take evasive action and he hauled Prospero off to the left, down the slight incline and into the long wet grass. The horse fell and twisted, hurling its rider to the ground with a dull bump. Maven felt the wind knocked out of him and lay there listening to the thudding of hooves on the ground nearby. Then, simultaneously, he heard a report from Audley's pistol and felt the rush of the ball skimming just a few feet past him. He let out a long breath and then looked up to see the back of the rider as he raced across the darkening marsh.

Carried by the light evening breeze from the bridge were the familiar wails of injured men, frightened men. Though he knew there could be no more than a dozen of them the noise they raised was similar to the nauseating legacy of the battlefields he had experienced often enough before. Some men moaned in agony while one cried for his mother. He sat up and looked around. Along the river, the redcoats were digging out the rebels and in the hand-to-hand combat the bayonets won every time. Thirty yards ahead he saw a redcoat who had discovered the wagon driver's mate. The rotund man had scuttled away at the first sign of danger, anxious to find a point at which to cross the water and make his way to safety. Now, the soldier stood over him, legs astride. All the pent up nervous energy of his tiny battle was released in his next action as the rifle was brought down bayonet first, spearing the victim in his ample belly. It was a necessary task in the absence of surrender but Maven was sickened nonetheless.

"Sir! Sir!"

The cry came from Maven's right and he recognised its owner immediately. He ran towards George, keeping his head down for fear of alerting the murderous bayonet-wielding redcoat or anyone who might fancy letting go with a firearm. He found the young couple huddled together in the shadow of the wagon.

"Keep your heads down," he said unnecessarily, "this will be over soon enough."

George's silent look towards the wagon reminded Maven what it was that it carried and he was urged into action. He rolled across the floor and his momentum brought him to the rear flap of the vehicle. He reached up and unhooked the catch. The flap was heavier than he anticipated and it slipped from his grasp, crashing loudly against the thick timber frame. He looked across the floor of the wagon then leaned in, arm outstretched and moving items aside until he found what it was he wanted. He tugged at a blanket that was wrapped around some metal object then pulled it towards him. Then with both hands he unwrapped his prize and breathed a sigh of relief that he had guessed correctly. Three rifles with bayonets fixed lay in front of him, the blades serrated and sharpened to malevolent points. He tore at the binds that held George fast to the lethal wagon.

"Get back there, as fast as you can," shouted Maven but George would not leave Claudette. Maven was non-plussed for a brief moment and then hurried to release the girl. George grabbed her by the wrist and dragged her across the road before their momentum sent them tumbling into a wet ditch. Maven followed them more sedately and sat down with them.

"I can't see Lancaster. Where is he?"

"He rode into the village first, sir. If he ain't dead then he must have gone straight through. Him and his mate."

The noise of gunfire and pained screams continued as individuals played out their own skirmishes.

"Captain! Behind you!"

One of the mercenaries, nothing more than a boy came at Maven with a pistol in his hand. As he got closer Maven recognised his assailant as Jess, the youngster who had followed him in Westminster.

"Put it down boy, you'll get yourself killed."

"You don't understand," shouted the Scot, blinded by rage.

"I understand enough to know you are on the wrong side, boy!"

"No sir, I do this for my countrymen. The English have failed us again!"

Jess came at him, his desire for revenge on Maven and the English in general outweighing his sense of reason. Maven sprang forwards and upwards and rushed the youth, hitting him hard in the midriff with his shoulder. Winded, Jess hit the ground and clutched his rib cage, groaning in agony. Maven hurled the pistol away and turned to look for George but found himself face to face with the redcoat who had recently slaughtered the driver.

"Put down your weapon soldier, the job is done," ordered Maven.

There was fear in the soldier's eyes and rational thought was crowded out by the desire to survive. The redcoat eased the weapon back, the better to get a good firm thrust, his bloodlust not yet sated. A voice called out, urgent and shouting from the river, accompanied by splashes as heavy boots ploughed their way through the water.

"Stop yer bleddy killin', damn you!"

The force of the Sergeant's voice carried on the breeze. Trescothick appeared beside Maven, wheezing with the effort and the fear of it all. He grabbed the soldier by the arm of his coat and dragged him away, hurled him to the floor and watched the rifle drop from the man's hands. Trescothick marched twenty yards down the road, confident that, with the battle, such as it was, over, he was now quite safe.

"Stand yerselves up and yer won't be shot!" he shouted.
Nothing happened. Maven signalled to George with his palm to stay where he was.

"Come on, I haven't got all bleddy night!"

There was movement then, as first one then two of Audley's men stood and raised their hands above their heads. They called to Trescothick that they were unarmed. A third man stood and made a great show of throwing down a musket.

"Cowards!" cried a familiar voice from the long grass.

Maven saw what was about to happen and launched himself at Trescothick, knocking him to the ground. At the same instant there was a small flash from the side of the road followed by a sharp report and the ball whistled over their heads. The opponent cursed and hurled his weapon aside before raising a second pistol and taking aim, this time at one of the men who had just surrendered. It was Dench who held the pistol out in front of him. He fired and the ball hit the deserter squarely in the centre of his chest and he fell back, arms outstretched. A group of redcoats had crossed the river now and, instinctively, they began shooting at the source of the action, a futile and disorganised volley.

"Stop!" Maven shouted at them, anxious that they should not ignite the powder wagon with a stray bullet and they would have turned their fire on him had Maddox not ordered them to desist. Dench was in open ground but hidden behind tall tufts of grass. His green and brown apparel combined with the worsening light gave him an effective camouflage and if he played the game correctly he would succeed in following his master to safety. Maven ran to the stricken wagon and seized another bayonet. He ran towards the area where he knew Dench to be. The Corporal moved then, running across the uneven ground bent double. He was trying to stay as close as he could to the road, away from the wet marsh that would suck him in. Maven watched him go then ran in the same direction, cutting off the Corporal's route to safety. Maven lay low in the grass. Dench stumbled and fell and let out a yell of frustration as he twisted his ankle. Maven stopped and turned towards him. They were no more than twenty yards apart but were invisible to each other.

"Give it up man! There is no way out of here for you."

"Damn you, Maven. You've no idea what you're involved in."

"Audley has abandoned you, Dench. He doesn't need you any more. Give yourself up."

"And hang for your pleasure? I don't think so."

The silence that followed concerned Maven for it could mean only one thing. He was proved right when Dench stood and took aim with his pistol, pointing the barrel directly at him. Instinctively, Maven made himself a moving target and ran first to the left and then to the right getting further from a weapon whose range was limited at the best of times. There was a loud bang and a ball whistled through the air grazing his upper arm. The strike stung him viciously and he felt the warm blood seep through his tunic. Ignoring the pain, he turned and ran directly at Dench and leapt upon him before the Corporal could prepare another shot. Maven swung his right fist and caught his enemy squarely on the jaw but instead of recoiling, Dench hurled the pistol aside and came at him with his fists clenched. His first blow was a calculated one, striking Maven on the arm where his blood had stained the fabric of the clothing. The pain made Maven cry out in agony. As he rolled over and readied himself to pursue Dench he saw Trescothick standing nearby with a musket and taking aim but Maven was angered and he wanted Dench for himself. In three long strides he was on the fleeing man again and this time the pugilist would not be allowed to get a punch in. The pair rolled over and Dench struggled to get out from under the taller man. Their eyes met briefly and neither man betrayed the slightest hint of fear. Maven raised the bayonet above his head and brought it down into Dench's neck. Blood spurted over the pair of them and Dench smiled up at him as the life drained from his body.

When the first shot had rung out the surly landlord threw himself to the floor and scrambled behind the safety of a heavy table. He had known as soon as the redcoats arrived there would be trouble. You cannot put weapons in men's hands and not expect them to be used, he had said to his wife. Bolingbroke had surprised himself at how calmly he had reacted, though he would admit to having been taken by surprise. To the landlord's evident alarm, Bolingbroke went to the window, his only concession to danger being to crouch low and drag himself across the stone flags on his hands and knees.

"Get yerself away from that window, sir. If there is gunfire then you shall be hit."

Bolingbroke waved the landlord away. He wanted to see who it was the soldiers had fired at. He could see that a ruffian had been struck but the gentleman he searched for could not be seen. Then, at the first full volley, the roar and the shock of the noise sent him reeling away from his vantage point. There was shouting and screaming just feet away from him and he was separated from it only by thin pieces of glass. His heart beat briskly and the adrenalin coursed through his body. The shots made the tavern tremble and fine brick dust settled on him like tiny snowflakes. Where was Audley? Not in the vanguard where he should have been, that was for sure. Bolingbroke had seen the one with the eye patch before and he knew him to be Audley's man but he was concerned by the master's absence. Only then did Bolingbroke drag himself away and slide across the floor to join the landlord where his agile politician's mind calculated the consequences of what he had just witnessed.

"I must get away."

"I bet you must. But you ain't goin' nowhere for the minute, sir, unless you wants your 'ead knocked off yer shoulders."

Then the landlord reached out a long arm and rescued from the dresser an almost full bottle of brandy and handed it to his guest, who swigged it greedily. Out of habit he checked the label. It was not of the quality he would have expected in Westminster but in the circumstances he felt it would do. He would wait to speak with the officer in charge.

It took a matter of minutes to round up the remainder of Audley's tiny army, but Corporal Dench had created enough of a disturbance and a delay to enable a small, wiry man to effect an escape across the river and into the northern edge of the village. By the time they realised Pinchbeck was missing it was too late and whilst the tavern had horses, the lack of able riders meant that they could not pursue him. In any case, Maddox decided, Pinchbeck was only a servant. In the meantime, the Lieutenant detailed his men efficiently and there was a roll call when the remaining prisoners were lined up against a wall. The corpses lined up on the road were proof enough for Maddox of the success of the mission until Maven pointed out that Audley was missing. The mercenaries who remained alive and chained together made a sorry sight as Maddox walked among them, illuminating each one with a torch and warming their cold faces with the flame.

Trescothick went to George and the older man hugged his son but could think of no words that might communicate what he felt. Instead, brushed some imaginary dirt from the front of the youngster's jacket then stroked his hair.

Maddox had detailed one man to keep an eye on the coach at all times while they hunted down the remaining men and his scout was sure that no one had gone in or out of the inn. Battle shy as he was, even Maddox knew that his men deserved a reward. He gave the order and the voracious pack descended on the front door of the inn. At that moment the side door opened and Bolingbroke eased himself out, checked left and right and walked to this carriage. From the loose box at the back of the yard appeared the face of Wentworth, the driver whom Bolingbroke had hoped might be his protector. He still shivered from the shock of the gun battle and the presence of redcoats with murderous intentions.

"Time to go, I think," hissed Bolingbroke.

Then Bolingbroke recognised Maven.

"Captain, good afternoon. This is not how it seems, you know."

"And how does it seem?"

"I was lured here under false pretences."

"Of course you were."

"Now I plan to take my leave."

Wentworth had assembled the horses and awaited his instructions. Maven looked at Maddox. As the serving officer and the one who carried the order, Maddox had precedence. The youngster stepped forward and opened the door of the coach and helped the Viscount into the vehicle. Then he reached into his tunic and withdrew a piece of paper that bore a red seal and handed it to Bolingbroke.

"Outside the village you will come across a company of my men. You will have seen them on the way up, I think. Give them this order. It will grant you safe passage."

Maven looked on incredulously as the coach turned in the yard and made ready to leave.

"Should we not have taken him with us?"

The equipage eased forward and the nervous horses pulled the coach up the hill then turned left towards Hackney and the city.

"Orders, Maven. Who are we to seek reason in them?"

"Orders from who?"

"The Duke."

"Which one?"

There was some calling and shouting from nearer the bridge, then Maddox walked over to them holding a blazing torch.

"Captain, would you like to do the honours? I can't very well take that lot into the City and I dare not leave it here."

Two of Maddox's men had gone to the wagons and, in the torchlight, had unhitched the still terrified horses and pushed the vehicle back down the road so that it sat in open space. Maddox handed his torch to Maven.

"Get down everyone!"

Maven walked down the slope to the wagon and threw his torch under the load bed then sprinted back up to the village and crouched behind the first of the stone sheds next to George. The powder wagon was ablaze quickly, the wood drying under the force of the flames, cracking and splintering. Bodies still lay on the floor, the skin glowing in the shadow of the flames. Then the powder went. The explosion rocked the ground and rang in their ears such that they thought they might not have got far enough away. A yellow ball of flame leapt fifty, sixty feet into the air and hung there and the draught of the heat scorched their faces. The Sergeant slid alongside Maven clutching the bottle of cheap brandy that Bolingbroke had discarded.

"Wet yer whistle on that. Tis a bit rough but it does the job after 'ard day's work, I'd say."

Maven swigged greedily. It was indeed the coarsest brandy he had ever tasted.

"Shame about yer bugger with the eyepatch."

Maven was suddenly alert.

"Maddox said he was in the front. Was he not hit?"

"Barclay was grazed in the arm but the pair of them ran through the line. Like bleddy cavalry they was."

"But that was ages ago. They could be anywhere."

"Calm yerself down, boy. Yer toy soldier there has men down in 'oxton guardin' the road. They shan't get far."

24

The prisoners were to be marched into the city where they would spend the night in the cells at Artillery House. This time Maddox would not chance putting his charges into a compter. The enemy now numbered only six walking and one of those was unlikely to make the distance. They made for a sorry and defeated outfit as they trudged dejectedly along in the dark, greatly outnumbered by their guard. In the wagons lay the dead and the dying and, at the rear the remaining redcoats, including those who had stood guard on the road to the village and had heard but not seen the action. Maddox had lost two men and had two more with superficial injuries. He was sad for them but it remained a good day's work. The boy had survived and Maddox was relieved that he would have the young culprit to hand when the blame was being passed round. He made sure the youngster remained close to him for the whole journey south. When they linked with the company guarding the road Maven had enquired after Lancaster and Barclay but they had not, it seemed, taken that route. By common consent there was no other way into the city unless they had the use of a good local guide and, since both men were not Londoners, it was agreed they had run north like cowards naturally would.

Maven decided it was time to take their leave and head for Hatton Garden. The group of four rode past the short line of prisoners and into the darkness. Once their eyes had become accustomed to the night the moonlight showed them the way. To their rear they could hear the sounds of triumphant soldiers singing, the songs helped along by the generous supply of ale that had been given them by the tapster at the tavern. Soon the sounds faded to silence. Claudette sat behind George and clung on with her arms around him. As they reached the outskirts of the city the countryside was replaced by an unbroken line of houses, workshops and inns. They all sensed many pairs of eyes watching them from the dark recesses of the courtyards that occupied each side of the road.

When they reached Hatton Garden the road and all of the houses bar one were in darkness. Maven's heart began to pound and he stirred Prospero to a gallop for the last hundred yards. The sound of hooves on the ground must have roused Sarah for, as he pulled up, the front door opened and she stood in a state of some alarm. Blood had run down the side of her face and it had merged with her tears so that it looked as though it was she who had spent the day crossing the Lea Marsh. Maven dismounted and ran towards her. It looked worse than it really was. There was no sign of Kathrine.

"Sarah, tell me what happened."

"Oh, he was horrible, Captain. An evil man. The work of the devil!"

She could barely get the words out and while she spoke Maven ran the various possibilities through his mind. It was impossible that Audley could have got here quicker than him. He may not have even made it back to London at all if he had become stranded on the darkening marsh.

"What was he like, this man?"

"He had an eye patch. Like a robber he was, waving pistols about and shouting and swearing."

He looked past her shoulder into the house.

"Are you alone?"

"Mr Hammond is here, sir, but he caught him a fearful blow about the 'ead with the back of a gun. The poor man is having a lie down."

The others caught up then dismounted and tied the horses. Maven beckoned Trescothick towards him.

"Sarah, Sergeant Trescothick is going to clean your wound and then I would like you to help him take care of this young woman. She has burned her foot and it needs to be bathed. Can you do that for me?"

Maven's presence was reassuring and she was pleased to have someone else attend to the decision making. Maven went inside. The hallway was full of shards where the large looking glass in the hall had smashed and splintered. The light from the wall lamps flickered and the glass sparkled as the breeze disturbed the candles. The china ornaments that usually sat on the half-table under the mirror were broken and lay in pieces at the foot of the stairs. He crunched through the debris and went into the drawing room to find Hammond lying flat out on the good chaise, clutching the back of his head and weeping silently. He looked up when he saw Maven enter.

"I am sorry, Captain, but he ..."

Maven knelt at his side.

"Don't worry yourself. There was nothing you could have done. Did he give any clues as to where he went?"

"No, sir, not a thing. The only thing he was talking about was Lady Kathrine. I only put my hand out to stop him from striking Sarah then before I know it he had hit me with his gun."

Maven felt Hammond's head.

"You've a nasty bump there, man. Bigger then the one I had. You must rest, though. Try not to sleep just yet. We will get you right soon enough. Now then, where did he take Lady Kathrine?"

"No, sir, I'm sorry, you don't understand. Her ladyship wasn't here. That's why he got so cross and broke everything up." Maven looked around and even in the poor light could see that Lancaster had set about this room in much the same way as he had the hall. Moonlight shone on the portrait of the General. It had been torn, as if with a sword and it was rent from top to bottom."

"Your Mr Peck, sir. I think he took the full punishment."

"Peck? Where is he?"

"The kitchen, as far as I knows."

Maven leapt up and made for the back of the house. Mr Peck, Trescothick's much-maligned pot man from The Star was sat down and he looked straight through Maven with a vacant stare. Most of his clothes were missing and he had in front of him a bowl of water and a blood stained cloth that he dabbed slowly and repeatedly to cuts on his neck and above his eyebrow. His white undershirt was stained a deep and darkening red and Maven had a momentary flash back to Smithfield, for Peck had been cut about the throat, albeit his wound was superficial. He was, though, in a state of catatonic terror. There was a noise and a bustle in the hall and the others joined him then.

"Oh bleddy 'ell, what they done to you, boy?"

Trescothick went over to tend to his employee and Sarah, now repaired, joined them to lend a hand and fussed about him. The room was not large enough for all of them so Maven pulled Sarah aside and withdrew to the doorway.

"Sarah, where is she?"

"I don't know sir. She got herself dressed in Mr Peck's clothes and rode off by herself. As to where she went, you best ask your friend Mr Crouch, for it was his being here that caused her to go."

Kathrine thought she looked authentic, especially after she had reached down to the road and smeared damp earth on her hands and, for good measure, glanced her palms across her face. That poor man had been terrified, though it seemed his most significant fear was of being ordered to undress in the presence of a lady. Peck was not a large man but his clothes were still a generous fit on her. She had had to stuff the toes of his boots with torn sheets to make them fit and his breeches were loose enough around her waist to warrant being tied with a makeshift belt made of some string she had located in the scullery. The jacket was heavy and weighted down her shoulders so she found it difficult to sit upright on the horse. She had pulled the wide brim of the hat down over her face and focused on the road ahead of her. She rode in the masculine style, astride the horse and the sack like material of the breeches chafed her thighs as she rode. It may be made to last a lifetime, she had thought, but I shall be glad to replace it with something a little more comfortable. Riding along Holborn in the darkness of the October evening there were few carriages but a regular parade of pedestrians kept her from being alone. Those that were abroad seemed to be mostly drunks rolling to and from their taverns and even they went about in groups, wary of the dangers. She passed a watchman and was startled when he called the hour in a voice booming enough to wake the whole city.

She was cold now and wondered if she had done the right thing in telling Crouch she would make her own way, but she needed to be sure and when she looked into those eyes she could find nothing to trust. She could not believe she was the only one who found Gideon Crouch peculiar. She had been faced with a man possessed of a strange, contorted body who was unable to make direct eye contact. She had had to lean forward to hear him better when he began speaking as the raspy, almost feminine pitch of his whisper had proved almost inaudible. Maven had earlier warned her to beware of anything that seemed out of the ordinary and the presence of Gideon Crouch standing on the front step in the darkness was very much out of the ordinary. She had not permitted him to enter the house, an act to which he took immediate offence, especially as Hammond, whose job it was to answer the door after dark, was all for letting him in and keeping the cold outside. The strange little man had called her "her ladyship" in terms so obsequious that she could not remember having been on the receiving end of such a toadying presence ever before. He had bowed and smiled and waved his hat at her all in one odd movement that was at once as frightening as it was funny.

"My lady, you must leave here at once," he had said, "we believe you to be in great danger. Would you permit me to escort you in my carriage?"

He must have expected it to play out rather differently to the manner in which it did, for he was left without an answer when she asked him why she should not simply remain locked in her house with a rifle primed and ready.

"No, my lady, Audley is abroad and you are not safe. The Duke wishes to ensure you are protected. It will be more appropriate for me to take you somewhere safe. I think you are aware of who it is that places you in danger."

Where was Maven when she needed him? Must I rely on this pathetic twisted specimen to defend me, she had thought. So she had sent him away and Crouch was not happy. He begged her to reconsider and make ready with a bag of, as he put it, essential female apparel. Damn him. Damn the lot of them and in her mind she decided that the day she had feared would come had arrived.

In his defence, Peck had been quite persuasive about accompanying her and, certainly, his experience of the night-time London streets was considerably greater than hers, standing as it was at none at all. Only now, as she rode down the centre of Holborn did she realise quite how terror felt. This was quite unlike the fear she had felt about being left alone after the General's death. That feeling had been more of a nagging loneliness. No, what she felt now was immediate and urgent, like someone could leap out from the noxious shadows at any second and pull her to the ground, perhaps believing her to be a wealthy traveller in town for the coronation festivities. She could lose her life. Many such thoughts went through her mind and she heightened her mood by conjuring ever more terrifying scenes of robbery and the debauchery that would certainly follow when her attackers found her to be a woman. No, she thought, she had not tasted such fear since she was a child.

She cursed the names of everyone who had got her to this point. She cursed the General and she cursed God for taking him from her and leaving her independent in a world where women seemed destined forever to be nothing more than goods to be owned and traded between gentlemen. Most of all she cursed Maven, who was supposed to be her protector, her paid guard no less, but even he had deserted her and gone off in search of the tapster's son. She placed her hand on the pistol that Peck had impressed upon her. It was not primed. She had been frightened of killing someone accidentally and Peck, forgetting his lowly rank, had said she stood more chance of shooting her own leg off. She could use it only as a threat and that would have to be a sufficient defence. If he ever came back she would get Maven to teach her to shoot the damn thing and she would despatch Audley herself. And Bolingbroke. Damn them all.

Crouch had insisted on giving her the address of, as he described it, the safe house, and she was thankful that she had, after a moment's hesitation, ran to the bureau and written it down as soon as the door closed. She would go there, she thought but she would wait nearby first and see who came and went. It was surprising that Mr Crouch would wish her harm. After all, he could simply have brought force to bear when he was at her home. Westminster remained some distance away and though she had been there many times in her coach, the view she had now was one she was experiencing for the first time. She found herself at the hackney carriage rank by Charing Cross. There were just two cabs waiting, their drivers huddled together in conversation on a bench by the first of the vehicles. As she passed, they looked up at her, anxious for some amusement before they were called upon to take the theatre crowd home. One of them called a greeting to her and she ignored him, not wishing to effect an artificially deep voice for their amusement. Her reticence brought forth a stream of foul abuse and a lump of mud, which missed her shoulder by inches.

"Damn Jacobite! You'd have spoke with us if we'd addressed you in French, sir!"

She kicked and quickened her pace, pleased that they had not taken her for a woman, at least. She reached King Street. The road was well lit and there seemed to be a watchman every few yards. There was more activity here with many soldiers and civilian gentlemen about, some in groups and others escorting ladies on their arms. Some of the female companions betrayed their true profession, she thought and the gentlemen must have thought so too for they hurried to their destinations. At the corner of the street she paused again and checked the address. It was dark off the main road and she struggled to count the front doors in the gloom. Crouch had said he would leave a lamp up by the door and it seemed that he had done so, for a light burned about fifty yards down. She twisted left and right in the saddle to check whether she was followed then urged her mount slowly down the side street. The horse was suddenly skittish, like she had seen something that unsettled her. Kathrine peered ahead but she could see nothing and nobody and she scolded the beast. Then, within a few yards of her destination she saw movement in the middle distance, a shifting of a large dark shadow and she wondered whether it was a cat or a dog skulking there and forcing tricks from the moonlight. The mare was nervous again and began wheeling, anxious to return to the lit street. Kathrine struggled to keep it steady. Suddenly she heard hooves clattering on the ground and then two dark shapes heading towards her at a gallop, one of them shouting. They slid to a stop beside her and dirt from the road surface spattered over her. One of them withdrew a pistol.

"You there! Halt! State your business, sir"

She was speechless and was sure she was about to be robbed. They arranged themselves so the road in front of her was blocked. The mare began to edge backwards, keen to get away.

"I asked you a question. Give me a damned answer!"

She mumbled something in a deep voice about having taken a wrong turn and apologised for troubling them. She cursed inwardly at her helplessness. Then one of them, the one with the eye patch sidled up to her and, with his free hand, knocked the brim of her hat away from her face.

"Well, what do we have here then, Mr Barclay?"

Lancaster stroked her cheek menacingly.

Gideon Crouch must have been alerted by the noise for the front door of the house opened and the peculiar little man stood there, as if to welcome her in. He looked up at the two assailants and there was pure fear in his eyes. The parties stood there, as if wondering who would make the first move. Crouch was rooted to the spot, silent in his terror. Kathrine looked from Crouch to the bedraggled pair of footpads in front of her. Lancaster looked at Barclay and the former was about to speak when he was disturbed by the presence of another man in the doorway. He stared at Kathrine like a father might stare at a wayward daughter; or a gentleman might stare at the young woman who had betrayed him some years before.

"Leave her alone," said Bolingbroke sharply, "this ridiculous game is over."

"Damn your eyes, you dandy," replied Barclay and raised his pistol in the direction of the statesman, "from what I hear there ain't many gentlemen left who would care much if I was to put a bullet in your belly. Get back in the 'ouse damn yer."

She had a fraction of a second to make her decision while Lancaster's attention was diverted by his colleague. From where in her subconscious the choice came she was unable to tell but she knew that to stay here was more dangerous than running away. She turned the mount away from the house, away from Crouch and Bolingbroke and their dubious acquaintances, wheeling the horse around and galloping back to King Street and the lights and the soldiers and the gentlemen and their whores. There was a shot behind her, a sharp report that echoed through the empty street and she wondered whether this was it, whether she would at last be reunited with her beloved General but there was nothing, no pain, no whistling of a lead ball past her ear, just the wind rushing into her face and the terror of her fleeing mare. Instead there was a male shout, pained and strangled, then fading quickly, over-taken in its volume by the sound of her mount's hooves on the road. She could not hope to see it as she slowed and looked back but Gideon Crouch, unwinding his twisted body had extended his arm and fired a pistol directly at Nathaniel Barclay, striking the man in the heart, the ball tearing a wide hole in his coat and making an exit through his shoulder.

Lancaster did not stop to wait on his colleague but instead kicked his mount into action and charged towards King Street in pursuit of the woman, cursing her name loudly. He left Barclay in his wake, dangling from his horse with one foot in the stirrup, the beast terrified by the shot and turning round and round upon itself so that if Barclay had stood a chance of surviving the assault it was gone now as his head was dashed repeatedly on the hard road. Bolingbroke looked at Crouch, who went into the house then returned almost at once with the green-coated servant, who was despatched to obtain assistance. Crouch stepped forward and captured the skittish horse and tied its reins to a post. Neither man could bring himself to deal with the body of the mercenary who hung from the horse before them, his dead weight resting sickeningly upon his neck.

In the crowds of King Street, Lancaster did not wish to draw attention to himself by galloping in pursuit of Kathrine. In any case, carriages, riders and pedestrians impeded his momentum. Up ahead in the gloom he could make out her shape but, in truth she had been dressed in such a way that any one of four riders might be her. Then a rotund gentleman dressed in what appeared to be his former army uniform and much the worse for drink, tumbled in front of Lancaster and the stallion reared and turned away.

"God damn you, man. Get the hell out of my way. Fool!"

The outburst caused several disapproving pairs of eyes to settle upon him and Lancaster found himself staring into a watchman's lantern and he was forced to wait while the drunkard was heaved to his feet and dusted down by a companion. A small crowd formed to enjoy the spectacle and laughed when the rotund gentleman directed his ire at Lancaster.

"You wants to be more careful, sir. There's a lot of folk abroad this evening and you ain't gonna make too many friends by shouting at 'em. Especially with you having just the one eye and all. You sure you can see where you're going?"

Lancaster was aggrieved on two counts: first, that he had given this man an opportunity to mock him and that the disturbance had diverted his attention and given the woman an opportunity to escape. He subdued his desire to get down and strike the man hard and, instead, kicked the horse and shrugged it round the obstacle, just failing to avoid the edge of the watchman's lantern so that the much abused mount was startled by the heat of the flame and took off at a gallop that Lancaster could barely control. Kathrine, meanwhile, had managed to negotiate a passage through the growing crowd, which seemed to have no common purpose that she could see. It was not a night for promenading and yet people of all sorts of backgrounds, ages and sizes perambulated like it was a Sunday afternoon in Vauxhall Gardens. She wondered how many would miss the coronation through drunkenness and the need to recuperate tomorrow. But she was reassured by the size of the crowd, which did not, as she had feared, thin out when she reached the Strand. As she executed the right turn she stole a quick glance behind to see whether her follower had kept pace. In the darkness, she could not see very far but neither assailant was visible. Nonetheless, the rapid pulsating in her ears would not subside and every fibre of her being was alert with fear. She wondered then where she should go and in her mind ran through the limited list of possibilities.

Maven set out for Westminster but he was unsure why. A sixth sense, perhaps, drove him towards the Blackbird Club or was it towards Gideon Crouch? He rode along Holborn and looked as closely as he dared at the other lone riders. There were more people around than he expected and he wondered how soon it would be before a gentleman would question why he peered so intently into the faces of strangers. It is, sir, to see whether you might be a woman. He imagined swords being drawn.

Kathrine had left of her own volition and Crouch had not travelled with her, had merely caused her to flee after he had left. Would they meet? And, if so, where? He decided that Crouch's house in Westminster was the correct choice but it was not the only option. Kathrine thought herself part of London society and Crouch was also a senior member of that fraternity. He would be trying to get her to a place of safety but had failed in convincing her to trust him. He wondered briefly whether she might head for Bolingbroke's house, a large mansion on Golden Square. Maven could not resolve the nature of their relationship but there remained a nagging doubt that while there was something between them the attraction was in one direction only.

*

She rode as quickly as the crowds permitted. At Temple Bar a mob had gathered and the road was blocked. Several taverns existed close together here and men spilled out from each of them, forming a large, unruly circle that stretched from one side of the street to the other, its depth increasing by the second as more bodies joined the throng. She got as close she dared and from her high vantage point she could see that the crowd was watching a fight. Two men, both uproariously drunk, had stripped to the waist and their flabby white bodies reflected the light of many torches. Other men, makeshift seconds, egged them on. There was also a pair of raucous and foul-mouthed women, their size as notable as their coarseness. It did not take long to understand the nature of their disagreement for the air was thick with accusations of Jacobitism and counter-accusations of being in the pay of Dutch spymasters. In her sobriety Kathrine could see that the vast majority of the crowd were less interested in the finer points of the politics and much more concerned with seeing some blood shed. Money changed hands and a side argument erupted when a gentleman had his wig torn off his head. He turned to accuse the thief of being a Papist, the twisted logic of the accusation merely exciting the mob further, and they set about both men with fists and feet. At this point the melee erupted once and for all and it seemed like everyone in the street was intent on striking his neighbour.

She allowed the horse's fear to carry her away from the chaos. Until then the fact that she was dressed as a man had not occurred to her but she was brought to her senses when she felt her ankle in the firm grip of a ruddy-faced man who had the complexion and strength of a stevedore. She pulled herself away firmly and kicked the horse as hard as she could, slipping the grip of the man, who stood gawping when he realised that the slender ankle he had just had hold of belonged to an attractive woman. He paid for his hesitation when he was hit on the back of the head by a heavy wooden stool that flew through the air from a nearby doorway. Kathrine's assailant crumpled to the ground. She turned to ride in the direction from which she had come, barging through a group that surged towards the fighting.

The congestion was backing up now, carriages were stationary in the street unable to move forward and their occupants craned necks out of vehicles to gain a better view. Her excitement gave way to a basic, primeval fear, surrounded as she was for the first time in her life by the uncontrolled violence of the mob. She felt a lump rise in her throat and she was close to panic for whichever way she turned there were people, men mostly, pushing, shouting and punching. Then, as she shoved her mount through the crowd and reached the junction with Thanet Place she saw him.

Lancaster saw her at the same time. Like a starving street dog plotting the catching of a rat, the ragged half-pay officer shifted his position quickly then hung back in the shadows and watched as she turned this way and that trying to pick out the horse and rider in the crowd. She was lost and alone in the crowded and terrifying London street and through the tumult she could not see where he had gone. Then she made her decision, coaxed her mount back into action and rode west, away from the mob. The street split here, and if she stayed on the main road, as he was sure she would, it would return her to Charing Cross. There was a second option, though, a dark and narrow passage known as Butchers Row that took its user behind the church. No, he thought, she would not choose that way because she would not know where the road ended up. Trusting her to do as he expected, he waited for her to pass then moved out behind her and set off at a gallop into the narrow darkness, his plan to loop north and head her off when she appeared on the other side of the church. There was nobody about and though there was only an occasional lamp to light the way he made rapid progress and found himself in the churchyard facing her some time before she had negotiated the tide of people. The great stone church loomed over him and gave him shelter and only the snickering of his horse could give him away. He reached for his pistol and then, recalling his orders, replaced the weapon and, instead, retrieved from his saddlebag a length of rope.

As she rode she twisted in the saddle to search for him but could not see him. Surely he had seen her. She convinced herself that her disguise had held good and she would get away after all. Then Lancaster rode alongside, barging her horse and grabbed her arm. She was too startled to react and too weak to prevent him from steering her into the darkness that was Arundel Street.

"We can do it easy or we can do it hard. You choose. Either way, you are coming with me."

His grip was firm and her arm hurt. There was no way out, although she had enough of her senses about her to know that he could not escort her through the streets like this. He must have read her mind.

"Listen, bitch. I am going to tie your hands. As far as the rest of the world is concerned, you are my prisoner and I am taking you to the magistrate. It is a common enough sight and will be all the more so as this night progresses. Lucky you chose that disguise, eh? Now give me your hands."

She refused.

"I will tie them, whether you allow me or not. I do not wish to damage you madam but if I tie you firmly you will feel the pain of that experience for many weeks to come."

Then he appeared to think of something more unsavoury and stroked her thigh.

"'Course, I could always tell his lordship you got away. No reason why I shouldn't have you then leave you in a ditch, eh? Now, are you going to give me your hands?"

She looked briefly into the darkness and was enveloped by a wave of defeat. She cursed her own pride. Why had she not simply trusted Crouch? In truth, she knew no more of whether Crouch could be trusted than she did this brute who leaned towards her with his foul breath and stinking clothes. She tried desperately not to cry. On no account, she resolved, was she to show him how terrified she really was. She held out her hands and he began to tie them. When he was finished he took the reins of her horse, shortened them and looped his hand through so he could control both horses.

"We have to ride up and around that mob. There will be no way through to Fleet Street for a while yet. Don't even think of trying to draw attention to yourself. If I have to shoot you then I will."

They rode shackled together and progress was awkward until the horses ordered themselves into a natural rhythm. They turned off the Strand and went north.

Afterwards, Maven decided it was not so much of a coincidence after all. The route to Westminster meant it was sensible to use Holborn, one of London's natural arteries. He had wondered, as he travelled west, why there was as much traffic this evening as there normally was during a working day but then he was not to know about the disturbance at Temple Bar. His inquisitive stares at other solitary road users had now become just occasional glances and he accepted there was very little chance of finding an individual soul in this city that teemed with life. He swayed with Prospero's gentle rhythm and they made slow progress. The people about him were full of the excitement of the coronation and there was a joyous revelry in the taverns along the way. Shouted conversations and peaks of laughter punctuated the relative quietude of the dark street. There was an inviting warmth about the alehouses that beckoned in passers by but he was not tempted to curtail his journey. Then, in the distance, riding towards him he saw what appeared to be a constable mounted on a large horse, an unusual sight, for most city law men went about by foot or made use of a carriage of some kind. This one had with him a prisoner, some poor wretch no doubt, guilty probably of nothing more than thieving a loaf. But the scene troubled him. It was the usual practice to tie the prisoner by the hands and force him to walk, rather than afford him the luxury of a ride. No, he decided, this was wrong and, instinctively, he knew he should be concerned. From his location, the duo were too far away to see the detail of their faces but there was something about the larger of the two men that raised his nerve ends. Maven halted and dismounted then tied the reins loosely to a metal post that held a gently flaming lamp. He backed away and stood in the darkness of a narrow passage.

Maven had, for years during his military service wondered about his luck in surviving skirmishes without so much as a scratch. Colleagues, both supporters and detractors, had decided he had about him some divine presence that intervened at just the right point to save his soul. He had always treated such thoughts as pious nonsense peddled by soldiers who needed to go into battle armed as much with superstition as with rifles. On this occasion, though, the thought occurred to him again that he was, somehow, just plain lucky.

He tracked the pair as they rode towards him. It was Lancaster, of that there could be no doubt for he would recognise his some time ally anywhere. But if that was Kathrine she had done well with her disguise, for he had to look hard at her to see that the prisoner was a woman rather than a male of slight build. Maven considered his options. They were still thirty or forty yards away and moving slowly, part of the procession that ambled slowly toward the city. Maven looked back down Holborn for signs of Barclay or Pinchbeck. He was surprised that Lancaster worked alone. He decided then that he would wait until they had passed and then he would ride up behind them and deal with the problem quickly and with the minimum of fuss. One swift blow ought to do it and if the force should prove too great then Lancaster's departure from mortality would not be too onerous a loss for the world to bear.

But then Kathrine made a decision that changed his simple plan into something more complicated. During the journey she had succeeded in wresting her hands free of the lightly tied bonds and had sat patiently, biding her time until the opportunity presented itself. Now, as they halted again behind a queue of traffic, she decided that this was her chance. She reached up to her head with, removed Peck's hat and flung it to the side of the road, being sure to hit the tall, officious looking gentleman who stood there in conversation with a friend. When he turned to see where the hat had come from she swept her long hair out of her collar and swung it too and fro, enhancing the scene with a friendly, beaming, utterly feminine smile.

"I say!" exclaimed the stranger, at first none too pleased at being assaulted then calmed by the sight that greeted him. Lancaster was once again pitched into the centre of an attention he did not desire. He looked around for an escape route but could find nowhere to go. Maven, startled into action, strode forward from his hiding place then broke into a run. Kathrine was now at a loss as to what she might do next for, having gained the attention of the crowd, she was surprised to find that no one came to her aid. Instead they merely spectated from the side of the road as if waiting for a show to start. She swung herself down from her horse as Maven skidded to a halt and whilst she could see that someone had approached she did not realise it was him until he called to her.

"Run! Prospero is over there. Get on him and ride home," and then, when she hesitated, "Go now!"

The years of pent up rivalry and hatred for Marlborough's man erupted and drove Lancaster's next decision. He reached for his scabbard and drew his sword, fancying himself in the position of a cavalry officer and ready to strike down his opponent from above. Maven stepped back and drew his knife but Lancaster was impeded by having both horses tied together and they pulled him away from his intended victim, as if sensing that where Kathrine went was a safer place. Lancaster, unbalanced, could not manoeuvre both horses and he fumbled with the rope, attempting to release the second beast.

"Give it up, man, there is nowhere for you to go. Do you think you are going to fight me in the street with all these people looking on?"

Suddenly Lancaster was free of the burdensome animal and it seemed that street fighting was exactly what he had in mind for he spun his mount around and charged directly at Maven. He adopted a pose he had seen so many times used by the cavalry. He pointed his sword forward and aligned his arm with his shoulder so that the full force of his momentum might be brought to bear on his victim. But Lancaster was no cavalry officer and not only had he insufficient momentum to strike a meaningful blow he had also shown his hand too soon and Maven easily side stepped the onrushing horse and rider. Lancaster rode on for some yards then turned laboriously and again rushed at Maven. This time he abandoned the discipline and merely waved his sword about in the air like a sabre, his face awash with anger.

Maven was pleased that Trescothick had seen fit to re-arm him. The ivory handle felt warm in his grip and he braced himself for what he was about to do. He was transported now and in his mind he was no longer in a London street but in some continental town where he had fought hand to hand with bayonets and knives so many times in the past. The onlookers might as well be French or Flemish. In his mind the action slowed. He watched and waited and allowed Lancaster to build his momentum to a point where he would be unable to stop or turn aside. Maven leaned back and wound his arm to ready the throw. Lancaster was at full tilt, his sword raised high behind him and ready for its slashing motion. As the steel was about to hurtle down upon him, Maven released the knife with full force and, in the same movement, stepped out of the way so that the swinging metal of the sword, meeting no resistance, continued on its arc and struck Lancaster's mount a glancing blow on the neck, drawing blood and causing the horse to rear up and scream. Its rider, impaled in the ribs by Maven's knife, was powerless to control the passage of the horse, which galloped off towards the west. Lancaster slipped in the saddle and, after being dragged on the ground for several yards was finally jettisoned when his shoulder cannoned sickeningly into the iron wheel of a carriage. The lifeless body snapped back and wrenched itself clear of the stirrup and the horse, now free of its rider, galloped away to liberty.

Maven ran towards Lancaster and, as he did so, he became conscious again of the people around him. He could hear mutterings of discontent, horrified wailing from ladies, who were being shielded from the gruesome sight by their escorts. He caught the words constable, magistrate and murderer as he passed them by but nobody dared step out into the street and impede his progress. Lancaster was not dead, but he could not be long for the world. He lay there moaning in pain but Maven felt nothing, not even the regret that had begun to creep up on him in his final campaigns. His instinct had been right, the world would be no poorer for Lancaster's passing. That did not alter the fact that there would be some explaining to be done and the sensible course now was to make himself scarce. He crouched down and retrieved his knife. It had worked loose when Lancaster fell to the floor and Maven withdrew it from the folds of his enemy's coat easily. Quickly, he wiped the blood on Lancaster's jacket and stowed the weapon.

Kathrine had untied Prospero and, ignoring his earlier order, had waited for him under the lamp. One or two gallant gentlemen had now ventured towards Lancaster to investigate but nobody had tried to restrain Kathrine. As he ran to her the only words he heard were from women, wondering who on earth this hussy might be and who did she think she was, going about town dressed as a man. Then he climbed aboard Prospero and helped her up to ride behind him. She looped her arms around his waist and he kicked away. Kathrine's long hair flowed out behind her as they galloped away and she gripped with her legs and her arms with more effort than she had ever done anything before and her tears ran down the back of his jacket as she wept silently.

25

In Westminster, Crouch set the glasses upon the polished wood of the table and poured the wine, a good red from the Bordeaux region of France and he was pleased that his masters had invited him to share in their refreshment. Shrewsbury and Henry St John Bolingbroke sat in opposite corners of the room like prizefighters readying themselves for their next round. There had been very little conversation since the incident in the street. Crouch had gone about the business of tidying up the situation with his usual discretion while the senior men had retired to the back room. A pair of redcoats had removed Barclay's body and a third had taken the horse. Very soon two loyal men of the parish would have their coronation celebrations interrupted so they could wash away the blood that had splashed onto the step of the house. Crouch reasoned that the morning dew would deal with any stains that currently lay on the road, although in the darkness it had been difficult to make an accurate assessment. The Duke struggled to contain his fury and, though he remained seated and silent, he shifted in his seat and glared at both Bolingbroke and Crouch. Finally, he could contain himself no longer.

"Henry, how could you possibly have let this get so out of control? You assured me that Audley was restrained and that we would hear nothing from him. Now here we are a matter of hours from crowning the new King and we discover the madman trying to march into London with a wagon full of gunpowder and enough rifles to equip a regiment. What on earth was he thinking? Did he seriously believe he was going to parade through St James's with that cargo? And why the devil were you not able to restrain him? You were there, I understand?"

"He drew up the plan, as you know."

Shrewsbury lowered his voice.

"At your instigation. You failed to keep him on a short leash. You said you could control him. Personally, I think a lunatic like that should have been carted off to Bedlam before he could do any damage. You gave him his head, Harry, and it was up to you to stop it. What force does he have at his disposal now?"

"Nothing to speak of. There are three of them, we think -"

"You think? You mean you don't know?"

"Your man was there as well. I am sure he has already given you this information. Now that Lieutenant Barclay is no more there are three who remain to pose a threat: Audley himself, of course, his servant, Pinchbeck and the other half-pay officer, the one with the eye patch. "

"Is that it?"

"The group that was to have joined them were persuaded to abandon their plans. They will be no of threat to you."

"Harry, it is not the threat to my person that most concerns me at this minute. Can you not see beyond your own coat tails for once? Mr Crouch, what have we done to increase the guard on the King?"

Crouch had allowed himself to drift into the role of observer and was startled to be suddenly drawn into the conversation.

"There is an extra company of Life Guards, sir, to come in from Chelsea under General Stimpson and the entire militia from the City to Westminster is available to us. Indeed, sir, it was a company from the Honourable Artillery Company that prevented Audley from bringing the gunpowder into the city earlier this evening."

"Lieutenant Maddox, you mean?"

"Indeed, sir."

"Then we shall recommend him for a promotion. He has done a fine job."

They paused then as the bells of St Margaret's chimed midnight and the steady rhythm of the toll seemed to last for ages.

"Very well," continued the Duke, "we can, I suppose, do no more. Harry, you will be in the Abbey during the coronation?"

"Yes, of course."

"I meant, sir, that you will not take the opportunity to slip away?"

"Charles, do not insult me with such talk."

Bolingbroke paused, as if concluding an idea.

"You know, it is Audley that needs to escape."

"He already has his strategy planned, does he not?"

"Indeed he does, but he never planned to leave alone, remember?"

"The woman?"

"If we give him the woman I believe we can persuade him to make good his departure before the coronation."

Shrewsbury looked at Crouch as if seeking his approval then reverted to Bolingbroke.

"Getting Audley away from London would no doubt reduce the risk to the King. Crouch, what do you think?"

Gideon Crouch glowed with pride to be included in such an important discussion.

"Well sir, it is said that Audley cares more for Lady Cooper than he does for the monarchy."

Shrewsbury harrumphed in disapproval.

"He has sufficient funds that he will not return to these shores?"

"You authorised the payment yourself, sir," replied Crouch. Crouch realised his mistake immediately and Bolingbroke, alarmed by the answer, suddenly realised how exposed he had allowed himself to become.

"Very well," went on Shrewsbury, as if nothing of any import had been said, "if there is even so much as a rumour of an attempt on the King tomorrow then I fear we shall all be for the gallows. We must take any and every step to protect the King. That includes you Harry."

Then he turned to Crouch. "It really is a damnable nuisance that you let her escape, Crouch. Where will she go?"

"Home, I expect." He looked at Bolingbroke and continued, "Does she have anywhere else to hide?"

"I do not shield her, if that is your insinuation, sir."

"Harry, there is gossip."

"Damn your tittle tattle. I am a married man. The widow is nothing to me."

"Ah, but that was not always the case, was it?"

"That is no secret."

"They say you still love her. I wonder whether your pride would be hurt if she were to go with Audley."

Shrewsbury poured each of them a glass of wine and sat back in his chair. The others waited for the coughing fit they could see was fast approaching. Shrewsbury raised a white handkerchief to his mouth. His rasping cough and bright red complexion alarmed them but they remained seated until he had finished. Shrewsbury cleared his throat with a large swig of wine.

"Harry, I should like you to tell me of Her Majesty's letters. Many gentleman speak of them. It would be best for everyone if they were kept under lock and key. I should like to have them at your earliest convenience."

Bolingbroke paused momentarily, wrong-footed by the change of subject.

"What letters, sir?"

"I want none of your nonsense! Give me the letters, damn you!"

Bolingbroke blanched at the temper and the insult.

"They are safe and I am wise enough to understand that their continued existence is all that prevents Bothmer from impeaching me."

"Then you should trust me, sir. It is in no one's interest to impeach you, however much Bothmer might wish to do so."

Bolingbroke eyed Crouch suspiciously.

"Might we continue these conversations alone? Has my station sunk so low that I must converse with servants?"

"You already know the answer to that question, Harry."

"Then I shall take my leave, sir. I have no further use for this discourse. I do not have the letters and you may rest assured that if I am threatened then they shall be made public. I doubt Bothmer will evade the mob. "

He stood and bowed and Crouch showed him out before returning to the office.

"Where are the letters Crouch? Does the widow have them? Does she help him?"

"We do not know, sir."

"You do not know? Bloody well find out then! This matter cannot be settled unless we have them. They are the final piece in our puzzle and once we have them we may remove that damnable schemer from the scene once and for all."

"Is he in danger from Bothmer?"

"Undoubtedly, Crouch. At least I have the good sense to keep him alive. We should never underestimate the value of clemency, especially when a traitor is involved. The new administration shall be seen as merciful champions of the personal freedoms the modern gentleman holds so dear. Bothmer and Marlborough, on the other hand, would dearly love to see him swing. They are savages and if he dies all hell will reign."

Once they were away from the crowd of onlookers, Maven slowed Prospero to a walk. Kathrine did not relax her grip on him nor did he encourage her to do so. He could feel the side of her head resting on his back and could hear her tiny sobs. When he turned the horse in the road and began to ride back towards Westminster she stirred.

"Where are we going?"

"I had thought it wise to take you home as we are so close but I am not so sure. That is where Audley will go first and we shall put the whole household in danger again. There is somewhere else you will be safe."

The bells of St Andrews rang out their midnight chimes then and they heard a watchman calling that all was well. Maven begged to differ. He roused Prospero into a trot and at the watch house turned right into Grays Inn Lane. It was quieter here as the mostly residential street was untroubled by taverns. It was lit well enough, though, and they made good progress until turning left onto the Kings Way, a path that crossed an open patch of parkland and took them towards Bloomsbury and St Giles. The moon was hidden in cloud and they were enveloped by a complete and total darkness such that the only light was from the houses in Red Lyon Street, away in the distance. Maven trusted Prospero to find his way, though progress was slow. Not wishing to venture any nearer to Holborn than was absolutely necessary, Maven stayed in the quiet darkness of Theobalds Row before dropping down the narrow Kingsgate Street. If they were minded to they could have reached out and touched the timber of the houses on each side and with the darkness above them it felt as though they proceeded through a tunnel. The stench of human life was almost overpowering. Occasionally, they heard the sounds of married life seeping from the houses they passed, lovemaking, babies crying, arguments. There were no secrets for these people, hemmed in like prisoners on a transport ship.

At the junction with Holborn, he stopped and took a few seconds to look up and down the main road. There were more people about than might normally be the case at this late hour but that had been the case all evening. What he sought were clues that the constables or the militia might be searching for them but he saw nothing that troubled him. They crossed into Great Queen Street and worked their way through the narrow passages until they found themselves on the busy Drury Lane. He was on home ground now and Prospero seemed to sense Maven's relaxing mood.

In Southampton Street, the black carriage drew up outside the front door of Mother McGrath's. Its arrival raised no questions at this time of night for it was merely the latest in a parade of gentlemen's carriages that had paid a visit this night. Bolingbroke swept down and had Wentworth drive on and wait at the corner. He rapped on the door and the bawd herself let him in.

"Is she here?"

"Whatever are you asking, sir?"

"You know damn well who I am asking for. Is she here?"

"I should not like to - "

He slapped her across the face with his open palm. She reached up to her swelling lip and felt blood where her skin stung from the blow.

"Do not mock me, woman or so help me I shall knock the very life from you."

He slapped her a second time, harder, and she fell to the ground in a state of genuine confusion. He stood over her.

"She has nowhere to go that is safe. She is bound to return here and when she does you will send a boy to me with news of her arrival. I shall wait all night. If you fail me then you will not see the end of the month. Is that clear?"

Maven used the narrow passages around the back of Long Acre to enter the yard of The Star. The tavern was in darkness. Trescothick had lost out on the takings from the eve of coronation celebrations. He would be grumpy for weeks, thought Maven. They slid off the horse and Maven tied the animal to the wooden post while he went in search of the key. This was not a part of London where it would be safe to use any other than the most secure locks, for the mob would make short work of Trescothick's store of liquor if it could gain entry. She was alarmed when he left her alone and ducked into a small shed. She heard him rummaging about and then he returned brandishing a large iron key.

"Security," he smiled.

Inside, the tavern was cold and he could not recall it ever feeling this way, even in the early mornings. There had been no topers in this place tonight, the fires had not been lit and there had been no need for lamps. He shivered and the thought occurred to him that his friends must still be in Hatton Garden. Maven poured two large glasses of brandy.

"Drink this. It will warm you through."

He lit a candle and went to the fireplace and brought the fire to life but then thought better of it. He turned, took her by the hand and led her upstairs. She resisted.

"It's not so cold upstairs," he said, "it will take an age to get warm down here. "

Maven's room was to the left and they walked past it. He led her into one of the guest rooms that overlooked Long Acre and she sat on the bed. The bedclothes were damp and the room smelled musty. Maven got the fire going and she sipped her brandy. She watched him as he worked, this big man, who had rescued her from the half-blind kidnapper. She wondered where she would be now if she had not had the front to accost him in this very street just a few days ago. She put such thoughts from her mind as the warmth from the fire began to reach her. She slipped to the floor and sat next to him and the light flickered across their faces.

"Thank you," she said.

"For allowing you to be taken by a brute like Lancaster? Don't mention it. Nice disguise, though."

She smiled and at once he felt himself recoil. He felt instinctively for the pewter box in his inside pocket.

"What do you keep in there?"

He stared back as if not understanding.

"I have seen you. You treat that little metal box as if it contained the Queen's jewels."

She reached into his jacket and felt for the box. Instead she put her hand on the bundle of papers he had rescued from the Webb house.   She withdrew them. They were stained where the rain had got at them and where he had rolled on the wet earth with Dench earlier on.

"God alive, do you know what you have here? Where did you get them?"

"They were at your sister's house. In the floorboards."

"Matthew must have hidden them there. The poor man must have been out of his mind with fear."

Maven turned the papers in his hands and stared at them quizzically. He unfolded the letter and began to read then stopped after a few seconds as if he had strayed into forbidden ground.

"Are these why he died?"

"It would seem so."

"Who gave them to him?"

He could see the guilt in her eyes.

"Where is your sister? Doers she know she is widowed?"

"She is safe but she will be ignorant of Matthew's death."

It was her turn to withdraw a letter from her pocket and she presented it to him. It was written on an altogether poorer quality paper but the handwriting betrayed a solid education.

"I had this in my hand when Crouch called this evening. I suppose I couldn't face leaving it behind."

She handed Maven the letter.

Woodford Wells
Essex
1st day of October 1714

My dearest Kathrine,

This is, I fear, the last occasion you shall hear from me for some time. Although I have written this letter at home, I have brought it with me to London and I shall arrange to have it delivered to you from there. By the time you read this we shall be on our way.

I must ask you for your confidence for my husband does not know that I write you this note. Matthew has returned to our house in a state of high alarm and has insisted, issued a direct order, in fact, that we must leave immediately. So urgent is our need to depart that we are to sneak away at dawn tomorrow and head directly for London, where we shall meet a ship that will deliver us to, of all places, Virginia. I cannot say I am at all pleased to leave behind all that we own and, indeed, I am more than a little frightened.

The cause, need you ask, is he whom you know. As if his continued approaches toward you were not reason enough to doubt his honour, it would seem that he has set in motion a plan that threatens poor Matthew's very existence should he not lend his support. In truth, I have never seen my dear husband so distracted.

I shall write again when we have arrived in that far off place. Meanwhile, I pray that you will go with care and, especially, keep a great distance between yourself and that evil man.

Your faithful and loving sister,
Elizabeth

"She has gone?"

"Yes, though whether she enjoys a safe crossing we shall discover in a few weeks' time. May I see your tin box now?"

He withdrew the pewter container and held it like it were a trophy.

"May I?"

She took it from him without waiting for his reply and opened the clasp. He felt belittled, like a child on the brink of adulthood might feel when it was discovered in possession of some childish toy that helped it cling to the past.

"You must have loved her."

He looked away, then, unsure of whether he was able to have the conversation but she persisted.

"What was her name?"

"Ruth."

"Was she beautiful?"

"Yes, I thought so."

"How long is it since you lost her?"

"Ten years."

"How did she die?"

"She was with child. At labour."

He told her, as best he could with his faltering and inadequate vocabulary, of his pacing outside the closed door, of the to-ing and fro-ing of the women and the increasing concern for his wife's welfare. He left out the screams and the helpless anguish that still woke him on his restless nights but Kathrine seemed to understand that they were part of his experience. As he spoke she stroked the lock of Ruth's hair and held it to his cheek and the softness melted him. She replaced the lock and closed the lid of the box then placed it inside his jacket. She did not remove her hand but instead caressed his chest. He raised his hand to stop her but she leaned forward and kissed him and then they were rolling in front of the fire.

Crouch answered the knock at the door himself. The liveried servant had long since been dismissed for the night and nobody but its occupants would know who called at this late hour. Audley did not wait for the door to open completely but barged through, flinging Crouch against the wall and sending a delicate piece of china crashing to the hard floor. The clerk regained his composure and checked in the street to see whether any of Audley's adjutants were waiting outside for their leader, but Audley had come alone. Crouch smiled. So the plot had faltered and Audley was indeed isolated and seeking a way out. The visitor had, by now, found his way to the Duke and burst into the small room with much the same gusto. Crouch scuttled along the corridor and caught him up in time to hear Shrewsbury take the initiative.

"I hope you are pleased, Edward. Bothmer and I gave you an opportunity to redeem yourself and you failed. Your escape route was there, in the palm of your hand. I should have known that you would let us down."

Shrewsbury poured a glass of wine and handed it to Audley as if the new arrival were a polite dinner guest. Audley gathered his thoughts quickly.

"Your redcoats were too damned keen to shoot us. If they had waited just a minute longer I should have had him trapped and your man could have made the arrest. Surely his presence there is enough to justify an indictment. There were enough witnesses for heaven's sake."

"He will argue that he went to prevent you from carrying out your plan. Nothing that happened today gives the lie to that defence. No, sir, your instruction was to have him ride with you. Instead, he returned alone."

"I have been let down by so many people," said Audley. "I shall deliver him tomorrow."

"How on earth do you propose to do that?"

"I shall find a way."

Bothmer slid silently into the doorway and remained unseen by their guest.

"You shall do more than deliver him, Mr Audley."

Audley turned to face the familiar voice.

"Do you understand what is required of you?"

"I-I fear that indeed, I do, sir. And my escape? I shall not leave empty handed, sir."

"There is money aboard the ship. More than was agreed," said Shrewsbury.

"Not that ..."

"The woman?"

"Kathrine, yes."

Shrewsbury looked at Bothmer and thought he saw in the German's eyes a look of relish. He ignored it.

"We will bring her to you."

"She was meant to be here already. That was the agreement."

"As your plans have changed then so have ours. These things happen. She will be brought to you when we are sure of your acquiescence and when you have delivered the traitor."

Maven woke to the return of Trescothick, trailing behind him a caravan of injured colleagues, though in the case of Peck the injuries were now mostly to his pride, especially as both the Trescothicks had extracted maximum capital from his predicament and poked fun at the poor wretch all the way from Hatton Garden. Maven left

Kathrine sleeping, pulled on his still damp clothes and went downstairs to greet the party, who were setting about the best victuals The Star had to offer. Trescothick watched as the door opened and Maven entered the room.

"Thank bleddy 'eck for that, I thought we 'ad the burglars in. What are you doin' here?"

Maven took him to one side and explained the evening's events. Trescothick reacted in the way that Maven knew he would.

"Where's the rest of 'em? And if you is goin' out to find 'em then we is comin' with you."

"You will do no such thing, Tresco. You have done more than enough. Once we have Audley then the business is done. I'd wager that he is out there searching for us, so it may prove easier than I think."

"Aye, tis as maybe but just you be careful, sir."

George and Claudette had taken themselves off to one side of the group and were engaged in hushed conversation. Trescothick followed Maven's line of sight and raised his eyes heavenward as he and Maven exchanged smiles.

"Kathrine is asleep upstairs, Tresco. She has had a busy night."

"Oh, Kathrine is it, now? How busy she been then, you rascal?"

"Just leave her in peace until the morning, there's a good chap."

Maven and Prospero struck out for Westminster and a meeting with Gideon Crouch. It was time, thought Maven, to clear up just what the clerk had intended when he called on Lady Kathrine. It was late enough that most of the lamps had burned out and had not been replaced. He was unsure of the time but guessed that it must now be past two o'clock. There were no watchmen about to confirm it and the streets were empty, the stamina and funds of the London mob having been run down by the earlier celebrations.

In the shadows opposite The Star a man waited. He was short and wiry and had about him the air of one for whom standing in the freezing, foetid streets of London was considerably beneath his station. Gabriel Pinchbeck had the cat-like ability to remain perfectly still and silent and to blend into his surroundings such that no witness was ever able to recall his being present. He took pride in this skill and had perfected it over many years. His employers paid handsomely for the privilege of having on their staff one so talented and Lord Edward Audley paid more handsomely than most. But then he wanted so much more.

Pinchbeck looked out onto Long Acre. The narrow street was empty and, now that that bumbling oaf of a soldier had gone on his way, silent. He had followed the old man and his entourage from Hatton Garden. It had not been difficult, their noisy presence and the volume of traffic sufficient to allow him the luxury of being able to drop back a considerable distance and still not lose sight of the Lady's coach. From his position opposite he had seen them light the candles and fall upon the liquor like it was their last chance to seek oblivion. Pinchbeck did not touch alcohol and he often wondered whether he was the only human being in the world who abstained. Filthy, low-life scum, he thought. They deserve what they get. He had been concerned about the whereabouts of the woman but when he had seen Maven enter the tavern Pinchbeck had clenched his fists with joy at his good fortune. She was in there, he knew it.

Pinchbeck stood at the back door, sheltered by the coach. Apart from the breathing of the horses, all was silent in the yard and he offered up a prayer. He tried the door. Yes. The crowd had been so desperate to get at the victuals they had not locked the door behind Maven. He slipped it open just enough to make his entrance then pulled it to. He had a good view of the entire downstairs room and the woman was not there. He turned to the right and crept up the stairs, pausing once when his boot settled on a loose board. The creak went unheard among the din of the conversation in the main room.

In the darkness of the corridor, he tried each door, none of which were locked. The first of the rooms appeared to be occupied, for clothing hung in the wardrobe but the bed was tidy and the room empty. Further down he entered another room, this one lit faintly by the moonlight. At first it appeared to be empty and he was about to withdraw until he heard a light murmur, the sound a woman might make as she turned in her sleep. He waited to make sure she still slumbered then went closer. He stood over her. She lay on her back, her dark hair spread across the white pillow and she seemed to smile. So, the bitch dreamed pleasant dreams, perhaps of her soldier boy. Hussy. He knelt down beside her and withdrew from his jacket a stiletto, one of the weapons of which he was most proud. It had served him well, this innocuous piece of metal and he was loyal to it.

Then he was disturbed suddenly by voices in the corridor outside and he swung his head around to check that he had closed the door. It was the youngster and his whore, giggling together as they made their way to the boy's room, no doubt to indulge in some peasant rutting. They are no better than animals, he thought, unable to keep the sneer from his face. The sound had been enough to wake Kathrine as well and she stirred, her arms out of the bed now as she stretched. Then she saw him and froze.

26

The closer he got to Westminster the more soldiers there were and, for the first time, he was stopped in the street by a pair of redcoats who prevented his progress until he convinced them that he was senior to them and was going about his lawful business. Though he was reassured by their presence he was nonetheless glad that they had not insisted on searching him for the result would surely have been a night in the compter or a musket ball in the back if he had turned away. Close to the Abbey preparations were already underway despite the darkness of the hour. By moonlight and inadequate torches, men moved benches, stools and, in fact, any other item of furniture that might offer a vantage point that could be charged for.

Maven left them to it and continued. He paused some yards from Crouch's front door. Parked immediately in front of the house was a grand coach. He went closer, searching for the confirmation and, as he reached the vehicle, he found it, the crest on the door the sign that he sought. Maven's presence disturbed its driver, who turned around to look hard at the stranger. Inside, the gentleman leaned forward to look through the window at the rider who had broken the silence. When he saw who it was the passenger threw himself against the seat back and rapped on the wooden coachwork with his cane.

"Come on, damn you!"

The driver did not respond to orders from anyone other than his master and, as Maven began to realise, though it was Audley who occupied the passenger compartment, the carriage belonged to the Duke of Shrewsbury.

Pinchbeck relished his job. On occasions, he merely enjoyed it but this was one of those times that he was so happy that he almost smiled. The bitch had been so compliant and getting her out of that den of vipers had proved far easier than he had expected.

The stiletto had glinted in the moonlight and it had looked all the more threatening for it. He watched her as she dressed, a lascivious grin on his face, though she turned her back to him to preserve some of her modesty.

"I have nothing to lose," he said, "if you make a sound I will kill you. You know that I speak the truth, madam."

"Where will you take me?" she whispered.

"To meet your husband, of course. There is at least one plan that we will see through. And then you shall join him on his voyage and enjoy your new life together."

She had trembled then and yearned for Maven to return but could do nothing except follow the orders of this madman. Would he really kill her if she screamed? If Audley had sent a stranger then she might have tested his resolve but Pinchbeck was a different matter. She knew he had killed and she knew that he saw it as his profession to do so. Even Audley held the servant in some reverence. He bundled her into her own carriage, which she was surprised to find parked in the yard of the tavern. He produced a length of rope, thin enough to bind her hands and feet but rough enough to chafe her wrists. He tied the bonds more tightly than Lancaster had done, all the while staring into her eyes with a look of undiluted malice. Finally, he produced from his pocket a filthy rag that had once been a piece of white muslin and used it to gag her. He flung her onto the bench seat and closed the door quietly. There was no need for him to warn her again.

Their departure could not, of course, be executed in silence so Pinchbeck manoeuvred the carriage as quickly as he could, turning in the tight space and expertly guiding it through the narrow aperture of the gate and onto Long Acre. He whipped the horses then and startled them into urgent action, heading for Drury Lane. In the room above the yard, George had heard the closing of the door and scrabbling of boots as Pinchbeck climbed onto the driver's bench. He flung open the window to get a better look at what was happening.

"You there! Halt, I say!"

But his cry was in vain and by the time he had pulled on his clothes and got to the ground floor the rest of the group were already by the door cursing the thievery of Covent Garden for their effrontery in stealing a coach and two from under their very noses. None of them thought to check on the well-being of Lady Kathrine.

The roads were empty and the darkness was all enveloping. Pinchbeck kept up a brisk pace and reached the southern end of Drury Lane in just a few minutes. He turned left and headed for the City, past the church where Kathrine had been taken by Lancaster earlier on that evening and past the tavern where her progress had been impeded by the street fight. There was no evidence now of the altercation that had blocked Fleet Street and as she looked out from the carriage at the passing city her heart sank. Taken prisoner in her own vehicle and being carried off to the mercy of a lunatic. Audley was a peer of the realm, held in high esteem and feted, it seemed, by the new business class that sought knighthoods for themselves. All of them men, she thought, their poor wives nothing more than chattels. Is that all I am, she thought? An attractive piece of furniture to be bought and sold or, like tonight, stolen?

She became over-powered by the stench of the river. She had been on the Thames many times and had not known it this bad. No, she thought, as she looked out, this is the Fleet. Unable to reach for a perfumed handkerchief she received the full force of the noxious odours. They were at the bridge, close to where the ditch joined the Thames and the waters slowed, causing the contents of the open sewer to ferment: the butchers' offal from Smithfield combined with all the waste of human life that the stream collected as it ran south, stale food, dead dogs and excrement from thousands of London slums gathered here as a monument to the great City and its too rapid expansion. Her stomach turned and she wretched, the rank atmosphere finally detonating the pent up fear. She thought she would choke but managed to control herself and then fell onto the floor of the carriage, sobbing.

They continued and she was thrown left and right as the carriage executed a series of sharp turns. Pinchbeck stopped the carriage and the thought crossed her mind that he was going to throw her into the Fleet. Was that to be her punishment? The door opened and she was no more than three feet from a small front door of a house whose timbers hung over the street. She thought of Maven and decided he would have to stoop to get into the house, such was the height of the door. Pinchbeck did not touch her, merely raised his chin to indicate she should get out. Still bound by the wrists, she shuffled across the floor of the coach. Pinchbeck untied the binding at her ankles and she eased herself down to ground level. There was no step and no helping hand.

In the seconds that it took Maven to dismount, Audley jumped down from the carriage. Maven blocked the way to King Street and his large frame would have easily prevented Audley from making any headway in that direction.

"Captain Maven, how nice to see you again. Tell me, what progress do you make with the challenge I set you?"

Maven laboured to recall the conversation he and Audley had had in Woodford what seemed like an eternity ago. Audley detected Maven's memory loss.

"Lady Kathrine. My wife."

"She is not your wife, sir, in case you had forgotten."

"She is betrothed to me, Maven. It is much the same thing. Have you seen her since your return to London?"

"No."

"Really? I should have thought that searching for her would have been your first priority. You seem to have forgotten my request: deliver her to me and you shall be spared. If I have to find her myself then you will have failed to meet your side of the bargain, sir."

For a man who was somewhat shorter than Maven, Audley seemed to grow in stature while he spoke, as if inflated by his status. So many years of getting your own way, thought Maven. It cannot be a good thing. Maven drew his sword and called up to the driver of the coach.

"You there, climb down and help me."

The man looked from Maven to Audley and then back to Maven. He did not move. Audley smiled.

"What on earth are you doing you fool?"

"I am arresting you, sir."

"Don't be absurd, you cannot arrest me. I am a member of Parliament."

"You are a traitor who plots to kill the King."

"Hah! The King, sir, resides in France. I am in London as you can clearly see. No, Captain, the King is in no danger from me."

"There will be some crime you can be charged with. Carrying all that gunpowder on a public highway. Shooting at the militia."

"Captain, the actions of the Government have inflamed tensions all across this great nation. There is a great deal of unrest. And you should be careful with your accusations, sir. I have not shot at anyone."

"No, you have your henchmen do it for you. Corporal Dench is dead, did you know?"

There was not the slightest flicker of concern.

"He gave his life providing cover for you to escape."

"He was a soldier. That was his purpose. Now you, Captain, what is your purpose? You have already been elevated to a rank far beyond the one to which you were entitled. I suggest that you do not get involved in affairs of state. You would not understand them and will only end up looking foolish."

Maven's temper was beginning to boil but he retained enough self-control to understand that he was being played by Audley.

"I see you draw your sword, sir. I think then that I shall draw mine and I shall have satisfaction. What do you say?"

"Duelling is illegal and, as you say, I am much your inferior. You shall not earn your satisfaction that way."

"So you do understand the rules, Maven. Now go and find Lady Kathrine. You shall be well rewarded."

"What did you do with her sister?"

"Her sister?"

"Elizabeth Webb."

"Elizabeth is safe and well, Captain. Elizabeth has done me no harm."

"Where is she?"

"In the colonies, I expect. She sailed ahead. Kathrine shall be reunited with her sister very soon."

"Without a husband?"

"As I have tried to tell you so many times, Maven, I am a man of honour. People who do not cross me will prosper."

"Matthew Webb crossed you?"

"I will not be robbed, Captain and I will not be cheated. Webb was no better than a common thief."

"So you had Pinchbeck kill him."

"Mr Pinchbeck, like Corporal Dench, has his profession and he is very good at it. If Matthew Webb had not been dishonest then he would still be with us."

There was silence then. Audley looked uneasily at the house, willing its occupant to conclude whatever business detained him and send the carriage on its way. The long wait seemed to sap his confidence and his nerve was beginning to fail. He was shaping to run and at that moment he made his decision.

"You have failed to deliver her, Maven. You have disobeyed me and I am dishonoured. Like the others you will pay, sir. You have my word on that."

There was no room to get past Maven. Instead, Audley turned and ran west into the darkness unaware of whether the street had an opening at that end and, if it did, where it might take him. All the while, the driver remained on his bench, staring ahead resolutely trying as hard as he could to avoid witnessing the scene. At least, thought Maven, you didn't help him get away. Maven was two strides into his pursuit when the front door opened and Gideon Crouch appeared, peering out furtively to see if the coast was clear. Maven's presence took him by surprise, all the more so when the bigger man stopped his pursuit, turned and strode towards him. Maven grabbed the clerk by the lapels of his jacket.

"W-what...?"

"I think you need to be explaining some things."

Then there were two other gentlemen approaching from within the house. Shrewsbury recognised Maven.

"Put him down Captain, please. Your temper does not help the situation. Am I to assume that our guest has fled the scene? Do come in. This, Captain, is Herr Bothmer."

Bothmer shuffled his feet then bowed slightly. Shrewsbury busied himself briefly with a whispered instruction to his driver that Maven did not hear.

"It is a pleasure to meet you, Mr Maven. I have heard a great deal about you."

Then, with unseemly haste, he barged past and clambered into the coach, slamming the door behind him. With evident relief, the driver acknowledged a nod from Shrewsbury and whipped the horses into life. The vehicle clattered away.

Not only was the darkness total and the stench of the air as foul as it had been outside but she was cold, chilled to the bone. The room was small, perhaps eight feet square and it had a single, damp, foetid cot wedged into one corner under a small, glazed window, the bars of which were silhouetted against the night sky. She had stood for a while then, tired, had sat on the floor. She could hear the gentle lapping of water against the wall outside. The thought of what foul contents might be held by the Fleet at this point made her stomach turn again and she fought the urge to vomit. But what concerned her most of all was the malevolent figure of Gabriel Pinchbeck, who squatted in the corner of the room staring at her. He had no intention of disobeying his master's order to not let the woman out of his sight.

"Maven, he is a man of honour!"

They had retired to the drawing room and the Duke had taken issue with Maven's assertion that Audley was a madman who needed to be locked up. He had stopped short of accusing the Lord Treasurer and Bothmer of being in league with Audley, though Shrewsbury understood where the conversation was leading.

"You cannot seriously expect that he will simply melt into obscurity. He is hell bent on preventing the coronation from taking place."

"The King will be guarded by hundreds of armed soldiers, He has no hope of getting close enough. Audley is alone now, all of his acolytes have deserted him. Or they are dead."

"Why did you not stop him sooner?"

"Maven, we have stopped him. That is all that matters. None of us could have foreseen that the ... situation would come this far. Let us not forget that it was you who helped to prevent the outrage. I will ensure the Captain-General hears of it."

"Damn the Captain-General. If he knew the risks you had taken he would have the pair of you lynched."

"Maven you speak out of turn. Moderate your tone, sir, or I shall have you removed."

"With respect, sir, the King remains in danger and a young woman's life remains threatened."

"Ah, yes," said Shrewsbury, grateful to change the subject, "you seem to have developed a fondness for Lady Kathrine. Do you know of her whereabouts?"

"She is safe enough."

"So you do know? Please tell us where she is."

Maven hesitated.

"So we can send a guard to her, man, a detachment of troops to make sure she is safe. Mr Crouch, how soon can we have her protected?"

"If she is in London, sir, within the hour."

"There. If the lady is guarded and the King is protected then our problems are solved are they not?"

"What will you do with Audley?"

"He will be dealt with."

"Dealt with? How?"

"That is not your concern, Captain, your job is done."

"He remains a threat to Lady Kathrine."

"Maven, how many times do I have to tell you? She can be protected. Where is she?"

"I would rather not divulge where she is. She is in safe hands."

Crouch left them briefly for a fresh supply of red wine and clean glasses. The Duke took the opportunity to leave the room on some personal errand and Maven was left alone. He could not rid himself of the nagging doubt that he was somehow the dupe in a game and he felt a compulsion to return and lie beside her again in the warm bed.

Crouch returned with the drinks and placed them carefully on the desk. He twisted his body around and looked at Maven, looked through him, it seemed, such was the odd way that the clerk carried himself.

"She remains in danger," he said quietly.

Maven took a second to understand the information the little man had just provided so low was the murmur in which it was delivered.

"What do you say?"

"Shh! The lady is in danger, sir."

"How so?"

"She is his prize, his compensation ... for loss of office."

"Audley's?"

"You should tell me where she is so that I might arrange for her protection."

"I shall go to her myself, then."

They were interrupted by Shrewsbury, accompanied by a young officer in a red coat.

"I believe you are acquainted with Lieutenant Maddox, Maven."

Maddox saluted and Maven returned the acknowledgement without thinking. The youngster seemed none the worse for his experience with the gentle skirmish on the outskirts of the City.

"The prisoners are delivered safely, sir."

"Maddox has been detailed to help us, Maven."

"Audley was outside in the street a few minutes ago. He cannot have got far."

"I have asked the Lieutenant to take personal charge of protecting this office. Protecting me, one might say. Maven, you should not worry yourself about Audley. Events have moved on and there are other ways of dealing with him."

Maven stood, anxious to leave. Maddox withdrew his pistol and was joined immediately by two subordinates who had been lurking in the hall. Maven recognised them as members of the company that had seen action on the marsh. Shrewsbury stood before him.

"Whilst I do not expect you to understand affairs of state, Maven, I regret that right now I am most in danger from you and the actions you might take."

"I do not threaten you, sir."

"Oh, but you do. You just cannot see how."

Shrewsbury turned to Maddox.

"Take him away, Lieutenant."

Maven watched the late October dawn break. There was a window, or more accurately, a hole high up in the corner of the wall that had been hacked from the bricks and it offered an open invitation to the elements. The wind chased the grey clouds across the sky and, from his vantage point, it seemed unlikely that the sun would find a way through for some hours, perhaps not at all. At least this prison had proper walls, he thought. He passed the time wondering whether Kathrine had missed him when she awoke, whether she had turned to where he had lay earlier and what she might have done when she had realised he was not there. He had spent the hours locked in his cell questioning how she could have allowed herself to become the plaything of politicians. The power of the politicians was intoxicating and it must have felt good to be a part of that circle, to be on first name terms with such important gentlemen.

When they had escorted him here it had still been dark and the full horror of his surroundings had been invisible, though the low moaning of other inmates and the foul smell of humanity had left him in no doubt of where he was to be detained. The Gatehouse was reputed to be one of the capital's more enlightened penal establishments. He shuddered at the thought of what Newgate must be like. His moaning neighbours had maintained an unceasing chorus of lament, ignored by the warder, and their cries had become so much a part of the night that they blended in to the stone walls and damp floor and became, in the end, inaudible, a mere background.

He had left his pewter box at The Star, its contents discarded carelessly on the rough table by the bed and he was disturbed by his sense of betrayal at having shared the contents with Kathrine. He stood and paced about the room, determined not to let the damp transmit itself into his bones. He knew that his stay here would be a short one. Whatever horrors the British judicial system threatened, he knew that he had not only done nothing wrong but, more importantly, he knew too much about Shrewsbury and the company he kept. He knew that if he were to be disposed of then it would not be through official channels. He wondered what would be the price of his freedom.

As if drawn by nature to the freshest of the air, he found himself standing under the window. It was set high up but if he dragged the putrid cot across the room he could stand on it and see out and take in some deep breaths of clean air, cleaner at least than the noxious odours that pervaded the inside of this gruesome establishment. The small bed was shackled to the wall with hemp and the damp had got into the rope, rendering the knots immovable. The bonds had enough play in them to be able to move the bed to and fro by about a foot, nowhere near enough to get the thing to where he wanted it. From nowhere, the anger came upon him again and suddenly he could not contain his temper. Spurred on by the resentment of losing Ruth and of being toyed with by his superiors his fury welled up from deep within him and spilled over, enveloping him in its dark thunder. He hurled the cot against its bonds over and over in a desperate attempt to snap them, watching the pathetic piece of furniture bounce back and forth against the wall. He could hear the rope tearing but only slightly, so he pulled hard against it, determined that he would break something, the hemp rope, the foul bed or his own body.

Inevitably, it was the bed, the weakest of the three that gave out first. The wood around the joints splintered, slowly at first then surrendered completely so that he was left holding a piece of timber about two feet long while the rest of the cot collapsed hopelessly to the floor. He held the length of wood in his hand for a second as if unsure where it had come from then hurled it as hard as he could against the cell door. It struck with a ringing echo then cartwheeled back to land at his feet.

The Judas hole burst open. A pair of old man's eyes appeared, swivelling left and right for a second before he spoke.

"Whatever you break, boy, you'll be paying for. If you can find anything else in there to destroy then you go right ahead. Ain't no care of mine."

Maven bent down and picked up the piece of wood then hurled it once again at the door. The warder withdrew instinctively and the weapon clattered to the floor without harming him.

"And just fer that you ain't getting no grub."

The warder slammed the flap shut and tramped off down the corridor, the sound of his boots on the stone flags receding into silence. Then the moaning of Maven's neighbour recommenced and all was back to normal. He went and stood under the window again. Despite the early hour there seemed to be a great deal of activity as Westminster prepared itself for the coronation of the new King of England. King of Great Britain, he corrected himself, as like so many people of his age and older, he instinctively overlooked the relatively recent creation of the Union. We shall have a King who speaks no English and who, by repute, cares little for this land. Though Maven cared not at all for politics he was troubled by the thought that if the Hanoverian was the most suitable choice to replace the Queen then how bad must the others have been. Not bad, he reminded himself, merely of the wrong faith and then he lost the thread of his thoughts since he had long since lost his own religious convictions.

He walked to the far wall and leaned back against it. He sprang off the bricks and ran at the wall then levered himself up, generating enough lift to get off the ground so he could reach up and grab the lip of the window. He clung on and scrabbled up the wall, his boots finding the slightest of undulations in the rough masonry. The depth of the wall was such that he was able to lean his weight forward and, provided he held on with both hands, he could just about rest there with comfort. The window offered no possibility of escape, though. His cell was on one of the upper floors and, even if he could wrestle through the small space, the sheer drop on the other side would surely kill him.

Outside, the hawkers called and shouted to anyone who would listen and the volume drifted up to him so he could hear what they said quite clearly. They had staked out their pitches early. Fruit, meat and drinks were available in plentiful quantities and, judging from the growing tumult, business was brisk. There seemed to be a swell of pride, a common purpose to the London crowd made up of locals and visitors who had swarmed into the capital for the occasion. Much the same as there is on a hanging day, he thought.

Such was the noise outside that he did not hear the warder unlock the door and only the change in the current of air disturbed him from his eavesdropping. As he turned, Maven lost his balance and slithered down the wall, his hands rubbed on the stone and he grazed his wrist. He landed heavily and cursed. He turned and was confronted by Gideon Crouch, his diminutive frame dwarfed by the warder who stood behind him, a lardy man with hands like fleshy joints of raw meat. The reddish eyes that had spied on Maven through the slot in the door now stared hard at him, full of contempt. Crouch stepped away from the warder.

"You may leave, us. The Captain is not a threat to me."

The warder was not convinced. Then Crouch pulled some coins from his pocket and passed them across. The jailer looked down at his prize and was pleased with the reward. Reluctantly, he left the cell, allowing the door to swing free on its hinges.

"What the hell is going on here, Crouch? What possible harm can I do to Shrewsbury? All I want is for Kathrine to be safe. The rest of you can go to hell."

Crouch let him get the frustrations out of his system. There was silence when Maven had no more left to say.

"The warder says you broke his bed."

"I did him a favour."

"I should say. That will cost me ten shillings. Have you eaten?"

"No."

"Probably a good idea. How is your arm? I heard you took a bullet."

"Only a scrape. I shall survive. Are you going to explain to me why I am here?"

Crouch looked around the cell with some disdain. His gaze settled on a pile of what appeared to be excrement that a previous occupant had tried to hide under the straw that covered the flags.

"I am sorry."

"For what?"

"Sorry that you were forced to undergo this. The Duke has no idea what conditions are endured by prisoners here, or anywhere else for that matter. I shall ensure he learns what sort of institution he has as a near neighbour."

There was silence again, as though Crouch was waiting for the right moment to tell him something and the little man fidgeted and jerked his awkward frame in sharp movements. Then suddenly the news burst forth.

"I must congratulate you on your choice of establishment for Lady Kathrine. She must hold you in high esteem for I fear that a few days ago she would not have entertained the thought of crossing the threshold of the Star Tavern. However, I have some bad news. She has gone. Disappeared, I mean, despite your best efforts." Maven was struck by the thought that she might have left the tavern to look for him then dismissed it as vain and absurd.

"Did you frighten her away again?"

"No, Maven and I will thank you to keep a civil tongue in your head. She was taken. You must have been followed."

"No."

"Your friends then. It seems that the Sergeant's son was disturbed by someone he thought was stealing her coach. That must have been how they got away."

"Who took her? Audley?"

"Even he cannot be in two places at once."

"But I thought he was alone now. Have we not accounted for all his accomplices. Is Barclay still abroad?"

"No, Captain, Barclay was killed earlier in the evening … not far from here."

"And Dench was killed on the marsh and the others were taken prisoner. Who else is there?"

And then as soon as he had asked the question, he realised who it was that had taken her and he was instantly carried back to Smithfield and the house and the blood. He shivered. He paced about the cell like a caged animal.

"How long must I remain in this hell-hole?"

"Until the coronation is over. Then you may leave."

"But that is ridiculous."

"The Duke has arrived at the view that you have dishonoured him with your opinions. You were rather robust, Maven."

"I spoke honestly."

"Indeed you did. But a gentleman of his status is not used to being addressed in such a way."

"Does the Duke have no care for Lady Kathrine at all?"

"She is but a bargaining chip."

"And he has offered her to Audley. In return for what?"

"In return for Audley leaving these shores and not returning. He has been given the opportunity to start a new life in the colonies."

"With her money?"

"No, no, no, Captain, though I suppose if the marriage laws are the same over there as they are here then what is hers will become his in due course. No, Audley has been well rewarded from the public purse. He shall have no cause to return, at least not for financial reasons. Her sister is already there you know."

"Elizabeth? Yes, I know. And when Kathrine and Audley reach America what use will he have for her? Elizabeth will also be a burden to him."

"Maven, I do not believe that Lady Kathrine's life is in danger. Far from it, the man is utterly besotted. The sister, yes, would be superfluous. But not, perhaps, to his friend."

"Surely not."

"They say it is a place to make a fresh start. Who is to know whether one's name is Audley, Pinchbeck or Webb?"

"Does the Duke know of this?"

"He has chosen to overlook it. In matters of state the happiness of two sisters is some way down the list of priorities."

"But surely there is a risk that someone so committed to his cause might choose to return. If the tide turns and the King falls from favour then …"

"Quite so, Captain. And Audley has something of a following in the country, not to mention among his colleagues in the House. Of course, none would dare show his hand without being completely sure of his own safety first."

"And Audley is to be sent abroad? It seems a lenient punishment. Why not lock him up?"

Crouch paused and considered whether to share the information.

"Audley had a task to perform for the Duke. It concerns Bolingbroke."

Maven was silent for a moment.

"Bolingbroke? What is his role in all of this?"

"The legendary Henry St John, a master politician. And something of a ladies man."

Maven looked at him blankly, lost for the moment as to what the clerk might be getting at.

"She didn't tell you?"

Maven was embarrassed by his assumption that Kathrine was an innocent. He raised his fist to his mouth and turned away, as if in thought, but, in reality, nothing came to him.

"She rejected him to marry General Cooper. He was not pleased. He was ready to keep her in some comfort. His wife, you see, prefers Berkshire to the busy life he leads in London."

"And Bolingbroke despises Kathrine so much that he is happy to let her go to the other side of the world with a lunatic?"

"I should not think so. But he is a proud man, Captain, that I will grant you. I gather she, how might one say it, did not rebuff his advances when she became widowed. For once, he has found himself a female companion who has reliance on him for financial assistance. It has given her more …leverage than he is used to."

"Good for her."

"Quite."

"But what of his role in the Audley affair? They are acquainted."

"Indeed, but I would not read too much into that, Captain. There are many gentlemen in high places that seek to maintain dialogues with both sides. Bolingbroke is well practiced."

"Whose side is he on?"

"Right now, who knows? He has survived this long by not sharing his thoughts with the likes of me and I do not suppose he is about to start now."

"And your spies? What do they say?"

"About Bolingbroke? Surprisingly little."

"And what do they say of Shrewsbury? What is he to Bolingbroke?"

"The Duke and the Viscount are enemies, at least they have become so since the death of the Queen."

Maven looked at Crouch quizzically.

"The lady died at what, for Bolingbroke, was a most inopportune moment. He had, it seemed, persuaded her to reconsider her choice of successor. If she had survived for just a few more weeks, days even, he would have gone public."

"Never. There would have been a civil war."

"Probably. But fate has a way of resolving these things, don't you find?"

"Her death left him isolated?"

"Quite stranded."

"Did she die in …"

"Suspicious circumstances? No, there is no doubt that the poor woman died naturally and they say that never did such a sad soul welcome death so readily. She was a troubled woman and a stranger to happiness."

"And Bolingbroke's enemies have moved against him. Why has he not been arrested? It is well known that Marlborough detests the man also. If he has no friends then now, surely, would be the time for Shrewsbury to punish him?"

"The Viscount has made sure that his death cannot occur."

"How?"

"He has, he says, proof that the Queen changed her mind about the Hanoverian. Some letters that, according to her ladies of the bedchamber, she kept with her at all times. She even slept with them under her bolster."

"And the letters have been lost?"

"They were not with her when she died. If they exist then Bolingbroke took them. They are his protection."

"Why are you here Crouch? If Shrewsbury knew that you betrayed him then you would be finished."

"You will have seen that the Duke of Shrewsbury is quite ill. He is not long for this world. One must make alternative arrangements if one is not to be reliant on a meagre annuity in the future."

"Who do you work for?"

"All in good time, Maven. For now, I should like you to trust me."

Maven reached into his tunic and retrieved the bundle of papers with the red seal. They rested neatly in the palm of his hand.

"Ah, very good. May I take them?"

Maven nodded his assent and Crouch swept away the papers into his own pocket.

"Is Bolingbroke to die now?"

"He believes the letters to be safely hidden somewhere. He believes that Kathrine has them."

"Will Shrewsbury and his German friend move against him?"

"If they find out that I have them then, yes, they probably will."

"I judge that you do not plan to tell them."

"It is better for everyone if the letters are never found. One cannot have statesmen holding each other to ransom. It would not be good for the country. Imagine the chaos that will ensue should that come about."

"So Bolingbroke is to survive. Will he be forgiven for his associations?"

"His dismissal in August was but the first step in a plan to ease him out of harm's way. Bolingbroke has more punishment to come. The Captain-General will see to that."

"What is Marlborough to do with this?"

"The Captain-General returned to England as soon as he heard of the Queen's illness. Once again, the great man will ensure the safety of this country."

"Is Shrewsbury his man? He makes for an unlikely ally."

"The Captain–General has taken steps to ensure that he understands what is happening close to the Viscount."

"You are a spy for Marlborough?"

"Sh, sir. It is not to be stated in those terms. Like you I love my country, at least I love it enough to want to avoid meddling politicians plunging us into a war we do not need. It rather makes us comrades, Maven."

"That may be exciting for you Crouch but it hardly helps me or Lady Kathrine, does it?"

Crouch then put his hands behind his back and set off on a tour of the cell, pacing around the confined space, his body adopting a pecking motion, like a hen at feeding time.

"There are two matters with which, um, the Captain-General, that is to say, your country, requires your assistance."

Maven was not impressed with Crouch's strangled approach to communication but elected to wait and, in so doing, forced the man to continue in his struggle to get his request across.

"You see, Captain, though Shrewsbury chooses not to see the risk that presents itself, well, there are, you see, others. And by others, I m-mean the Captain-General ..."

"Come on, man get it out."

"… who is c-concerned at your treatment at the hands of the Duke, your plight, as it were …"

"What do you want?"

"The Captain-General believes that Audley has it mind to, um, finish the original job, as it were, before he flees the country. That would implicate Bolingbroke and Shrewsbury and facilitate his revenge upon a nation he now despises."

"And what do you want me to do about it?"

"Well, we cannot very well task the militia with such a delicate assignment. All that weaponry in such a confined space. Perish the thought. No, this job requires someone with skill in close combat, some cunning…"

"Go to hell."

"Yes, I thought you might say that."

They were silent then, the noise outside growing as the crowd swelled. There was laughter, raucous and uproarious and the sound of singing in the distance. Crouch moved to the door.

"I have a bargain for you."

"Go on."

"I am told that the lady is down near the Fleet at one of the marriage houses. She awaits his lordship for their nuptials."

"Which house?"

"Genuinely, I do not know but it should not be difficult to discover. Second, the bridegroom has unfinished business, as I say, before he departs these shores for good. He would love to leave his mark on history, I am sure."

"And how do you propose that I can solve either problem while I am locked in here?"

"Thank you Maven, I knew you would see sense. Give me five minutes. The outer door is guarded by a young soldier, a token gesture against someone such as yourself."

"And this door?"

"As you can see, it has remained open during my visit and I am sure it will continue to be so after I have gone. Provided you promise not to break anything else."

He smirked at his attempt at wry humour then turned and fled, leaving the heavy door to swing free again. The warder did not return and Maven stared at the open door, a most welcome sight.

The poor wretch in the adjacent cell resumed his low moans, as if he had paused in his caterwauling to listen in on their conversation. It seemed louder now. Maven waited by the door for what seemed like five minutes but was, in truth, nearer three.

In the corridor outside the cell the grey flags were swept clean and there were torches on the wall at regular intervals. There was a large, rough-hewn desk at the end of the line of cells and, behind it, an empty chair, only recently vacated, it seemed, for there was half a loaf of bread and a large cup sitting in the centre. Maven helped himself to the bread and tore into it ravenously as he walked. The staircase that in the darkness had felt narrow and claustrophobic was, in a better light, wide enough for him to descend without brushing against either wall. There was a tight turn at the bottom and he paused when he heard male voices. He pulled back into the shadows and watched as two jailers ambled past the foot of the staircase and into the bowels of the jail. Behind them was the main door that gave out onto the open space. The square in front of the Abbey thronged with people and the noise of the crowd drifted gently into this desperate place. He stepped forward and, about halfway to the main door, he stopped as a young redcoat stepped across the opening then turned and strolled back. Not so difficult, he thought.

The opening was about twelve feet high, a grand entrance, even for a parish building. One of the doors was open, tied back with a chain to the stone wall. The other remained firmly locked, though the iron hardware looked like it was released several times in a normal day. The young soldier had adopted a rhythm now, amusing himself and relieving his boredom with his choreographed routine. Through the gap in the planks, Maven watched him take ten steps to the left, turn on his heel then step slowly past the opening until he reached a fruit seller before turning again and retracing his steps. The youngster feigned to steal an apple from the trader as he turned. The boredom of guard duty.

On his next circuit, a large hand reached out from inside the jail and grabbed the young redcoat by the collar. Maven dragged him backwards into the gloom so suddenly that there was no time to make a sound other than a sharp intake of breath. The rifle clattered to the floor and the soldier tumbled over his sword so that he was off balance when Maven struck him hard in the midriff.

Maven stood behind him and pulled him upright by the collar, causing further pain to the boy's stomach muscles, and twisted his arm behind his back.

"That's for not doing your job properly, soldier. I will leave you with your dignity intact. You will stand here facing the wall and count to a hundred, if you are able, then you will resume your guarding as if nothing has happened. I am your senior officer and I report directly to the Captain-General. If you raise your weapon to me you will be court-martialled and hanged. Do you understand?"

The boy was terrified and in a matter of seconds his trembling had resulted in a pool of warm liquid at his feet. He nodded lamely. Maven thrust him into the corner and slipped through the open door to join the coronation crowd.

28

As dawn broke near the Fleet Bridge it brought with it the pungent aroma of morning. The foul air drifted into Kathrine's room, making her feel nauseous. She looked to the corner and saw that Pinchbeck was gone. Through the window she watched a group of boisterous, laughing boys throwing stones into the water, aiming at what appeared to be the carcass of a dead sheep whose path into the Thames was blocked by a discarded bedstead that rested at the buttresses of the bridge. The boys were impervious to their surroundings and she stared at them for a long time wondering why it was that the human spirit could adapt so readily to the most debasing and shameful surroundings. She felt sick to the stomach and placed the palm of her hand on her abdomen. Then one of the youths, disturbed perhaps by her movement, saw her spying on them and shared the information with his fellows. Each of them turned to look in her direction. She stared back. The largest of the boys took aim with a stone and it crashed through the window, taking out one of the small panes of glass and sending shards spattering across the floor. The small lump of masonry landed with a thud near the door. Instinctively, she had turned herself away from the window as the missile flew towards her and by the time she had regained her vantage point all she could see were their backs running towards the filthy, decaying buildings that were, presumably, their homes. Kathrine retrieved the stone from where it lay and, after turning it her hands for a few seconds, concealed it under the bedclothes.

There was a knock at the door and when it opened she was almost caught withdrawing her hand from under the filthy counterpane and her face bore the guilty expression of someone who had broken a house rule. The visitor did not pause to wait for an instruction to enter. It was a servant, a girl no more than fourteen years old. She strode in carrying a tray, the contents of which were covered by a towel. She was short and thin and the pallor of her skin betrayed her poor health and lowly status in society. Her brown hair was tied at the back but it was so lank and dirty that it broke free from its bonds and strands of it hung loose over her shoulders, brushing against the tray. Kathrine wanted to reach out and hold her.

"Breakfast, miss. Ain't much but it's better than nuffing, eh."

The girl saw the glass on the floor.

"What's 'appened here, then?"

She placed the tray on the table and kicked at the pieces of glass with her slipper.

"Oh, some boys, I think ..." said Kathrine.

"Rascals, ain't they, miss. Do anything for some sport round 'ere. I'll fetch a broom."

Hungry but preparing herself for the worst, Kathrine rose and went to the table, her queasy stomach demanding some sort of sustenance to subdue her appetite, which gnawed away at her. She would settle for a stale piece of bread.

As the girl brushed past her, Kathrine caught the faint whiff of perfume or perhaps scented water and the pleasant aroma took her back to a different, better place. The girl sensed the reaction and turned to look at her.

"You all right, miss?"

"Yes, yes. I was just surprised by your perfume. It seems so ... out of place."

"Yeah, it's a bit smelly round 'ere but you gets used to it. Don't mean I can't dab a bit of cologne about meself, though. Cheers me up. I'll bring you some, if you like. Let's go and get that broom."

The girl swept from the room with an air of controlled efficiency. She took the opportunity to look Kathrine up and down but betrayed no judgement. Kathrine turned to the food tray and lifted the greying towel, forcing herself to overlook the stains of the damp cloth. It concealed, as she had expected, a large hunk of bread. Alongside the loaf were a pat of butter on a clean white plate, two apples and a small jug of what appeared to be ale of some kind. She was suddenly ravenous and set about the bread with a desperation that betrayed all the deportment that had ever been schooled into her. It felt good to tear at the loaf with her teeth, to gorge herself on the doughy mixture. She paused and sipped at the beer, which she thought was revolting. It took her back to a different time. Turning to the door to make sure no one could see her, she turned to the corner of the room and spat the disgusting liquid onto the floor, feeling somehow liberated by the action.

When she had finished eating she still could still smell the perfume. She found she could subdue the aroma of the foul river by concentrating on the pleasant scent, which lingered in the room. Kathrine paced around and stood by the window chewing on the bread, taking care to remain one pace away from the glazing lest she was seen again. A cockroach clambered across the windowsill and she watched the black insect as it scurried to and fro, eventually reaching its destination after coming perilously close to dropping off the edge.

The girl returned with her broom, a home-made, long handled thing with twigs tied about its base with thin twine. This time there was no knock and the door opened to reveal the child holding the equipment as if it were a rifle, the handle resting against her shoulder.

"I'm sorry, miss. It was the best I could do."

"I beg your pardon?"

"For your wedding breakfast. It's not much but I got all I could with the money 'e give me."

The girl seemed unfazed by Kathrine's shocked expression.

"We get all sorts through here. Don't you worry none. Once the ceremony is out of the way you'll be all legal and within a few days you'll forget you was ever in this 'orrible place."

She continued to sweep while Kathrine regained her composure and sat down on the bed to finish the bread.

"What is your name?"

"Charlotte. Charlotte Thomas, miss."

"Charlotte, is it your job to wait on … brides-to-be?"

"Amongst other things, yes, miss. There's always a load of weddings but not many of 'em involve proper ladies and gentlemen like you, miss. Serving you today is a real honour."

"And what sort of people do you normally see here?"

"Mostly they is poor couples who can't afford the licence. Yeah, we get loads coming in from outside the wall: Whitechapel, St Giles and the like. It's cheaper, see."

"And what sort of wedding is mine, would you say?"

"Oh, miss, yours is the best kind of wedding. Proper romantic, like. It's how I would like me own wedding to be."

"And how is that?"

"Oh, I fall in love with a handsome lord but he is divorced from his barren old 'ag of a wife. He loves me but society disapproves so we have to marry in secret then sail away to a new life overseas. I get to live the life of a proper lady and I get to have servants of me own. You must be so excited."

"Is that what you've been told, Charlotte?"

"Yes, course. There can't be any other reason why a lady like you is sitting here in a hole like this ..."

Her voice trailed away as Kathrine's expression gave her the answer.

"But your gentleman, he's such a ... gentleman."

"Have you seen him?"

"No, but I've seen his servant or footman, whatever you call 'em. He is a proper aristocrat's man is Mr Pinchbeck."

"You should not allow yourself to be fooled by appearances, Charlotte."

The sound of boots tramping up the stairs disturbed them and seconds later a gnarled old woman stood in the doorway, glaring at Charlotte. Immediately, the child's shoulders sank and her head bowed. She shuffled the broken glass into the corner with the broom, curtsied to Kathrine and departed.

In the open space between the Gatehouse and the Abbey crowds filed in and milled about with no obvious pattern. Families struggled to remain together as they made their way to their chosen vantage point and as fathers lost their tempers with fractious offspring, mothers fretted at the sheer scale of it all. Around them older folk worked hard to retain the pitches they had carved out for themselves when they had arrived early for the day's entertainment. At the fringes of the assembly, as was always the case when a London crowd gathered, men with questionable motives loitered or roamed about slowly, smacking their lips as they sized up the opportunities presented when such a huge number of people congregated. On the far side, by Westminster Hall, some makeshift benches had been arranged in tiers to afford the spectators a better view. Every space was taken but, despite the lack of room, new arrivals continued to squeeze themselves in, resulting in a series of arguments as the incumbents defended their places. Fists flew and the language gave no quarter to the presence of women and children.

The chattering, arguing and laughter created a volume the like of which Maven had never before experienced as a civilian, as sections of the crowd competed with each other to see who could raise the greatest racket. He struggled to find his way through and the swell and heave of the mass of bodies drew him first left then right until he had to look up at the Abbey to be sure of the direction in which he was being swept. Once, his feet were lifted off the ground as a rush of people swarmed in, perhaps disgorged from a boat that had docked on the nearby river. In the panic a small child sped across in front of him, bounced off several pairs of feet and found itself spat out on the edge of the crowd, closely followed by its distraught mother, cursing the strangers around her. The bells of the Abbey began to chime but the pealing served only to torment the crowd and it circulated the false rumour that the tolling of the bells indicated the start of the ceremony.

Maven pushed on, no longer bothering to apologise as he shoved past the onlookers. As he got closer to King Street, he became aware that his was now the only body pushing away from the Abbey and the hundreds, perhaps thousands of souls in front of him were attempting to cram themselves into a space that was already more than full. A hawker, bearing a tray of Coronation favours was upended and beaten by the mob when he tried to increase the price of his wares, the next customer in line taking violent exception to being the victim of his free enterprise. Relieved of his goods, the hawker collected his now broken and useless tray from the floor and struggled to his feet. A quick-witted youth had taken advantage of the trader's fall. With the malicious efficiency of a fox dismembering a chicken, he had rested his knee firmly in the small of the man's back and lifted the day's takings from his pocket, all the while keeping a scurvy eye out for anyone who might apprehend him or, worse, rob him of his bounty. By the time the victim had regained his composure and patted down his pockets the robber was long gone, enveloped by the mob. Now a graze on the cheek was all the reward the trader had to show for his morning's work but his withering and pathetic look cut no ice with Maven, who resumed his journey.

At the corner of King Street a group of red-coated soldiers had their bayonets fixed and tried in vain to clear a path to the Abbey gate. Their officer, a man Maven thought to be too young to have seen any meaningful action, struggled to make himself heard above the din. His cause was not helped by a nearby householder who was doing a better job of attracting the crowd's attention. He was auctioning viewing points from his property. Looking up, Maven could see the windows of the house, and those either side of it, thronged with onlookers, merry with the occasion and, of course, with drink even at this early hour. He wondered how long it would be before one of the spectators fell from the window and he had no doubt that their place would be taken rapidly.

From the periphery, Maven could hear a familiar voice calling his name. He stopped and, in doing so, unwittingly attracted the attention of the auctioneer's wife, a round woman with rosy cheeks and fat hands, who took him for a potential customer. Maven tried to move towards the calling and had to manhandle the insistent creature out of his way, causing one of the soldiers to start in his direction when she let out a cry. Maven averted his eyes and swept past towards the voice that was now familiar. In the chaos, the soldier quickly aborted his pursuit.

"Where the bleddy 'ell you bin? Don't you know there's work to be done?"

Maven stepped along beside Trescothick who was already waling north.

"Are we on foot?"

"No, the coach is up there. Senseless bringing the thing this far down."

They walked quickly. Either the crowd had thinned because everyone who wanted to see the new King was now beside the Abbey or the rest of the mob had given up and turned back to continue the revelry closer to home. Either way, they were able to make brisk progress. At the corner of New Palace Yard, Trescothick pointed to a smart black coach drawn by a pair of finely groomed horses. Sitting on top, whip in hand, Hammond sat poised and impatient for work, still bearing the bruises from his encounter with Lancaster.

"Belongs to your important friend," said Trescothick in response to Maven's enquiring look, "the funny little bloke with the 'ump. Ours for the day, if we can get it around the town with all these bleddy people about."

They jogged the last few strides and Trescothick flung back the door of the coach. Hammond did not wait for them to close the door or even for the pair to be seated before he cracked the horses into action and they were away, north towards Charing Cross, the vehicle swinging wildly on its springs. It took a few seconds for each of the men to regain his composure. Maven leaned forward and looked out of the window.

"Where are we heading Tresco?"

"Figured you'd have two choices. Stay 'ere and find the buggers 'fore they try and kill his majester or get ourselves down the Fleet to 'er ladyship. Did I guess right?"

"Tresco, you know darn well you did."

"Aye, bleddy foreigner can bleddy well look after himself."

The Right Honourable Lord Edward Audley of Waltham Abbey admired his reflection in the full-length mirror. Draped over the winged armchair in the corner were his ceremonial robes. His servant, an elderly gentleman who had recently entered his seventh decade of loyal service to the family, had assumed that the peer, like his dear father before him, would join the members of the House of Lords at the coronation and had risen early to prepare the outfit. This particular peer, though, had told the servant that today he had no use for ermine and red velvet. Instead, the disappointed and confused attendant had been reassigned to dress his master for some other engagement, although it was not his place to enquire what that engagement might be. So, with his disapproval hidden behind a cloak of respectful silence, the manservant helped his gentleman to dress in white stockings and breeches and a blue brocade waistcoat.

Looking into the mirror, Audley fancied himself the dandy in his newly acquired attire. In the corner, Pinchbeck stood silently holding over his arm Audley's latest foray into high fashion, a delicate china blue coat. Pinchbeck had collected the made-to-measure garment from the Jermyn Street tailor two days previously and he knew how excited his master was to be wearing it for this most auspicious occasion. His malignant expression suggested he did not share Audley's excitement.

"I shall breakfast now, I think. I do hope the lady slept well. I should hate to think of her suffering at all today."

For the first time in his employment, Pinchbeck could not tell whether Audley was making a joke at Lady Kathrine's expense or whether, genuinely, the peer had no idea of the conditions in which his reluctant bride now found herself. Pinchbeck had done his best to describe the term "Fleet Wedding" but Audley had listened only to the part concerning convenience and discretion. Pinchbeck's descriptions of the Fleet Bridge area and the sights that would greet them this morning had fallen on deaf ears. He now realised that he should have taken his employer there personally, for that would have been the only way he could have conveyed the full horror of what he was going to find. He feared a backlash once they got there, but he had done his best. He had personally made sure the bitch was installed in the cleanest room in what was, after all, a most putrid establishment. He had threatened the bawd and made it clear that her life depended on the lady's comfort. He had paid grossly over the odds for the freshest food they could find in that nefarious quarter and he had secured the services of the best maid the philandering old clergyman had to offer. And he had several from which he could choose. No, he thought, he is in for a shock, the stupid misguided fool. And, then, looking on disdainfully as his dandy employer continued to preen himself in the glass, he thought to himself, you'll be lucky if that outfit makes it through the day.

Pinchbeck left the room to retrieve the breakfast items from the kitchen in the basement. When he returned, he found Audley pacing about in a state of distraction, as if he had been disturbed by some event in the street outside. Pinchbeck stole a sly glance out of the window but Lincoln's Inn Field was quiet, even for a Saturday.

"Is something the matter, sir?"

"Mm, what? Yes, something is the matter."

Pinchbeck looked at him quizzically.

"That mercenary half-pay officer Shrewsbury set upon me is still out there. I'd wager that he has paid him to shoot me. Those fellows will do anything for a guinea. Look at the pair we hired. Those two would probably do it for less. Shrewsbury fears me, you know, he fears what an honest man can do to him. I shall bring the whole house of cards crashing down around his pathetic, petrified ears. What do you say to that, hm?"

Pinchbeck, as usual, said nothing but deposited the tray of food onto the polished sideboard.

"Talk to me, man. I value your opinion, and I should like to hear it."

Pinchbeck glanced at the older attendant and Audley followed his eye line.

"Yes, quite, get out. I am done with you for now."

The servant bowed as deeply as his ageing back would allow and left the room, closing the doors behind him. Audley stepped briskly to the food and tore back the pure white cloth that protected the meal on its journey through the house.

"So, come on. What are your views?"

While he listened he set about the first of the pair of boiled eggs, tapped the shell lightly on the edge of the tray then tore off the casing with unseemly haste. When he was left with a clean white ovum he held it up to the light as if to examine its qualities then, in two bites, disposed of it and pronounced himself pleased with its quality. The exercise was repeated with the second egg.

"It seems to me that Maven acts alone, apart from the straggling group of camp followers that has attached itself to him and they are far from his equal. So, in that respect we outnumber him."

While he spoke, Pinchbeck allowed his right hand to wander into the inside of his tunic where it found the trusty stiletto that had so terrified the woman. It would no longer be a mere threat to gain him an advantage. He would put the weapon to the use it was designed for before the day was out, he thought, and that thought pleased him a great deal. Suddenly, he realised Audley was speaking to him.

"If Shrewsbury thinks he can send an assassin after me the man is more of a fool than the colleagues he has betrayed take him for. Do you know, Pinchbeck, it is as if the man had denied all knowledge of ever having been a Tory. Of ever having been a proper Englishman! Changes his colours at the merest hint of a challenge, the blackguard."

Audley continued his breakfast as he spoke.

"Like Bolingbroke," said Pinchbeck.

"Now don't get me started on him. Heaven only knows whose side he fights for these days. I should be surprised if he even knew himself, given how he jumps from one to the other. They say he is a spy, you know. Who the devil he spies for and who would be foolish enough to trust his information is beyond me. How I should love to meet him in Hyde Park one morning. Would you be my second? Eh, would you? That is the honourable way to deal with traitors like him."

"Of course, sir."

At his house in Golden Square, Henry St John Bolingbroke also admired his reflection in the full-length mirror. His elderly servant had also spent several hours arranging his attire and every piece was cleaned and polished so that it looked brand new. He wore the crimson velvet mantle lined with the purest white sarcanet, furred with miniver and powdered with ermine. He held in his hand a cap made of golden cloth. Bolingbroke gazed at himself for several minutes, beginning with his black pumps, which were made of the softest leather, rising through his white stockings and breeches to the pale gold waistcoat. He heard the tolling of the Abbey bell. Instinctively, he took out his fob watch and checked the time for the umpteenth occasion this morning. He sighed deeply and dismissed the servant with an irritated wave of the hand. The man had spent too long around the viscount to object to being treated in this manner. He gave a cursory bow, turned on his heel and left the room.

Bolingbroke walked to the window and looked out into the street. He was two floors up and had a good view. Was it his imagination or did there seem to be a cleaner air today? There seemed to be less smoke hanging above them due, he thought, to the rabble congregating here in Westminster. He wondered how successful the soldiers would be in getting the parade from the Hall to the Abbey. Perhaps the people would rise up and show their true colours. Then he dismissed the thought as absurd. Damn them all, he thought.

There was a knock at the door.

"Yes, what is it?" he called curtly.

The door opened and his father came in. He was dressed in the same manner as his son and had taken just as much care with his appearance.

"Decent day for it, Harry."

"I don't see what there is to be so happy about, unless you've secured yourself an annuity."

"Come on, man, if Bothmer had any plans for you then you would have found out about them by now."

"Do you know where I am to be seated? Do you? Of course you do. How could you have let them do such a thing?"

"I think you overstate my influence. It hardly matters where you sit. All eyes will be on Him."

"I am sitting next to the Countess of Dorchester, for heaven's sake, right in the middle of the Jacobite nobility. I might as well stand up and shout "off with his head!" They shall have me. Mark my words, they are playing with me and they plan to drive me out of my own country."

"Harry..."

"Just you wait. They toy with me. When all this has calmed down I shall be done for. Damn their eyes."

In the distance they could hear the kettledrums and trumpeters practising across the park, as they had been practising daily for the last two weeks.

"Shrewsbury must be pleased with himself. Today all his planning comes to fruition. It will be a success, undoubtedly. Even the rain has held off."

Bolingbroke looked out onto the street as a detachment of troops wheeled left and out of his sight, on their way to join their musical colleagues and form up the procession. There were redcoats everywhere.

"You forget, Harry, that you have friends in important places, even now. "

"Like you, you mean. A lot of good your influence has done me, father."

Bolingbroke's pacing disturbed the powder of their robes and wigs and his father sneezed violently then followed up with a burst of coughing, its intensity causing Bolingbroke such concern that he had him sit down while he called for the servant to fetch a cup of water. The elder St John dabbed at his mouth with a white handkerchief and waved away his son's concern with the other. There was a further knock at the door and it opened without the visitor waiting for approval to enter. Bolingbroke was about to vent his fury once again on his hapless servant then checked when he saw who it was.

"Oh, it's you."

"Indeed, sir. Are we well?" asked Gideon Crouch.

*

Less than hour later, Crouch had returned to Westminster and awaited his instructions from Shrewsbury in the Lord Treasurer's office.

"Where is my wife?"

"She waits for you downstairs, sir. We shall be called presently."

"Very well. Come, we must not be seen to be dragging our heels. Especially you, eh Crouch!"

"Very droll, sir."

They started for the stairs.

"Crouch, where will you be during the ceremony? Don't tell me you have to fight your way through the crowds. Shame there isn't room with us."

"It really wouldn't be the done thing, sir."

"True enough. It has been a task enough keeping the numbers down to manageable proportions as it is. I wonder how many Abbeys we should require if we had granted a seat to every tradesman of the middling sort who chanced his luck with a petition. We never had this sort of behaviour with the Queen's coronation, did we? No Jacobites there, eh? I hope the King recognises how popular he is amongst the social climbers."

Crouch nodded his assent and they left the room.

29

Charlotte Thomas returned to collect the breakfast things and stayed to chat, perched on the end of the bed. Tiredness had forced Kathrine to give up on her determination to stand for as long as possible and now she sat on the bed. She found that if she remained in one position her body heat had the effect of negating the cold of the mattress.

"Charlotte, you don't seem to understand. I am not here willingly. I do not want to marry Lord Audley."

Charlotte understood quite clearly the position in which Kathrine found herself since she had been detailed by the madam to look after this lady. Kathrine was not the first woman to be married here against her will and nor would she be the last. And a lady with property and no husband was in the most dangerous position of all.

"Is yours a chattels wedding, miss?"

"A what?"

"A chattels wedding. It's where the man marries you for your money and your house. It's the law of the land, innit. What's yours becomes 'is."

"No, Charlotte, I do not believe it is that type of wedding. Does it happen often?"

"Often enough, miss. The last time was about two months ago. I knew summink was up when they brought the poor girl in during the night. They'd forced a load of gin down her throat to keep her quiet but she was just sick all night."

"What happened to her?"

"The parson only marries 'em between eight and twelve in the morning. It's the law, see, so they had to keep her here. Screaming and carryin' on like the bears they have at Bartholomew's Fair, she was. Nearly tore the place to pieces. The parson, he got her married off good and quick about ten past eight and then they was off."

"What happened to her?"

"Dumped over the side of a boat in the estuary for all I know, miss."

"Did they find who did it?"

"Course they did, on account of the legals. But they'd stripped her 'ouse and sold everything that was in it. Horses from the stable and all. People reckon they've gone abroad but I wouldn't be so sure. They'll be needing to nick more stuff soon enough I shouldn't wonder."

Kathrine paused while she formed the words in her mind.

"Charlotte, I need you to help me get away."

The girl swallowed and looked at her as if she was the first bride who had ever made such a request.

"I don't know about that, miss."

"Surely you understand that I am a prisoner here, Charlotte?"

"Well, yes, miss but ..."

The girl looked towards the door as if expecting the return of her employer any minute and she rubbed her hands together as if to warm them up in this chilly room.

"If I marry that man I fear I too shall end up dumped overboard, like the bride you just described."

"Miss, I'd love to 'elp you but they'll kill me. I ain't worth nothing to 'em, see and they'll get someone else 'fore the day is out. I wish you hadn't asked me."

"Come with me then. I must be able to offer you a better life than the one you have here. It's an escape for you as well."

Charlotte did not appear attracted to the thought of leaving. Are your horizons so low that you cannot even consider the notion, thought Kathrine?

"If you are not prepared to help me then I must ask you to leave me alone. Now. But please don't tell anyone what I plan to do. They won't ever know. I'm sure you will not be blamed. Tell me, how easy is to reach ... the Strand?"

It was the only street she knew by name that was anywhere close by.

"You got to get out of the building first, miss and madam keeps the door bolted."

Charlotte followed Kathrine's glance at the window, where a cold draught now blew in through the broken glass.

"It's a drop to the ditch, miss. You'll be killed by the plague if you fall in there."

"The front door it is then. Go now and leave me alone. Make yourself busy elsewhere and you will not be involved."

With some reluctance, Charlotte got up and edged toward the door. Kathrine tried to impart her most disapproving look but she could not summon up anything other than pity for the child and anger at the life that enveloped her. Then Charlotte was gone and the door hung ajar. Kathrine tried to recall whether the door had been unlocked since her arrival and reproached herself for not finding out. From the floor she picked up the largest of the shards of glass from the pile that Charlotte had created earlier. As she collected the piece she nicked her forefinger and cursed under her breath as the pain made her wince. She looked at her finger and watched as the blood began to ease out of the small cut. She put the makeshift weapon on the bed then tore at the cotton sheet, allowing all her rage and frustration to be channelled into the violent action. When she had a long strip she wrapped the material around piece of glass. From her hair, she took two pins, working the small pieces of metal so as to fasten the material. She had a knife now, the blade of which was no more than two inches long.

She tucked the weapon into the pocket of her skirt and walked to the door. She eased it open briskly so as not to alert the household with the squeaking of the hinges, then looked out into the narrow landing that led onto the stairs. There were three other doors, one of which looked like a cupboard. She walked to the top of the stairs and peered over. From below, she heard Charlotte chattering about nothing in particular to another girl and then the old woman admonished her servants with a cheerless insult that sent them out of earshot to complete some domestic errand. The downstairs of the property was small and there seemed to be only one other room that the old woman entered and then left again in rapid succession. The parlour gave out onto the street, which meant that at least one of the rooms by her side must do the same. She chose the door directly opposite her own. It was unlocked. As she stepped inside the floorboard creaked and she stopped dead to wait for a reaction from downstairs. None came. She walked as lightly as she could to the window. The glass was filthy, caked in grime and she could barely see out. Below her was a narrow street.

She turned back to the bed and hurled the blanket and counterpane to the floor. There was a top sheet and a second piece of linen that covered the mattress. She tore them off and began knotting them together, trying as best she could not to move around in case her footsteps were heard downstairs. She tugged hard from each end and the fastening held well enough. At the window her heart sank. The handle was stuck fast with mould. She clenched her fist around it and pushed as hard as she could but she was unable to shift it. Panting from the effort, she lay back on the bed and took a deep breath. She drew back her foot and kicked with her heel as hard as she could. The handle gave way immediately, so much so that the cheap metal object broke free of the opening and flew across the room, clattering onto the floor. Still in a prone position she kicked again at the window until it swung free brining the chill air bursting in. She tied one end of the sheet around the bedstead then hurled the other out of the window and sat herself on the windowsill. She was grateful she still had Mr Peck's clothes on for the aperture would have been too narrow for her normal skirts. Even so, she struggled to turn herself around so that her legs dangled in the air while she clung on with her fingertips. The drop did not seem very far and she wondered whether she needed the makeshift rope at all. Then the door to the room burst open and the wretched old woman stood there smiling and watching her as if this sort of thing happened every day. The hag turned and ran for the stairs. The bottom end of the sheet dragged in the dirt of the street so she was sure about not having to drop off the end. She was not sure, though, about how strong the bedstead might be. In truth, she did not care. All that mattered was that she got to the street and ran to the corner to hide amongst the people she could see there. She edged out backwards and let out a scream as she slid down the rope. The sheet swung back into wards the house and she hit the ground close the wall.

She had her back to the street so she did not see the man who caught her and then steadied her by placing his palms on the tops of her arms. Startled, she turned to face him.

"Having second thoughts, my dear?"

Pinchbeck gripped her firmly and hurried her back into the house.

As the servant had expected, the journey, or at least the last half-mile of it, had been difficult for his master. It was the first time Audley had ventured into this part of London and he had gawped in awe at the degradation and human detritus that propped up the wall of the capital. What did he expect? Pinchbeck had thought. He had warned him, of that there was no doubt. A gentleman cannot expect to flaunt himself around this part of town dressed at his most dandyish without there being some reparation to the insult felt by these poverty-stricken people. They had had to leave the carriage on the far side of the Fleet Bridge, as the footman had failed miserably to negotiate the furore of traders that blocked the way.

The first time Audley had doubted his plan was when he took his first step down from the carriage and was accosted by a garrulous fishwife, a huge barrel of a woman with a wicked tongue that could lift paint from the hull of a ship. She had taken him to task for his wearing of white stockings and found the golden buckles of his shoes rather fetching. So fetching, in fact, that she called to her friend, an equally enormous woman, and the pair of them had set about ridiculing the peer, who had no answer, so dumbstruck was he at their effrontery. Pinchbeck had to take him by the arm then led him across the bridge, the catcalls and mocking laughter of the women ringing in their ears.

Entering the Rules of the Fleet, Audley had stiffened again and the horror of the place had repelled him. Pinchbeck wondered whether his master feared more for himself or if there was genuine affection for the bitch after all. Perhaps the dandy fool had softened after all. Then the inevitable had happened, as Pinchbeck had feared it would. Walking towards them along the narrow thoroughfare was a group of six or so boys whose ages ranged from perhaps fourteen down to no more than perhaps five years old, tough it was difficult to tell. Streetwise, loutish and filthy with the grime of the place, they first of all hollered obscene insults at the pair of gentlemen. Greeted only with silence, they chanced their arm with something a little more threatening. The oldest of the group saw his opportunity to cement his seniority and barged into Audley, catching him a glancing blow on his left side.

"Oi, look where you're bleedin' goin'"

Audley hesitated and Pinchbeck withdrew his sword and stepped in front of his employer. The boy backed off immediately and there were catcalls and insults from his band of brothers. Amid laughter and more obscenity the boys continued on their way. Pinchbeck watched them until he judged that they were out of harm's way, but as soon as they turned away one of the gang shied a large lump of horse manure at them, hitting Audley between the shoulders and staining his new blue coat.

At the end of the Strand their way was blocked by crowds of people and by the time they reached Temple Bar the road was impassable. Unlike the night before, when Kathrine had been impeded by the drunken mob, the crowd this morning seemed full of good cheer and posed no threat. Maven leaned out of the coach. He was disheartened to see that the congestion stretched in both directions all the way down Fleet Street.

"Out!" he barked at Trescothick and then flung back the door.

"Hang on a minute, Captain. Let's get ourselves sorted 'ere."

Trescothick pulled the door closed and sat down next to him. The sergeant removed the bench seat opposite and leaned the leather upholstery against the door then retrieved from the hollow space a pair of pistols. In his haste to leave the Gatehouse Maven had not missed the knife that was normally stowed in his boot and was now locked away in some cabinet under the not so watchful eye of the jailer. Trescothick passed him an inferior but nonetheless still useful blade. Maven held the lethal weapon in front of him. It shone as he turned it in the light and the small scratches down its edge indicated that it had been sharpened recently. He replaced the knife in its leather scabbard and slid it into his boot. He peered into the treasure chest of violence that Trescothick had assembled and was amazed at the variety of the arsenal. The older man picked up a musket with his left hand and, exchanging looks with Maven, waved his right hand in a should-we-shouldn't-we manner and they decided to leave the musket behind.

"There is no way we'll get that thing through the streets without drawing attention, even around here," said Maven.

The bench seat replaced, they leaped from the vehicle and told Hammond where to meet them.

"You want me to wait for you there? You must be joking," and then, when Maven's look of disapproval suggested otherwise, "Right you are, sir."

"Just get yourself there Hammond, don't let us down."

They looked ahead of them at the crowd and then they looked to the right, into the dark and narrow passageways of Alsatia, the forbidding territory around the Temple that claimed itself to be above the law and, even in daylight, was off limits to all but the bravest of souls.

"It will take us ages to get down Fleet Street, Tresco. Sorry, but we have no choice. Come on, we only need to skirt around the edge."

"Aye, come on then, let's get on with it. I'd wager we've seen worse. I 'ope you know your way."

They took the first passage that looked as though it might be wide enough to lead beyond a tenement yard. This close to the river the aroma was ripe, not helped by the sewage and other detritus thrown out by the householders into the gulleys that ran down the centre of the streets. The buildings on either side of them, not especially well constructed when they were new, now betrayed their years of neglect, damaged by the short-term tenants and ignored by the landlords. They knew the demand for accommodation was so great they could let any of these rat infested holes in just a matter of days. Windows broken so long ago that there was no longer any trace of glass allowed the sound of hard London lives to drift in the air. They heard a wife shout at her hapless husband and further on they heard a drunken, brawling couple hurl insults at each other as their hungry babies' screams for attention went ignored.

They found themselves facing a group of six boisterous youths who marched towards them with purpose. They both expected to be challenged but the boys were more intent on reaching Fleet Street than indulging in sport. They stood aside to allow the gang to pass. They both knew that to be strangers here was bad enough. To have to attempt any kind of self defence was an act that would draw out yet more of the ragged army.

They marked their progress and direction by occasional glimpses of the great dome that, from here, behaved like a refined Chelsea gentlewoman, averting her eyes from the stinking mass that dwelt at her feet. The enormous cathedral could only be reached by crossing the Fleet and entering the city through Ludgate but the size of the building made it seem as though Wren's great monument sat alongside them. They pressed on with urgency. Eventually, they found themselves in a narrow street lined on one side by more slipshod and untidy buildings. On the other was a wall about four feet high and they did not need to go closer to know that protected them from the stinking Fleet ditch. Maven noticed that none of the nearby buildings had their windows open. To their left and across the foetid ditch was what they sought: the Fleet Prison. They turned left and in less than a hundred yards had reached the bridge. As usual, the main thoroughfare into the south of the City was crowded with people and vehicles trying to get through Ludgate and they vied with those who travelled in the opposite direction.

Traders and mountebanks, drawn to the location by the slowing of the crowd, constricted their way. The sale of remedies for the ills that troubled society were especially popular here even though most of the medicinal cures amounted to nothing but sweetened water, or worse, a tincture that would punish the buyer for his naiveté by laying him low with an ague. The street was noisy, though not at the volume they had experienced in Westminster. It was as if the people here had not heard there was a coronation this morning or, if they had, they cared not be involved. The mob had its own cares and worried not at all about a German King and the tribulations and favours of his Court.

They made their way slowly across the bridge, trying as best they could to maintain the middle ground and, in so doing, steer away from the dubious individuals who staked their pitches with their backs to the stonework. They were as threatening a crowd as Maven had seen anywhere and he sensed that he was sized up and valued more than once as they crossed. Serving at The Star, Trescothick had heard sailors commenting that here was a place more dangerous than any port in the Indies, for in the shadow of the greatest city in the world were men who would slit a traveller's throat for the price of cup of gin. And yet it did not stop the sailors returning here for their entertainments, he thought, as a group of three tars, still merry from the night before, stumbled past with a pair of giggling whores.

Maven and Trescothick turned left and stuck close to the Fleet. On the right was the gate to the prison, open now, of course, for it was daylight and the jailers made money from renting a day's freedom to the sorry inmates who were forced to make this their home. Maven had had the misfortune to come here just once before and he had vowed never to come searching for anyone in this parish again, such was its proximity to hell. For Trescothick, though he had heard tales of the Fleet he had never had cause to set foot here. He looked about him, a foreigner in his own land.

Maven knew only one marriage establishment that would fit the bill for Audley and there was no time to worry about what sort of reception they might receive. Rather than go there directly he needed to check his theory first for the putrid den was deep in the bowels of the Rules and he had no wish to enter unnecessarily. At the second house after the prison gate he rapped on the door with his clenched fist and, when there was no reply after a few seconds, he rapped again, only louder. The door opened just a few inches and the dirty face of a young woman appeared. Before she could close the door Maven had his boot in it and then leaned hard against the wood to force it open. Trescothick followed him in and they found themselves in a bare parlour, dirty from neglect. The girl stared at them sullenly.

"Where is Miss Elizabeth?"

"Elizabeth who?"

"You know dam well who. Dirty Liza. Come on I don't have time to play your stupid games. Tell me where she is."

The girl was plainly terrified but he could not be sure that he was the cause of her fear. Her anxious glances toward the inner door gave him his answer but before he could get there the door opened and a middle-aged woman stood before them. She was short and stout and her face had been a stranger to water for many months. Her unwashed and straggling hair fell about her shoulders, where it rested on a grubby brown shawl.

"Never thought I'd see you again, Captain"

"Nor I you, a pleasure though it is, Liza. I need your help."

The woman laughed mirthlessly.

"I need some information and I need it quickly."

"Cost ya."

"I'll pay."

"How much?"

"Enough to keep you in gin for a year."

She was interested but pretended otherwise and Maven did the best he could to speed up the game.

"I'm looking for a woman. A lady."

"Ain't we all dear."

"She would have been brought down here last night."

"Not in here she wasn't. Don't you go accusing me of nothing, Captain."

"Which of these rat holes is she being kept in?"

"Can't afford to tell you. Not for all the money you got."

He had assumed that financial reward was all that it would take. He had not believed that Audley and Pinchbeck could have influence down here. Then it occurred to him that, for all he knew, Audley was the landlord who owned these God-forsaken slums.

"You'll be safe Lizzy. Whoever has threatened you is leaving today. Leaving the country. All he is concerned about is his own safety. You will be the last of his worries."

She was not convinced and stood looking at him silently.

"I don't owe you nothing."

"I'm not asking you for a favour, Lizzy. I've said I'll pay you. And a woman's life is in danger."

"And mine's not? Get away with you. You've no friends 'ere."

Trescothick pulled one of the pistols from the inside of his jacket. He held his arm out level, pointing the weapon directly at the woman's head. She laughed at him.

"Tell the monkey to put that away. If he blows me 'ead off all the dregs of London'll come runnin' to see what's become of me. And you won't get the tart back neither."

"Put it down, Tresco."

Trescothick lowered the weapon, slowly and with barely concealed reluctance. Maven stepped towards the woman and, with the back of his hand, brushed her cheek. Her skin was surprisingly soft and she was warm. He felt her breath on the back of his hand. He towered over her.

"Tell me. Is it the grey parson that has her?"

He looked her in the eyes so he could judge her response.

"Nah. He's long gone, that one."

But the momentary, involuntary flick of her eyeballs had confirmed it for him.

"Thank you. I'll give him your regards."

When she realised she had betrayed the man she most feared she began to tremble and Maven felt her skin go cold to his touch.

"You've killed me, sir."

"Hide yourself until morning. You will be safe enough. There must be a hundred and one hovels to choose from around here."

Dirty Liza was suddenly unsteady on her feet and she began to faint, reaching out with a spindly arm for the fireplace, then falling and twisting dramatically toward the fire. The young girl ran to her mistress and caught her before she fell into the weak flame.

"Here you go, Lizzy, you come and sit down here."

Then she turned and stared at Maven.

"Damn your eyes," said the girl malevolently, "Get out of this 'ouse and do your searching somewhere else."

He nodded to Trescothick and the pair left the warm fug of the kitchen. As they paused outside and decided which way to turn the door slammed shut behind them with enough force to rouse the attention of several of the locals who were hanging about in the street.

"Come on, Tresco. We need to be quick. These people will get a message out and we shall lose them. If we find the parson he will lead us there. As long as we're not already too late."

"And you know where?"

"I can hazard a good guess."

They set off into the narrow and forbidding passages of the Rules. Maven explained to Trescothick as they walked.

"There are about forty marriage houses round about here. The parson only works in two of them. But I reckon we shan't find him in either just yet."

"How so?"

"His is neither an honest nor a legal trade, Tresco. He bides his time in a tavern, more of a private parlour, really, then he steps out and does his duty, collects his money and disappears again before anyone has noticed he was ever involved."

"And you're sure he's our man?"

"It's a guess, but it's an educated one. He has the reputation of being available to the better classes when they need to be married in a hurry, discreetly."

They passed the first of the more open marriage houses. The broken down building was sandwiched between two private homes. Above the doorway of the sorry looking establishment hung a sign depicting a man's hand holding that of a woman and the words underneath read Marriages Perform'd Within. Or at least they would have done if the sign were not so weather-beaten that most of the white lettering had blended into the pale green paint of the sign.

"Can't say as I'd be overly pleased should any offspring of mine decide to get himself 'itched in such a rotten place. I thought there was a law against such behaviour."

"There is, Tresco. The trouble is the man we seek resides in the Fleet Prison, up to his eyes in debt. Getting fined another £100 for performing weddings without a licence is hardly going to trouble him."

"And his creditors are probably keen for him to do so if they gets to see a bit of the lucre, eh?"

"Quite, if he hasn't drunk it all first."

They continued on their way.

"How do you know him then?"

"He isn't overly concerned to check who it is he marries. Often, he is too drunk to notice. Do you remember the work I did for Richard Breton, the silk merchant who lives in Spittle Fields?"

"Aye. All a bit hush hush, as I recall."

"With good reason. His daughter made a little too much of the freedom Breton granted her and she fell in with bad company. One morning, when she believed she was going for a ride to Vauxhall Gardens she ended up here instead. Breton had only hired me the day before to keep an eye on her."

"Lucky Maven. And you sorted it?"

"By the skin of my teeth."

"You ain't told me about that one before."

"He swore me to secrecy. I can't say that I blame him. If word had got out then he would never have got her married off. Bit fussy, the middling sort."

"Bet he paid you well to keep your mouth shut, eh?"

"Less than he would have paid the kidnappers to get his daughter back and annul the wedding."

"And this Grey Parson, he's round here is he?"

"Strictly speaking he's not allowed out of the Prison but he greases a few palms and they let him roam as long as he stays within sight of the walls. If we find the tavern then we'll find him."

"And if he's not there?"

"Then we're too late."

They were well away from the hollering and bickering of the Fleet Bridge now. They reached a corner. Maven halted and pulled Trescothick back. They were alone except for a tall, thin man dressed from head to foot in black and carrying a book bound with red leather. The stranger was about thirty yards in front of them, staggering with every other step and swaying from side to side. His black hat had a wide brim and it sat on his head at what, on a summer Sunday afternoon, would have been a jaunty angle, revealing a long grey mane of hair. Maven pushed Trescothick into a narrow crevice between two buildings then followed him in.

"That our boy?"

"Yes, Tresco, that's our boy. He must have found somewhere else to get his liquor. Let's hope he gets to where he's going soon. I reckon Dirty Liza will have sent someone out to warn him."

"But I thought …"

"There's more in it for her if he doesn't get caught."

"And we're gonna let her warn him?"

"It's not our job to arrest the parson. In fact, that's probably the last thing Shrewsbury wants us to do. So let's just concentrate on getting Kathrine out safely. It will be a good enough day's work but I wager that we'll still have some explaining to do when Shrewsbury finds out."

They followed the drunken minister at a discreet distance as he stumbled left and right through the maze of tiny streets. Maven noticed another marrying establishment, this one even more decrepit than the last. It was handily placed next to a down at heel inn called the Jack Tar and, true to its name, the alehouse seemed to exist for the pleasure of sailors and, perhaps, their future wives. It was decorated with ropes and various ephemera that had found its way ashore from the ships in settlement of beer bills. To their surprise, the parson stumbled past and continued his journey unmolested. Shortly afterwards, he reached his destination. The grey parson was a wily individual and he paused a few yards away from an unmarked house and stood in the middle of the street looking all about him. They were far enough away to be out of his sight and the tall grey man betrayed no sign of having seen them.

30

In the parlour of the shabby, rundown house, Audley looked around at his surroundings. He reconciled the disgraceful scene with the thought that as soon as the minister was here they would conclude the ceremony and be on their way, the first task of the day duly despatched. He looked at Kathrine and saw the unbridled hostility in her look.

"Why do you run? Can you not see that I love you? I am merely fulfilling a promise."

"It was a lifetime ago. Go to hell."

"Such spirit. Clearly, the General was too soft on you. I hear that life in the colonies can be harsh. If we are to live there together in peace then you would be well advised to moderate your attitude."

"If you think I am going anywhere with you then you are very much mistaken."

"You cannot very well remain here, can you? All of London knows we are betrothed and half the women at Court would give their right arm to change places with you. Why on earth can you not see sense?"

He turned away from her now and caught the attention of his servant.

"Pinchbeck, where the devil is that parson? Let's have this damned ceremony over so we can get away from this hell hole."

At this, the old woman, who had remained in the corner in silent deference, bristled with barely disguised indignation. Pinchbeck caught her insolence and shot her a glance that silenced any backchat before it had begun. Charlotte Thomas hovered behind the woman, a guilty look about her as if it had been her fault that Kathrine's escape bid had taken place.

"Where is he? Eight o'clock we said," asked Pinchbeck.

"He'll be 'ere soon enough. He needs to be sure."

"Sure of what?"

"Sure you ain't been followed. Can't be too careful round these parts. There's plenty would 'ave 'im hanged soon enough."

Pinchbeck moved alongside her and whispered in her ear.

"He, like you, has been paid in advance, much against my better judgement. If he doesn't turn up then I shall start to claw it back. With interest."

Despite the undiluted menace in his tone she was utterly unfazed, though he was unsure whether it was through strength or stupidity. Audley took to wandering around the small room. He settled at what appeared to be an entrance of some kind.

"That's the chapel," said the crone.

"Then I say we should wait in there, what?"

Audley threw open the doors and looked at the scene that presented itself. The room was barely twelve feet square but its purpose was immediately clear, for it was impossible not to focus on the huge wooden cross that adorned the far wall. Immediately in front of it was a lectern, a sturdy piece that had found its way here after a robbery at a country church in Middlesex. In front of them, set out in a mocking copy of a church were four rude wooden benches. In one corner, on a tall table, was a vase of dead flowers; in the other was a smaller table that sported an inkpot and pen and was intended for the signing of the certificates once the ceremony was complete. There was no ventilation and, as a result, the room reeked of decay and mildew. The old woman detected Audley's annoyance.

"Ain't easy to give it an airing. But 't was only used on Wednesday and we don't normally get no complaints. In the circumstances."

Kathrine, hanging back in the shadows behind the two men, eyed the front door. Charlotte edged nearer to the door, perhaps with the intention of unlocking it. Her progress was checked, though, by a thud as though a heavy dead weight had been hurled against the door. This was followed by a slurred pleading and a tapping. They all turned to see what it was but it was the old woman who moved to deal with it.

"That'll be the parson."

Loitering in the gloom created by a darkening sky and the overhanging buildings, Maven and Trescothick saw the grey parson stumble and then fall against the front door of the house. He thumped the door repeatedly with his fist but his cries to be let in were barely distinguishable. After a few seconds, the door opened, but not before a series of knocks and bangs that betrayed the presence of a series of heavy locks. This was why the place enjoyed such a dubious reputation, thought Maven: it took no chances.

Once the door had closed they sauntered past the front of the building as slowly as they dared, in case anyone should be keeping watch. The upstairs window was open and, given the importance of their guests this morning, it was reasonable to assume that a watch had been posted up there. The house, for a private house was all that it was, was abutted on one side by a warehouse and on the other by a narrow alley, which ran down to the rear of the property. They walked on and then, with an air of diffidence, turned and made their way back. As they passed the alley, Maven slipped away from Trescothick's side and made his way down into the darkness, leaving the Sergeant to stand guard at its mouth. The old soldier leaned against the house and took out his clay pipe, the better to blend in with the surroundings. He tamped down the tobacco and lit the device, sending smoke twirling into the air above him. He allowed his gaze to follow the smoke trail and settle on the open window. The scant light reflected on the glass and he could just make out the interior of the room. He could see nobody there.

In the alley, Maven reached a dead end and was faced with the flank wall of a taller property. There was a back door to the wedding house but wooden boxes had been stacked against it and it was clear from the state of the timber that they had endured four seasons of weather. The only way into this place seemed to be through the front door. He walked back to the street and joined Trescothick, who had read his thoughts. Silently, the older man looked up at the window and pursed his lips.

"What d'you reckon?"

"There's no way in through that door as far as I can see. Doesn't seem that we have any choice."

Trescothick looked up and down the street. Sure that nobody was going to see them he shifted to his right and, with his back to the house, cupped his hands at waist height. Maven took a step into the street. Then, in one deft movement he strode forward and lifted his left boot into the makeshift stirrup, levered himself up into the air and grabbed hold of the windowsill with both hands. He lifted himself onto his elbows and rested there briefly while he checked to see whether the room was empty. It was, but a faint waft of perfume provided a pleasant contrast to the stench that he had grown used to and suggested that the chamber had been occupied quite recently. He pushed himself up further then struggled to squeeze his bulk through the opening, getting his foot trapped momentarily as he twisted around. He turned and allowed himself a brief glance at the street below. Trescothick had resumed his sentry duty at the side of the house.

Downstairs, Audley had flown into a rage at the sight of the drunken minister and Pinchbeck had had to restrain him from striking the pathetic toper. The crone forced a glass of beer onto the guest, an act that left the assembled group speechless but, oddly, had the effect of bringing the parson closer to sobriety. He placed his red book on to the table and rearranged his hat so that it rested on his head with more dignity. Then he looked lasciviously at Kathrine and took in her complete form, beginning at her waist and ending by looking directly into her eyes. He smiled, revealing browned and untidy stumps of teeth. Though from a distance he gave the impression of being an alcoholic fool, the parson had a look in his eye that betrayed naked evil. Audley stepped between them.

"Come on, damn you. Moderate your behaviour, sir, or I shall run you through with my sword. Let us get on with this ceremony before I really do lose my temper with you."

Audley grabbed the parson by the shoulder and propelled him through the double doors into the chapel. There was a moment of panic while the parson forgot where he had left the red book and there was much arm waving and mumbling until he had found it again. Then, suddenly, it was as if the drunkenness had worn off, for the parson assumed his position under the cross and, book open on the lectern, looked for all the world like a country pastor about to deliver his Sunday sermon. Only a vague look in his rheumy eyes betrayed his true state.

Kathrine decided to make one last attempt at freedom. She turned and ran the few steps to the front door, shouting at Charlotte on the way.

"Get this damned door open, will you!"

Charlotte, quaking with fear, looked from Kathrine to her mistress and back again and held the keys close to her chest. The girl stepped back until she was hard against a heavy cupboard and could recoil no further. Kathrine heaved against the door, causing it to sway back and forth but such was the strength of the wood and the locks that there was no way through it by the use of force alone. Outside, Trescothick could hear the shouting and the banging; he could see the movement in the door but could only look on helplessly.

Maven ran lightly across the floor to the top of the stairs and, though he could not see into the chapel, he could hear the words clearly as they floated up the stairwell. He stayed where he was until he was sure who else was down there.

"You are wasting your time my dear."

He recognised Audley's patronising tones.

"Now do come on. We do not have time for this."

Kathrine shook the door again but the force was no longer there. She began to cry and slapped helplessly against the door with her open palm. Pinchbeck came out of the chapel and walked towards her. He withdrew the stiletto and held it in front of her face. His body leaned against hers and he whispered menacingly, "If it comes to it then you'll get this, bitch, and don't think I don't mean it. His Lordship has greater work to deal with today than marrying a hussy like you. Face it, my dear, the only way you are leaving this house is as his wife or in a box. The choice is yours."

Then, to emphasise his point he allowed the cold steel to rest against her throat. When she looked up at him he was smiling.

"Bring her in here. For God's sake let's get this thing done."

Maven stood at the top of the stairs. Audley and Pinchbeck were the main danger, although the old woman would no doubt have a weapon of some kind to hand. The young girl was terrified and the parson was insensible. Pinchbeck was the cleverer of the two men and, of course, he would be the more vicious. Maven shivered once again as he recalled the evidence of his handiwork in Smithfield. On balance, he reckoned Pinchbeck would harm Kathrine for sheer spite. Maven returned to the bedroom. He picked up the sheet that was lying on the floor and was surprised to find that it was two sheets tied at each corner. He began to piece together the events of the morning. He took the sheet to the window and tied it, as Kathrine had done, to the bedstead, realising now why the bed was so close to the window. Then he leaned out and tapped lightly on the outer sill to gain Trescothick's attention. The older man caught the end of the sheet as it tumbled down.

Maven walked back to the top of the stairs and primed his pistol. He walked down three stairs and peered around. The parlour was empty now, with everybody present in the chapel. The parson slurred some words. Maven reached the ground floor and went first to the front door. It was bolted with the sort of hardware designed to keep the militia and other unwanted visitors out for some considerable time. There was no way through here without the keys and wherever the escape route was he had been unable to locate it. Everybody had their backs to him except the grey parson and he was focused entirely on what appeared to be two men standing before him, for Kathrine still wore Peck's clothing. Pinchbeck sat in the front row of seats to the right. The madam and the girl sat nearest the door to the left. With the pistol in his hand he strode into the chapel, moving as lightly on his feet as he could. He fired into the wall behind the parson, hitting the cross, the bullet grazing the minister's ear on its way past. The report from the firearm was immense in such a confined space and all of them were deafened and disoriented by the explosion. Pinchbeck was the first to react and he twisted and jumped towards Maven, who swung the pistol at him, catching the servant a blow full in the face that sent him spinning to the floor with blood pouring from his nose. Without waiting, Maven grabbed at Kathrine and seized her by the waist of her breeches and the neck of her tunic and dragged her towards him. At the foot of the stairs he forced her to go first.

"Upstairs then out the window. Do it now."

She paused, in a state of alarm. He thrust her in the small of the back and followed her up.

"Tresco will catch you. Go, for heaven's sake!"

She stumbled up the stairs, catching the edge of the tread, finally reaching the first floor on her knees. She recovered and ran, more or less bent double, into the room and sprinted to the window. She looked out and found Trescothick smiling up at her, his pipe hanging from the side of his mouth.

"Come on, lady, you just jump an' old Tresco'll do the rest."

From below she could hear the sound of locks being opened in a panic, of Charlotte trying the wrong keys and the old woman hurling obscene abuse at the girl. She swung her legs over the side, tearing her breeches in the process but not caring. She dangled from the sill by her finger tips then closed her eyes and let go. She fell backwards into Trescothick's outstretched arms, the force of her fall knocking him down onto his back. He pushed her off and she rolled in the dirt. He was up before her, extending his arm to help her stand. She wanted to wait for Maven but Trescothick would not let her. Instead, they ran in the direction from which he and Maven had walked earlier on.

In the house, Pinchbeck had recovered and he and Audley pursued Maven to the stairs. The Captain turned to block the way and stood on the first step, increasing his height advantage. Audley drew his sword.

"Get out of my way damn you. I shall run you through!"

Maven aimed a kick into his midriff and caught Audley just below the ribs. The peer stumbled backwards, cursing. It was Pinchbeck, though, that created the most anxiety. Suddenly the servant had something in his hand. It was the stiletto, the first time Maven had seen it but it took just a fraction of a second to understand the threat it posed. He reached down to his boot and thanked Trescothick silently for having the good sense to arm him earlier. The presence of the knife made Pinchbeck smile. He seemed to relish the situation. Maven kicked out again but the slim man dodged the boot expertly. Then he lunged upwards, forcing Maven to climb a stair. There was no way that Maven could strike a blow with the knife from here. He tried again to kick the weapon from Pinchbeck's hand but this time the servant's swing coincided with Audley rejoining the fray and the deadly implement caught the peer a glancing blow on the side of the face that drew blood.

"Agh! God damn it."

While Pinchbeck was distracted, Maven seized his chance and sprinted up the stairs and into the bedroom, slamming the door behind him. He heaved the bedstead across the room and blocked the door then ran to the window and swung his legs over the edge. As Kathrine had done, he clung on by his fingers and then dropped the remaining few feet to safety. As he landed, the bawd had the front door open and there was a split second when he saw Audley, blood running down his face and onto his smart blue coat staring at him, eyes raging, and Pinchbeck loitering just behind his master. Neither man, though, left the house to come after him.

31

Outside Westminster Hall, Shrewsbury stood in the fresh air with colleagues from both Houses. The air was thick with gossip and intrigue, of reputations and opportunities. The Duke took the first available opportunity to disengage. Spying the King's advisors, Bothmer and Robethon, Shrewsbury strode across to them and attached himself instead to their conversation. He had earlier alerted them to the news of yet another possible plot unearthed by his spies a few days ago and their presence here among the crowds of noblemen, rather than with the King was testament to how seriously they took the risk. The Germans scanned the faces, essentially ignorant of who among the throng might pose a risk. If they were reassured when Shrewsbury told them of the presence of extra soldiers from trusted regiments who would be guarding each yard of the short route then they did not show it. The Duke added that the soldiers had orders to shoot on sight anyone who threatened the monarch's wellbeing.

There was a small rumpus in the area where the Tories had congregated. Bolingbroke was at its centre. The group of about twenty men and a smaller number of women were drinking toasts to the health of each other and of the country when one of their number announced the toast, "To the King."

"To the King" they answered, in unison.

"… across the water," added a low, dissenting voice, whose owner remained unknown.

There were murmurings of discontent from the guests around them and from within the group. Bothmer heard it but could not see who it was that had uttered the oath. His eyes met those of Bolingbroke, who shrugged in a gesture of embarrassment.

"Any minute now," said Bothmer to a smiling Robethon, "the fools will announce the arrival of Louis and all their troubles will be ended."

Robethon laughed and Shrewsbury permitted himself a smile.

A fanfare of trumpets that silenced all conversation greeted the arrival of the Prince and Princess of Wales. Heads turned and necks craned to get a better view of the royal couple. They walked together and exchanged pleasantries with people as they passed.

"They seem rather prompt," said Robethon, "are we to receive Georg August already?"

Shrewsbury was also concerned that events seemed to be running ahead of schedule and excused himself to go in search of Gideon Crouch, who had been stationed inside with two fob watches to help ensure the procession departed at the appointed hour.

Maven continued running, retracing the steps that he and Trescothick had taken earlier. Within a minute he had caught up with the Sergeant, who was gallantly shepherding Kathrine past the worst of the obstacles in the street whilst still trying to maintain a rapid pace through the putrid and narrow byways. Maven pulled alongside them as Trescothick turned to check whether anyone was following. Maven's presence, a matter of a few feet away, startled him and he let out a short cry of alarm.

"Come on, old boy, I thought you'd be further away than this by now."

"You frightened the bleddy life out of me, you bugger."

They continued walking.

"We need to get away from this place as quickly as we can. We're being watched all the way."

"Don't bleddy start. I ain't as young as I was. And you is puffin' a bit an' all."

The exertion of the fight and the subsequent escape meant Maven could feel his chest heaving with the effort. Smoke from thousands of London chimneystacks hung in the air and also made it harder for him to breath. He coughed to clear his throat and spat on the ground. Kathrine turned to face him. Her normally pale skin tone was enlivened and her cheeks glowed a bright red as if she had enjoyed nothing more challenging then a vigorous walk on a windy day. Her eyes, though, were alive with terror and her hands trembled. She gazed at Maven but could find no words. He reached out a hand and rested it on her forearm. She looked up and smiled at him but her mind was elsewhere.

"Let's hope that Hammond has got that damned coach a bit nearer."

They walked on at a brisk pace and soon reached the prison. The gate yawned open as before and they could make out bodies in the wide entry, some standing and talking, others lying prone, as if resting in this most unlikely of places. They hurried by and headed for the Bridge and all its repellent London life. In a doorway sat a scrawny man, dressed in the black of a priest with a white lace neckerchief. He rested himself on a rude wooden box. He leaned his back against the building, for he was so drunk that it would have been impossible to stand. In his hand he held a stone jar that doubtless contained his gin ration. His grey periwig had slipped from his head and rested on his shoulder. As they passed, he spied Kathrine and waved at her and smiled. Kathrine looked askance and the toper's resemblance to the grey parson was suddenly quite striking. She grabbed Maven by the arm and had to run to keep up with him.

"Are they chasing us?" she asked.

"Apparently not, but I don't understand why. He seemed to give you up quite easily."

"Perhaps he realised finally that I don't want him."

"Perhaps."

Hammond had managed to park the coach at the side of the road in the shadow of Ludgate, in the only place that did not impede the progress of the other road users, though he had had to argue for his right to park there with a pedlar who saw it as an ideal pitch from which to sell his wares. The three of them reached the coach and startled the driver by opening the door. Hammond just managed to prevent himself leaping upon the new arrivals as he saw, just in time, that it was not a street boy who climbed aboard but his mistress. Immediately, he got down and went to her assistance, taking her other arm so that he and Maven shared her light weight and lifted her into the coach. Trescothick clambered in behind her and left the door open for Maven but the Captain stood there in silence for a moment.

"Come on, y'bugger, get yerself up 'ere. This is no time for contemplation."

"They didn't follow us."

"Bleddy good job, I say."

"Which means that someone else will. They didn't need to follow, don't you see? Tresco, Hammond, you as well, go home and barricade yourself in. No one gets in or out until I return, is that clear? Shoot 'em if you have to."

Maven turned on his heel and ran away from them, pushing out of his way a colourfully dressed mountebank who was trying to whip up some enthusiasm for a clear liquid he claimed would cure gout and all manner of seizures. The importunate individual cursed and Maven barged him against the wall on his way past. Trescothick and Hammond looked at the retreating figure in disbelief, then the Sergeant pulled the carriage door closed and peered out through the window.

"Come on, boy. Sometimes he thinks of stuff and don't share it wi' me. I say we head for 'ome. He'll find us when he wants us."

Hammond did not need to be told a second time and jumped back onto the board. He whipped the horses into life and turned the coach in the road, hollering at the pedlar who wheeled his handcart through the gate.

Maven knew that to run through the Rules was to invite attention and trouble. Instead, he walked briskly past the prison and the drunken, sleeping pastor and once again entered the maze of streets, ignoring the menace that surrounded him. Arriving at the marriage house he found the front door wide open and Charlotte Thomas sitting in the street outside, her head resting on her knees. She sobbed silently. He was unsure quite how to approach the situation of a tearful child, so he nudged her thigh gently with his foot. She looked up at him. Her eyes were red with tears and, like Kathrine's, empty with shock. Her pale skin was almost white now, as the colour had drained from it alarmingly. She recoiled slightly, as if she feared Maven would do her some harm. Then, realising she was safe, she jerked her head toward the house and resumed her pose, resting against her knees in a futile attempt to shut out the horrors of the world.

Maven stood in the doorway of the house and, seeing nothing untoward in the parlour, walked into the chapel. In front of him was the huge cross, still ridiculously out of place on the wall of such a small room. The lectern, with the red leather bible still resting on it, faced the wall on the right, as if it had been shoved aside in a struggle. Beside it, slumped in a seated position with his back against the wall was the grey parson. His throat had been cut and blood still oozed from the wound. The darkening red liquid found the path of least resistance to the cleric's waist, laid a stain across his lap and formed a pool upon the floor beside him. He was quite dead. Maven looked around for the madam, deciding that unless she had been quick on her feet then she, too, would have paid the ultimate price for the humiliation that had recently occurred here. He wheeled around and, sure enough, in the opposite corner, he found her. The wretched woman had done her best to escape but she had been unable even to reach the door of this ridiculous effrontery to organised religion. She lay on the floor, her outstretched hand, desperate for freedom, rested on the floor and her neck had been twisted so that her face stared up at him at a sickening angle. The fear that still showed in her eyes was proof that she had died in a state of terror. At least they spared the child, he thought.

Maven went back to Charlotte, who was still sitting in the street. This time he was more guarded and knelt down beside her.

"Tell me," he said, softly, "which way did they go?"

Charlotte Thomas turned and stared at him.

"Please. It's very important."

Slowly, she raised her left hand and gestured vaguely in the opposite direction that Maven had taken earlier. He rested his hand lightly on her shoulder.

"You're safe now. They won't hurt you but you need to get yourself inside. Do you have anywhere to go?"

She looked up at him, her eyes still red from the crying and still she could find nothing to say. He left her, gently withdrawing his hand from her shoulder. From somewhere deep inside the impulse welled up to hold her close to him, as a father might comfort his daughter, but so unfamiliar was the urge that he allowed it to pass unheeded and backed away. He walked quickly in the direction she had indicated, scouting into the unfamiliar territory ahead of him, aware all the time of the danger that may be hidden around each corner, not merely from Audley and his murderous henchman, but from the local populace, many of whom would not think twice to jump him. If he allowed himself to be attacked in this place then there was no telling how long it would be before he could be rescued.

At each junction he selected the route that appeared the most likely to take him to the main road, deciding that Audley and Pinchbeck would have little idea of where their flight might take them and, like he had earlier on, would merely retrace their steps. To his surprise, he soon found himself alongside the walls of the Fleet Prison, this time at the rear of the ugly building that so dominated the area. He followed the perimeter of the jail and was once again at the junction near the Fleet Bridge. Then, in the distance he saw them, Audley's blue coat disappearing down the slope towards the Thames with Pinchbeck scuttling along beside him. He quickened his pace and ran after them. He was baulked as he crossed the road by the same mountebank he had barged into a short while before who had now succeeded in attracting his crowd. Maven had to skirt around them in order to maintain progress and briefly lost sight of Audley as he did so. Maven looked around quickly for the black coach. He was relieved that Hammond had got the vehicle away safely. The coster who had so coveted the space had assumed squatter's rights on the pitch immediately it had become vacant.

Maven could see Audley and Pinchbeck talking to a boatman, apparently negotiating a fare. The waterman seemed to be surprised that the usual prolonged negotiations took no time at all, his undoubted demand for an inflated fee being accepted without question. The pair climbed into the wherry and the boatman pushed the craft away from the shingle with an oar. Maven ran down the slope to the river, bouncing off passengers who had recently disembarked from a larger vessel, catching his wounded arm on a heavy wooden box that was being lugged blindly by a small man who had to peer around the load to see where he was going.

When he reached the shore, still cursing the pain, Maven searched in vain for a suitable craft to hire and go in pursuit of Audley. To his right he could see them making good progress up river towards Westminster. He ran along the foreshore towards the City and finally found a boat. Perched on the bow of the craft was a small wooden sign, bearing the name of Benjamin Toldervey and indicating that the said Mr Toldervey was available for hire to transport goods and people anywhere along the Thames at competitive rates. The waterman, who Maven presumed was the eponymous owner of the business, dozed on the boat, resting his head on his folded arms and he cursed when Maven shook him awake.

"Come, sir. I need a ride. Urgently."

"Be off with you, I'm on a break."

"Never mind your cursing, get yourself awake there and look lively."

"Bugger off, I said."

Maven withdrew his leather purse from an inside pocket and tossed a guinea at the waterman who, despite his supposed tiredness caught the coin deftly, examined it for authenticity and pocketed it quickly. The belligerent owner roused himself finally, frustrating Maven with his slow progress.

"Where you goin' then, young man?"

"Do you see that boat?"

He turned as he said it and then realised how stupid the question had been. As always, there was a flotilla of craft on the Thames and the main artery of London thronged with boats going about their business. Toldervey looked at him silently, as if mocking his customer. Maven stretched out his arm and pointed.

"The wherry, there. It has a passenger in a blue coat."

"Aye, I got it."

Maven did not believe him.

"We must catch it. Come on, quickly. There's another guinea in it for you if we get to them before they reach their destination."

By now Audley and Pinchbeck's craft had passed Temple Pier and was almost lost to his sight amongst the other boats.

"And where might that be?"

"Come on, man, what does it matter? Westminster."

The waterman spat on the ground.

"'Tis a long way to be rowing quick, I'd say."

Then suddenly, and to Maven's surprise, the waterman got up from the boat and disappeared into a small, rudimentary hut that existed for the purpose of storing materials used in the repair of the wherries. Before Maven could go in pursuit, Toldervey was back, dragging behind him a younger man. The new arrival was foreign, perhaps from North Africa and Maven recognised his

Mediterranean colouring from the men he fought against during the war. The foreigner was enormous. His shoulders were broader than Maven's and his forearms were as thick as hams, testament to a life spent fetching and carrying goods on the river. Toldervey was pleased with himself at finding a solution.

"This is Mr Stephen. He's a good lad. Guinea each if we catch 'em."

The payment of the earlier sum had been forgotten.

"Done. But come on, we have to go now."

The reward agreed, Toldervey was now galvanised into action and he cajoled the oddly named servant into the boat then darted back into the shed for a second pair of oars. Any thought Maven may have had about being a passenger disappeared immediately when Toldervey handed him the oars and told him to get in and get settled. The boat was narrower than the usual passenger carrying river craft and, judging by the layer of grime that sat on the surface of the timber, it was not often used for the transport of people. The craft rocked alarmingly to and fro in the shallow water as Mr Stephen got himself into a comfortable position, far enough away from Maven to ensure their oars did not snag. The waterman, a long and heavy pole in his hand, pushed them away from the side and then jumped in. His intention, it seemed, was to steer the boat and keep Maven posted on where they were in relation to Audley.

Maven had not rowed for many years, so many, in fact, that he struggled to recall exactly when. His lack of expertise did not, however, impede them, such was the strength of Mr Stephen. Toldervey squinted ahead, trying to locate Audley and his distinctive clothing and, because he was looking forwards so intently, he did not see the coal barge that cut across towards them from the southern bank. The larger boat, its billowing sail stained with black dust, was attempting a turn into the mouth of the Fleet. Maven could see the inevitable collision about to take place. Mr Stephen, sitting a few yards behind him seemed to ignore it entirely. Somehow, Maven found his rhythm with the oars and, together with a series of rapid strokes from the North African, they avoided a collision. The larger vessel turned into their wake, missing the stern of their flimsy craft by a matter of inches. A coal-stained seaman leaned over the bows and cursed them.

The presence of the larger vessel upset their progress and there was a pause of a second or two while Maven and Mr Stephen regained their composure and began to row in something resembling an orderly pattern. Toldervey cursed them and urged them on, suddenly taken with the sport of the race or, more likely, with the thought of the two guinea reward, for Maven was sure that Mr Stephen would see little, if any, of the money.

They cut through the water at a searing pace now, passing other craft. Occasionally they were baulked and knocked aside the other craft as oars clashed. Toldervey was in his element, haranguing the other boatmen with a range of obscenities impressive and varied even to a soldier's ear.

"We is catchin' 'em, sir!"

Audley and Pinchbeck were alongside the Savoy now, by the stairs.

"They is only one and we is two," shouted Toldervey, "and he is tiring."

He is not the only one, thought Maven. His shoulders ached with the exertion and his upper arms were on fire, burning him deeply. His chest heaved in and out with the effort and he felt a rasping in his lungs that turned to wheezing.

"You ain't so strong for a big man," scolded Toldervey.

Mr Stephen continued to beat out the strokes as if he pulled against nothing heavier than air. It was an impressive sight. Looking beyond Mr Stephen's left shoulder, Maven could see Audley's back, sat low in the wherry and he was closer now than at any point in the pursuit, perhaps fifty yards away. Between them there were three other craft, all wherries carrying people in the direction of Westminster.

"Where's me guineas?"

"We're not there yet. Catch 'em and you can have your reward."

"Hand it over, boy. We shall be there soon enough."

They passed the first of the other craft and, it was true, they were closing on their targets rapidly. While Toldervey bantered with the other boatmen Maven spun around fully to get a better look at Audley. He and Pinchbeck sat in the boat like a pair of City gentlemen out for a Sunday afternoon excursion. Their boatman, tired and stroking slowly, was making little progress and a heavily laden shallop passed him. Now there was just one boat between them and Audley. Mr Stephen pressed on, no break in his rhythm, cruising now, it seemed, as he beat out the strokes.

"Money please, Mister, or I shall turn us round."

Maven deemed it safe to hand over the cash and took the coins from his purse. Toldervey snaffled the money away in some secret place about his person. Then they were past the remaining craft with clear water between them and Audley.

"Pull alongside and stop them, will you. Tip them in the water if needs be."

"I ain't damaging my boat, sir, not for you or no one, whatever your business might be."

Maven decided it would not be wise to tell Benjamin Toldervey what he thought the pair planned to do in Westminster.

"Just get as near as you can. Try and force them into the shore."

They were alongside the Tudor Yard now and, ahead of them, Westminster was in their sight. Around the White Hall Stairs there was a crowd of boats disgorging people then jostling for position for the return legs of their journeys. Toldervey stared ahead, weighing his chances of securing some passengers and gaining a lucrative return journey to the city. Maven turned to see what it was that intrigued him. He found himself exchanging looks with a startled Pinchbeck, about twenty yards away. The servant alerted Audley and the peer turned in his seat, craning his neck to look at Maven, as if to make sure that his man was telling the truth. Maven heard Audley scold the boatman, urging him to go faster. Suddenly Audley had a pistol in his hand and was priming the weapon. Pinchbeck urged his master against taking foolish action. Toldervey had seen it as well and let out a cry of alarm.

"Keep going!" shouted Maven.

Mr Stephen kept up his relentless pace. Audley stretched out his right arm, aiming as best he could at Maven but they both knew that the shot would be a lottery, so choppy was the water, and Audley was as likely to hit any of them or none of them as he pitched to and fro. Pinchbeck spoke to Audley and must have said much the same for at last the peer rested the gun. Audley's boatman could find no additional strength and was obviously frightened by the presence of an armed man. Mr Stephen had them alongside in a matter of seconds.

"Pull over!" cried Maven

Audley stared straight ahead, intent on reaching Westminster, pretending that Maven was not there.

"Pull over, I say!"

The boatman, an old gentleman nearing the end of his career on the water and probably better suited to life as a hackney carriage driver, was keen to comply with the request and his stroke rate slowed considerably then stopped altogether. Audley, at last, turned to face Maven.

"Get away from here, damn you. This has nothing to do with you. Leave me alone and you shall be left in peace."

"What can you possibly hope to achieve? Westminster is crawling with soldiers. You cannot ever get close enough."

"That is my problem not yours. Get back to your damsel in distress."

"You will be hanged for what you've done. Both of you!"

"How naïve you are, Captain. I shall no more hang than you, sir. I am a member of the House of Lords. They won't hang me."

"You are a murderer, sir! You and your servant there. Surrender now and I am sure you will be shown leniency."

"Go to hell! Boatman, get this damn craft to the shore as quickly as you can. I have work to do."

Pinchbeck, who had remained silent throughout this exchange, turned in his seat and quietly confirmed the order with his usual menace. The boatman, now rested slightly, eased his left oar around and the craft began to turn towards the northern bank and the Hungerford Stairs.

"Mr Stephen, get me close enough that I can jump across."

The boat turned sharply towards the north shore and the boatmen snagged their oars. The strength of Mr Stephen overpowered that of the smaller man who hurt his wrist in the collision.

"I am arresting the two of you for murder! Get the boat to the shore and surrender yourselves."

"Damn your eyes!"

"And hand over the weapon!"

Suddenly, Pinchbeck stood and turned on his boatman. He held him by the scruff of the neck and then lifted him bodily out of his seat and into the water. The craft tilted over so much that it was on the brink of capsizing. Audley, though, leaned against the angle and the boat righted itself, rocking in the water. Pinchbeck had the oars now and he hesitated, his experience of rowing seemingly no greater than Maven's. He pulled hard on his left hand and the boat turned away from his pursuer but no sooner had Pinchbeck straightened out the craft than Mr Stephen had caught him and they were once again alongside. The older waterman floundered in the river, his arms flaying, and he cursed his passengers roundly.

"Save your friend from the water, sir," said Maven in the direction of Toldervey and Mr Stephen turned the craft towards the stricken boatman. Maven leapt over the side into the river to pursue Audley. Mr Stephen glided the boat away and was soon alongside the boatman, who gladly grabbed the proffered oar.

Maven swam alongside Audley's boat and reached for one of the oars. Pinchbeck swung it wildly, trying to knock Maven about the head but his control was poor and he missed by some margin each time. On the third pass, Maven grabbed at the oar with an outstretched hand and held on, using it to pull himself closer to the boat. Holding onto the boat with his other hand he saw that Audley was once again raising the pistol. Ignoring the burning pain in the muscles of his arms, Maven hoisted himself out of the water and hung over the side of the boat, tipping the vessel to an angle of forty five degrees as he did so. Pinchbeck leaned out the other side, almost falling out of the boat. The sudden shock of being lifted into the air destabilised Audley and he had to hang on with his right hand so that the pistol hung hopelessly in his left. Maven reached out and lifted the weapon off Audley's hand. He slithered back into the water and the boat righted itself, pitching alarmingly once again. Maven aimed the pistol at Pinchbeck as the servant regained control of the oars. This time the heavy wooden oar would not miss and it swung through the air towards him. Maven pulled the trigger and there was a loud explosion that made his ears ring. The recoil threw him back and he went under the water. As he fell the face of the oar swung across, just inches in front of his eyes. Filthy river water entered his mouth and stung the back of his throat. Instinctively, he recovered and got his head above water once again. Pinchbeck stared back at him, unharmed by the ball, which landed harmlessly in the water beyond him.

Pinchbeck stood then and leapt over the side, the stiletto clasped between his teeth. His bony hands grabbed for Maven's face and he clawed with his fingernails. Maven threw a punch and missed. Both men floundered in the deep water, each struggling to reach his opponent. Then Pinchbeck got hold of Maven's throat and clung on, attempting to squeeze the air from him and drown him. Maven clung to his attacker but could not shift his grip. With his spare hand Pinchbeck withdrew the stiletto from his mouth and raised his arm above his head to administer the coup de grace. Maven summoned his last ounce of energy and pulled himself under the water, dragging Pinchbeck with him. The servant spluttered and took on water as Maven kicked out, making contact wherever he could, finally striking Pinchbeck in the groin and the pain made the servant release his grip. Maven swam away and grasped for the surface. He looked around for Pinchbeck. In the brief second that he allowed himself to look away from the water he saw Audley in the boat, pulling away from them, halfway to the bank, rowing expertly and strongly. Pinchbeck surfaced about ten yards away and gasped for air. There was a look of horror on his face when he saw that his master had abandoned him. He was caught between following his master and finishing off his victim. He swam towards Maven.

Maven's throat throbbed with pain where Pinchbeck had had hold of it and he struggled to breath. Suddenly his attacker was upon him again and stiletto reflected the light as it arced above them. Then Mr Stephen's oar swung towards him and Pinchbeck and his weapon fell to one side. The stiletto spun from his hand and floated on the choppy surface. Maven grabbed for it. Pinchbeck gasped for air and threw himself upon Maven, who thrust the stiletto upwards to greet its owner. Pinchbeck screamed in Maven's face as the point embedded itself in his chest then he fell upon his attacker, a dead weight. The unconscious Pinchbeck was in danger of dragging Maven down but he managed to scrabble out from beneath the lifeless form and get back to the surface, where he splashed about and sucked in air.

Maven looked up at Toldervey and his assistant and was incapable of saying anything, though he knew that he owed them his life. The North African leaned his long and muscular arm from the boat and grabbed Maven by his sopping wet coat. Too weak even to hold onto the side, Maven allowed the strong man to lift him bodily from the water and hold him under his arms while Toldervey swung his legs over the side. Maven lay in the boat and gasped lungfuls of air. Still unable to speak he rested his hand on the African's and nodded his acknowledgement.

After a minute, he raised himself up and looked over the side. Pinchbeck still floated lifelessly, face down in the water, his coat filled with water. The river would deal with him as it usually did, gorging on the body then spitting it out on tomorrow's tide. To his dismay, Maven saw that Audley's boat rested empty on the shore, its oars cast aside on the shingle.

32

Outside the hall the dignitaries were formed up in the appropriate and designated order. They awaited only the arrival of the King and a suitable space had been left for his group near the front of the line. Last minute jostlings for position had earlier been anticipated and rejected with Shrewsbury's customary efficiency. Precedence had been dictated over many generations and it was not his place to subvert the true nature of things.

Gideon Crouch was being addressed by Shrewsbury in what he considered a most unprofessional manner. As he tried to explain to his employer, it had been necessary to circulate among the various elements of the procession to ensure that every man knew his place and his timings and that he had considered it necessary to see to these arrangements personally. That the Duke had spent an hour trying to locate him was hardly his fault. The stress of the occasion was affecting them both and, for once, Crouch was not inclined to forgive his master. The Lord Treasurer stood before him coughing into his handkerchief, bent at the waist with the exertion.

They walked away from the head of the column, bowing to the Prince and Princess of Wales as they departed. After a few steps, Shrewsbury slowed and nodded his greeting to the Lord High Constable of Scotland and the Earl Marischal. In the past few weeks the wrangling with these important noblemen had vexed Gideon Crouch considerably and it had only been after several tiresome negotiations with the High Constable of England that the infernal matter had been resolved to both their satisfactions. It irked the clerk that men who were otherwise the epitome of common sense could create the most ridiculous of scenes merely to prove a point of precedence as to who should walk closest to the Sword of State. And this at a time when all eyes would be on the King. He smiled benevolently at both men. Then Crouch tapped Shrewsbury on the forearm and drew his attention to the appearance in the large doorway of the King's servants, Mustapha and Mahomet.

"Aah, the abominable Turks are here. The King shall not be far behind, then. Go and see that everything is order, will you, Crouch?"

With that, Shrewsbury flipped open the lid of his fob watch. Crouch bowed briskly and departed, covering the ground quickly. Today the Turks were the King's personal guard, as if there were not enough armed redcoats about the place. The accepted wisdom at Court was that these two ruffians were usually charged with the responsibility of organising the King's various mistresses so as to maintain an air of respectability. The King, at Bothmer's insistence, had requested that the Turks walk alongside him, one on each side. Their height and size formed a barrier between the new monarch and his people. Shrewsbury had wasted several frustrating hours explaining to Bothmer how the London mob would react to such a show but his remarks were in vain.

Shrewsbury turned to see what transpired between Crouch and the minders and saw that Herr Bothmer had stationed himself between the two giants and was engaged in earnest conversation with the clerk. Strangely, it seemed to be Bothmer who was nodding as if it were he who received the instructions.

Mr Stephen got the boat past the clogged White Hall Stairs and they were soon at the Westminster Steps where a sizeable crowd of river craft had formed and was jostling for position. Mr Stephen set about easing the other boats out of the way with his brute strength. Toldervey had been for putting Maven ashore at the same point as Audley then turning tail and returning to Puddle Dock as quickly as they could. The sight of Pinchbeck's body bobbing face down in the murky waters of the Thames had frightened him considerably and the manner of its getting there meant the consequences of any investigation vexed him even more. In his experience, when there were gentlemen involved it was the usual form for them to look around for someone from the lower orders to blame.

To both of their surprises, the reticent Mr Stephen took the initiative and made his decision as soon as Maven explained where Audley was likely to be heading. His taciturn manner was suddenly replaced by a fierce determination. In the mind of Mr Stephen, it seemed, Maven was right and Audley was wrong and there should be no need for negotiation. Despite Toldervey's furious protests the craft had cut through the choppy waters and made its way upstream. As they neared their destination a discreet, satisfied grin crept onto the face of the North African. There were three passenger wherries between them and the steps but such was Toldervey's haste to get Maven off his boat that he grabbed the Captain by the shoulder and pointed.

"Them blokes will be there for an age yet, blockin' up the steps. You can step across 'em. Lightly mind, else you'll be in the sup again."

Maven had recovered his breathing now and the pain around his throat had eased, though the wound on his arm continued to throb. He stood and steadied himself as the boat rocked on the water. He was still damp from his earlier dunking and had no desire to repeat the experience, especially in front of an audience. Unlike Toldervey, these watermen wore official red frock coats and displayed their licences under the coat of arms wrapped around their left sleeves. It felt as though he invaded a club of which he was not a member. He stepped onto the adjacent craft and the first waterman's cry of protest that there was a lighterman in their midst alerted his neighbours. Maven made the second boat safely and, once again, annoyed its owner with his trespass. As he stepped onto the third and final barrier the aggrieved boatman grabbed hold of his ankle so that Maven stumbled, rather than walked, across the boat and fell onto the steps, grazing his hand. He kicked out against the boat and, in doing so, he caught the boatman full in the face with his boot and the red-jacketed troublemaker fell back, cursing, into the bowels of his small craft.

Maven scrambled up the steps. At the top he eased aside a portly gentleman who had appointed himself controller of the queues for departing boats. The queue at the moment was comprised of a line of scruffily dressed urchins who had been paid a penny each to hold the place while their employers enjoyed the procession. Maven ran into New Palace Yard but the armed guard that stretched in a line from Westminster Hall to the Wool Staple prevented him from continuing his journey. They were stood at ease with their rifles to the front, each weapon essentially a threatening ornament rather than a practical defence against invaders.

"Halt! Wait a while there, sir."

A burly Sergeant strode towards him, resplendent in a clean and pressed red coat and grey breeches. His black boots had been polished to perfection. As the Sergeant walked towards him Maven looked through the line of soldiers and could see the line of noblemen dressed in their red velvet cloaks, indistinguishable from each other at this distance. Just a few feet from the door of Westminster Hall was the unmistakeable form of Gideon Crouch and, without thinking, Maven attempted to break through the cordon to reach him. Suddenly, weapons were raised and he faced the joint threat of a steel bayonet from one Life Guard and the hard, wooden butt end of the weapon belonging to another.

"Steady there, steady, sir!"

The Sergeant was alongside him and casting anxious glances into the yard, lest he should cause a fuss and draw the attention of his betters at this important time.

"State your business, sir," he demanded brusquely.

"Let me through, Sergeant. I need to speak to that man, there," said Maven, pointing in the direction of Gideon Crouch. Then Shrewsbury began yet another bout of coughing and Maven saw the Duke. He added, "and the Duke of Shrewsbury. I have urgent news for …"

"Now then, sir, you can't seem to make your mind up. If it's a view you're after then I suggest you takes your chances with the rest of 'em round at King Street. But I warns you, sir, 'tis mighty crowded and you is unlikely to see much."

"No, you don't understand …"

"Don't get me started, young man. We is very busy …"

"I am a Captain in the Duke of Marlborough's office and I order you to let me through!"

"And I am 'is majesty's long lost lover. Now stop wasting my time and move along. Ain't no one coming through this way without a warrant signed by the Lord Treasurer himself. Now bugger off."

Maven knew it was pointless to argue. He ran along the line to try and get as close as he could to Shrewsbury but the riflemen were grateful to move and welcomed the opportunity to inflict some physical harm on this uppity stranger. Maven wondered how best to obtain Shrewsbury's attention and settled on, "Your Grace!"

Shrewsbury genuinely did not hear him.

"Your Grace!" he called again, only louder. This time the Duke, along with several of his colleagues, turned to see who shouted. Only Shrewsbury maintained his gaze and it was clear that he recognised Maven immediately. The Lord Treasurer froze momentarily and the Sergeant, who had pursued Maven, monitored his actions lest he should somehow have offended the nobleman by refusing Maven entry. Then Shrewsbury turned away, his red velvet robe billowing slightly in the wind adding a dramatic flourish to his gesture of rejection. The Sergeant had his arm on Maven's shoulder.

"Looks to me like he don't know you after all, sir."

Then the whole assembly in the yard was called to order as the two trumpeters on the steps of the hall stood to attention and raised their instruments to their mouths. As the fanfare began, the crowd that had been milling around in the area between the yard and the steps swarmed forward to catch a glimpse of the King. The Guards braced themselves for the onslaught and their line held firm despite the jostling and complaints of the mob.

Maven was caught in the crush between the soldiers and the spectators. He fought his way through the crowd, back towards the river and the further he got from the yard the easier his passage became. At the Stairs one of the wherrymen recognised him and the men joined in a chorus of obscene mockery as he turned left and ran towards Manchester House. A few yards from the stairs the ground was no longer paved and the earth was damp and clung to his boots, slowing his progress. He turned left again, into Wool Staple, a street he knew would take him around the back of New Palace Yard. Over the roofs of the houses he could hear more fanfares and the beating of the drums. From the crowds, he heard cheering interspersed with occasional booing and shouted insults as the cumulative anticipation began to find its release.

His way into the yard was blocked and he was forced by a further line of soldiers to turn right and go through the market, an open space that usually thronged with traders but which, today, was oddly quiet. Suddenly he was at King Street at the exact point where, earlier, he had narrowly avoided an altercation with the landlord who had been renting his house as a viewing gallery. The crowd was surging toward another barrier of soldiers at the corner of New Palace Yard, where the royal procession would make a left turn on its way to the Abbey. Maven was swept along in the rush, deafened by the chatter of hundreds of voices. All the while he searched in vain for Audley.

The drums beat out a different pattern, more urgent now that the fanfares had stopped. Gideon Crouch stood to one side of the great doors. In front of the Prince of Wales was a space that would shortly be occupied by the King and his officers of state. In front of this space stood the herb woman, holding a sizeable basket of specially picked leaves. Around her, bored by the interminable wait, scampered six children, three boys and three girls, dressed in virginal white. They danced around their own baskets of flowers that they had placed on the floor and ignored the look of thunder that Shrewsbury directed towards them.

The unsmiling Bothmer reappeared in the doorway and looked left and right, searching for anyone who looked out of place. He looked directly at Crouch, who nodded in response to the unspoken enquiry. Bothmer turned his back to the crowd and made a signal with his hand, beckoning the King toward him. He clicked his fingers and the Turkish servants took a step toward each other, creating a narrow space, into which the King would step. To Bothmer's evident annoyance, the pair glanced at each other and exchanged smiles then turned to face their eyes to the front, intent on enjoying their finest moment. Crouch felt a tug on the sleeve of his coat and turned to see who it was that disturbed him. One of the many liveried footmen that he had stationed around the yard and along the route had come and found him, as they had been instructed to do in the event of any suspicious behaviour.

"Mr Crouch, sir, there is a mob, misbehaving down by St Margaret's church, sir."

"What sort of misbehaviour? I told you, we are not interested in the usual drunkenness."

"No, Mr Crouch, there is a crowd that has set up its own procession," said the servant hurriedly, "but you had best come and see for yourself."

Reluctantly, Crouch departed while Bothmer looked on with concern. As Crouch limped along the edge of the yard he heard the cheer raised for the King, who had arrived in the doorway and paused between his minders. The clerk turned briefly and saw that, on cue, their lordships hurled their golden caps in the air to celebrate the arrival of the monarch. But Crouch had other, more important business to attend to. He scuttled as quickly as he could in the wake of his informant, turning a sharp left and then arriving at the rear entrance to St Margaret's. Crouch struggled to keep up. The man waited for him by the altar of the church, clearly impatient with his superior.

"This way Mr Crouch, come on."

In seconds they were on the steps looking out into the Sanctuary. The Abbey loomed to their left and made an imposing neighbour. The servant beckoned to Crouch to stand alongside him.

"See there," he said, indicating a group of men to his right, "they is the ones I was telling you about, sir."

Crouch was immediately disappointed. The group of six men were dressed entirely in black, which is what, presumably had alarmed the servant. He had not, of course, wanted to alarm the guards by warning them of an impeding assassination attempt but he had hoped that the young man would have brought him something more important than the tomfoolery that was evidently taking place. The group had dressed one of its number in a mocking tribute to the king, including a turnip set on top of a wand. The idiot was marching up and down in the space that had been cleared by the militia for the official procession. It was not the fool that concerned Crouch so much, since he was evidently keeping the crowd amused. Instead, he was more concerned by the jester's serious looking companions. Not only had they put the man up to the mischief but they were now standing at appropriate points to ensure that nobody broke up the show. Then one of the group stepped into the space to join his colleague. He took the fool by the arm and introduced him to the audience, shouting, "Here's our George, now where's yours?"

This was greeted with laughter from some but, Crouch was pleased to note, consternation by the majority.

"At least they recognise this Jacobite stunt for the pathetic joke that it undoubtedly is," he hissed at the boy.

"Are we to take any action?"

"No, leave it alone. But if there is any hint that these ruffians are armed I want them removed. Keep watch and alert the redcoats if you see anything to alarm you."

Crouch set off at a pace, being sure to keep to the right of King Street and away from the fool who now performed an encore for his spectators. Crouch headed for a group of soldiers who loitered there, chattering to the crowd. Lieutenant Maddox recognised him as he approached and snapped to attention.

"Never mind all that, Lieutenant. Do you see that idiot with the turnip?"

"It is only some innocent fun, Mr Crouch."

"See to it that they are removed before the King arrives. Give them another two minutes to entertain these fools then get rid of them. But watch where they go, especially the ringleaders."

Maven was penned in at the corner of the Sanctuary. As soon as it became apparent that the King had joined the parade armed guards formed into lines and marked out the route, pushing back the bystanders to create a narrow path. He looked back up King Street, a narrow enough thoroughfare at the best of times but now there was just enough room for the parade to pass. Their lordships, walking in pairs, would have an easier passage but would remain at the mercy of a crowd that was within touching distance, soldiers or no soldiers.

The herb woman turned from New Palace Yard, followed closely by the children, all of them gently throwing petals and leaves into the road in front of them, maintaining the tradition to ward off the threat of plague. Maven thought they might do better to douse the street with some clean water. The newspapers had made a great play recently that the King would wear Queen Anne's crown, suitably adjusted for his larger head. They were correct, for immediately behind the herb woman walked Shrewsbury carrying the crown on a plump red cushion. The Lord Treasurer's serious expression confirmed that this was his proudest moment and he plodded slowly forwards, oblivious of the noise around him, concentrating on the crown. Then, carrying the orb, the sceptre and the sword of state came three more officers, the Dukes of Dorset and Argyll and the Earl of Abingdon, though neither Maven nor anyone else in the crowd could have put a name to their faces. Behind them were three bishops carrying a paten, a chalice and a Bible. There was a gap and, as the King and his Turkish servants turned the corner an enormous roar went up to greet his arrival.

The King was dressed in a sumptuous golden cloak, the train of which measured about twenty feet and was held by an army of pages all marching slowly in step. The Turks walked either side of the King, carrying out their instructions to block him from the London populace, lest any members of the unruly mob should find a way to hurl something and cause him harm. Then the Prince and Princess of Wales turned into the street and Maven could see the coronation canopy held by the Noblemen of the Cinque Ports just behind them. The King was directly in front of him now and looking much the same as he did when Maven had met him; or rather when he had stood behind the Captain-General while Marlborough had exchanged pleasantries in the French language with the Elector. The monarch, shorter and plumper than Maven remembered, looked neither left nor right but stared at a spot on the ground ten feet in front of him and plodded on slowly, morosely toward the Abbey. How unregal you seem, he thought, how ordinary. How vulnerable. Maven scanned the faces in the crowd.

Then came the Prince and Princess of Wales, more accessible to the mob, since they did not have anyone walking alongside to block the view. The young Prince even took a chance of inciting the crowd by waving and smiling. In response, he received a huge cheer, drowning out the shouts of protest that seemed to be orchestrated by small groups of radicals who pushed through the multitude on the far side. Maven eased away and walked along the back of the crowd, his great height enabling him to see over the heads of the people in front. He looked around for signs of trouble and the thought crossed his mind that this was none of his business. Shrewsbury had, after all, so blatantly ignored him a few minutes ago. He toyed with the idea of walking away, of walking back to Kathrine.

Then Maven a small gap opened up in front of him and he stepped forward. Shrewsbury walked within a few feet of him, his eyes directly ahead, pacing slowly and deliberately, proud of the attention but willing the torture to end quickly, desperate to keep the crown steady on the cushion. Maven did not try to attract his attention again. He thought of Audley and decided that if the peer were minded to attack the King he would have do so by now, for this was the most exposed section of the parade. Maven was reassured by the presence of an enormous number of soldiers, some of whom, he had noticed, were not in uniform but mingled with the mob.

The parade of noblemen, perfectly turned out in their state robes and marching in order of seniority, seemed to continue for an eternity and the crowd was becoming restless. Then Maven saw the Duke of Marlborough who, true to his nature, defied the convention and looked not at the ground ahead of him but all around, soaking up the atmosphere. Occasionally, one of the spectators would recognise him and would let on to his neighbours that the Captain-General, their great military hero, was amongst them and there would be a cheer. Marlborough looked across and, to Maven's surprise, recognised his former subordinate. The Duke touched the corner of his cap in a subtle gesture of comradeship and several pairs of eyes turned toward Maven to see who might be the object of the hero's warmth. Then the Captain-General was gone, replaced by anonymous men in red velvet cloaks, all of whom stared morosely at the ground ahead of them as they plodded towards the Abbey.

Disappointed by the brief glimpse they had been granted of their King, some of the spectators embarked on some sport at the expense of the peers who walked before them. Soldiers broke from the line and took to arguing with the worst of the offenders then pushed them back as best they could to maintain a wide passage for the noblemen. In places, the cordon remained broken as soldiers went to each other's aide in dealing with the spectators who were too much of a handful for one or two men. Maven felt himself being shoved in the back and heaved forward then pushed back the other way as the soldiers did their best to keep order. The royal party had now safely entered the Abbey and Maven relaxed.

Then he saw him.

The last of the noblemen were quickening their pace now, perhaps in a desire to take their places inside the Abbey or, more likely, in their haste to escape the mob. In front of the third pair from the back a gentleman walked alone. He appeared to be dressed the same as the others in the red velvet cloak and golden cap and he walked with his head bowed. An observer with a keen eye would have noted that the markings on his ermine differed from those of the peers around him and, therefore, Lord Audley was in the wrong place, walking with men of a lesser rank. Maven, however, merely recognised the facial features. Casting a glance down to Audley's footwear, he saw that the peer had not had time to change properly and his shoes were those that he had worn and ruined on his jaunt to the Fleet and subsequent escape on the Thames.

"You there!"

Audley ignored Maven's shout and walked past without altering his pace, but Maven had attracted the attention of the soldiers immediately in front of him.

"Shut your mouth, sir. We don't want no trouble."

Maven pushed forward and, of course, the cordon pushed back. There was no way through.

"You don't understand. That man," he pointed in vain at Audley's back as he made his way to the Abbey, "is a major threat. You must stop him."

Maven moved along the cordon, shoving spectators aside as he went. Suddenly he found himself face to face with a Guard of his own height. The soldier had earlier noticed the greeting from Marlborough to this upstart stranger. He raised his weapon above his head and, before Maven could react, pushed it butt first into Maven's chest. The pain was immense and he collapsed to the floor, clutching his ribs.

"Do as you're bloody told."

When Maven had recovered, the riflemen had been ordered away and the crowd had swarmed across the street, a cordon no longer necessary to restrain them. Some people headed for home, drifting away from the Sanctuary to the boats on the Thames or the hackney cabs at Charing Cross. Maven rolled himself into a tailor's doorway and sat with his back to the shop, watching the movement of the people.

He thought about Audley and whether he would dare to strike in a holy place in front of so many people. Would his misplaced sense of patriotism over-ride his religious convictions? Maven had no clue. Perhaps he would wait until after the coronation, when the mood would become more relaxed and the guests were partaking of the celebratory banquet in Westminster Hall. He sat back and exhaled slowly rubbing his sore ribs gently.

33

In the Abbey Bolingbroke took his seat amongst the Jacobite nobility and his expression betrayed his sour mood. He saw Bothmer staring at him with a wry smile. Alongside Bolingbroke, King James' former mistress, the Countess of Dorchester muttered under her breath, making suggestive and disparaging remarks about anyone she considered fair game. Then she very nearly caused herself to be ejected when she whispered just loudly enough for Bothmer to hear, "Everybody seems pleased, or at least they pretend to be pleased," which she clearly felt was very daring indeed.

Bolingbroke shot her a scathing look and even that redoubtable lady realised she had overstepped the mark. She cut short her commentary, duly chastised. Bothmer had witnessed the exchange and whilst he did not understand the double meaning it was clear enough that some sort of seditious comment had passed. Bolingbroke wished the ground would open up and swallow him or at least that some other event would take the attention of the spectators away from this corner. He got his wish moments later when there was a scene a few rows away. Lady Cowper was shoved from her seat by Lady Nottingham, who objected to her sitting amongst the Tory grandees when her husband had so recently and so treacherously accepted the position of Lord Chancellor in the Whig administration. The twittering and giggling of the ladies who should have known better turned to a stony silence when Lord Cowper himself departed his position to show his wife to a prime location at the front of the congregation. It was the only time since he had entered the great building that Bolingbroke had had cause to smile.

Near the door, Gideon Crouch loitered with the Turks. The tanned servants looked like awkward prizefighters dressed in ill-fitting suits. They towered over Crouch and he had to look up at a peculiar angle in order to speak to them. The three of them were biding their time while the King received his personal and private blessing from the Archbishop in the tiny Confessor's Chapel, accompanied by the officers and all twelve of the regents. The great doors of the Abbey were closed now and the congregation was lit by the magnificent glass windows. The whispered mutterings of the enormous crowd rose into the high vaulted space and merged into a steady, impenetrable murmur punctuated by occasional laughter as high spirits got the better of dignified patience.

Outside, Maven had recovered enough to be able to stand and walk. While he was propped against the door of the tailor's shop he watched a young man who he had at first taken to be George Trescothick. The youngster had evidently lost contact with his sweetheart and now that the crowd was thinning the pair had reunited with a public display of affection. Kathrine, who had not been far from his thoughts since her rescue, once again preoccupied him. He looked at the Abbey and he looked toward Charing Cross. There would be no more sights of the King today for his route would surely take him out of the eastern end of the Abbey and directly into Westminster Hall under a canopy that had been erected for the purpose. If Audley made his move on the King now then he would be killed before he could do any harm, whether he acted in the Abbey or in the Hall. Maven breathed in deeply, stood up and strode out for Hatton Garden, expecting to walk the whole way. In the street lay the detritus of the parade, the crowd now dispersed for the most part with the occasional pocket of activity as groups of revellers chatted and enjoyed the remainder of their day before they set off for home or for an alehouse. An abundance of paper blew in the breeze and mixed with the petals that had been tossed in the air in advance of the King's footsteps. The remnants of picnic lunches, crusts of bread and empty bottles, lay in the gulley. A pair of rats had dared to venture out for the spoils.

To his right was Whitehall, proud and upstanding against the early afternoon sky. He could see the river just beyond the building and on it crowded the boats, ferrying passengers back toward the city or over to the Lambeth side to meet the waiting carriages. Maven resolved to seek out Benjamin Toldervey in a few days to thank him for his efforts. And to thank Mr Stephen, of course and perhaps engage him to provide lessons in the art of rowing if the African's employer should have no objection. Suddenly, in his mind he had a clear picture of Pinchbeck, floating face down in the putrid water. How devoted a servant must have to be to his master to lay down his life and how callous that master would be to turn his back on one so loyal? Maven stopped suddenly. Then he turned and began to walk quickly back to the Abbey. As his mind raced so he quickened his pace and broke into a run. Past the rubbish that lifted and twisted in the breeze, past the rats that gorged themselves on the husks of bread with a dozen of their fellows and past the young lovers. He ran through the open space and stopped when he reached the northern door of the Abbey. It was guarded by a pair of ageing militiamen and the rifles they carried would have been rejected as unfit for service as long ago as Blenheim.

"Halt! State your business, sir"

"I must go inside. It is a matter of emergency."

The older of the two soldiers smiled at him, revealing a graveyard of teeth.

"You ain't goin' in there, sir. Tis for the toffs only today, zur."

"Look, get out of the way, will you. I need to see the Duke of Marlborough."

"Our orders is to –"

But he was gone then, sprinting to his right, crossing the closely mown grass in search of another way in. The guards were torn between deserting their posts and going after him but, in doing so, leaving their door unguarded. The longer they dithered the more sure they became that they would remain where they were. He reached the western side of the building. The gothic façade loomed over him, its porch cold and unwelcoming. The heavy doors were closed and locked and there was no need for a guard here. He stepped back and looked up, as if he were searching for some way in through an upper floor. He craned his neck round and settled on the odd-looking extension attached to the main wall. He recalled that it was known as the Jerusalem Chamber and he remembered being brought here by his father to be shown the location of the place where the church had been officially reformed by the Committee of the Divines after the civil war. What odd facts the mind stored away, he thought. Now he was less interested in its history than in his ability to gain entry to the Abbey. He tried the door and found that it sat awkwardly on its hinges not locked but merely wedged closed. He pushed against it. It would not budge. He shoved it harder with his shoulder and released it with a scraping of wood on dry wood.

Inside, the Jericho Parlour was as he remembered it from years before, mostly dark wood and several large portraits that stared down on him. He scanned the room quickly for a human presence but he was quite alone. He went through into the Chamber itself, a larger room dominated by a huge dark table with eight chairs arranged on each side. There was a large, ornamental fireplace but no fire had been lit for some days and the room was bitterly cold. In the far corner, the door was open and Maven walked towards it. As he reached the door, he heard a fanfare of trumpets, followed by the cheering of the congregation, louder than he expected given he was separated from the nave by two thick stone walls. He skipped through the small hallways and remained undisturbed. Right now all eyes would be on the conclusion of the Coronation ceremony. He went into the deanery, a large non-descript room and peered out through the window to the vaulted walkway known as the west cloister. He paused and looked around. To his right, in the north walk two figures both dressed in the red velvet of the noblemen had detached themselves from the ceremony and sat on the stone bench that was built into the length of the wall. They hunched forward in urgent, whispered conversation. He watched and waited, needing to be sure.

At least three pairs of eyes watched Audley slip away from the Jacobite group and although he kept his head down and stayed in the shadows, those same three pairs of eyes tracked him to the door in the south aisle that led to the north cloister. Gideon Crouch scanned the congregation from the south aisle and Bothmer watched from the north. The third observer was Bolingbroke, who had sat three rows behind the peer. When it was clear where Audley was going, Bolingbroke rose from his seat and eased himself out of the cramped row, apologising quietly as he went.

Audley eased the heavy door open and slipped through, closing it again behind him. The walkway was covered, preventing the sun from warming the stone flags and the corridor was cold and unwelcoming. He turned left and followed the cloister along its eastern side. Bolingbroke reached the door a few moments later and let himself out. Bothmer moved silently along the flags and reached the door in seconds. He removed from his inside pocket a large iron key and locked the heavy door. Bolingbroke followed Audley, who appeared to be searching for a route through the Chapter House or, to Bolingbroke's alarm, the South Transept, where he would have direct access to the newly crowned monarch.

"Edward! Enough. Leave this ridiculous plan alone."

Audley turned. When he saw who it was he paused for a second and made as if to advance on Bolingbroke. Then he changed his mind and set off along the cloister, his shadow flickering in and out of the stone columns. Bolingbroke ran after him, calling, and finally Audley stopped and turned. Bolingbroke, breathless from the exertion, grabbed at Audley's red velvet sleeve and bade him sit down.

Maven watched the two men. Though they made little or no sound they were clearly involved in a dispute. Maven went to the door of the Deanery and let himself out onto the vaulted stone walkway. There was no direct route to the pair across the lawn and he had to walk first a hundred feet along the west cloister and then turn left. He paused at the corner. They were about fifty feet away and, though they still spoke in aggressive whispers, the acoustics of the corridor served to amplify their voices.

"Damn your eyes, sir!" said Audley. Then he stood and pulled back his red velvet cloak and withdrew his sword, a fine, stout thing that was designed perfectly for its lethal purpose. Bolingbroke, shocked at the threat to his life, stared at his former conspirator.

"What are you doing you fool? Put the weapon away."

"Too late, Harry. Your double dealings have caught up with you at last."

"Surely you are not serious. Do you mean to duel with me here?"

"No sir, this is not the time for me to have my satisfaction with honour, for you have sunk too low for that to be a worthwhile course of action. No Harry, your peers have decided that today you shall be punished for your treachery and you shall die."

"But you searched for the King. All the while you have spoken of nothing else but replacing the Elector with your true King. You have changed your allegiance?"

"I have learned from a master, Harry. My only allegiance is to myself."

"So leave. Walk away. You would be welcomed at the Pretender's court."

"My safe departure is promised but there is a price I must pay to secure it."

Bolingbroke looked for an escape route, first to his right and then to his left. He saw Maven loitering in the shadows and fixed his gaze on the Captain. Audley span around to see what it was that Bolingbroke had seen and the Viscount took his opportunity to scuttle past Audley to the corner of the cloister. Audley found himself in the centre between Bolingbroke and Maven.

"I told you earlier to keep your nose out of my business, Maven. You should learn to do as you are told."

"Put down the sword before anyone else gets hurt."

"You fool. One word from me and you shall be arrested. There are witnesses who saw what you did to my servant. He was fighting to protect my life and you killed him, Maven. That makes you a murderer, sir."

Bolingbroke edged away slowly, his face a deathly pale shade. From the nave there was an increase in volume. The ceremony had ended and voices that had remained silent for so long suddenly found they had the opportunity join in conversation. The King would be departing for the Hall and the guests would be expected to follow. Bolingbroke looked from Audley to Maven and was slow to react as Audley turned and ran and went after him, swinging the blade wildly, slashing in two wide arcs, missing each time but, with the second, catching the red velvet and slicing through the noble garment as Bolingbroke finally began to run. In his panic to get away, Bolingbroke tore his cloak away, making the rupture longer. He grabbed at the material and heaved it towards himself, finally freeing the weapon from the folds of velvet. Audley went for him again but by this time Maven had covered the ground and had him around the neck with one arm while he wrestled the sword free with the other. Bolingbroke made off towards the door to the south nave but found it locked. He rattled wood against wood and looked left and then right for another way out.

Crouch saw Bothmer secure the door to the north cloister and sped along the aisle towards the west entrance. On his way he passed Marlborough and answered the Duke's enquiring look with a discreet nod of the head. The Duke slipped out of his pew and went after Crouch. He walked quickly but not so rapidly as to alarm any of the other dignitaries. Crouch crossed behind the final pew and slipped into the Deanery. He held the door open for Marlborough then closed it shut behind them. He remained with his back leaning against the door while the Duke stood in the doorway.

Maven had a tight hold on both Audley's throat and wrist and eventually the peer relented and dropped the sword, which clattered to the floor.

"I am arresting you, sir, for the murder of ..." but he could not for the moment recall the names of the disreputable pair that had been despatched so viciously in the Fleet."

"You see, Captain, they were so worthless that you cannot remember who they were. The world is no poorer without them, nor any of the others who crossed us on our mission. And do you know why? Because we go with God."

It is a strange and offensive God that allows to take his name someone who would force an innocent woman into a marriage she would rather die than consummate. "I have no interest in your religion."

"Your harlot. I had forgotten how you dote on her so. You are welcome to her. A whore is what she was and a whore is what she will always be. Damn her."

There was movement in the far corner as a door opened and, briefly, a small group of bishops appeared, being shown around the Abbey like tourists from abroad. Audley tried to wrestle free and shouted, "Help! Murderer, I am attacked!"

The group's host, an elderly nobleman in the customary red velvet shuffled along the stone floor in his slippers and stopped at the corner where he was confronted by the sight of a fellow peer being restrained by a tall stranger who may or may not have been a robber. He turned and called to his friends to raise the alarm. Audley took advantage of Maven's hesitation and slipped away from his grasp. He picked up the sword and ran towards the elderly peer, who recognised Audley immediately. Audley ran at the old man, waved the sword at him and then brushed him aside rudely. The shocked man fell to the floor with a moan. Maven ran after Audley but paused as he reached the fallen gentleman. He knelt down to check on his welfare but in reality, to reassure him that he was in no danger.

"Please go and find Charles Talbot and, if you can, his clerk, Gideon Crouch. I have urgent business with them. The King's life is in danger."

The man hesitated, overwhelmed by the gravity of what Maven had just said.

"Go now, please."

At the entrance to the Deanery, Bolingbroke ran into Marlborough, who did not yield.

"I should allow Audley to complete his work for your fate, sir, seems entirely justified," said the Captain-General, "This is the only door to freedom that remains unlocked and one you have crossed with your treachery and underhand diplomacy stands between you and safety. What say you?"

"You are part of the plot that would see me murdered?"

"Is that what you believe?"

"Well, are you?"

"It would be deserved, would it not?"

"It was diplomacy. And it brought an end to your butchery."

"It is very tempting to allow Bothmer's plan to proceed but, no, your death would cause complications."

"What the devil are you saying?"

"We cannot have members of the aristocracy killing each other within the confines of a holy institution such as this, can we? The people would be most offended."

"Then let me past, sir, else what you describe will surely come to pass."

"I should like the letters the Queen entrusted to you."

"I do not have them."

"I am surprised you shared such a valuable commodity with someone else, however much you trusted them. No matter. I have the originals. I need to know, are there copies?"

"No, sir, but I shall die in any case, surely?"

"You have my word that your life will be spared."

"You are my enemy."

"I am also a gentleman, sir and in my world that counts for something of significance."

Marlborough saw Audley turn the north eastern corner of the cloister.

"There is none so murderous as a friend betrayed, sir. You have but a few seconds before he reaches us."

"Then he shall hang for his crime."

"Such a penalty requires him to be taken and I have no intention of being implicated in the arrangement Audley has made with Bothmer. Shrewsbury and the King's man have outwitted you and not merely in depriving you of your office."

"But you restrain me. You are as good as plunging the dagger in with your own hand."

Marlborough looked at Crouch.

"My man here swears that I never left my seat except to void my bladder in the street."

Crouch nodded his confirmation.

Marlborough held out his hand.

Bolingbroke looked over his shoulder at the approaching figure of Audley then reached into an inside pocket and withdrew a small bundle of papers, identical to the letters that Maven had rescued from the Webb house, even down to the red wax seal. He handed them to the Captain-General.

"Now, for pity's sake will you let me through?"

Marlborough stood aside then closed the door on Audley and held it fast. Crouch opened the door at the other end of the room and loped along in his awkward fashion in advance of Bolingbroke to the Jerusalem Chamber and then out into the fresh air of the Sanctuary. When Bolingbroke was clear of the building, Crouch slammed the door shut as best he could.

Marlborough returned to the south aisle, walked across the rearmost pew and resumed his seat, ensuring that the letters were secured inside his tunic.

Maven left the old gentleman to complete his task and went in search of Audley. Maven ran in Audley's footsteps. He stopped in the doorway and pushed open the heavy door, checking in case Audley waited behind it. The room was quite empty. He retraced his steps into the Jerusalem Chamber and was just in time to see the Audley's back as he entered the ante-room. Audley's progress was slow and he was no more familiar with the layout of the Abbey than Maven.

"Give it up, man!"

Audley was by the door that led to the western entrance. It was stuck fast and Audley struggled to heave it open. Maven stepped forward to restrain the peer. He turned and faced Maven, brandishing the sword threateningly.

"You have made yourself an enemy, Maven. You know the punishment for those who cross me. History will prove me to have been right. You mark my words, Captain. Who are you to stand in the way of history? You are nothing but a peasant."

On the other side of the door Gideon Crouch attempted to prevent a group of gentlemen entering and Maven could hear their voices through the thick timber. The gentlemen outranked the clerk it seemed. Someone outside thudded against the door and tried to force it open. Suddenly they succeeded and the door swung open. The room was bathed in the weak afternoon sunlight. A bishop and two curates stood aghast at the scene that confronted them. Audley sensed his opportunity for freedom and charged past them, pushing one of the curates aside roughly. The area in front of the great doors that had been empty just a few minutes ago now teemed with coronation guests, stretching their legs after the ceremony and taking the air before they joined the banquet in the Hall.

Maven followed Audley outside and saw Gideon Crouch skipping away towards the Gatehouse. Then a redcoat, watching the scene from about thirty yards away decided his presence was called for and ran towards them, withdrawing his sword as he ran. He lunged at the peer and Audley reeled back, dodging the lethal metal of the weapon. Maven closed in and blocked the getaway. Audley span like a fox searching desperately for an escape route from the dogs but a sea of red velvet was all around him and his eyes shone with panic. The great door to the Abbey was open now and in his distress, Audley decided it was his only route to freedom. His eyes were wide with terror, the eyes of a man who no longer had a plan. Maven moved in but Audley darted through the crowd and, as he did so, he grabbed a woman by the neck and turned on his pursuer.

"Don't touch me, Maven. She will die first."

There was a gasp from the guests. His prisoner was silent but her eyes screamed panic and she raised the palm of her hand, silently imploring Maven not to come forward. Audley held his sword in his right hand and his left gripped the woman by the throat. Audley stepped backwards into the Abbey, looking over his shoulder as he went. His face was red and his eyes were wide. He darted his head left and right, searching out his enemies and reached the last row of benches, empty now that the occupants had departed. The few guests that remained standing in the Abbey watched the scene unfold. Audley searched to see whether the door at the other end of the nave was open. That was the door that would take him into Westminster Hall. Maven recognised the plan that formed in Audley's mind. Audley continued to walk backwards then halted, looked at Maven then back again to the far end of the nave. Along the south aisle marched Bothmer, menacing in his black garb. Striding towards them along the north aisle was Shrewsbury and beside him was a red-coated officer. The officer had a pistol in his hand. It was Shrewsbury who called.

"Edward! Stop this. Let us end it like civilised gentlemen."

"Leave me alone you traitors."

Audley scanned the faces. His prisoner began to weep.

"You are all traitors. Can't you see what you have done?"

Shrewsbury was close enough now not to have to raise his voice. Maven could see that the officer was Lieutenant Maddox.

"Come along Edward. The lady has done you no harm. Please release her and let us settle this some other way."

Audley's eyes were wide open, wild, almost primeval, and his head darted in different directions. Then he seemed to sense an opportunity for escape. He shoved the poor woman towards Maven, who caught her safely. She shook in his arms and suddenly burst into tears at the relief of her freedom and the safety of his strong arms. Audley sped past him, still with his sword in his hand. Gideon Crouch stood in the doorway and blocked the way. Audley skidded to a halt on the stone flags and started up the stone stairs that led into the gothic portico above the doors. At the far end was a door that led off, perhaps onto the roof of the Jerusalem Chamber. It was his only hope of getting away. The enclosed stairway was narrow and they could hear the sword clanging against the stone wall as Audley turned on the spiral steps. Maven was the first to react and went after him. Maddox, pistol at the ready cleared a space in front of him and waited for Audley to appear above them in the narrow gallery.

"Kill him when you get a clear shot."

The voice was Shrewsbury's. Maven, though, did not hear the order. He was bounding up the stairs two at a time, his wide shoulders scraping against the walls. Ahead of him, Audley was tiring and the prolonged chase had sapped his stamina. As a result, he entered the narrow gallery on his hands and knees with Maven holding tightly onto his left ankle, trying to haul him back.

Then Maddox fired the pistol and the sharp report echoed through the Abbey. There was a scream and footsteps echoed on the flags as men came running. Maddox, though, did not have a clear view. His shot missed Audley and grazed Maven's right arm as it ricocheted off the stone wall, sending dust and tiny fragments showering down. In the surreal silence they heard the bullet click down the stone steps before it came to rest. Audley turned and kicked out at Maven and caught him on his wounded arm. The pain made Maven shout in anger and release his grip. Then, as Audley turned to stand and berate Shrewsbury once again, Maven reached out to grab him and caught hold of the velvet robe. As Audley tried to release himself from Maven's grip he caught his sword between the wall and the wooden railing of the gallery. The weapon created a makeshift barrier, which tripped him and he stumbled forward. Audley's momentum carried him over the balustrade and he span thirty feet onto the floor, landing face first with his arms outstretched. The sword followed him down, falling in an arc before clanging noisily to the ground beside its master. Maven leaned over the balustrade and saw that Audley lay with his head twisted sickeningly. Blood seeped from his ear, wending a black stream across the grey flagstone. Shrewsbury, Bothmer, Maddox and

Crouch looked up at Maven. The Captain sank back against the stone and swore.

34

In Waltham Forest on Mr Child's estate there was a tree, a huge oak whose great age could only be guessed at even by the verderers and woodmen whose fathers and grandfathers had known it to be there. The tree was at a point where four paths converged and, for many years, the oak had been an illicit meeting place for traders, robbers and lovers. Approaching from the south was a carriage, a black coach drawn by a pair of bay mares. Inside, facing forwards, Lady Kathrine Cooper watched the forest pass her by. She was deep in thought and her companion left her to her silence. Maven still found the carriage an uncomfortable place to be and a ten mile journey was not a pleasurable experience. He would sooner have ridden alongside on Prospero but she would not hear of it and had insisted that he should accompany her as her equal and not as her employee. It was late on the Monday morning and they had shared the northbound road with a straggling procession of coronation revellers returning to their homes. One or two had dared to flaunt the convention that forbade travelling on a Sunday but most, it seemed, had found something to amuse them on the Sabbath and returned to their East Anglian homes today. They had paused at the cage and Kathrine had expressed her horror at his confinement in such a barbaric manner. Finally they had stopped at her sister's house so that her personal papers might be retrieved.

He recognised the clearing from the description she had given him at the house before they had departed. Hammond, it seemed, did not require an instruction to bring the vehicle to a halt.

"Is this it?" he asked.

"It is but I should like us to go somewhere else first."

She pulled aside the leather curtain and gave Hammond his instruction. The driver roused the horses for a final half-mile trot. Looking backwards at the great tree, now shorn of its foliage, Maven thought its branches pointed the way to several different directions.

"There seem to be a great many ponds here," said Maven as they passed a small lake filled with muddy water. A heron stood at the water's edge on the far side and eyed them suspiciously.

"They are clay pits. When all the clay is dug they are abandoned and they fill with water."

Presently, Hammond drew the vehicle to a halt. He had driven her here before and he did not need to wait for an instruction. They halted in front of a small cottage, no more than a hut that had been created from odd-sized clay bricks. She nodded at Maven's unspoken enquiry. He opened the door from inside, descended then allowed her palm to rest on his hand as she got down. There was a stiff breeze blowing and he sensed the first chill of winter. Around them the noise of the wind in the trees was the only sound. Fallen leaves had blown inside the hut through the open door and unglazed windows. A carpet of green, gold and dark brown lay upon the floor. She led him inside. It was a single room with, at one end, a brick fireplace and chimney. A rough wooden table sat in front of the fire but there were no chairs. To their left was an open space and he guessed that this would once have been the sleeping quarters. A string hung from the wall and attached to it was the remnant of a thin curtain, much of which had been chewed away by mice. The cottage was cold and had not been used for a long time, it seemed.

"This was my home," she said and he was taken by surprise because he thought she was showing him some secret meeting place. "My father dug clay and fired it in the brick kiln you see over there," she said, indicating an oven-like structure about twenty yards beyond the kitchen window. Maven struggled to reconcile her life of luxury in London with what he saw before him.

"All four of you lived here?"

"Something of a difference between this and the parties in Chelsea, wouldn't you say?"

From one side to the other merited six of his long strides and the cottage was about half as deep.

"Your parents. Where are they now?"

"It was hard labour ... "

In a matter of seconds his assumptions about her had unravelled and he wondered whether she wanted his admiration for how she had adapted to her new role or his pity for what she had

had to endure. He could not fathom her and she was a stranger to him.

"I'm very sorry. I had thought your parents were of the middling sort. I had not imagined …"

"There is no need to be embarrassed, Maven. If I have affected certain mannerisms and a more appropriate accent then it was to ensure that I could be certain of making good my escape. They are buried not far from here in the church at High Beach."

"With this as your father's livelihood I should have expected a pauper's burial."

"Your expectation is correct, Maven, though at least they have a stone now."

"It is a better monument to their lives than this."

"The only reason it still stands is because my father built it himself. Even so, I do not expect it to last more than another winter or two before it is swallowed by the forest. His only wish is that he would leave something behind to be remembered by. A monument to Samuel and Mary Naylor, born into poverty, dug and fired clay and then died without otherwise leaving a mark upon the world."

"They left you as their legacy. And your sister."

"Just. I made some judicious choices and had some luck."

Maven felt hemmed in. He kicked at the dead leaves and pretended to admire the view from the window.

"When did you escape?"

"When I was fifteen. Elizabeth and I discussed it and we made the decision. The arrogance of youth. It broke mother's heart, of course, but she understood. She had always borne the guilt of providing two daughters but no sons. She made up for it by teaching us to read. Father could not see the reason in it but she insisted it was our only way out."

They went outside and she looked around, turned a full circle and, satisfied that she would never again visit this place, returned to the carriage. As they travelled back along the narrow and uneven path between the trees she held the curtain back and looked out and he could see the pathetic dwelling still held her like an umbilical cord.

Hammond stirred the horses into life. The coach rocked and bumped over the ground and they travelled in silence. This time they halted at the great oak.

"There is something else I must show you."

They stood at the foot of the huge tree. Maven reached out a hand and rested it on the damp, greying bark and looked up. The canopy was mostly bare now for the autumn winds had taken away all but the most enduring leaves and they too would soon be lost to nature. She had given him precise instructions. He walked around the trunk without removing his hand. Then he looked about him to check they were alone. She was not dressed for the climbing of trees so he went up alone, though it seemed to him that she came close to joining him before decorum got the better of her. He hoisted himself up and caught the lowest branch with his left leg and levered himself into the tree. It was a struggle but it could be perfected with practice. She directed him higher and to the right. He sat with his back resting against a firm bough and looked down at her.

"Is this it?"

"Do you see it? Look on the trunk. In the shape of a heart."

He found the heart. It had been carved deeply into the bark. It bore two sets of initials, the lower pair read quite clearly, KN, and it seemed as though the heart had been the subject of repeated carving for the marks were quite fresh. Above them, the letters were less clear but he made them out. He looked down at her.

"What are you telling me?"

"Back then his family owned the western side of the forest."

"EA?"

"We were tenants. We paid his father rent."

Maven climbed down and jumped the last three feet. They walked together, away from Hammond, who remained with the carriage.

"My God, you were childhood sweethearts?"

"Perhaps. But there was no future to it. Can you imagine how his father reacted when Edward said he wanted to marry a girl from the claypits? We were lower than the serving staff in the house, not fit even to grace the building with our presence."

"But he was the second son. Allowances are made, it would not have been that unusual."

"That is what Edward said, but I was still a child. So was he really, just two years older than me. His father arranged his marriage, perhaps a little earlier than he might otherwise have done. It was a business deal and the union brought with it considerable lands in Norfolk. Edward flew into a rage and told his father he was having none of it. They did not speak for months. Edward and I would meet secretly in the woods. Then one day Thomas, his brother, saw us. Right here. There was an argument. You have seen how quarrelsome Edward could be. His temper was always uncontrollable."

She looked away from him and stared across the open grassland.

"Edward hit him very hard. Thomas fell and dashed his head on the hard ground. It changed things forever. Suddenly it wasn't a game any more."

Maven struggled to find the appropriate words to break the silence but could think of nothing to say. Instead, he stepped forward and rested his hand gently on her shoulder. She welcomed his touch and sank back against his broad chest. She looked away into the distance.

"But why did you hate him so much?"

"I am not sure that I hated him then. I feared him, certainly, for his rage. When his brother lay there bleeding to death his only thought was to find a way to blame me for the fight. He strode about in a panic, shouting and swearing. I managed to calm him down and we agreed that we would have to share this terrible secret for ever."

"But there had been a murder. That could not have been overlooked, surely, even out here?"

"Edward told his father that Thomas had fallen from his horse. He told the story so often that in the end he believed it himself. He found that telling lies came easily to him. He made a career of it, in fact. Each time he saw me he was reminded of his brother, I suppose. I was frightened. So I ran, got as far away from him as I could. Elizabeth packed all she could find into a square of cotton and we set off together for London. One of the girls at the house had said she knew of a woman who would find us work."

Maven squeezed her shoulder gently and she lifted her hand to place it upon his.

"It is time to go. I wanted to see it one last time and to show you where I came from. Thank you for coming out here with me."

"When we first met you gave me a task that I refused. You wanted me to kill Audley. Nothing you have told me here gives you a motive for wanting him dead. Now that he is gone only you know the secret of his brother's death. What else do you need to tell me?"

"You saw where I was born and how we lived. When I left Edward told his father that I had stolen something that belonged to him. It was an insignificant thing, a watch, I think, but the accusation allowed him to bully my father. The rent went up so that the value of the watch might be repaid, but of course, it was impossible to meet his demands. This extra burden coincided with a severe winter. They starved and then they froze to death."

"The forest must be teeming with life and with food. I have never seen such a plentiful supply of firewood."

"Everything belongs to the estate, Maven. They were forbidden from cutting firewood or even collecting it from the floor. Audley would send someone out to make sure they had not poached. Sometimes he would come himself. It was his way of punishing me. So you see, I did have good reason to revenge him."

"Yet he still wanted to marry you?"

"Men do foolish things in the name of love."

"Are you glad he is dead?"

"No. I had thought I would be satisfied by his death but I am not. I derive no pleasure at all from his demise."

Bolingbroke sat with his father in the drawing room of the Battersea manor house. The customary bottle of red Burgundy had been opened and half consumed. The fire roared in the grate and his father twirled the glass in his hand and inhaled the aroma of the good wine.

"Escaped by the skin of your teeth I would say, Harry. Who is this Maven fellow? I suggest you find him and shake his hand."

"He is Marlborough's man, I think. Or he belongs to that sly administrator. The result is much the same. I am alive only because Marlborough has deemed it propitious for me to remain so."

"Then you should shake Marlborough by the hand."

"Do stop being so naïve father. If the warmonger thinks I am to be in his debt he is very much mistaken."

"How many people know of this situation?"

"Barely a handful, thank goodness."

"The knowledge, though, is as much a barrier to your return as any castle wall, I would say."

"Indeed. It seems as though I shall be required to return to Bucklersbury once again. It is becoming a habit."

"And your dear wife. I am sure she shall be pleased to have you about the place once again. The Berkshire air will do you good." Bolingbroke looked at his father crossly but only encouraged him further.

"Throw yourself into the management of the lands, Harry. There is much less likelihood of losing your head. Celebrate being alive, man."

The coach clattered on the cobbles of Southampton Street, which was busy with shoppers traversing back and forth to Covent Garden. Among the crowds it was easy to lose the front door as it blended shyly into the background. After dark, when the street was clear of foot traffic it seemed to develop its own identity, to stand out, pushed forward perhaps by its infamy and reputation among London's gentlemen. In the daytime it was merely another unremarkable front door. They waited in the carriage for a minute. Patronage of Mother McGrath's was reserved for a certain class of gentleman and Maven was not among them. He did not recognise that the infamous brothel was directly in front of them, for it bore no signage of any kind.

"Maven, you shall have to negotiate my arrival."

He looked at her quizzically.

"It is not seemly for a lady to approach the front door."

She told him where they were and suddenly her life story fell into place and he could not help but stare at the beautiful woman who sat in front of him and he was ashamed of himself for being taken by surprise, for how else could the orphaned daughter of a clay brick maker come to own a house in Hatton Garden? The pleasure she had given him recently at The Star changed in seconds from a memory of blissful pleasure to one of mere gratification. It was a judgement he would return to again in the future but for now he needed to leave the carriage and be away from her. He jumped down to the street and strode to the front door. It being daylight the door was opened immediately. Maven was surprised at how young the girl before him seemed, though she was clean and dressed well enough.

"We're not open, sir. You should return in the evening."

"No, you do not understand. I have a visitor who wishes to meet with the … proprietor."

At that moment, Mother McGrath bustled into the hallway and opened the door further, the better to see who it was that disturbed her girl.

"And who the devil are you, sir? I should thank you to stop drawing attention to my front door."

Maven stepped aside and allowed the bawd to look directly to the window of the coach. Kathrine held aside the leather curtain and looked directly at her hostess, who stared in silence for a moment at the familiar face.

"Well, I never. It is a rare thing to find a bitch that wants to pay a visit to this God- forsaken refuge once she has escaped it. And you, sir, are her current meal ticket, are you?"

She appraised him from head to foot.

"You do not look like one of their lordships."

Maven ignored the insult.

"I can assure you that my mistress does not wish to draw unwarranted attention either to your house or herself."

The woman paused but then intrigue got the better of her.

"Very well," she said, raising her voice and aiming her instruction directly at Kathrine, "get yourself in here as soon as you like."

They sat in what Maven thought was a remarkably comfortable drawing room for a whorehouse. His experience of such places had been limited to the rougher end of the market and he surmised that such an establishment as this would have it as a rule not to accept soldiers unless they were of a very senior rank indeed. Generals, perhaps, would be acceptable. He thought of the Blackbird Club and its threadbare armchairs and worn carpets and decided this was an altogether more welcoming environment, though it gave no clues as to its real business. Mother McGrath stared at her former charge with barely concealed contempt but she spoke to Maven.

"I made her what she is, you know. Did she tell you that? I'll wager half a piece she did not, sir. They never do. They forget as soon as they walk out of here that if it wasn't for me they'd be nothing but common nightwalkers and usually dead within the year. I protect 'em, see, give 'em a roof and fine threads and some schooling in elocution and other more private matters. And what thanks do I get? Absolutely nothing, sir, nothing whatsoever. They would see me hang rather than stoop to help me."

Kathrine spared him the task of thinking of an appropriate reply.

"Madam, you ensure that you are rewarded for your labours well enough. Your house is a fine establishment and I am sure you eat and drink plenty, so let us not mislead ourselves into believing you are penniless. I should like my stay here to be brief and then I shall leave you to your business."

"So you've not come to ask for your job back?" cackled the bawd, "I'd heard your old man had upped and died and then your old beau had gone and fallen off Westminster Abbey, the ninnyhammer."

She laughed loudly at her witticism. Kathrine took from her purse a note.

"Mother," she said and then reproached herself silently for her unintended slip into old habits, "I should like to buy one of your girls."

"You what, my dear? For an hour or for the night? What am I a slaver?"

She looked at Maven.

"Is it to be you reward, sir?"

Kathrine ignored her and continued.

"There is a girl here who is ready to move on. I should like to help her. You can trust Captain Maven. Nothing of what we say here today shall be repeated. Am I right Captain?"

Maven nodded.

"Now then, to business. The girl calls herself Claudette."

"Had a girl by that name once. She has absconded from me, like they all does. Like you did. Quarrelsome little bitch she is. What do you want with her?"

"That is my business and not yours, madam. I should like to release her from whatever contract she has with you so that she may begin a life of her own."

"How very noble. I warrant she'll be back afore the year is out, though, for she is a playful little baggage. Popular with the gentlemen she is. Especially so with your old acquaintance, Mr Bolingbroke."

"I am sure she is, Mrs McGrath. I shall give you fifty guineas if you will release her into my custody."

There was a brief hesitation while she considered the size of what was, by any measure, a generous offer.

"Comin' into the profession yourself are you?"

"Fifty guineas, Mrs McGrath, and I shall ask you for your confidence in protecting her honour. In return she shall remain discreet about her employment here."

"She is worth a guinea a trick."

"There is to be no negotiation. You know I am sparing you the trouble and the cost of searching for her."

"Damn your eyes. You always was a one for the money. Give me the lucre, then and if I ever see the bitch in Covent Garden I shall have her put in the river for the rats and the watermen, you see if I don't."

The business done, they left the brothel and Hammond took them around the market to Long Acre and The Star, where Trescothick had insisted they go for luncheon. The tavern was quiet and as they walked the sound of Maven's boots on the flags was the only thing that disturbed the low murmur of the topers' whispers. As was his custom, Maven sat with his back to the wall and looked into the saloon. Trescothick had set aside the snug area in the corner, swept it clean and covered the table with a white linen cloth of a luxurious thickness, the only time Maven had known him to do so. The cutlery was laid out neatly and sparkled in the candlelight. The host had bathed and shaved this morning and sported an apron as white as the tablecloth. His cheeks shone red.

"Bin busy in the kitchen, we has, ma'am. I hopes you are pleased with the result."

"I hope you're not planning on serving coffee, Tresco. I am not sure that would make for the best start to a long journey."

"Now then, Captain, I shall thank you to keep those sorts of comments to yourself if I may." He turned to Kathrine and continued, "We has a piece of the very best Scotch beef for you ma'am fresh in from the market this morning and a lump o' Cheshire that is to die for. May I fetch you a drop of Burgundy wine?"

"Would this be part of the haul you filched from the Blackbird, Tresco?"

The Cornishman signalled with his hands for Maven to keep his voice down then leaned forward to continue in a conspiratorial vein.

"Well that lot ain't got no use for it now, has they? Besides, it's too bleedin' good for traitors, eh? Aye, you shall sup well 'ere today mark my words. I has some good victuals that you may take with you and all. Ain't no tellin' what you is gonna find away over theres."

He scuttled off to retrieve the wine from the replenished cellar. In the kitchen George and Claudette busied themselves. Kathrine took great pleasure from what she saw as they moved to and fro. She was dressed drably, in grey with a white smock thrown over and she wore a white headscarf. She looked like a puritan's wife but she smiled and there was a brightness to her eyes that had not been present before. George was demonstrating how to plug a tap into a fresh barrel and Claudette was failing miserably to comply with his instructions, using far less force than was needed for the task. The metal tap bounced off the wood. Then she got it at the second attempt and the tap was inserted with only the slightest spillage of ale. She smiled broadly at her achievement. Maven disturbed Kathrine's thoughts.

"Did you need to buy her out of the brothel?"

"This place is barely a stone's throw away. If Claudette is seen in the market by one of Mother McGrath's boys then she will disappear and be sold on as part of some scheme the old witch will arrange. She will be away from here in no time at all, that is for sure."

"And she will be saved, you think?"

"Look at her. She found George before she went too far. She is a little too feisty to attract a gentleman of means so before long any respect she had for herself will be drowned in drink. And once the drink takes hold they are done for."

"It is you that has saved her."

"Let's look upon it as a penance for my sins."

*

The following morning dawned bright and dry and the light clouds were blown across the sky by a strong wind. Gideon Crouch bade his wife good day and left his Westminster house, pausing to take a deep breath of the London air. He was able to reach St James's Square by walking solely on pavement and he thought to himself how much more civilised the world was becoming. At the south western corner of the square he paused and watched the men at work. The company of Life Guards that had been guarding the club since the eve of the coronation had now been had been detailed to empty the establishment of its more sensitive contents and had formed a human chain, which passed from hand to hand the muskets, rifles and pistols that had lain in the storerooms. The final link in the chain had become bored by his duty for he threw each item into the back of the large covered wagon in such a way that it landed with a noisy clatter and the noise drew the attentions of his Sergeant, who hollered at the Private to take more care. Summersby's widow had agreed to sell the lease and the building would doubtless pass into a more desirable use now. Crouch smiled and moved along, dragging his leg slightly as the effort of the walk caught up with him.

He reached Pall Mall then turned right towards Marlborough House. The red brick of the Duke's residence dominated the landscape and Crouch thought it the grandest house in London, even though Lady Sarah had requested a plain and convenient residence from Mr Wren. He felt the warmth of the unseasonal morning sun on his back as he walked and then turned left. How ironic, he thought, that the building next door to the House should be the German Church. He smiled at the humour of it and was still smiling when he knocked at the green door. He was admitted to the Duke's private chamber and waited in an anteroom where he admired the furniture and the paintings. He rather hoped Lady Sarah might be at home and toyed with ideas about how he might address her.

In the end, the Lady did not present herself and Crouch was shown through to the Duke's grand study. He bowed but Marlborough did not stand.

"Sit yourself down, man," boomed the Captain-General and Crouch found himself a chair, a smart piece made of mahogany with satin upholstery. He felt himself shrink in the presence of the senior officer.

"Tell me of Bolingbroke. Is he humbled?"

"Never has a man's reputation crumbled so rapidly, sir. He has retired to be with his father and then he shall return to Bucklersbury."

"Does he scheme? We need to know whether he continues to be a threat."

"If he meets with the Jacobite element then we shall know of it soon enough."

Marlborough played with the pen and ink well on the desk.

"Tell me what you think of Captain Maven."

"Well, sir, I – I am not all sure in what context you wish me to express an opinion, sir."

Marlborough's impatience got the better of him.

"I know about Maven's skills on the battlefield. I want to know how he measures up in England."

"Well, sir, I am not at all sure what projects you have in mind for the Captain, but he would be an asset to your office. I might say that he seems a little unknowing, especially of gentlemen and the ways of politicians."

"That does not seem to me to be an insurmountable problem and I would add, sir, that it is your job rather than his to understand the motives of gentlemen. If I ask him to knock heads together can I still rely on him to do it?"

"Undoubtedly, sir."

"Excellent. We shall have to find a way for Shrewsbury to make his peace with Maven. And Lady Kathrine, has he fallen for her charms?"

Crouch blushed.

"I may not be the best judge of that particular situation, sir."

Maven sat in what he assumed was the captain's chair and stretched out his long legs so that his boots rested at the foot of the panelled wall opposite. The chair was made of strong polished timber and was upholstered in dark green leather, which gave off a pungent but not unpleasant aroma, albeit not enough to mask the foul stench of the river and the Kentish marsh. They had come down by lighter from the Pool and their moods had changed as they made their way down to Gravesend, the point at which the river became the sea. They had stood on the deck in the stiff breeze watching the city recede, to be replaced by the long green grasses of the marshes on the north and south banks of the river. The traffic had thinned out the further they went and it had not taken long before they were in a rural setting. She had asked him the question in Hatton Garden and he had annoyed himself by not being as definite with his answer as he wanted. Now she was asking him again.

"I cannot see myself as a farmer and I have no trade. I should not think you would want me to return to being a soldier."

"Indeed not. But I should think that you could make a success of managing the land, Maven. You should have no need to get your hands dirty with manual labour or military matters."

The chair was bolted to the floor and, having noticed this, his mind raced back to the occasions on which he had crossed the Channel. Regardless of whether he travelled as an enlisted man or as an officer he suffered sea crossings badly and right now he felt the queasiness building in his stomach, though the Mary Edney seemed to be anchored so tightly that the swell of the Thames gave rise to barely a gentle rocking motion. Perhaps, he thought, if he could spend the whole voyage in this cabin then he might be able to force himself to get used to sailing. The captain had very graciously offered to vacate his usual accommodation as soon as he heard that he was to carry Lady Kathrine Cooper to the colonies. He considered it an honour and would not countenance her travelling in any but the most comfortable cabin.

She turned and stood looking out onto the river, as if fascinated by the comings and goings of the craft and of the men who made their livings here. He wondered whether she was sad to be leaving and then she spoke as if she had read his thoughts.

"I shall not be disappointed to put London behind me, Luke."

"It is a huge step, though. A whole new continent."

"A fresh start."

"Four weeks in this thing won't be the most pleasant of journeys, either."

"Oh, I don't know. Perhaps we shall meet pirates and have wonderfully exciting adventures. Oh Luke, don't pull such faces, I was only joking. We shall be as safe as God decides."

His expression conveyed his disapproval and she smiled. There was a knock on the cabin door and he leaned across to open it. Kathrine turned to see who it might be.

"Oh Charlotte do come in."

"I brought your boxes, ma'am."

The girl tried to negotiate her way through the narrow doorway but the size of the luggage precluded her from doing so.

"They is awkward rather than heavy, ma'am."

Maven took them from her then wondered what he might do with them in the confined space. Only when he had stowed them in the corner of the cabin was there enough room for the three of them to stand together in comfort. Kathrine continued their earlier conversation, "And besides if we meet pirates I am sure that Charlotte will protect me."

There was nothing more that he needed to say to her and though he wanted to leave he could not bring himself to go. The silence was broken by another knock at the door. It was the lighterman who had brought them down the river, a ruddy faced beaky individual with the dirtiest hands.

"I is goin' back to London, sir. You comin' or what?"

"Wait for me in the boat," said Maven, "I shall be with you shortly."

Charlotte Thomas realised her presence was not required and slipped away to collect luggage she knew was not there.

"I must go."

"Is there room in that little metal box you carry?"

He reached into his pocket and withdrew his most treasured possession. Kathrine removed a silver ring from her right index finger. She placed it in the palm of his hand and her fingers rested there for a moment longer than was necessary.

"Don't worry, I am not going to embarrass you by crying."

"I am not worth spilling tears over."

"No, of course you are not."

He examined the ring thoughtfully then placed it inside the pewter box and closed the lid gently.

Historical Note

It is well known that Queen Anne favoured the Empress Sophia as her successor rather more than she liked the son. It is quite possible that Anne changed her mind about the succession when Sophia died but, politically, it would have been impossible to bring about a change to the Act of Succession without the support of her Government. Queen Anne died before Bolingbroke could engineer such a change, if, indeed, that was the outcome he was aiming for. The letters she kept with her did, by common consent, exist, though most accounts have Bolingbroke destroying them immediately after the Queen's death. In his dealings with the Queen, Bolingbroke was outwitted by Shrewsbury and the latter can claim the greatest credit for the peaceful accession of the House of Hanover.

Bolingbroke was driven out of England following the elections of 1715 when he went to offer his services to James Stuart. Whilst there, however, he behaved unwisely and spent generously on loose women. He was never trusted at court and found his way back to England in 1723 when he had been pardoned. At the same time he was able to regain all his rights and estates, which had been confiscated by Act of Attainder. Forbidden from speaking in parliamentary debates, he took retired to his desk instead and became a critic of Walpole's government.

Shrewsbury worked on in his position of Lord Treasurer until he retired on account of his ill health in 1715, though in truth he would have felt out of place in the world of Hanoverian Whiggery. He died in 1718. The Whigs triumphed in the election of 1715 and, under the leadership of Walpole enjoyed several decades of power. By the middle of the century, almost all Tories had accepted the legitimacy of the Protestant accession and there was very little to differentiate the parties ideologically.

There is no evidence to suggest that a plot to assassinate the Elector ever existed.